SEKRET
MACHINES
BOOK 2
A FIRE
WITHIN

SEKRET MACHINES

From the imagination of **TOM DELONGE**

with *New York Times* bestselling author **A.J. HARTLEY**

BOOK 2
A FIRE WITHIN

To The Stars, Inc.
1051 S. Coast Hwy 101 Suite B, Encinitas, CA 92024
ToTheStars.Media

To The Stars... and *Sekret Machines* are trademarks of To the Stars, Inc.

Cover Design by Jesse Reed
Book Design by Lamp Post
Managing Editor: Kari DeLonge

Manufactured in the United States of America

ISBN 978-1-943272-41-9 (Trade Paperback)
ISBN 978-1-943272-35-8 (eBook)

Distributed worldwide by Simon & Schuster

*As I travel within my own consciousness and
rebuild my own soul to handle the next part of
life that is served to me, I wish to dedicate the
themes and learnings that I achieve
to my children, Ava and Jonas . . .*

*And within the Sekret Machines franchise,
these stories contain bits and pieces
of a soul well traveled.*

TOM'S ACKNOWLEDGMENTS AND THANKS

A SPECIAL THANK YOU TO AJ HARTLEY FOR BEING A WONDERFUL teammate, co-author, and friend.

A.J.'S ACKNOWLEDGMENTS AND THANKS

THANKS TO TOM DELONGE, JIM SEMIVAN, HAL PUTOFF, AND Peter Levenda for their input during the drafting of this book, and to those who have shared their insight on aspects of the story, including Janine Spendlove, Gray Rinehart, and Kerra Bolton, as well as those whose input has to remain anonymous. Special thanks to my agent, Stacey Glick, and my family, Finie Osako and Sebastian Hartley, who are also my first readers.

SEKRET MACHINES

BOOK 2
A FIRE WITHIN

WARRAD-MURIM
Uruk, Sumeria (Iraq), 3216 BCE

WARRAD-MURIM, FIFTEEN-YEAR-OLD APPRENTICE to the mason, Bakshishum, rose from his bed and stretched.

"Amar," he muttered, "get up. The world didn't end after all. You have work to do." He trudged across the stable where they slept on straw with the goats and rinsed his face at the water trough. They would need to ferry water up from the canal to the building site today, a tedious and miserable task that became only more tedious and miserable as the hot day went on. The sooner they got started, the better.

"Amar?" he said again, irritated now. "Leave your nasty little dreams and get up or . . ." He hesitated, studying the empty straw mattress where his workmate slept. "Amar?"

1

Maybe he has gone ahead, he thought. *Got started on the work, sharpening the chisels or fetching water . . .*

That was too much to hope for and, realizing it, Warrad-Murim cursed colorfully. If Amar was late today of all days, after all the other delays, the mistakes in the deliveries of materials, the constant confusion over what was being ferried in and out of the work site, he was on his own. Warrad-Murim would not cover for him. Not this time, and particularly not after last night.

He shuddered at the memory.

The Eanna district was the city's religious and administrative center. It stood northeast of the Kullaba block at the heart of the town, a place of power, luxury, and impenetrable defenses. But as the city swelled, the temple complex had begun to seem—according to the administrators—not grand enough, and though the great, ornamented structures seemed plenty impressive to Warrad-Murim, they had been ordered to be pulled down and replaced with something more fitting the glory and might of the gods. So being behind—months behind now—was not good. Was, in fact, Bakshishum had pronounced just the day before, insulting, an outrage to Inanna, Queen of Heaven.

And then there had been the portents.

There had been rumors of divine discontent for weeks. The Euphrates was unusually low for the time of year, and that affected everything from crops to basic sanitation. Some of the city's canals and water sources were entirely dry, and when an earthquake shook carved statue heads from the buttresses of the royal palace, the goddess's name was spoken in hushed tones. Warrad-Murim had seen worse, and his solution had been to keep his head down, do what he was told, and try to keep the rest of his team on schedule, if only so that when they were sitting around with nothing to do they could point at the vacant ground where the imported red rock was supposed to be and say what Bakshishum himself said on such occasions: "Bring us the stone and I'll work. Without it I am just empty hands."

He liked that. It was pompous and annoying when Bakshishum said it, especially when he was blaming the apprentices for the absence of materials, but when Warrad-Murim said it, it sounded different, adult.

So he had tolerated the rumors of divine displeasure and the threat of beatings from his master, though he had avoided the hard gaze of the overseers when they came to do their weekly progress examination, and everything had been fine till last night.

It had begun an hour or more before the first cock; a great light had appeared without warning over the city. Warrad-Murim might have slept through it, but Amar had woken him to show him what the goats were doing. In fact they weren't doing anything but standing in silence, unblinking and utterly motionless which, for creatures that were naturally both skittish and belligerent, was more than unusual. It was as if they had stopped being goats and had turned into something else entirely, retaining only the shape of the animals. The light came in at every crack, reflected off every surface so that even the dim and shady stable seemed to glow. Nor was it the golden light of day, but a hard white radiance leaning to blue.

The two boys had left the statue-like goats and gone outside, glad to get out from under the beasts' blank, uncanny stare, shading their eyes against the light over-head. The streets had filled with people all gazing upward, some of them praying to Inanna, some weeping, some even running to get away, though where they would go to escape such a thing, Warrad-Murim could not say. They had climbed to the highest point of the city, marveling at the way the light sparkled on the surface of the river, and it was as if the moon itself had swung low to inspect them.

But when the light began to move it was clearly not shaped like the moon, but long and narrow like a pipe or, Warrad-Murim thought, a wand. Amar had liked that word, and his eyes had flashed with more than the reflection of the goddess above. When the light began to move, drifting silent as a soaring eagle out over the desert, Amar had followed it with his eyes, and gasped when a new beam of light, not a general radiance but a golden spear, lanced down to the earth.

"That is by Sidu's place!" said Amar. Sidu was a trader, mostly cloth and beer, a slovenly brute of a man, but one with a head for business. His home was a mess of huts and storage cabins down by the riverbank. "We should go there!"

"Are you mad?" Warrad-Murim had said. "We should go to bed and get up extra early and get on with our work so that the goddess is appeased."

"Come with me," said Amar.

But that had been madness and, in truth, Warrad-Murim hadn't really believed his friend would go. Amar was a clever boy, but he was too fanciful, too much in love with stories and tales of danger and adventure. He had not yet learned that the only way for a boy of his rank to make his way in the world was to use his hands for someone else's profit. So Warrad-Murim had gone to bed assuming that Amar would wander the now-darkened city for an hour and then sneak in, his head full of rumor and mystery about seeing the goddess in the city's streets, stories he would embroider throughout the following day till Bakshishum threatened him with the lash.

That Amar wasn't here and clearly hadn't returned to his bed at all was annoying and, if Warrad-Murim was honest, worrying.

He skipped breakfast and ran up to the site on the off chance that the boy had indeed gone there early, but there was no sign of him. Warrad-Murim considered the way the sun was inching up over the horizon and, with another muttered curse, set off running down through the streets to the river gatehouse and out, along the bank to Sidu's place, rehearsing the furious words he would heap on Amar's head when he saw him.

More than words. He'd earned a beating this time.

It was still early, and Sidu's wife, Asharru, was fetching water from the river when he arrived. She did not speak but regarded him coldly, as if his very appearance was an impertinence. He bowed, and asked politely if she had seen a boy, an apprentice a couple of years younger than he, but she shook her head.

"Last night," he added on impulse. "There was a light in the sky. It seemed to point down around here. Do you know where exactly?"

He felt he was taking a risk even asking, and her eyes were wary as she considered her response. At length she made a ritual gesture to ward off evil, then pointed out back over a ridge of rock and sand. Warrad-Murim thanked her, bowed once more, and recommenced his running.

He was weary, hot, and angry by the time he crested the ridge, but his feelings evaporated as he looked down and saw the boy sitting cross-legged on the baked earth. He was hunched over, engaged in some careful practice, scratching with a stick into the sunbaked clay which was, from time to time, part of the swollen river bed. He was positioned in the center of a blackened ring that looked scorched into the earth, and beside him was a square slab of stone whose edge was set with what might have been metal, though it was bluish in hue and sparkled strangely.

Saying nothing, Warrad-Murim took a few faltering steps down toward the circle. Hearing his approach, Amar looked up. His face showed every sign of exhaustion, the special delirium of heat and sleeplessness, but his eyes were alive and focused. Around him, etched into the ground with the stick in his hand, were lines and symbols. Not the pictures they used to tell inventory but something else entirely, and as Warrad-Murim got closer, he saw that they mirrored the strange, fine carvings on the slab of stone.

"Amar?" he said, cautious and watchful. "What is this?"

Amar considered him and smiled.

"It is everything," he said, and his face was full of something holy and exalted, as if he had indeed met the goddess and heard her truth. "Not just lists. It is all things on earth and in the heavens made usable, beautiful. It is people and trade and resources. It is story and worship. It is the end of error, of miscommunication. It is the prelude and avoidance of war. It is the stuff of peace, of love, of all things."

Warrad-Murim shook his head, baffled, looking at the strange carved lines and symbols, many of them repeating, sometimes with variations. They spread out around the boy like a carpet. Hours of meticulous, bewildering work.

"I don't understand," he said. "What is it?"

Amar smiled again, this time his usual, ordinary, boyish smile.

"Words," he said. "Not pictures. Sounds."

"How can you draw a sound?"

"Like this," said Amar simply. "This," he said, "is a gift from the goddess. It is writing. It will change the world and everyone in it."

JENNIFER
Fox Smokehouse, Boulder City, Nevada. Present day.

IT WAS SIX DAYS SINCE THE EVENTS THEY HAD COME collectively to refer to simply as "the incident." Three days of separate interrogations had followed. They had not, they had to agree, been badly treated. Timika Mars had huffed about personal liberties, but her heart wasn't in it, not given all they had gone through. All they had seen. Alan Young and Barry Regis, being military and used to similar, if less protracted debriefings after far more routine missions than this, thought they had gotten off lightly. Jennifer Quinn kept quiet, swirling the straw in her Diet Coke without drinking, lost in her own thoughts.

The events themselves had become faintly dreamlike to her, like something she had seen in a movie on a plane as she picked at unappetizing food, got up to stretch, or slid in and out of sleep. She was left with moments—some of them striking and vivid—but no clear sense of story line. As she had recounted everything that had taken her to Area 51 and to the stone-faced, uniformed men and women who had probed her account over and over for the previous three days, the events receded, became still more remote and hard to comprehend. Within minutes of the interrogation beginning, she had decided to tell the truth, all of it, holding nothing back. She couldn't know if the others had made the same decision, but they had not had time to agree upon any coherent string of lies, so the truth seemed the only viable option. More to the point, she had no idea what she would be trying to hide from these people who, almost certainly, knew all of it already.

That, after all, was the one thing she had emerged from the incident sure of. The strange lights in the sky, the impossible craft: they would not be surprises to the men and women who ran this installation. They knew them well. They had built them themselves. But they had not done so alone.

And there, as they say, was the rub. Because the one image she had tried to forget would not fade from her mind's eye. It burned there, like the trail in the brush left by the brass-colored sphere as it came down under Alan's weapons. It had been cracked open and she had seen inside. She had looked in and seen the blasted remains of the cockpit, the two seats and their occupants, both unconscious, possibly dead, one a man in a flight suit not significantly different from Alan's, the other . . .

Not.

That was all she was prepared to say. The other figure had been smaller, childlike, but her mind told her in no uncertain terms that what she had seen was no human child.

Since the four of them had been reunited and turned unexpectedly, bizarrely, loose at the gates of the base, they had talked about everything that had happened, except that. They saw it in each other's eyes when they caught each other unawares, but no one wanted to say anything, as if keeping silent meant it wasn't real, that they could each dismiss what they had seen as a trick of the light, an effect of stress and panic. They could believe that the sphere had been flown by two human pilots. Not by one man and one . . .

Even now she couldn't bring herself to say the word, even in her head.

"Who wants to start?" asked the waitress.

"I'm the hungriest," said Barry, the heavily muscled black soldier she had met only at the height of the chaos. "Ribs, please. Full rack, cowboy beans, fries. And a beer. Thanks."

He sounded . . . together. Unfazed. Jennifer looked at the menu in front of her as if it had just appeared on the table, as if she couldn't read the words in front of her, and waved the waitress on to Alan while she tried to get her mind around the prospect of ordering food. In the end she just copied Timika, who ordered the Chicky sandwich and a chopped salad with such flair and certainty that you'd think she'd been eating here for months. When it arrived, the food was a surprise, not just because it was good, but because Jennifer couldn't remember what she had ordered.

She needed to sort herself out, and fast.

It wasn't like the last few days had been hard, she told herself again. After she had agreed to sign the nondisclosure agreement on the morning of the second day, her interrogators had been positively polite, their questions seeking clarity rather than seeming to come from disbelief or the sense that she was holding anything back. Timika, whose brand of bullheadedness was a little different from her own, had held out till the final day before signing, only doing so when they warned her she could be held indefinitely according to special provisions within the law concerning national security, but Jennifer had been, she felt, compliant throughout. They had brought her coffee, and though she had been obliged to eat alone in her quarters—more a low-budget hotel room than a cell—the food had been reasonable. On the third day they had even allowed her to make phone calls, though she suspected those were monitored. She had called Reg Deacon, who had been her father's personal assistant and was now her estate manager in the UK. He had been frantic about her silent absence, but she had rolled over that, telling him in no uncertain terms to dump all stock, investments, and business ties to the Maynard Consortium which, she suspected, was about to have a very bad week. In deference to the document she had just signed, she was sparing on details but adamant, finding a reserve of strength and moral certainty that she had otherwise lost in the bewildering fog of all that had happened at the base.

When they had been released and returned to their vehicles, the four of them had experienced a kind of disbelieving euphoria, laughing hysterically at the smallest thing as they drove and drove in vague search for somewhere to stop and regroup. A few hours ago they had stood on the massive walkway of the Hoover Dam like a bunch of tourists, gazing down the great sweep of concrete to the strangely luminous turquoise of the water below, as if nothing could be more normal. Now they were talking about how good the brisket was, and she was almost certain that Timika was flirting with Barry.

It was surreal.

"And we both had this doc when we were kids, right Alan?" Barry was saying. "Dr. Vespasian. Guy had a weak R. Called me Bawy. Bawy Wegis. '*How are my favowite patients, Bawy and Awan?*' he used to say. We thought it was hilarious. We used to come up with reasons to make him say words he couldn't pronounce. Really not cool. Sometimes I want to write to the guy to say sorry."

"That is so mean!" said Timika. "I didn't think you were so mean."

"I know," said Barry, grinning nonetheless. "We were terrible. But he was always sticking us with needles, drawing blood, pumping us full of stuff. It was our little revenge, I guess."

"Pass the salt, please," said Alan.

"*How have you been feewing?*" Barry said. "Man, poor guy. I wonder where he is."

"You should find out," said Timika, scolding, but with the ghost of a smile she couldn't quite conceal. "Thank him for all he did for you."

They had been turned loose with no directives or requirements, sent back to their lives as if nothing had happened, or rather as if what had happened had been put into a locked box like the one that had been at the end of Jerzy's treasure hunt in a concrete vault under an abandoned airstrip. The interrogators had thanked Timika for her trouble, locked the metaphorical box, and pumped the vault full of cement. It was over. Even Alan and Barry had been given an indefinite leave of absence, told to return "when they felt ready." When Alan told them he didn't think he'd be back, the guy interviewing him had apparently just smiled to himself and said he should take as long as he needed. They had seemed, Alan said, pretty confident he'd be back. Weirdly so.

Barry was laughing at something Timika had said that Jennifer hadn't caught, but then it hadn't been meant for her. The two of them might have been at another table for all the attention they paid to Alan and Jennifer, their eyes never leaving each other's faces. Timika had spent most of the previous day on the phone to her boyfriend Dion in New York, but it had gone badly. Timika had, she confided, said some things that had been on her mind for a while, but that she hadn't intended to say. Something about what they had gone through had sent a jolt through her life and "some stuff just came loose," she said. Whatever she was now playing at with Barry seemed to be her way of unwinding, shedding some of the tension and strangeness. Whether it was more than that, or would become more, Jennifer had no idea. After today, who knew if she would ever see the woman again.

"Can I have the salt?" asked Alan again.

Jennifer came to, or came about halfway, turning a quizzical look on him.

"What?" she said.

"I asked if you would pass the salt," said Alan, his politeness strained. His eyes still looked a little sunken from tiredness, but his other injuries seemed to have healed quickly.

"You want salt," she echoed, listening to herself speaking in the silence between Timika's playful laughter and Barry's encouraging rumble. They were bickering in that flippant way that sounded more adversarial than it really was. Something about music. Jennifer's brow furrowed and for a second her eyes closed before she said, "We just left the airbase where we've been held while we were quizzed about a battle with UFOs, piloted by . . . by an *alien*, and you want me to pass the salt?"

Her voice rose as the sentence climbed. Timika and Barry stopped talking and turned to give her a look that mirrored Alan's: surprised, but also anxious, warning. Barry lowered his head and murmured, "You want to keep your voice down?"

"My voice?" she replied, unable to keep the shrillness out, knowing that she was beginning to sound hysterical and unable to stop it. "He wants the salt and you want me to keep my *voice* down?"

A middle-aged woman two tables over half-turned her head toward them, and Timika made a calming motion with her hand.

"I know we've all been through some weird shit . . ." she began.

"Yeah?" Jennifer shot back. "You don't say! Well, I'm sorry if I'm not quite ready for sightseeing and . . . whatever the hell you two are talking about . . ."

"Timika said that Marvin Gaye was better than Smokey Robinson and I was like . . ."

"I don't care!" Jennifer snapped, slamming her hands to the sides of her head as if trying to hold it together. "How can you just sit here and talk like it's a regular day?"

"Because it is," said Timika, not laughing now.

"What? How?"

"Because it has to be," said Timika.

"This is nuts!" Jennifer gasped, sitting up as if about to rocket out of her chair and storm out. "Everything has changed. I mean . . . Everything! And you're just sitting here *chatting*."

"What are we supposed to do?" Timika returned, stiffening now and tilting her head like a bull considering a charge.

"I don't know! Something! Anything! Not just pretending the world is the same as it was!"

"It is," hissed Barry. "Nothing has changed. We just know more than we did a week ago."

"I just wanted the salt," said Alan.

It was supposed to be a joke, a wry lightening of the mood, but Jennifer wasn't there yet.

"You were in this from the start, Major," she said, looking malevolently first at him, then at Barry. "Me and her? We got dragged into it."

"*Her?*" Timika echoed, the bull starting to paw the ground.

"You know what I mean," Jennifer snapped.

"I think you're not used to not being in control," said Timika, staring her down, "and it's wigging you out."

"Oh, don't start," said Jennifer.

"Start what?"

"I'm in control because I'm rich and white but you're rolling with it because you're used to getting screwed over."

"You know," Timika responded with a little steel in her voice, "there may be something to that."

"Yeah, I thought there might be."

"Excuse me?" said Timika, matching Jennifer's volume and upping her swagger. "You think I'm getting too uppity, your highness?"

"Woah! Woah! Woah!" said Barry, spreading his hands between them. "Can everyone take it down a notch? That's not what she meant."

"Oh you know that, huh?" Timika fired back.

"I don't know what you're talking about," said Jennifer sulkily. "All I know is that . . ."

"Will someone please pass me the damn SALT!" said Alan, punctuating the end of the sentence by snapping his hand open.

It happened instantly. As the others stared in astonishment, the salt shaker, a little glass thing with a silver screw-on cap, slid rapidly across the table as if shot over by some invisible force and slammed into his palm.

The sparring stopped. Wide-eyed and baffled, everyone looked from the salt shaker in his hand to Alan's face in stunned silence.

"What the hell was that?" whispered Barry at last.

Alan shook his head, but when he tried to speak the words wouldn't come out. Carefully, he set the salt shaker down on the table, as if it might explode, and when he finally spoke, he sounded badly spooked.

"I have absolutely no idea," he said.

TIMIKA
Grand Canyon National Park, Arizona

ALAN HAD TRIED TO DO IT AGAIN, THAT THING WITH THE salt shaker, but it wouldn't work. He stared at it, one hand open to catch it if it slid suddenly, then tried squeezing his eyes shut and focusing with his mind till it looked like he was going to have an aneurism. The salt didn't shift an inch. Timika watched him warily, not sure what to believe.

Her first response had been to think it was a trick, a joke to defuse the rising tension, but he swore blind it wasn't and, eventually, she believed him, mainly because he looked freaked out. He was either one hell of an actor, or it had been as much a surprise to him as it was to the rest of them and, cool though it kind of was, not a pleasant surprise. It made him uneasy and he kept glancing at his hand like it belonged to someone else and might start doing things all by itself, like that guy on that *House* episode who kept slapping his girlfriend even though he didn't mean to. Season five or there-abouts. That was pretty cool.

Alan still had no explanation.

"I don't know how I did it," he said about fifty times. "I was angry and I wanted it and it was just . . ."

"We saw," said Timika. "You're quite the David Copperfield."

"The Dickens character?" asked Jennifer, bewildered.

"He's a stage magician," said Barry quietly.

"An incredibly famous one," said Timika. Jennifer shrugged and looked away.

Timika wasn't sure why the Englishwoman kept setting her off. They were, she supposed, both stressed, on edge after all they'd gone through, though they expressed themselves differently.

Different as chalk and cheese, she thought, not for the first time.

Alan's little magic show with the salt shaker had killed more than the brewing squabble. They had eaten their food in virtual silence, keen to get out of the restaurant, though for Timika's part she had no clue what she was going to do next. After the calamitous call to Dion she had spoken to Marvin back in the office, but even that had left her with a cold anxiety that sat in her gut like a cannonball. *Debunktion*—the skeptical website she ran—had been her life, her pride and joy, her face in the world. But after what she had experienced in the last couple of weeks, how could she go back to it? She had considered modulating the site's content, dialing back its scornful cynicism and doubt, but that *was* the site! It had been built around her hard-edged logic, her critical eye, and her barbed wit. She couldn't simply rebrand the site as some-thing that tolerated all it had formerly derided. That would leave it, at best, weak, tamed by its more measured approach, and at worst, an industry joke. She couldn't bear that. Better fold it outright.

And do what? Return to New York to her cratering relationship with Dion to live in overpriced real estate with nothing to sustain her, and employees—friends—to lay off? She would have to explain to them why she was doing what she was doing, which would be excruciatingly embarrassing. And, she reminded herself, given the papers she finally signed, illegal.

Figures.

But there was one thing she still had to do. She hadn't mentioned it to the others yet because they had all instinctively told the truth to their interrogators. That was a smart call, if only because it kept you from tripping yourself up, and it was what Timika had done for the most part. But there was one thing she had held back, one thing she hadn't been prepared to give up.

Jerzy Stern had come to her in New York and brought her a book: his book, the account of his life and directions to that Nevada airfield. She had found what he wanted her to find at the foot of a concrete shaft, a seemingly ancient item in a metal box, but then it had been whisked away from her again.

Except that she had snapped a picture of it, and uploaded it to a private drop box before giving up her phone to the soldier who had demanded it. As a reporter and, if she was honest, as a black woman, she had a constant wariness of authority that buzzed in her ears like a witch's insect familiar, always on watch. It was second nature to her to preset her phone so that it would delete all information after each use. That meant she had to carry numbers in her head, but it was worth the inconvenience. In the instant the soldier had demanded she finish her conversation with Marvin out there in the strobe-lit desert almost a week ago, she had stared him down and, when he looked away, she had thumbed open the phone with practiced fingers, slid out the SIM card, and dropped it. As she stepped up to him, the useless phone extended, she had deftly kicked the tiny plastic panel into the sandy earth.

She wasn't sure what they'd get off her phone. They might have returned to the spot and searched for the SIM card, but even if they found it she wasn't sure they'd be able to piece together all she had done, though she supposed that if anyone had the equipment and skills to do so, it would be them.

In any case, she had simply not referred to the picture she had taken or the message she had sent, and no one had prompted her. They'd asked her if she'd looked in the box and she had said she had, but hadn't had a chance to make sense of what was inside.

"Something old," she'd said, shrugging. "Weird looking."

One of the women in the room, a dishwater blond in her early thirties, had watched her closely at that, her eyes narrowing a fraction as if she didn't trust Timika's pretense of thoughtlessness, but if she'd rung any alarm bells in the blond's head, the woman hadn't pressed further. It was easy to pretend you were stupid when other people wanted to believe it.

Even so, Timika was surprised when she had picked up a disposable phone in Boulder City that morning and found the picture still in the drop box she'd sent it to. She downloaded it to her new phone but hesitated to send it to Marvin. The nondisclosure agreement she had signed was nothing to fool with. Even if she said nothing about where the image had come from, Marvin would put two and two together and that could get her into serious trouble. They might already be monitoring her account, waiting for her to screw up . . .

She'd keep the image to herself. For now.

But there was more. Her earlier call to Marvin had raised another possibility, one that might direct her next actions.

Apparently in his reorganizing of the office ransacked by the Maynard Consortium's goons he had turned up a single sheet of paper with a series of handwritten numbers on it. He had photographed the page and e-mailed it to her. It matched the faded, old-fashioned paper of Jerzy's notebook, and Timika, her heart in her mouth, guessed that it had been left in the bottom of the little box in which the notebook had arrived the day it all began. Dimly, she remembered sitting outside, slipping the book into the pocket of her long red coat. She missed that coat. She'd left it in some store while running from the fake Homeland Security agent, "Cook."

She closed her eyes, trying to remember what she had done with the box the notebook had come in, but her mind was blank. Maybe she'd left it in the park and Marvin had picked it up. Or she might have handed it to him. She couldn't remember.

But she recognized the string of numbers as a set of coordinates like the ones that had led her to the carved artifact in the bunker. But these numbers were quite different and that meant . . .

Another hidden object?

Possibly.

"Hiya."

It was Jennifer, looking sheepish. Keen to leave Nevada behind and with no clue what they were going to do next, they had left Boulder City and driven the two hours over the Arizona border to the Grand Canyon park entrance. It had been Jennifer's idea, and since the mood was already utterly bizarre, it made about as much sense as anything else. Strangely, none of them had visited the Grand Canyon before.

"Hey," said Timika.

"So," said Jennifer, gazing out over the lookout point through the blue air to the stripes of layered pink and russet stone. "This is the Grand Canyon. You Americans do like everything to be . . . big."

Timika gave her a sidelong look, took in the Englishwoman's half smile, and said simply, "Yep."

There was a moment of silence as a family of over-padded white people looking flushed and unhappy waddled past. Then Jennifer said, "Listen, about before . . ."

"It's cool."

"I know, but I'm sorry. I suppose everything was just getting on top of me and I was feeling a bit het up . . ."

"Het up?"

"Upset. You don't say that?"

Timika shrugged. "I don't," she said.

"I was feeling . . . out of it, I guess."

"Out of what?"

"The loop," said Jennifer, sighing at herself. "You all seemed so relaxed about it all. I felt," she paused, struggling for the words, "like the English person."

"Ha," said Timika. "Well, you are, you know."

"I know. It just felt we had the Atlantic between us right there at the table."

"Really?"

"Kind of. Not really. I don't know. I felt like the spare wheel, the odd one out, the fish out of . . ."

"I get it."

"Barry's military. Alan flies those things. Even you've been in one. I saw it! But me? I feel like everything is happening to me but I'm not doing anything. I don't know where I fit in. Does that make sense?"

"I guess. Though for what it's worth, I was mostly on the receiving end too."

"I suppose so," Jennifer agreed. "And I don't know why I took it out on you. I'm sorry."

"I know. I guess I was a bit *het up* too." Timika frowned. "Oh, that doesn't sound right at all. You English are so weird with your English."

"What are we doing here?"

"It was your idea," said Timika. "You wanted to see the Grand Canyon. So. There it is."

"I mean, what do we do next?"

"Is there a next?"

"You mean, just go back to our lives?" said Jennifer. "Pretend it never happened?"

"You could." Seeing the fractional tightening in Jennifer's face, Timika added, "not just because you're rich. I didn't mean that. My job, my life in New York . . . I don't know if there's anything to go back to. You could at least pick up where you left off."

"In my castle, you mean," said Jennifer grinning.

"I assumed it was a palace, but okay."

"A palatial castle," Jennifer deadpanned. "Best of both worlds. Comfortable, but you can still throw the servants into the moat."

Timika laughed and considered her.

"I really am sorry about before," she said.

"It is, as you would say, cool," said Jennifer, smiling.

The decision was made in a second. Timika pulled her phone out, called up the picture, and showed it to Jennifer.

"What's this?" she asked, shielding the screen from the sun.

"Jerzy's buried treasure. It's what was in the lockbox before it disappeared."

Jennifer gaped at her.

"Do they know you have this?" she asked.

"Not sure. I didn't advertise it and I don't intend to. Just keeping it within the family for now."

Jennifer's mouth flickered into a smile, but her eyes went back to the screen.

"What do you think it is?" she asked.

The image showed an irregular slab of stone scored with intricate carved lines, the whole thing edged with a band of bluish metal.

"Writing," said Timika. "I'd guess some early Near Eastern civilization, but I don't really know. Older than ancient Greek. You can't tell from the picture but the metal around the edge, which looks like it was added later, gave off light and energy, like it reacted to touch or closeness. I'd seen something similar before. An old woman claimed to have a piece from Roswell."

Jennifer looked at her.

"If you'd said that to me a couple of weeks ago . . ." she began.

"I know."

"What are you going to do with this?"

"Find someone who can read it," said Timika, pocketing the phone. "And I think there might be another."

"What? Why?"

Hurriedly, with no sense of taking a risk, she told the Englishwoman about Marvin's extra page and the numbers on the back. Jennifer considered this thoughtfully, then nodded to where Alan and Barry stood apart, gazing out over the great gulf. They seemed farther away than mere physical distance would allow. But that was men for you, military men in particular.

"You going to tell them?" asked Jennifer.

"No," said Timika, another snap decision. "Not yet at least."

"Well, I need to go back to the UK, but I can help."

"Yeah? How?"

"The way people like me always help," said Jennifer. "With money."

Timika gave her a look.

"I don't want to impose . . ." she began.

"Please," said Jennifer. "You are effectively out of work. You have nowhere to live. Do you even have a laptop? Are you going to blow your savings on hotels and car hire and flights?" Timika looked down. "Do you have any idea how much money I'm in control of?" Jennifer went on.

"Okay. No need to rub it in."

"I'm not rubbing anything in. I'm just telling you the truth. I've reclaimed my father's assets. I have literally more money than I could ever spend and now I want to know what that picture means. I'm not entirely sure why, but I trust you. We've been through something. Shared the kind of experience few people ever do. So. Consider yourself a freelance investigator. With one phone call I can set you up with a per diem, a substantial credit line . . ."

"I thought we were living under the radar? Credit cards will bring them down on us like . . ."

"Who? Maynard is done," said Jennifer, not bothering to keep a vicious flash of triumph out of her face. "They are finished. My interrogators said that on the second day. The ones who aren't dead are under arrest pending charges. Deacon confirmed that this morning. And not because of lawsuits from me. The US Department of Justice is after them, and that's about as serious as it gets. If Maynard and their nasty little friends still have field agents, they are burrowing a bloody long way out of sight right now. You are free as a bird."

"The DOJ?" said Timika, awed.

"The legal equivalent of the United States cavalry," said Jennifer. "They are flying the flag of national security and everyone is getting the hell out of the way. Anyone touched by Maynard is in the path of the freight train, and so long as you don't piss off your own government, you can do what you want. No one is coming after you, Timika. Not now. As soon as we're done here, I say we get you set up to re-enter the lists."

"Lists of what?"

"It's a jousting term, I think."

"Knights in armor and shit? Not sure I like the sound of that."

"Then let's just say we're going to get you back up on the horse."

Timika nodded thoughtfully, then grinned.

"You're on, Princess. Timika Mars, investigative journalist, reporting for duty."

Jennifer offered her hand, but as they shook on the deal, her face became suddenly serious.

"I want to know how they got my father involved," she said. "And what they thought they were after. If whatever was at the end of Jerzy's treasure hunt is relevant to that, I want to know."

"Got it," said Timika. "And thanks."

"Sure," said Jennifer. "It's what people like me do. We're the bank."

She said it ruefully, and there was a flicker of something in her eyes that was more than self-deprecating. It was sad.

"You won't regret it," said Timika.

"Never occurred to me that I would," Jennifer replied, rediscovering her uncomplicated smile. "You sure you're not going to tell the guys?"

Timika looked over to them again and shook her head.

"They have enough to deal with," she said. "And I think they'll go back to the base. If they don't know what I'm doing they won't have to keep it secret."

"Alan said he wouldn't go back," said Jennifer, considering him through scratched sunglasses.

"That was before he started making the condiments dance," said Timika. "He might not have realized it yet, but he'll go back. They are the only people who will be able to make sense of what has happened to him."

"You think it's because of what he did, flying that ship?"

"Don't you? He said he flew it with his mind. This can't be a coincidence."

Jennifer nodded thoughtfully.

"You ever watch *Doctor Who*?" she asked. Timika shook her head. "When I was a kid I was terrified of it because of these villains, the Daleks. They looked like salt shakers. Pepper pots, I called them."

"Doesn't sound too scary."

"They went around exterminating anything that wasn't Dalek," said Jennifer. "Shouting and shooting. They were like Nazis in their own private tanks."

"Okay," Timika conceded. "That *is* scary."

"About as scary as accidentally moving things with your mind," said Jennifer.

They watched Alan warily, and when Barry laid a hand on his shoulder and started talking to him, his face earnest and concerned, the women looked deliberately away to give them the privacy they seemed to need.

ALAN
Grand Canyon National Park

I F HE'D BEEN ALONE, HE MIGHT HAVE BEEN ABLE TO convince himself that he'd imagined it. Maybe. But he hadn't been. He'd been sitting at the table inches away from three other people. Two of them he felt sure he could trust, though they were really strangers, and the other he'd known all his life, and would trust him with it. He had examined the salt shaker and the tabletop for magnets or motors, transmitters . . . Anything. There was, of course, nothing. He hadn't expected there to be. So he tipped the salt out onto his plate and combed through it, grain by grain, till the server scowled at him and he, apologizing vaguely, decided it was time to go.

He tried to do it again, demanding things, concentrating on them, snapping open his hand just as he had in the restaurant, but nothing happened. It felt as thoroughly impossible as it would have right up to the second it had happened the first time. But in that second, the universe had changed.

It seemed like that anyway, and it was why he couldn't quite buy the idea that if there hadn't been witnesses he would have just gotten on with his life as if nothing had happened. Because he felt different. He couldn't put his finger on how and had absolutely no idea why, but he felt a strange, deep-seated rightness which he didn't trust himself to talk about in front of the others. Like it was natural. Like he had been waiting for the proper moment. Why the proper moment involved demanding salt while being ignored by his squabbling friends in a Nevada barbecue restaurant was less clear, but the certainty of it all had swelled in his mind. First there had been the panic, a fear of the weirdness of it, but then it had come, like a secret nodding smile that spread through his body like warmth.

This is how things were supposed to be.

It was an unsettling thought, and almost as soon as it had come, Alan went back to feeling nervous and apprehensive. He didn't like the sidelong way Barry—his friend from high school—watched him, considering him as if he was someone his buddy had never seen before. He didn't like the feeling of smugness he felt when he looked at their astonished faces. And he hated the fact that he couldn't do it again.

What, after all, was the point of superpowers if you couldn't control them?

Superpowers.

It was absurd. Of course it was. But that's what it felt like. It was worrying.

All the way to the Grand Canyon—why on earth were they going to the Grand Canyon?—he had wondered about it, but came up with nothing. He stared at the zipper on the bag at his feet, trying to flip the pull tab or move it an inch or two, parting the zipper's plastic teeth as it moved . . .

Nothing.

He couldn't do anything. But he *had* done something. Which left him where, exactly? Well, it left him gazing into the vast emptiness of one of America's great natural wonders, a metaphor if ever there was one. By the time Barry joined him at the rail, Alan was sinking back into doubt and confusion.

"Canyon's a little wide, don't you think?" asked Barry conversationally. "How 'bout you pull the other side a bit closer?"

"Funny," said Alan.

Barry grinned briefly, then said, "You doing all right?"

Alan shrugged.

"I guess," he said. "Not sure. Never had superpowers before."

"Oh hell, no," said Barry. "That salt shaker thing? I don't think so. When you can jump across the canyon or hurl your damn salt shaker hard enough to stop a tank, you can talk about superpowers, but for now, my brother, the Avengers are not taking your calls."

"You're just loving this, aren't you?"

"Better question," said Barry, "is why aren't you? You did something cool. It was weird, but it was cool as hell. What's with the angst?"

Alan shrugged again, eyes fixed on the blue distance. But Barry wouldn't let it go at that.

"You've dealt with weird physics before," he said.

"That was in a vehicle," Alan replied. "A craft that used technology I didn't understand, but which worked. This is different. It's in me. My body. My mind. So yeah, it feels strange."

"Is that all?" said Barry, probing. "I mean, I get that, but it feels like more."

Alan sighed.

"I was done, you know?" he said. "I felt like I'd paid my dues, done my duty. Above and beyond, man. I did my part and I earned the right to walk away. But now . . ."

"You think this means you have to go back," Barry concluded for him.

"Wouldn't you?"

Barry looked hard at his friend, then turned to stare out over the ancient rock formations and the long drop to the carving gash of the river so very far below.

"When?" he said.

"As soon as we're done here," said Alan.

Barry nodded.

"I'll drive you."

▼   ▼   ▼

AND HE DID. THEY WALKED AROUND THE PARK WITH TIMIKA and Jennifer, and listened in on a ranger talking about the geology of the region. They spotted a female elk stalking across the road and they stopped for a snack at one of the viewing lodges. Then Alan announced his decision, bracing himself for shock, even hurt, and explanations he didn't feel like giving. But the women seemed to have sensed this was coming and weren't the least bit surprised.

An hour later Alan and Barry arranged for separate cars and said their farewells, promising to stay in touch, though they were unsure if that was even possible. The women seemed to have a mission of their own but also seemed wary of discussing it, and Alan decided that the less he knew, the better. He had enough on his plate. Enough, indeed, that his parting from Jennifer, whom he had not long ago considered someone he might want to know a good deal better, seemed almost formally polite. Barry's goodbye to Timika, by contrast, included a real hug from which they both walked away grinning. Alan gave his friend an inquisitive look as they left, but Barry shrugged with his eyebrows and a pucker of the mouth that meant "who knows?"

Then they were driving again, west and north, back toward Nevada, back toward Rachel and Area 51, which he had been so glad to put behind him only yesterday. As they sped through the darkening desert in their rented Camry, Barry made small talk.

"Hell of a thing, huh? Two guys who went to the same high school still at the same base," he said.

"A good thing," said Alan, shooting him a quick look.

"Sure!" said Barry, eyes on the road. "Weird though, no?"

"Weird?"

"Yeah. I mean, we played football together! Now we're here."

"Just lucky, I guess."

"You think?" said Barry. There was something in his voice, a caution, as if there was something he wanted to say but couldn't figure out how to, something he had wanted to say for a long time. "I mean, it's been years. You're a major and a pilot. I'm a former pilot, former FAC, former MARSOC. Now I'm on base security."

Alan shifted in his seat. He had always believed that their difference in rank was a matter of interests and ambition, not aptitude, but he had never been comfortable with the fact of it. They were friends. He didn't always like what the Corps demanded of how they interacted based on their different positions.

"Both Marines," he remarked, trying to sound casual and glancing out of the window. "Both riflemen. Well, former."

They had both resigned their commissions to accept their Dreamland positions. They were CIA now, even if they still *felt* like Marines at heart.

"Always in each other's orbit, you know?" said Barry, like a dog with a bone he wouldn't give up. "I mean, I shouldn't even have been heading the ground team on that Afghan mission. But you were overhead, so there I was. You get transferred back stateside and whaddayaknow? There I am too. Same base. Then you're out of the Corps, and so am I, new intel assignments . . ."

"So?" said Alan. "You think someone wants to keep us together 'cuz we're friends?"

"Nah," said Barry. "But that's why it's weird, right? They shouldn't want us together. So why are we?"

"I think you're overthinking it," said Alan. "They probably don't even know how far back we go."

"They knew we were friends at Leatherneck and they knew we had a fight," said Barry, laying it out. Alan's instincts had been right. Barry had been thinking about this for a long time. "But when you were moved here, so was I. You don't think that's weird?"

"They said it was to help my transition," said Alan, hating the sound of the words. "Because of the new mission I had. The new tech. Messed with my head. I guess they were used to that and thought you being around would make me adjust better."

He didn't like to put it that way, but it was probably what had happened.

"The other pilots have old buddies around the base, did they?" asked Barry.

Alan frowned.

"Not that I know of," he said.

"No. Me neither."

The road stretched on in front of them, shimmering with heat even as the light faded fast.

"Okay, Barry," said Alan, pivoting in the passenger seat to consider his friend properly. "What are you driving at?"

"Nothing. I really don't know, Alan. I'm just saying it's pretty fucking odd, and that's coming from someone who saw an honest-to-God alien in the desert last week."

"And all *I'm* saying," said Alan, "is that on the scale of oddness you and I have been dealing with, it doesn't register, and I could do with one less thing to stress about right now, so if you wouldn't mind dropping it . . ."

"Won't go away just because we don't talk about it."

"There's nothing to talk about!" Alan shot back. They were both getting irritated. Unreasonably so. They were on the edge of something that had been rankling since Leatherneck, something they had kicked the dirt over but that was still there between them.

"And there you go," said Barry, his big knuckles whitening on the steering wheel.

"Where?"

"It's fine. Forget it. Everything is awesome and not weird at all."

"You got something on your mind, Barry, just say it."

"Is that an order, Major?"

"That's a bullshit response and you know it."

"Yeah? Well, being special, I guess you'd know."

"What the fuck is that supposed to mean?"

They were all but yelling now, and when Barry's eyes flashed toward Alan there was fire in them. The car was moving fast, too fast, but it was the heat of the argument that made Barry slow to see that the oncoming pickup had wandered from its lane. Even so the Camry braked hard, buying them a fraction of a second. Then Barry was twisting the wheel and the car was lurching over the rutted shoulder in a plume of grit and dust, tires biting as it came to a noisy, slewing stop. The pickup bounced away from them and came to a skidding halt forty yards down the road.

"You okay?" asked Barry.

"Yeah," said Alan, dazed and surprised by the truth of it. The pickup had been coming right at them. "What happened? He clip us?"

Barry shook his head uncertainly.

"Looked like it," he said. "But I didn't feel it. You?"

"No," said Alan, opening the door and sliding out.

"You fellas all right?"

It was the driver of the pickup, a middle-aged man with a leathery brown complexion and a steel-wool mustache. He was standing in the middle of the road looking back at them through the gathering gloom of the early evening. He looked spooked, wary.

"Think so," said Barry, walking toward him. "You?"

"Yeah. Guess I tagged you, huh?" he replied. He didn't sound exactly sure. His eyes kept flashing to the right fender of his truck, and when he stooped to run a hand along the bumper, he stood up looking merely confused.

"No," said Barry, after checking the Camry. "I don't think you did."

"Hit something," said the older man. "Felt it. Pretty sure, I felt it. Think I was getting on the drowsy side, to tell you the truth. These long roads, you know. May have closed my eyes. But something woke me right the hell up."

He spoke in a kind of daze, picking his way through the experience and trying to square it with what he found on his truck. Or didn't find. There was a little pocking from debris on the road where the paint was chipped, but it all looked old. There were no recent scratches or dents, and nothing like the kind of damage you'd expect from a head-on collision, however oblique, given their combined speeds.

"No," said Barry, stooping to consider the front of the Camry too. "I don't think you got us."

"Got something," said the driver, his brow furrowed, staring from the pickup to the Camry and back. "Don't make no sense."

"Let's go," said Alan in a low voice.

"You don't think we should trade insurance or something?" asked Barry.

"For what? There was no accident."

Barry heard something in Alan's voice and looked at him, realizing.

"You think you did it again," he said, matching Alan's murmur.

Alan shrugged and looked down.

"I thought he'd hit us," said Barry. "I was sure of it. I *saw* it . . ."

"You braked before he hit us," said Alan.

"I wasn't looking," Barry replied. "I was looking at you. How did I know . . . ? And then he kicked back across to his side like he'd bounced right off us but . . ."

"I think we're all good!" said Alan loudly and with a cheeriness he did not feel. He raised his hand to the driver of the pickup. "You okay to drive?"

"Yeah," said the other man vaguely. "I guess so. Damnedest thing . . ."

"Maybe get a cup of coffee at the diner over the hill," called Alan.

Barry was watching him, saying nothing.

"Yep," called the other guy, opening the door to the pickup. "Maybe I will at that."

And then it was done, and he was driving away and Barry was back behind the wheel of the Camry looking troubled, Alan beside him in the dark.

"You think you did that," said Barry quietly. "You think you did something to stop him from hitting us?"

"I think we both did," said Alan.

JOSH HARRUP
2014, Twenty Miles from Cedar Rapids, Iowa

JOSH HARRUP, 45, LAID DOWN THE PHOTOGRAPH OF Charlene, taken no more than eight months before she left him, and took another slug of Wild Turkey, which was kind of ironic, since it was because of the whisky that she'd finally packed her bags and left the farm for good. He had been working on the bottle for almost an hour now, long enough to find that fact both funny and sad in equal measure, but not long enough for misery to blot out anger. Not at Charlene. God knew she'd put up with a hell of a lot before she'd finally cracked, and in his cooler, more level-headed moments he really couldn't blame her for going. That kind of sucked because Josh liked to blame things: politicians, the economy, Wall Street—about which he knew little more than the name— talk radio hosts, liberals, competitive cyclists, Cubs fans.

It was a list that grew by the day without much logic to it. He knew that too, knew that his family (mostly estranged) thought him a loser who "never took responsibility for anything," and he had alienated most of the neighbors and the few friends he'd had when Charlene was still home. He only admitted it when he was in bed alone in the dark or, like now, when he was well into a bottle and not much caring whether he'd survive the night, but in those black, soul-sucking corners of misery he knew it was almost all his fault. He blamed and ranted and he pointed the finger, but in the deepest, darkest, coldest crevices of his soul, he knew that he had built his shitty life with one screwup after another. Everything was his fault.

Everything, at least, that wasn't Jimbo Styles's fault.

Josh considered the dingy, old-fashioned kitchen, the dishes stacked in the sink, the garbage can overflowing with the foil containers of frozen dinners and unrinsed cans of baked beans. Sure, he'd made some lousy calls over the last twenty five years or so, but none of it had been done in malice. He'd backed a couple of bad horses, figuratively speaking, but he'd never actually tried to screw anyone over. Not like Jimbo had. If his neighbor had been a different person, Josh figured, life might be very different. The farm would be twice the size it was now, that was for sure. Hell, Charlene might even still be here, reading one of her novels by the fire or baking bread for the morning.

God, the smell of Charlene's bread as it came out of the oven!

He smiled at the memory, then shuddered, and his face set hard again as reality seeped back into his head like the cold air that would stream in under the kitchen door all winter no matter what ham-fisted steps Josh took to shut it out. Right now that didn't sound all bad. It was Iowa in July and the AC unit in the window was busted, so the heat stood in the room close and still, like bodies in an elevator. Josh sweated in silence and took another drink.

Jimbo Styles was a lifelong bachelor who lived a mile north of Josh's westernmost field, lived—in fact—on land that had belonged to Josh's father, till Styles had pulled some legal crap and taken a prime slice right off the Harrup farm. Josh's list of people to blame had lawyers marked in big black letters, highlighted and underlined. He had never fully understood the suit. Something to do with a rental agreement made by his father just after Josh was born, a long-term lease, according to Styles—which he had called in on the death of Josh's father, when Jimbo's herd was large enough to need more grazing. Josh hadn't understood any of it. He had always thought the land was his, and had worked it accordingly. Suddenly there were men in suits at his door and then the fence posts were being moved and half of Josh's soy crop—his livelihood—was gone. A year later, so was Charlene.

You couldn't blame Josh for that.

For all he knew of the law, Josh's dad might have lost the land at a card game. A game at which Styles had cheated, rigged the deck somehow.

Yeah, he thought, refilling is glass unsteadily and knocking it quickly back. *That was it.*

Everything came back to Jimbo Styles, that slick, smooth-talking, Cadillac-driving bastard. He may as well have abducted Charlene himself.

Josh didn't like that last thought and usually tried to keep it in a strongbox bound with baling wire in some abandoned cupboard in his head, but from time to time it got out. It wasn't that Charlene might have been with Jimbo. She would never do that, though Jimbo would probably have jumped at the chance. It was that Josh had been made less by Jimbo. He felt smaller, weaker, unable to run his farm, or look after his wife the way a man should, all thanks to Jimbo fucking Styles, driving around with the top down—who heard of a farmer in a convertible?—smiling and waving and stinking of money and power and success, much of it stolen from Josh with words, some stupid paper his idiot father had signed years ago . . .

Josh lurched out of his chair, sending it shooting back so that it almost flipped. He put one hand on the table to steady himself, then took two long strides across the kitchen to the drawer by the oven where the bread wasn't baking. He plucked out a flashlight and a box of shells, which he upended on the table. He stuffed a half dozen into his pockets, then took up the old Browning 12-gauge from behind the door, broke it open, and pushed a shell into each barrel.

Just to make his point.

Maybe. Josh didn't have a plan, didn't know how the night would end and, in this particular moment, didn't much care.

He stormed out into the night, the whisky making his swagger wider, less certain, as he moved along the weedy path, clicking the flashlight on. Its beam was dim and amber, the batteries dying which, he thought furiously, just about figured. He focused on Jimbo Styles, who was the root of all that was wrong with Josh's world, and headed across the fields.

There was no point taking the truck. It took almost as long to get to the Styles' house by the convoluted road—laid out as it had been before the redrawing of the property lines—and besides, he didn't want his neighbor to hear him coming. He wanted to walk into the front door stinking of anger and justice, the shotgun in his hand. He wanted to see fear in Styles's face, to make him feel small and weak . . .

It was a hot night, the world alive with crickets and frogs, but there was very little wind and the sky was clear enough to see the stars. It was a steady, stifling heat, like a warm, wet blanket thrown across the state, and it was enough to drive some of the drunken certainty from him, though not to actually sober him up. He seemed to get slower but more sure of foot the farther he got from home. After ten minutes he climbed awkwardly over the fence across the field that had once been his and made a beeline for the pasture where Styles grazed his cattle, and for the farmhouse beyond.

If Josh's mind had been less dulled by drink, he would have noticed the silence earlier. As it was he was three quarters across the pasture before he registered the absence of the herd that normally stood around, breathing heavily, lowing from time to time in their sleep. He had been among them at night before, hating them for their owner's sake, and had once been reported when Styles spotted him, but tonight the field was empty.

It felt odd, and Josh Harrup's footsteps slowed, then stopped entirely as he flashed the weak beam of the flashlight over the hoof-trodden ground. It was a flat field, and if you looked closely, with the light held low, you could still see the undulations where the soy had grown, before Styles had seeded it for pasture, but now the field was dotted with irregular hulks like long mounds of earth, like . . .

Bodies.

Josh stared, suddenly cold, and fixed one in the flashlight beam. It was one of the cows, a red-and-white Ayrshire, lying on its side, unmoving. Josh kept very still, watching the animal's ribs for signs of breathing, but the beast was still as a statue. He rotated slowly and picked out another prone cow. Then another. And another.

The hair on the back of his neck prickled with the strangeness of the thing, but he couldn't help feeling a rush of savage pleasure. Jimbo Styles's herd was sick, maybe even dead or dying, struck down by some illness or poison in the very field he had stolen from Josh.

Maybe there was a God after all.

He took a series of steps up to the nearest cow, not troubling to be quiet. If it was sleeping he didn't want to be right next to it when it woke. Cows were big creatures and could do you a serious injury if they blundered into you.

But the animal didn't stir, and when he was close enough to touch it, Josh stooped and put the flat of his hand on the cow's flank. Beneath the stiff bristle of the coat, the beast felt still and cold.

It was dead.

Josh's former sense of triumph died on the spot and he felt a kind of pitying sadness for the animal, even if its demise would hurt his rival. He sighed, calmer than he had been, his anger muted now, and in that moment he turned his flashlight to the dead cow's face.

He recoiled, leaping to his feet and staggering back.

The cow's eyes were gone. There was no blood, but they had been neatly scooped from the skull so that the bone of the sockets gleamed pale in the struggling light of the flashlight.

What the hell?

He moved unsteadily, unthinking, to another, his heart beginning to race. For a moment he was relieved. The next animal had its eyes. But the face around the jaw had been flayed, the hide and flesh peeled carefully away to reveal the lower jaw of the animal.

Josh felt the sudden urge to vomit, and turned, puking hard and wet into the grass. As he raised his head he saw another shape in the darkness some twenty yards away. It was strangely vertical, and canted at a bizarre angle, so that he shone his flashlight on it even though he didn't really want to see it.

It was another cow, but this one was buried in the earth head-first up to the shoulder. The turf around it was churned up but showed a curious swirl pattern, as if the beast had been somehow *screwed* into the ground.

Which was impossible.

But there it was, hind legs in the air, body unmarked by gashes or any trace of blood splatter. In any other circumstance it might have been funny, but it wasn't. Not remotely. Over the strangeness and nausea came a new feeling, simpler and cleaner. It was terror. Something was very badly wrong here, and the only idea in Josh Harrup's head now was the desperate, blind urge to be somewhere else.

He half turned, dragging his eyes off the impossibly mangled Ayrshire, and as he did he tripped on a tussock of coarse grass and fell. The shotgun, which he had been cradling like a thing forgotten, went down with him and went off with a single deafening bang, a blaze of light and then another blaze, equally hot and savage, of pain.

Josh crumpled into the grass with a single cry. One hand flashed instinctively down to where the shot had torn open his boot. He felt the hot, sticky slickness within, and came close to passing out. The only thing that stopped him was the same desperate thought that persisted, even though he knew he had blown half his foot away.

Have to get out of here.

He couldn't stand, but he began a ragged, crab-like crawl, heading back the way he had come, the fire in his foot actually increasing as shock gave way to the agony of the damage itself. But he couldn't stop. He had to keep moving.

Have to get out of here.

And then, dimly, without really knowing what he meant, his addled, pain-ravaged brain added,

Before they come back.

MORAT
Somewhere north of Taraz, Kazakhstan

JEAN-CHRISTOPHE MORAT, OR THE MAN WHO HAD BEEN using that name for long enough that it felt real to him, lay in his bunk, staring at the ceiling, thinking back over everything that had happened since the debacle over Nevada. Try as he might, he couldn't put it completely behind him, even if his superiors would let him.

Which they wouldn't.

He had lost the fleet. The Americans had hit them with something new, something they shouldn't have had and which he would have bet serious money they didn't know how to use. But then there it was, slicing through the air, weapon systems flaring. The disk. Somehow, though he could not make sense of it, Alan Young had been at the helm. None of it should have worked, but it had, and Morat's fleet had been blown apart.

Decades of R&D gone at a stroke.

Morat's own arrowhead craft had spun aimless into the void and it was only good luck that had kept it from spiraling to earth or burning up on the lip of the atmosphere. For over an hour he had had no influence over the ship at all, and had only been half conscious for most of that time. He had drifted like an eggshell in a swollen stream, pulled by currents outside his control, rocked and tossed and buffeted till he had vomited his stomach empty and been forced to try what manual override he could as half his systems burned out, their surface controls puckered and black from the heat.

He remembered because he had relived it all in his dreams, though the real stuff, the things that had actually happened to him, always gave way to stranger, more unsettling images, the sense of being lost and hunted by . . . what? A pack? Something large, something at once single and multiple, though he did not know how that could be possible. Something of dread and terror and appetite. Something awful.

By comparison the truth of what had happened over Nevada and afterward was a cakewalk, even though it hadn't felt that way at the time.

He'd managed to reassert control of the rudder in a high-altitude drift over the Philippine Sea, retaining the most minimal of his operating systems to ease the arrowhead into a slow tracking orbit that kept out of the sun. After what felt like days he had limped back to the Kazakhstan base at something just north of stalling speed. By the time he could glide unevenly in to land—clumsily, tearing off a third of the port wing—the initial battle had been long over and Morat had been given up as dead.

Might have been better if he had stayed that way.

He could have evacuated the ship and set it to blow, gone into hiding, rejoined the world a safe year or more later with a new identity, outside the organization and determined to stay out.

Except that they would have found him. He was almost sure. Eventually they always caught up with you.

Or so it had been before. The full extent of the hit they had taken was only just becoming clear, and the loss of the fleet to the US triangles was only a part of the disaster. The Maynard Consortium was all but dead, key members of its board cut down in a gun battle with US security forces in the Nevada desert, its ties to break-ins and the attempted assassinations of Timika Mars and Jennifer Quinn causing shock waves to run through both sides of the Atlantic. Old protections and connections in law enforcement were breaking down, vanishing in the rush to cut ties, and it was said that money was leaking out of Maynard assets like oil from a ruptured tanker. Some of that was coming from Quinn herself who was, unaccountably, still alive and flexing what financial muscle her idiot father had bequeathed to her before the death that Morat had so expertly given him. It was a mess, though there was, as the English put it, no use crying over spilled milk.

Or, in this case, blood.

And in spite of everything, Morat had no regrets. He didn't particularly like killing and he had no special hatred for Edward Quinn, Martin Hatcher, or any of the other people—many of them nameless—whom he had dealt with over the years, but sometimes things had to be done and in such cases the world became simple: there were those who had the strength of will to act, to get their hands dirty and their consciences dirtier, and there were those who weren't. Morat knew his place in the world, his value, better than he knew his own name. The latter changed constantly. The former was firm, solid, and hard as diamond. He just hoped his superiors would remember that sooner rather than later. He was getting tired of being in the doghouse.

But there he was: confined to his cold quarters, banned from flying, fed and medicated in isolation and brought out to speak only to his interrogators, most of whom wouldn't last ten minutes in the field. Morat was no ideologue, no starry-eyed revolutionary or zealot. He was in it because he was well paid for his skills—which were remarkable—and he had no interest in whatever new world order his superiors wanted to bring about.

Superiors.

What a joke! They were an amalgam of corrupt financiers, politicians, generals, and other well-connected opportunists. Their names, faces, and wallets opened doors his did not, but otherwise they were no better than he was, and if any real test was made of their mettle he would best them all with one hand tied behind his back.

So this confinement rankled, as did their petulant remarks about his "operational decision making" and "professional expertise."

See if you can find better, he wanted to say, though he held the words in. This was not the kind of job one walked away from, and not only because the money was too good. People who left the organization tended to vanish from the radar and no one bothered to pretend they were in deep cover. Once you were in the organization, you were in. For life. That had always seemed fair to him.

But . . .

He was beginning to have questions he hadn't had before, and the more they berated him for their current situation, the more he wondered. After all, what was the value of being loyal to a doomed venture? They only kept him around because he was useful to them, but what happened when *they* stopped being useful to *him*? Perhaps in an attempt to make him feel guilt ridden and keen to prove himself they were overplaying the extent of the disaster and its various related collapses, of which Maynard was undoubtedly one. But what if they weren't? What if things were as bad as they said they were? How long could his paycheck hold out, and what would happen if they decided to seriously downsize?

These were questions worth thinking about. Jean-Christophe Morat—to stick with his current alias—had never been a man to walk into anything without a clear exit strategy. Staring at the walls of the concrete box which had been his home for the last week he decided to start building one. The place was getting him down and he was less and less sure that he wanted to remain a hired gun.

And besides, he thought, *there were the dreams . . .*

He pushed the half-memory aside, relieved by the distraction of footsteps in the echoing concrete hallway. Instantly on his guard he got quickly to his feet, arms at his side, elbows slightly crooked: ready. A warning rap on the metal door was followed by the chink of keys, the squeak of the handle, and the groan of the door pushing through its frame. There were two sentries, young, fit, nondescript, both wearing the vague almost-uniform of the base: unspecific olive and tan combat fatigues with matching belts and boots. On their heads were black berets sporting a blue and white badge with a gold sun motif. There were no words in any language or any insignia linking them to any official army from anywhere in the world. The hat badge might have been no more than the calling card of a private club. It was, of course, rather more than that, as their weapons showed. One had the heel of his hand rested on the sidearm holster at his belt, while the other cradled a squat-looking submachine gun that Morat recognized as an SR-2 Veresk. His eyes followed the gun barrel as the muscles of his legs tautened. If this was to be an execution he'd need to commit to his attack very quickly indeed.

But the gun didn't turn in his direction. The soldier kept it angled down toward the floor, ready, but not aimed. Morat hesitated.

"This way, please," said the one with the pistol, speaking in Russian and stepping back to free up the doorway.

Morat moved cautiously, still eyeing the Veresk. The soldier wielding it fell into step behind him and Morat switched focus to his ears: unless the guy was carrying it cocked and with the safety off—which would be stupid—he might hear the telltale click before it fired . . .

He needn't have worried. They walked him past a dozen similar doors and around the base's identical maze-like corridors, to a room more closely resembling a place of real human activity than any he had seen this week. There was a space heater in the corner, giving the room a welcome warmth that seemed to have soaked into its red carpet. The walls had been finished in Sheetrock and there was a long, black conference table polished to a dull satin finish so that it looked cast out of lead. Around it were padded office chairs on casters. The walls were stark and white, save where they were broken by a large, sleeping flat screen, but the overall impression was of a boardroom. There was no one else there.

"Have a seat," said the soldier who had brought them, and when Morat did, both troops stepped outside and closed the door. Though constructed of the same blued steel as the one leading to his own quarters, the inside of the door was paneled in charred and polished wood that matched the table. The door latched shut, and Morat was alone in the silence.

He immediately went to the TV and turned it on, feeling for the discreet buttons on its edge that allowed him to cycle through whatever stations were programmed in. Nothing came up, and eventually he turned it off and sat down again.

He waited. He was good at waiting. A good part of his job to date had been waiting, gauging the time to act. Sometimes it was a matter of months. Sometimes it was seconds. He approached the challenge as if it were a zen exercise, becoming truly still so that his heart slowed and respiration shallowed till an observer would barely know he was alive. It was an old sniper's trick and, for a while, the effort, the change it brought over mind and body, staved off the boredom he always felt nipping at his heels like a terrier.

He checked his watch as the door finally opened. He had been waiting thirty-eight minutes. If that was supposed to throw or rattle him, it hadn't worked. Two men and a woman came in. They matched the room, not the military escort who were asked to wait outside, and they smiled and shook his hand before unfolding laptops and drawing folders from attaché cases. He felt like he was back in some Maynard Consortium boardroom.

He knew only one of them, the elder of the two men, who called himself Rasmussen. It was not his real name. He had been part of the committee that had assigned Morat to the Maynard mission over a year before, and he had been one of those who had received his periodic reports throughout the proceedings. Rasmussen had also sat in—largely in silence—during Morat's post-Nevada debriefings. He was a thoughtful, soft-spoken man, studied and measured so that he was very difficult to read. Morat thought he seemed better versed in business than he was in military activity, though he had also liaised with the organization's air command wing and been privy to every operation Morat had undertaken over the last nine months, from street-level espionage and his dealings with Jennifer Quinn, to his missions in the arrowhead over Nevada. Fingers in lots of pies, then. Morat could respect that. He was, after all, something of a hybrid operative himself.

He burns very cool too, he thought. Another thing they had in common.

The younger man looked like a soldier, and not just because he had the physique and presence of someone poised to take control at any moment. He moved with economy, and though his face was neutral his eyes had a watchful, predatory edge.

Special forces? Maybe.

The woman was, perhaps, Chinese or Mongolian, tough looking, her skin sun- and wind-burned, her eyes unblinking. Her ancestors might have ridden to war with Genghis Kahn. She was maybe forty or forty five. She smiled at him as she took her seat, but it was the kind of formal smile that vanished so quickly and completely that it became hard to imagine it had ever been there.

She introduced herself as Gansükh Narantuyaa—not a Chinese name—and added that he could call her Narantuyaa. She spoke, surprisingly, in English, and if she had an accent he would have called it British RP, like the BBC announcers. The young man's English had a marked Russian inflection, while Rasmussen sounded so like a New Yorker that Morat had always assumed he really was one. Perhaps that was why they were all speaking English.

"Well, Mister Morat," said Rasmussen. "I trust you have been enjoying your down time at our little resort." He smiled bleakly to show Morat he was joking. "But now it's time we put you back to work. A change of pace for you, I think, and a challenge, though I am confident you will rise to it, if only to expunge the Maynard incident from your professional record."

"I regret the mission did not achieve all its objectives," said Morat.

Rasmussen's little smile peeked over the battlements once more.

"That's one of those *business-speak* irregular verbs, isn't it?" he said. "*I* did not achieve all my objectives, *you* failed, *he* caused unmitigated disaster." The smile stayed pleasant, despite the mockery, and Morat straightened in his seat, resolving not to respond. "So, moving on, we trust, to better things."

He pushed one of the manila folders toward Morat who responded by reaching for it, only to have Rasmussen lay his hand on top before it could be opened. Morat met his eyes.

"Tell me, Mr. Morat," said Rasmussen. "How have you been sleeping?"

The question was so unexpected that Morat stiffened, and when he said simply "Fine," shrugging, it was obviously a lie.

"That seems to me unlikely," said Rasmussen.

Morat felt the kind of creeping panic that men like him, used to navigating through lies and bullets, rarely experienced.

"What do you mean?" he said. "You've been giving me something? Poisoning my food or doctoring my meds?"

"Nothing like that," said Rasmussen, sitting back. "But let's take another run at my question, shall we?"

"I've been sleeping okay," said Morat. "Seven hours or so most nights. Longer at first. I was exhausted."

"And the nature of the sleep?" asked Narantuyaa.

Morat hesitated. Work meant money, and not working almost certainly meant a bullet. He had to handle this just right.

"I'm not sure I'm following," he said, stalling for time.

"She's asking about your dreams, Mr. Morat," said Rasmussen. "Or should we call them nightmares?"

NICHOLAS
University of Nevada, Reno

NICHOLAS TAN WATCHED HIS MENTOR, PROFESSOR Theodore "Ted" Jarret, as he looked over Nicholas's updated curriculum vitae, set it down, and stared at him across the cluttered desk. Jarret was teetering on the edge of retirement, at the opposite end of his career from Nicholas, who had just finished his first year as an assistant professor in the anthropology department at Reno, though it might be said that Nicholas's career had really started two years earlier with his appointment as an archaeology instructor.

It might also be said that his career hadn't really started yet at all, an idea confirmed by the look in Jarret's sour, whiskery face. Watching him read was like seeing the beginnings of a road accident: something slow and inevitable, like a bus driven by a drunk, coming toward you at low speed but leaving nowhere for you to go. At last the older man set the papers down and said simply, "Atlantis?"

The bus that Nicholas had been imagining sliding across the intersection in his head finally made crunching contact. As its wheels mounted his fender and rode up over the collapsing windshield, Nicholas scrambled to get out.

"The essay doesn't argue that I've *found* Atlantis, or even that I think Atlantis is there to be found," he said, blinking, his fingers twittering anxiously. "It's just a new angle on where the site might be—if it exists—using weather and ocean current mapping to examine the distribution pattern of the ash from the Santorini volcanic eruption."

He forced himself to sit back a little, hearing the whiny earnestness in his voice and wilting under Jarret's glacial stare.

"Hmm," said his mentor, unflinching. "Yes. Still. *Atlantis . . .*"

Nicholas swallowed and decided to go for broke.

"It's not like it's a new idea," he said. "Atlantis or the eruption. I'm just applying new computer imaging techniques to isolate a possible locale. I know we don't have the funding to explore it ourselves, but I thought that maybe if I partnered with a bigger institution, some place that had more overseas field resources, they might think it worth a preliminary sounding."

"To find Atlantis," said Jarret. He hadn't moved a muscle anywhere except his jaw since putting the CV down. It wasn't a question. "A city the world does not believe in. A city of legend which the discipline of archaeology does not think ever existed."

"People didn't think Troy was real till Schliemann found it."

"Modern archaeologists had not looked," said Jarret. "And much of what Schliemann claimed was just plain wrong. As you know," he added, though his voice didn't sound sure of that.

"According to Plato," Nicholas pressed, "Atlantis was . . ."

"A myth wielded by a philosopher," said Jarret, with a dismissive wave of his hand. "He was performing a lesson in hubris, not writing a visitor's guide." Nicholas went quiet at that. The old man's tone had been leaden, like the closing of a great door. "This is not a suitably serious focus for your scholarly research. You see that, I'm sure. The tenure committee will certainly see it. Now, you have just completed your first year. I'm sure you have summer plans that will generate more conventional academic publications, and that you can shift your concentration onto something in time to secure your continuance in this department at third-year review. Perhaps a sideways step away from the physical. Cultural theory is all the rage these days. Gender. Ethnicity. Those kinds of things. Your students like you. Your departmental service is commendable. There is just . . ." his eyes flicked to the CV again, "the matter of your research agenda."

Nicholas nodded vaguely and blinked. He did not trust himself to speak. He felt suddenly incredibly young and stupid, summoned by his father to be reprimanded for . . . what? It never seemed to matter. There was always something.

"I don't understand," said Jarret, leaning forward and giving him a sympathetically earnest look, "why you don't do something on China."

Nicholas blinked again.

"China?" he said. "I was trained in the archaeology of the ancient Mediterranean and Near East."

"Very fashionable, China," said Jarret, as if Nicholas hadn't spoken. "Perfect for you. No committee would say a word against your work if it was on China."

With a sense of vanishing beneath the wheels of the bus, Nicholas heard himself ask, "Why China?"

Jarret leaned still farther forward and said, in a low, conspiratorial voice, "Because you're Chinese!"

Under the tires, his body chewed up by the axle, Nicholas said, "I'm American. My parents were Chinese. I've never been!"

"There you are then," said Jarret, a white man whose family were from New England and whose academic specialty was Aztec Mexico. The old man sat back. His pronouncement had apparently ended the meeting.

Nicholas nodded and smiled and thanked the esteemed professor for his insight, then walked back to his pokey little office and closed the door behind him. In his mind, the bus caught fire.

For a moment he stood with his back to the door, his eyes tight shut, squeezing out the panic and despair. He was so royally screwed.

China?

God. The staff down at the Hunan Palace knew more about the archaeology of China than he did. They didn't even offer him the "real menu" they used to slip his parents, the one with the short ribs and those things they called chives or scallions but weren't either exactly.

God.

What had he been thinking? He knew Jarret would react like that. Well, not the China thing—the *racist* China thing—but his disdain for the Atlantis paper, sure.

He was still standing with his back to the door when someone knocked on the other side and he flinched, banishing his private angst like a man sweeping the clutter on his desk into the trash.

It's probably Jarret, come to suggest you offer Tai Chi classes to the faculty.

But it wasn't. It was actually someone about as far from Jarret as Nicholas could imagine.

She was tall, imposing, and black. She looked maybe in her early thirties, about his age, but she wore confidence like a borrowed coat that was slightly too big for her.

"Doctor Tan?" she said, offering a strong hand and smiling wide as a church door. He had opened the door faster than she had expected but she had recovered quickly. "I'm Timika Mars."

"Okay," said Nicholas, glancing down to see if she was one of those people who came trolling for textbooks, offering pennies on the dollar and then marking them up again for resale. She had no handcart. "Can I help you with something, only it's not a great time . . ."

"I'm a reporter," said the woman, missing or ignoring the hint.

"O . . . kay . . ."

"You're a specialist in the ancient Near East?" she asked.

"Depends who you ask," he replied, more honestly than he should, especially to a reporter. "Yes. Come in. What can I do for you?"

He went around his desk and sat down. Unlike Jarret's it was clear of everything save his computer and three carefully stacked books, their spines perfectly aligned. He gestured to the chair opposite him and she took it, which was a relief. She had been looming.

"I really hope I'm not wasting your time," she said. "But I don't know anything about this stuff."

"What stuff is that, exactly?" he said, trying not to sound too interested. He shouldn't have offered her a seat. He had a career to rethink . . .

She drew a sheet of A4 paper from a briefcase and slid it across the desk toward him. It had an image printed on it, a stone tablet covered in carved linear script and framed at some later date with a metal border. Nicholas pulled it into the light, and sat up.

"Where did you get this?" he asked.

"Can you identify it?"

"I can read it, or I could in time," he said. "It's a kind of cuneiform. Probably Ugaritic. Where did you get it?"

"I'm afraid I can't say."

Nicholas stared at the paper. The room went very quiet. For perhaps twenty seconds, neither of them spoke.

"I'm sorry," he said looking up suddenly. "What did you say?"

"I said I can't tell you where I got it. It's a journalistic integrity thing. Protecting sources. I'm sure you understand."

"Is it . . . stolen?"

"Stolen? Why would it be stolen?"

Was it him, or did she seem suddenly defensive, jumpy?

"I've never seen this particular fragment before," he said.

"I'm sure there's lots," she said. He was right; she had blushed and her eyes wouldn't hold his.

"Not as much as you'd think," he said. "The language comes from the second half of the second millennium before Christ, or before the common era, if you prefer, but Ugaritic wasn't discovered until the twentieth century. It's a pretty limited source pool."

"Ugaritic, huh? Where was it used?"

"A city called, amazingly enough, Ugarit," he said, managing a vague smile to show he wasn't trying to be a douche, "in present-day Syria."

"So . . . what does it say?"

She was still seated, but it was more like she was perching, ready to fly as soon as he gave her what she wanted.

"That will take a little time to determine," he said. "I'll need to share it with a colleague at another institution and do some research."

"I thought you could read it?" she said. It wasn't mockery or hostility so much as nervousness.

"I can, but I've read most of the other major examples before, so when I read them, I'm not so much translating as remembering. This is new, so I have to study it, and there are a couple of characters I don't recognize."

"Well," she said with an effort. "Take your time. You need a dictionary or something?"

He gave her a frank, appraising look of the kind he wished he had given Jarret. It was funny, the way he became more secure, more sure of himself while discussing his work rather than his career.

"Did you hear what I said?" he asked.

"Which part?" said the woman who had called herself Timika, still glancing around like a bird on a wire.

"I said, *this is new.*"

She waited for more, then said "So?"

"So? So it can't be! New examples of ancient Ugaritic text don't just appear out of nowhere. Most of them come from one place: Ugarit, also known as Ras Shamra. Unless this were from an active dig site, I should already know it. There just aren't that many, and with things as they are in Syria, artifacts are going missing and reappearing elsewhere. Illegally."

"I thought you said you hadn't seen this piece before?"

"I haven't, so I'm wondering if recent bombings have revealed a previously unknown cache or liberated pieces from private collections that had been hidden away. It's tricky ground, Miss . . ."

"Mars."

"Right."

"But it's real?" she said. "Not a fake? Or a copy?"

"Hard to say from a picture," he replied, still watching her calmly, though his stomach had begun to flutter. She was keeping something from him, but she had no idea what the object pictured was or why it might be important. "Though the metal has certainly been added to the piece, so it hasn't just been dug up."

"Maybe it was part of the original tablet."

He grinned at that.

"It's blue, like steel or aluminum, maybe," he said.

"Is that important?"

"You could say that," he replied. "If the metal was added at the same time as the carving it might be copper or bronze, possibly gold, but this? This is technology the Ugarit wouldn't have for a millennium. I have a friend at UNC Charlotte. Let me run it by them and see . . ."

"No," said Timika forcefully. "This stays between us."

Nicholas frowned.

"I really think you should tell me where it came from," he said.

"I can't," she said. "Not yet. But I can tell you where we might find another."

Tan became quite still, looking at her, saying nothing.

"Yeah?" he said. "Where? In a private collection?"

She shook her head.

He frowned.

"Then where?" he asked.

"I take it such a piece would be valuable?"

He gave her what was supposed to be a skeptical or apathetic shrug but she stared him down and his prevarication lost steam. "Maybe," he conceded. "But academic value isn't the same as cash value."

"I'm sure the tablet would be worth money to a collector," she said.

"If it's real," he replied, "but probably not as much as you'd expect. And I won't be involved in black market dealings."

"Not enough to fund a dig then," she said.

He knew it was a line tossed into the water, recognized the hook through the wiggling worm, but he couldn't stop himself going for it.

"It's still *in the ground?*" he said. His mouth had gone very dry.

"I can show you the general area," she said. "If you commit to exploring it, and to my terms, I'll narrow the search field."

He sat there, his mind racing.

"If you already know where it is, why do you need an archaeologist?" he asked at last.

"My information is incomplete," she said.

"How incomplete?"

"I need someone with knowledge of the period, the region and the language," she said. She was being evasive, he could tell, but he had already bitten down on the hook, and the fight in him was fading.

"Where is it?" he asked. "Because, in case you hadn't noticed, there's some stuff going on in Syria right now that might make a dig tricky."

It was her turn to look momentarily unsure. She seemed to consider him, and not just the man behind the desk. Her eyes moved over the walls, the museum posters, the framed diplomas, the Victorian archaeological lithographs, then came back to him. Somewhere in that little stroll through his career she had made a decision.

"Crete," she said.

He opened his mouth to protest, to dispute the idea that an Ugarit text would have shown up in Minoan Greece, but even as the words jostled for place in his mouth, ready to leap out like parachutists, another word rose up in his mind:

Atlantis.

The Minoan civilization, which blossomed on Bronze Age Crete prior to the rise of Mycenae on the Greek mainland and which fell just over a thousand years BCE, had long been considered a candidate for the city of Plato's myth. The Santorini or Thera eruption Nicholas had been debating—or attempting to—with Jarret had been 1600 BCE; too early to be considered responsible for the collapse of the entire Minoan civilization, but a viable candidate for the loss of some island outpost or principality. A tsunami triggered by the eruption would even fit many of Plato's details of rising water flooding the city. Whether they subsequently receded again and the devastated land eventually became home to other people mattered less than the idea that the flood was real. Nevertheless, in his secret heart Nicholas loved the idea that the eruption had led to some tectonic shift that had pulled Atlantis beneath the waves, partly because the image was so dramatically romantic, and partly because that meant that it may still be out there. Somewhere. Waiting to be found . . .

"You're talking about an actual excavation?" he asked, trying to sound dismissive. Trying, more to the point, not to sound breathlessly excited, even desperate for the possibility to be real.

"Yes," she said. "Interested?"

"Run by who?" he asked, still just this side of a sneer.

"There'd be documents to sign, agreements about the disclosure of findings and the like, but basically, if you want it, you."

"Me?" he said, the word coming out as a shout of derisive laughter that almost muted his exhilaration.

"Why not?"

"Because I'm not qualified!" he said. "Because I don't have a team and have precious little fieldwork experience in the region . . ."

"So it would be good to get more."

"Yes, but that's not possible!" he shot back, real exasperation showing through now as he faced the bleak reality of the situation. She might not intend it, she might not even know it, but this was just a tease. He wasn't about to run a dig in Crete! It was absurd. "I don't have the profile to head an expedition like this! We'd never get permission from the Greek government, and we sure as hell wouldn't get the money. I'm sorry Miss . . ."

"Mars. Timika Mars."

"I'm sorry Miss Mars, but you have no idea what you're asking and you don't have the resources to make the offer you are presenting. You need to take whatever you think you have to some more established scholar with the right kind of track record, the right friends, the right links to people who can supply the personnel and equipment, someone with a very serious practical research budget, and then, in a few years, maybe . . ."

"This summer," said the woman.

He stared at her, his mouth open, then managed an incredulous, "What?"

"I want to start now. I can set up flights, lodging . . ."

He'd heard enough. Whatever dream-like possibility had kindled briefly in his imagination had been doused and trampled into oblivion.

"I'm sorry," he said, holding up his hands to stop her. "I'm really very busy and have been having a lousy day. I'm not sure who you are or what you think you have, and I genuinely wish you the very best of luck in finding someone who can help, but . . ."

"I have money," she said.

"Not enough, believe me," he said, standing up, as if to show her the door.

"Actually," she replied, still level and, pointedly, still sitting, "I'm pretty sure I do."

He sighed.

"Look, Miss Mars," he said, "I mean no offense, but I'm guessing you have no archaeological background at all, right?"

"Only as a reporter," she said.

"Okay," he said, assuming she was conceding his point. "Overseas archaeology isn't an Indiana Jones movie. It's a slow, painstaking, scientific endeavor that takes place against a backdrop of diplomacy and political maneuvering. It involves huge numbers of people and generates, ninety percent of the time, little more than scholarly footnotes. No great statues or sealed tombs. We generate finds that wouldn't interest the most rabid of amateurs who like nothing more than looking for arrowheads or pacing Civil War battlefields with metal detectors. Above all, and I want to make this very, very clear since it will be my final comment on the subject, it costs a colossal amount: tens of thousands of dollars for the smallest of digs, and with every cent earmarked months, even years in advance. A medium-sized excavation might cost that much just for on-site curation and lab testing. You may have some backers, you may have run a couple of successful Kickstarter campaigns, you may even have some corporate sponsorship lined up, but I'm telling you, and you need to hear this because any other respectable archaeologist would tell you the same thing, you simply don't have and couldn't generate the funds to fuel even a small excavation in Crete."

The Mars woman—he liked that phrase: it made her sound like she'd just come in from another planet, which felt about right—nodded thoughtfully. But she didn't get up. At last, when he had begun to worry that he had been too hard on her and that she was genuinely upset, she said simply,

"How much do you think we could do with one-point-eight million dollars?"

DEPUTY DEWEY LARSON
2014, Twenty Miles from Cedar Rapids, Iowa

I T WAS FIVE DAYS SINCE THE CATTLE MUTILATIONS AT
the Styles farm. The sheriff's office had gotten word the
following morning when a feed delivery driver couldn't
get a response at the house and stumbled on the first of what
turned out to be eighteen dead cows. An initial search of the
scene had revealed a splash of vomit and, close by, the head
of a blood trail which, with the aid of the Coogans' hound
dog, Deputy Dewey Larson had followed all the way to Josh
Harrup's place. Harrup was found passed out fifty yards
from his own front door, half his foot blown away, presumably by the shotgun Larson had recovered at the edge of the
field. Harrup had lost a lot of blood, and would probably
walk with a stick for the rest of his days—which was no life
for a farmer—but he would live, though it seemed like he'd
spend whatever time he had left behind bars.

There was still no sign of Jimbo Styles, and from what Dewey Larson had heard down at Teddy's Barn and Grill the night before, the court of public opinion had already made its mind up as to what had happened. The bad blood between Josh Harrup and his more successful—and now missing—neighbor was old news throughout the county. The way the locals figured it, Harrup—who was usually drunk in the evening—went over to the Styles place to cause trouble, cut up some of the cows. He was disturbed by Jimbo, and in the struggle that followed, Harrup killed him and stashed the body. But he was hurt too and didn't make it all the way home before collapsing from blood loss.

Harrup had spent the next two days in hospital, where they had managed to graft one of his missing toes back on; better than nothing, Larson supposed, but maybe not by much. They had kept him sedated through the next day while they rehydrated him, pumped him full of painkillers, and fitted him for some kind of padded plastic boot that was supposed to help the tissue mend. He stayed in the hospital the next day—tired, but alert—and Larson had been one of those to grill him about what had happened at the Styles farm. Yes, he said, he had been drunk, and yes, he had been carrying the shotgun, though he insisted he wouldn't have used it, but he never harmed any livestock and never laid eyes on Jimbo Styles, alive or dead. When he stuck to his story through the fourth interview, and they still had neither a body nor any evidence tying Harrup directly to the cattle mutilations, they had to take him home. He'd be watched and was under strict instructions not to leave the county, and privately most of the sheriff's department figured it was only a matter of time before he was arrested on suspicion of murder with enough evidence to keep him inside.

Harrup moved like a sloth, but his face had developed a twitchy, hunted look, and when Larson had delivered him to his front porch, the man had stared off across the fields to the Styles farm. He was badly scared, and Larson would have put his wages for the week on a bet that the first thing Josh Harrup did once he had the front door closed behind him was reach for a whisky bottle.

Sheriff Tobias Burnhardt was being careful what he said, the political side of the job being the only thing he was really any good at, but it was obvious in the station that he couldn't wait to charge Harrup and move on. Murder was rare in Jones County, and unsolved murder rarer still. Burnhardt didn't want his record spoiled, not with an election coming.

Deputy Larson wasn't convinced. For one thing, a sustained search of the Styles farm had found no body, and no one had supplied an explanation for how Harrup could have so perfectly hidden the corpse away when he was himself badly injured. And then there were the mutilations themselves. Burnhardt had talked about the attack as if Harrup had gone crazy with a kitchen knife, hacking up the cattle where they stood, but that didn't make much sense, and not only because they hadn't found any such knife. The injuries were weird, precise and bloodless. Some of the dead animals had no apparent external wounds at all, though the preliminary autopsies had shown that some of them were missing internal organs, including in one case the heart. The hurriedly convened mismatch of medical examiners and local large animal vets had not been able to determine how anyone had gone in without leaving a mark. What seemed clear was that this was not the work of an amateur with a chef's knife. This was precise, skilled surgical work of the kind you might do with a laser scalpel, though even use of a tool like that didn't explain the absence of entry wounds.

Tob Burnhardt listened reluctantly to Dewey Larson's list of objections, his lips pursed and his face set, then drummed his pencil on the edge of the desk and shook his head in decision.

"Let's focus on finding Styles," he said, clutching at straws. It was uncomfortably warm in the office and Burnhardt was sweating through his shirt. "If this is a murder inquiry, the cattle stuff becomes secondary."

Larson hesitated a half second before saying his "yes, sir," and going back to his desk, but his boss's familiar tactics annoyed him: ignore whatever is inconvenient and hope no one notices. Joe Sanderson, the old sheriff, had been a pain in the ass, but he would never have done that. He always wanted the truth. If they hit an anomaly in a case, a detail that didn't quite fit, he'd sit there with his eyes half closed as he mentally picked at it till he forced some kind of truth out of it. It was—ironically—an inconvenient habit in someone whose job was at least partly political, and it had only been a matter of time before it had gotten him into trouble. He had been pushed out eight years ago and now spent his retirement digging into cold cases and investigating whatever nut job conspiracy BS he stumbled on. It was rumored that some of the more enterprising high school kids actually invented nonsense mysteries—Bigfoot sightings, reports of escaped exotic animals and the like—just for the amusement of watching him show up to investigate. Sanderson had never been great at telling good evidence from bad, and had wasted countless man hours meticulously eliminating crazy shit an ordinary cop would have thrown out the moment it was handed to him. But occasionally, just occasionally, he would niggle at some little weirdness for a while and it would turn into something real. Larson wished Sanderson was here now, and not only because his old boss had a nose for ferreting out the truth, no matter how long it took or how much grief he took in the process. Larson wanted him back because the word was that Joe Sanderson had seen this weird shit before.

It had been twelve years ago, only a couple of years after Larson had joined up. The farm had been down near Scotch Grove and the case had been almost identical: a dozen cattle killed, internal organs removed, no blood at the scene, and minimal surface lacerations to indicate point of entry. The details had been obscured because, as Burnhardt had suggested, what got done to a few cows got less attention than what got done to their owner. In the Scotch Grove case the owner had been a woman, Emily Swainson, a leather-tough widow who ran the farm with a few hired hands once her kids had gone off in search of altogether different versions of life in Chicago. The night of the event—that was what it was called locally, as if that dodged the weirdness of the thing—she had been home alone. No one found the dead cows for three days, and they didn't find her for another week, her body showing up in the woods of what was now the Indian Bluffs park. It had been treated as a murder inquiry, but at some point the guys from state took over, and a week or so later, they pronounced the death accidental. Emily Swainson had, they said, died of exhaustion, dehydration, and exposure, having become disoriented on the night someone took a knife to her herd. The official version, insofar as there was one, was that she had fled the scene, become lost and, having broken her leg in the woods, couldn't find her way out.

Old Sheriff Sanderson hadn't been happy with that verdict, and had—in his usual way—continued to drive out there taking pictures and asking questions, till it became a bit of local joke, an embarrassment even, at least once it made the papers. Went on for three years or more. State told him to leave it alone, but he kept on poking and tugging at it anyway whenever he had a spare hour or two, and then, all of a sudden, it seemed, Sanderson ran out of leeway. He resigned to save face, said the locals, but he did so under duress, though whether that was from state or from the mayor's office or what, no one seemed to know.

And now it was happening again.

Tob Burnhardt knew, of course. How could he not? That was part of the reason he was being so careful not to say anything that would be impossible to walk back. It was also why he was more than usually on edge, sitting at his desk, his eyes constantly sliding back to his phone, as if waiting for the call that would either save his ass or condemn it. Larson couldn't really blame the guy. The old case had been just old enough for its specifics to be largely forgotten, its details sufficiently confused that it had become a kind of myth, a fragment of colorful local lore on which no one really agreed because it was mostly just a campfire story. But the Internet, which had been in its infancy back in 2002, was an altogether different beast now, and every half-baked version of the old case was being dredged up and tied to the Styles farm incident. Those who could were taking to locking their livestock away at night, and there were rumors of vigilante patrols driving around in pickups with hunting rifles and God knew what else. The sheriff's office and its staff had become the center of what all law enforcement dreaded: they had become a story.

"We have to find that body and get a confession out of Josh Harrup," muttered Burnhardt, almost to himself.

Missy Singleton poked her head around the door, her face caught between dread and excitement.

"We've got the *Jones County News* and the *Monticello Express* asking if you have a moment to answer . . ." she began.

"No!" Burnhardt shot back, rubbing his forehead. "I told you. No interviews."

"They are very insistent, Tob," said the administrative assistant.

"So am I!" he returned.

She made an exasperated face.

"You can't hide in here forever, you know," she said.

Larson looked up from his desk, wondering if Burnhardt would go ballistic, but the sheriff managed to somehow shake his head and nod at the same time, a gesture that said that he didn't like it, but knew she was right. He caught Larson looking, met his eyes for a second, then beckoned him over. It was furtive action, and as he did it he turned his back on the room and sat next to his desk, huddled over. When Larson reached him, Burnhardt didn't look up but made a little head bob to draw the deputy in still closer. As Larson bent over, Burnhardt muttered, "Find Joe Sanderson."

"Seriously?"

The former sheriff's name was barely mentioned at the station these days.

Burnhardt met Larson's eyes and nodded once.

"Quietly," he said, mouthing the word. "Nothing official."

"Why don't you . . . ?"

"Because he doesn't like me," said Burnhardt, wincing at the truth of the statement and at having to say out loud what everyone in the county already knew. "Didn't like me taking over. He liked you. So talk to him."

"What should I say?"

"I don't care. Just . . . get this resolved."

And with that irritatingly unspecific instruction finally out, Burnhardt turned back to the laptop on his desk till Larson, dismissed, walked away, frowning.

IT TOOK LARSON MOST OF THE MORNING TO GET A BEAD on Joe Sanderson, and it came to him through the former sheriff's good-looking but permanently pissed off daughter, Jeanie.

"Why do you want to see him?" she asked when she returned his call.

"Work stuff," said Larson, cagey. "Just want to get his opinion on something."

"Jimbo Styles," she replied. It wasn't a question, and there was no point denying it.

"It's related to that," said Larson.

"You should leave him alone. He has enough problems without you sucking him back into that old nonsense."

"Problems?"

He heard her anger in the silence.

"You know," she said, and even that took effort. "Leave him be."

"Come on, Jeanie. We're not asking him to come back. Just to get his perspective on . . ."

"If they make a fool of him," she cut in, "if they put his picture in the paper looking goofy and give it some smart-ass caption, if they do anything, *anything*, to make his life more pathetic than it already is, Dewey Larson, I'm gonna cut your balls off and run them up the flagpole in front of the sheriff's office. You hear me?"

Larson stopped walking and took a breath.

"I hear you," he said.

"You'd better," she replied, then, softer, sadder, she added, "He's old, Dewey. Let the man have some dignity."

"Where is he, Jeanie?"

One last hesitation, then she said, "Over Maquoketa way. A farm."

Maquoketa? That was halfway to the Illinois border.

"What's he doing out there?" he asked.

"I'll tell you, but if you laugh I'm not gonna give you the address."

"Okay. I won't laugh."

"He drove out there to look at a crop circle. He got an anonymous e-mail first thing."

Larson looked at his feet but he didn't laugh. He needed that address.

JENNIFER
Las Vegas, Nevada

JENNIFER SPENT TWO DAYS IN LAS VEGAS, MOSTLY IN THE private office of a local bank that was part of a group in which her father had considerable investments. Lucia, the young Latina woman she dealt with, said that she spent most of her time discreetly funneling money to visiting foreign businessmen who had discovered the lure of the casinos. It made a nice change, she said, to help facilitate Jennifer's rather different plans. Still, those plans took time, much of it devoted to processing pass codes and identity documents, and Jennifer spent at least four hours in transatlantic phone calls to London, Oxford University, the British embassy in Athens and, most notably, to the department of history and archaeology of the University of Crete in Rethymno. But it got done. One-point-eight million dollars moved around and earmarked, just like that.

How the other half live, thought Jennifer with a grim smile, knowing that she *was* that other half, and it wasn't remotely a half. A thousandth. A millionth, more like. She didn't know why that made her feel lousy, but it did, as if it underscored the idea that all she was, was money.

Would the real Jennifer Quinn please stand up?

Without her checkbook, she wasn't sure there was such a person.

Jennifer wound up an hour and a half sooner than she thought she would, and was able to have a leisurely soft taco lunch before returning her rental car and boarding her nonstop American Airways flight to London Heathrow, satisfied that, in Timika's memorable phrase, all wheels were now greased.

It would be a ten-hour flight, not bad considering how much of the US land mass she had to cross before the long cold stretch of the north Atlantic, and she paid top dollar for first class in the hope that she might actually sleep most of the way. Vegas's airport slot machines held no allure for her, but she found she was also too tired to read, so she sat alone in a bar and drank a glass of wine very slowly, timing her departure precisely with her flight's first boarding announcement. She bypassed the worst of the sprawling departure gate chaos, got on board, and made the left turn she had come to disdain, looking right into the cramped main cabin to remind herself exactly why she had spent the extra money. One look at those seats, packed in tight as if they were earmarked for penned veal calves, and she knew she'd made the right decision. In first class her seat became the reclined pod she remembered from her flight from Africa, and after her takeoff champagne, she settled back and closed her eyes. She was asleep before they dimmed the cabin, missed dinner, and woke in time for a breakfast snack forty-five minutes before their final approach into the familiar grayness of London.

Though she had accumulated more on her trip than she had left with that terrible day when she had run across the fields to escape the murderous Mr. Morat, she hadn't enough to merit a checked bag, and was out of the terminal almost as soon as she had cleared immigration. Deacon, unsurprisingly, was waiting for her, and this time her gratitude was blissfully uncomplicated.

She hugged him, even kissing him quickly on the cheek.

"Welcome back, Miss Jennifer," he said, clearly glad to see her. Relieved.

"Thank you, and for picking me up. It has been a strange few weeks."

"That is," he replied, "if you don't mind me saying so, a considerable understatement."

She sat in the passenger seat beside him, against his wishes, staring out of the window as west London gave way to the dreary suburbs of Woking, but at Frimley, as if reading her mood, Deacon left the M3 and took the A331 to the edge of the South Downs.

"Should green up the view a bit," he remarked.

It was strange to be back, doubly so to pull up the long drive to the great house and know that her father's absence was now what everyone around her, Deacon included, considered normal. Not her. Her father had been this place. His death should have been marked with comets and earthquakes that left Steadings—the grand old pile she had been raised in—a hill of rubble. But there it was, imposing and elegant, rising above manicured lawns and the gravel forecourt where her father had fallen to his death.

At Morat's insistence.

Oh yes. She hadn't forgotten that. Her father was gone, but the man responsible, a man who had also tried to kill her, was probably still alive and free. Somewhere.

"You all right, Miss?" asked Deacon. He had shut the engine off but she hadn't moved.

"Fine," she said, coming back to herself and giving him a smile. "I'm . . . well," she said, more honestly, "you know."

"I do at that. Not the same place without him."

She nodded quickly but looked down and didn't trust herself to speak. Deacon gave her arm an avuncular pat, and she nodded silently again, then got out of the car.

"Perhaps after you have freshened up you'd like a bite to eat?" he asked.

Normally she napped for an hour or two when she returned to England to help her body adjust to the time difference, but she felt reasonably fresh and was keen to occupy her mind so that she wouldn't get lost in nostalgia and sadness.

"That would be great," she said. "Thanks. Give me a half hour."

THE SHOWER, CHANGE OF CLOTHES, AND SANDWICH OF GOOD, sharp local cheddar with Branston pickle all combined to keep her energy up, and she spent the remainder of the afternoon making what Deacon called "executive decisions"—mostly signing off on what he and her father's numerous accountants had recommended. All ties to Maynard were cut, though there were still some legal issues that would keep some of her father's documents and accounts tied up by investigators for the foreseeable future. To a lot of people in finance, this might have been crippling, but Edward Quinn had been the master of diversification, and there were plenty of what Deacon called "income streams" and holding accounts that had been firewalled from Maynard, and they were all still functional and available. Jennifer would not be short of money—even with her extravagant promises to Timika—for a long time to come. The idea would have made her younger self uncomfortable, but Jennifer had things to do, truths to uncover. There would be plenty of ways she could use the money to support the political and social initiatives she valued, but money would also be spent turning stones, chasing leads, digging in the metaphorical as well as the archaeologically literal sense. There were things she needed to know. Things—and people—she had to find. All of that cost money.

She wondered briefly if her father would begrudge her using his fortune like this, against some of the very people and initiatives he had been engaged with, but she felt in her heart that he wouldn't. He had always been essentially a good man. She was sure of that. It wasn't his success, his wealth that had poisoned him. It was something else, and that, whatever it was, was one of the truths she intended to uncover.

How had her thoughtful, loving father been sucked into the world of men like Saltzburg and Morat? What had happened, and when?

It was these questions that had haunted her in those moments when she waited to fall asleep over the last week or so, when the other, more pressing concerns of her own survival had receded like waves on a beach. What remained like traces in the sand were these deeper and more personal uncertainties, and now that she was home they glowed, as if heated till the sand ran together like molten glass.

Had that been about money too? she wondered. *So much of her life seemed to be . . .*

She spent an hour going over the timeline of her father's dealings with Maynard. It went back much further than she had realized, his ties to key holdings and people predating the official founding of the Consortium by a couple of decades. Was it that simple? He became enmeshed with them because of previous deals and relationships that had sucked him into their orbit? But then why hadn't he walked away when he knew what they were involved in? They say all men have a breaking point: something they want so badly that they will do literally anything to get it.

What had Edward Quinn wanted that badly?

And then there was the image she remembered from her childhood, the blueprint of what was surely the triangle ship—or something very like it—which meant that those activities, or his interest in them, predated Maynard too. So maybe it wasn't that old friends and working relationships had pulled him into Maynard. Maybe Maynard had been founded out of those very relationships, and her father's involvement had driven them. What, she asked herself again, had he wanted?

A rival space agency? Privately funded, independent of national interests and outside the great Cold War pissing contest? That made it sound vaguely altruistic, but she had learned too much of Maynard's methods to believe that the organization's guiding principles had been benevolent.

Power, then. Influence. They had been building a force beyond the limits of normal technology for purposes of their own. But what purposes, and why had her father gone along with so ruthless an organization?

She walked the long hall to her father's study, thought better of it, went down to the room with the model railway that had been his secret joy, switched it on, and set one of the engines running on the long loop that went around the room through a series of tunnels and over a girder bridge beside the little town center she had helped him build. She took the wheel backed chair he had always used and sat, listening to the sound of the railway cars on the rails. It was running slowly in parts. Model trains needed continual use or their tracks and motors got dusty. In time they developed a patina that interfered with the power transfer through the wheels . . .

She could almost hear him saying it.

There was a delicate knock on the door. Deacon.

She invited him in and told him they'd need to make sure the model railway got regular use.

"Certainly, Miss," said Deacon. "I'll speak to the staff."

"So long as I'm here, I'll handle it," she said.

"And how long will that be?" asked the man her father had called his Old Retainer.

"Not sure," she said. "I can manage a lot from here, with your assistance of course, if you don't mind."

"Glad to be of service, Miss, and glad, if I may say so, to have you back and involved. I'm sure your father would be most gratified."

Jennifer smiled and nodded, but she had no intention of wallowing in grief or nostalgia.

"What do you know about the triangles?" she said.

Deacon blinked.

"Triangles, Miss?"

"The . . . aircraft. Dad was involved in their development, their financing. Maynard was involved, but it started before Maynard existed, at least before the company was officially formed."

Deacon's face seemed to close for a second and then he looked down. He was going to need some coaxing.

"Tell you what," she added. "I'll give you what I know, what I've seen, and you can fill in the gaps."

"I thought you were under order not to disclose what you experienced?"

"I'll fudge the details. Maybe leave some stuff out."

"I don't know that I can tell you much you don't already know," said Deacon. "Your father trusted me on most things, including money, but there were some areas of his life he seemed at pains to keep to himself. I think he thought it a kindness."

"When did that start?"

Again, Deacon's face seemed to close, and this time it stayed that way for longer. His old, knotted hands clasped and unclasped. When he eventually spoke it was with a studied caution, as if the words were a tray of over-full drinks.

"What do you know about your early life?" he asked.

Jennifer made a face.

"What do you mean? Like what school I went to or . . . ?"

"Earlier. The months leading up to your first birthday."

Jennifer couldn't help but laugh.

"Before I was one!" she exclaimed. "No, not a lot of vivid memories from that period of my life. Was I a prodigy? Playing Mozart concertos on the piano or something?"

Deacon smiled faintly, remembering, but shook his head.

"You were a normal child," he said.

"Unremarkable, you mean," said Jennifer, grinning.

"Not to your parents," said Deacon, and the smile was clearly sad. "They adored you. Doted on you. Your mother would gaze at you in your crib for hours and your father . . ."

Jennifer held up her hand. She didn't want to go through all this again. It was too painful.

"Yes," said Deacon, cutting himself off with an understanding nod. "I'm sorry. But you asked when your father became . . . what's the word? Cautious? Private. Secretive, even."

"It was when I was born?" said Jennifer, stung by the idea. "All this stuff with Maynard, the shady deals, even his death was somehow *my* fault?"

She hadn't meant to sound so shrill but it came out that way, indignant, hurt. Deacon shook his head quickly and held up his hand to stop her from storming out.

"No," he said. "Not your fault but it was about you."

"How? What did *I* do?"

"Not what you did," said Deacon, clearly distressed. "I'm sorry. I'm not explaining this properly. I never thought I would have to."

"What?" she demanded. "What are you saying? What is it that I don't know?"

He sighed, composed himself, and said simply,

"You were kidnapped."

TIMIKA
Reno-Tahoe International Airport, Nevada

THE JURY WAS STILL OUT ON NICHOLAS TAN, AS FAR AS Timika was concerned. At times he seemed almost boyishly honest, naive, but then he'd get all excited about the dig she had talked him into and there'd be a foxy look that skulked into his face, something sharp and calculating and predatory.

Or maybe you don't trust anyone, said a voice in her head.

Given the last few weeks, she thought, who could blame her?

Tan was single and without family in the area. She got the impression he hadn't really bonded with his professional colleagues in the short time he'd been there, so the only real barrier to his agreeing to the trip had been a kind of nervous skepticism about throwing his lot in with this total stranger. He had, he said, to make sure his summer was productive, whatever that meant, or his teaching position could get precarious.

"A well-funded excavation overseas isn't considered productive?" she had asked.

"Depends."

"On?"

"What we find," he said, adding more ruefully, "and whether they think the excavation legit." Timika gave him a look and he shrugged apologetically. "No offense," he said. "But privately funded excavations without a university or professional organization backing them up . . ." He waggled his head noncommittally.

"You'll have the support of the University of Crete."

"Because someone gave them money and promised I wouldn't destroy anything valuable," said Nicholas bleakly.

"And you won't."

"Not a ringing scholarly endorsement, is it?"

"Does that matter?"

"If I find a cache of Minoan treasures or emerge with some groundbreaking theory about the decline of Cycladic culture, no," he replied. "But if I don't—and let's be honest, that's unlikely—I will have some explaining to do."

"You don't know what you'll find."

"No, which is why we dig, but most digs—especially brief ones like this—don't find much: a foundation that might have been part of a wall, a refuse heap. Even an important find will take months to classify. Mostly what archaeologists dig up is the need for money."

"We have money."

"For now, but I don't even really know what it is that's being funded."

"Nor do I," said Timika, frankly. "But I suspect it will be like porn." Tan gave her a bewildered look and she clarified. "I can't define it, but I know it when I see it."

He laughed at that and, for the moment, let it go.

They'd had a lot of those kinds of conversations over the last week as she had won him over, first in principle, then in practice, and had made the "unreasonably hasty" preparations—his words—to leave. In scientific terms, he assured her over and over, none of this made any sense at all and they were violating innumerable professional protocols and what he termed "best practice models." None of which would matter so much if, as he said, they found something. That constant litany was punctuated with various codas on the nature of academic publishing and the difficulty of turning actual finds into something worthy of a place in the larger scholarly conversation. She had half expected him to bail before the flight, and if he had, she wouldn't have blamed him. It was all a kind of madness after all, and his pulling out at the last second would have been no more than common sense. When he had greeted her sheepishly at check-in she had been just a little bit amazed, and stood there hunting his face for that glimmer of shared insanity.

It would be a long flight, first to San Francisco, then to Munich, Germany, for a killer thirteen-hour layover, then on to Nikos Kazantzakis airport in Heraklion, Crete. All told, almost thirty-five hours in transit.

Brutal.

But it had been the best they could manage at short notice. Tan said he would do some essential prep work en route, and had come with a laptop and a stack of books at least as unreasonable as their haste. Timika wasn't sure what she would do. She had picked up a couple of books of her own but was less sure how she was supposed to prepare for whatever she'd find herself doing when they landed in Greece. She had an uneasy feeling that she'd be doing a lot of improvising as she struggled to make sure the dig they had thrown together so absurdly quickly actually happened. Tan was the archeologist, but—per Jennifer's express wishes—Tamika held the purse strings and would be responsible for any negotiation with the locals. The thought gave her a mixture of fluttery butterfly wings in her stomach as pride, excitement, anxiety, and imposter syndrome fought for dominance. The last frequently won out, because it seemed the most measurably accurate. Having zero relevant expertise, she really had no business on this project. But there were things she had seen, things she knew, and she had earned Jennifer's trust. Taken together, they would have to be enough.

As they joined the line to board and she felt Tan's anxiety turn into giddy, schoolboy excitement, Timika found herself wondering again at the strangeness of what she was doing. Thirty-five hours sitting next to a man she had just met who gabbled about Hittite seals and *bulla*—which seemed to have something to do with ancient trade—and stele, and God knew what else! He kept reading and rereading his attempt at a translation of the Ugaritic cuneiform, making puzzled notations in the margins and glancing up from whatever he used as a dictionary with a faraway look on his face. It made her feel awkward, out of her depth. But then she had felt that way most of her life and had learned that the trick was just to keep kicking. So long as the water stayed below your chin, you were okay.

A part of her didn't believe they had shed the men who had chased her from New York across the country to Nevada, even though the ones she had seen—Cook and the fake cops who had searched the *Debunktion* office—were dead or taken by the Area 51 security detail. They had been well funded and coordinated. It was hard to believe that they were simply gone and wouldn't be replaced. A half memory from high school came back to her, a skeleton army grown from the teeth of a dragon who just kept coming till you found a way to turn them against each other. Or was it the serpent that grew two heads whenever you cut one off . . . ?

Some Greek mythology nonsense, she thought, wondering wildly if there was still time to get off the plane and leave Tan to fend for himself. She gave him a quick glance. He was poring over his books, his lips moving silently as he parsed out some new version of his translation, and she felt something almost like pity for him. Responsibility, at least. The hydra serpent and skeleton troops came back into her mind and she thought with a kind of deadpan comic misery, *Great. We're flying into some Jason and the Argonauts shit, him armed with his books and me armed with . . . what? Nothing so far as I can see. Awesome. Next stop Hades and the river Styx.*

But the next stop was actually San Francisco, a city she had always wanted to visit but that she could not see beyond the airport. She thumbed quickly through the inflight magazine, laughed aloud at what was for sale in the "skymall" and hoped to God there were decent movies to watch en route. Knowing her luck it would be *Jason and the* goddamn *Argonauts . . .*

The flight was, predictably, as close to Hell as was imaginable. She had shed a few pounds over the last month or so but was still no pixie waif and she was tall, so that while the seats were wide enough she had no room to shift her position or straighten her legs properly. The plane was, she decided, little better than a communal flying iron maiden. The food was flavorless gunk, and they billed her eight bucks for a rum and coke.

An hour after they'd dimmed the cabin lights, restless and unable to sleep, she raised the window shade and tried to see through the misty pane to the black Atlantic below, but could make out nothing beyond the blinking light of the wing. It reminded her of the other lights in the sky she had seen, and of the essential strangeness of what she was doing, pursuing leads she would—only a few months ago—have dismissed as the ravings of the sad, lonely, and deluded. Up here in the dark, flying to Europe for the first time in her life with a man she barely knew, that wasn't a reassuring feeling.

The movement in her peripheral vision snapped her head around, not toward the body of the plane, but out, so that she was peering forward toward the wing, her face pressed up to the cool plastic of the window.

Something was edging along the wing toward the body of the plane. It was a confused, blurred something the size of a Labrador retriever, but with black, twiggy arms and legs. The face—it had a kind of pointed face—was smeared and bluish, its features small and malevolent. Its limbs were spidery, but it had two arms and two legs, and its gleaming black eyes were humanoid. They turned and fixed on her, and she thought it grinned wickedly as it made its crab-crawl along the wing, though it seemed to shimmer and fade as if not quite in focus.

Timika gasped, horrified and confused, sitting tightly in her seat and then glancing desperately around for a flight attendant. There was no one, so she hit the call button on her armrest with an unsteady hand, her eyes flashing back to the ragged, impossible thing clawing its way along the aircraft's wing panel on splayed, sticklike limbs.

"Can I help you, Miss?"

Timika turned, startled to find one of the airline's uniformed attendants looming over her in the gloom.

"There's . . ." Timika began, but couldn't put what she had seen into words. She leaned back so the woman could crane across to the window and pointed, but as she did so, she realized there was nothing out there on the wing.

"What is it?" asked the flight attendant.

"There was . . . I don't know. I don't see it now."

The stewardess's concern, which had been genuine for a moment, evaporated immediately.

"Maybe you nodded off," she said.

"No," said Timika. "It was right there . . ."

"What was it?"

Timika couldn't answer that and suddenly found she didn't want to try.

"Sorry," she said. "Maybe I did dream it."

The flight attendant managed to smile and say it was no problem, but Timika felt stupid and embarrassed. She pulled the blind down and rested her head against it. Maybe she could get some real sleep.

She didn't. Not really. The dream—or whatever it had been—played on her mind, and she found herself periodically raising the blind and looking back out, and though the stick creature never reappeared, she could not settle, and sat there till the lights came on, her bored irritation blending with exhaustion to make her irritable.

As she got ready to leave she got down on her knees in the aisle, hunting under the seat.

"You lost something, Miss?" asked one of the perky, wooden flight attendants.

"The glamor of air travel," said Timika. "Got to be around here somewhere."

The only upside was that her misery took her mind off whatever difficulties lay ahead, and as she breezed through immigration staring down anyone who might think about giving her a hard time, she felt a little flicker of delight.

She was in Greece.

She met up with Tan in baggage claim and together, in weary silence, they moved through customs and out into the arrivals area, which was crowded with dark-suited men carelessly holding up signs. She scoured them. Almost a head taller than Tan, who was pivoting up and down on his toes, she was the first to spot their driver with his languidly held cardboard sign on which someone had written in black marker "MARS TIMCAL."

Close enough.

He was about sixty and truculent with a steel-gray mustache and a handful of English words, which he hoarded like gold.

But Timika was in no mood for small talk, and if the guy knew where they were going and how to get there, that was all she needed. Tan craned to see through the windows of the slightly boxy Mercedes, looking around like a baby bird that knows its mother is about to arrive with a beakful of worms. The University of Crete had two campuses, one in Heraklion and one in Rethymno, an hour or so up the coast. The latter housed the archaeology department. As the car sped along the coastal highway, Timika took a moment to take in the remarkable blue of the sea to their right, then closed her eyes and, remarkably, slept.

An hour later they were stopping among a complex of modern, cream-colored concrete buildings sitting on a low rise scattered with dusty trees and bushes. There were a lot of broad steps laid out like the terraces of an arena, and the mostly square angles of the buildings were occasionally broken by columns, some of them painted bright red.

"Huh," said Tan, pleased. "They're imitating the palace at Knossos."

Timika gave him a sleepy look but said nothing, then busied herself with getting her purse and other bits together. The driver was already out, the trunk popped expectantly.

"University," he said with a smile and a vague wave of his hand, as if he had built it during a free moment. The place was as deserted and silent as one of Tan's archaeological sites. The driver plucked a cell phone from his pocket, dialed, and delivered a few terse words of Greek, then hung up. "Coming," he said. "Bye."

And before either of them could think of anything else to say he was back in the Mercedes and pulling away. For a moment they just looked at each other, standing there in the hot, empty campus with their luggage, saying nothing. Timika was uncomfortably aware that Tan was looking to her to see what they were supposed to do next. She tried to look like this was all part of the plan, but inside she was kicking herself for falling asleep in the car. She felt disoriented and unprepared. Standing here by the empty road she felt like Cary Grant in the cornfields of *North by Northwest*, waiting for the crop duster to come strafing . . .

"Ms. Mars? Doctor Tan?"

A door had opened in the building behind her and a young woman was coming toward them, hand raised. She was slim and dark, with thick black hair tied back in a rough ponytail and big, liquid eyes. She was smiling as she skipped down the stairs.

"Hi! I am Elina Nerantzi," she said. "We spoke on the phone. You arrived okay? Good flight?"

"Long," said Timika honestly, but she was relieved and pleased by the woman's friendliness.

They shook hands and made small talk, but only for a minute or two, before Elina glanced at their luggage and said simply, "Okay, we go?"

"Sure," said Timika.

"Which of you is driving?"

"Me, I guess," she said.

"Okay. Come with me and I'll take my car. You can follow in the truck."

"Truck?" asked Timika, her apprehension waking again.

"It's no problem," said the Greek woman breezily. "It's easy."

Tan shot Timika a look and she forced a smile.

No problem.

Elina fished keys from her close-fitting jeans as they walked to a nearby lot, where she directed them to a battered Toyota pickup. It had once been white but was now coated with a fine gray dust and streaked with mud around the fenders. Elina caught Timika's glance and gave her an encouraging nod. "Is good," she said. "You can put your cases in the back."

They did so, laboring to shove them up over the tailgate among the picks and spades and other dirt-caked tools that were already there.

"Is it automatic?" asked Timika.

"Manual," said Elina.

"Right," said Timika. She gave Tan a look but he shook his head quickly. "Right."

"It's easy," said Elina again, still smiling as she opened the door to her tiny powder-blue Renault. She was beginning to get on Timika's nerves.

"Is there a GPS," Timika asked. "In case we lose you?"

"No. Once we leave town the phone signal is . . ." She waggled her hand: not great. "It's okay. I go slow."

"Right," said Timika again. "Figures." Raising her voice to be heard over Elina's engine she added, "I'm not sure about the manual transmission."

Elina shrugged with her face, then framed an apologetic smile.

"It's all there is," she said. "The other equipment was already committed to other work months ago. Miss Quinn's request for support came very recently. We can only loan what is going spare. People too."

"People?" asked Tan, catching Timika's anxiousness.

"There is only one available graduate student," said Elina. "She will come to meet you tomorrow."

Tan's face fell.

"One?" he said.

Again the shrugging smile, which repeated what she had already said: last minute, resources already committed, best we can do . . .

"Okay," said Timika, nodding decisively, determined to make it so, "We'll be right behind you."

She got into the truck and started familiarizing herself with the controls as Tan climbed in beside her. The vinyl of the dashboard was blistered, and a glittering line ran unevenly across the windshield to a little radiating spider web of cracks in the corner where something had hit the glass from outside.

"Okay," said Timika to herself, inserting the key and turning it. She pressed the clutch and found the reverse gear, rolling the truck back slowly into a turn, but as she tried to move it forward again she missed the gear and the engine whirred noisily.

"I think you have to . . ." Tan began.

"I know," Timika snapped, taking her foot off the accelerator and finding the clutch again. She started over, and this time brought the pickup behind the blue Renault which, with a cheery wave from the driver's window, pulled out onto the road. There was a plume of sand-colored dust as they left the parking lot, and Timika followed, hands gripping the wheel save when, nervously, she reached for the gear stick as if to check to be sure it was still there.

She had no idea where they went, though it took far longer than she had expected, almost half an hour. Her attention was entirely on the car in front and on the unfamiliar mechanism of clutch and gear change. Three times she left the truck racing completely out of gear and had to fumble it back into place—once with an alarming scraping noise which she feared was stripping teeth off the cogs—but she only stalled it once. The last ten minutes was the hardest, as they left the blacktop and turned onto a winding dirt road, which climbed dramatically over rutted and stone-strewn ground till the only buildings they could see were the roofs of houses below them and the occasional tower that might have been a church. She found herself holding her breath as they navigated each turn, the tires popping as gravel and stones spat up against the chassis, but they made it, and when they reached their destination Tan, who had been studiously, watchfully silent throughout the journey, said "Good job."

Where they had made it to was less clear.

It looked like a farm, and the rocky ground was broken only by stunted gray trees that Timika thought might be olive, though those that were still alive looked wild and untended. At the back of what, for want of a better word, she would call a field, Timika could see another tumble-down building, the roof of which was partially collapsed and weedy, and which sported a barrel-shaped tower with a ragged, crumbling top. Another tiny church, she thought, long abandoned.

They got out and joined Elina, who was leaning against a gate into the field and checking a folded map. It felt still hotter up here away from the sea breeze on the shadeless hillside. A desert heat.

As she heard them approach, Elina turned on her sunny smile.

"Okay," she said. "Here it is."

Timika blinked.

"Here what is?" she asked.

"The site," said Elina.

Timika considered the uneven ground with its falling-down buildings and blasted trees, scattered over an area at least a couple of football fields across and possibly much larger.

"Where's the dig?" asked Tan.

It was Elina's turn to look slightly bemused.

"You haven't started yet," she said, as if they might have forgotten.

"I know," said Tan, "but I thought there was already an excavation here."

Elina shook her head, pushing her bottom lip out for emphasis.

"It would have been much harder to get you access to a place where we knew there were Minoan remains," she explained. "But these are the coordinates you sent. This place has never been excavated."

Timika took a breath and, to fill Tan's darkening silence, said, "Okay. We have to start the dig ourselves."

"Yes."

"But that could take months . . . !" Tan began.

Timika cut him off, keen to convey that this was all within her capacity.

"Okay," she said. "So . . . where exactly do we dig?"

"Here," said Elina, nodding vaguely at the field. "This is the spot."

"Yes, but where specifically?" Timika pressed.

Elina shaped a larger shrug this time and blew out a puff of breath.

"Your coordinates did not have enough numbers to limit the range of the search," she said. "It's somewhere in here."

"It's huge," said Timika. "Where are we supposed to start?"

Elina said nothing. Tan dropped into a squat, his head in his hands and his eyes squeezed shut.

"Oh," breathed Timika, gazing out over the vast expanse of barren nothing, "you have got to be shitting me."

ALAN
Area 51/Dreamland

IT WAS AS IF THEY'D BEEN EXPECTED. THE GUARDS ON THE gate made their radio calls, checked their IDs, and showed them where to leave their vehicle, and then they were driven to the obligatory blacked-out bus and returned separately to their quarters. Alan's were exactly as he had left them. It was eleven p.m. and he wanted to lie down, but knowing they'd be coming for him, he sat on the edge of his cot and waited.

He listened to the silence of the base, smelling the desert air, which would sear the inside of his nostrils in the heat of the day but was now blessedly cool. It was all oddly familiar, almost reassuring.

It took them eight minutes. A duty officer came for him and, with an armed escort, they took a Humvee to a low, neutral-looking concrete box of a building a half mile or so away. Inside was a lot of empty space and an elevator, which took them down. There were only two buttons, but the lower level was considerably lower and the descent took the better part of 30 seconds. At the bottom he was escorted along a series of corridors deep beneath the desert, past identical doors, each marked with a number and code letter. They stopped at one marked 47C-5 SCIF, where another uniformed sentry checked everyone's credentials and unlocked the door with his handprint.

Only Alan stepped inside.

There were five people already inside waiting for him. One was the bald, blue-eyed CIA agent who had first introduced himself as Harvey Kenyon and who had been responsible for debriefing Alan after the incident. He was ranked General Schedule-15, roughly parallel to an Air Force Colonel, and was a CIA Group Chief. Flanking him were a white woman in a lab coat, who was Air Force, a black woman in the uniform of an Air Force Captain—the Counter Intelligence Officer—and two men, one white, one Hispanic, who were DOD and CIA scientists respectively. They stood and introduced themselves by name and role.

Alan barely took the names in, and though he nodded and shook hands, his eyes came back to Kenyon, who would clearly be running the show. He eyed the recording device on the table with its little red light and tried to look nonchalant. The room was bare to the point of austerity, and apart from the conference table and chairs the only other item in the room was a large yellow metal crate sitting in one corner.

"You seem unsurprised to see me, Mr. Kenyon," Alan remarked, shaking the Group Chief's hand, then taking his seat across the table.

"Well, as you know, I kind of had a feeling," said Kenyon, making a note on his pad with a blue ballpoint. "And please, call me Harvey. I am sure our Air Force comrades can unbend enough to handle that much informality." He glanced around the table and everyone smiled and nodded in silence. Alan had been right. This was to be Kenyon's show. "But that's as good a place to start as any," Kenyon continued. "You seemed pretty distressed when you left, Alan. Like you might be walking away not just from this table but from your career. What brought you back?"

Alan had known this was coming and kept his face neutral. He could feel everyone watching him, however much their hands hovered over notes and laptop keys. He didn't want to answer in terms of how many years' service he'd done, mostly with the Marines, the years to retirement, the benefits he'd banked on, but he didn't have a better answer.

"What else am I going to do?" he asked. Kenyon's lips pursed slightly, so he added, "It's tough to go back to the real world after the things I've seen."

"Real world?"

"Ordinary world, then."

Kenyon nodded sympathetically.

"No doubt," he said. "But about that, and in the interests of . . . *clearing the air*, shall we say."

He turned to the black woman beside him—the Air Force Counter Intelligence captain, whose name badge said Forsythe—and bumped his head in the direction of the yellow crate in the corner of the room. Alan thought she held Kenyon's eyes for a split second and there was a question in them—*are you sure?*—but he nodded again, and she got to her feet. She dragged the wheeled crate toward the table and keyed a pass code into its lock. It beeped once and Forsythe turned her attention on Alan.

"Mr. Young, if you wouldn't mind. Something we'd like you to see."

He got out of his chair and moved slowly, warily, toward the metal box, sensing the tensions and anticipation in the air. His eyes moved from Forsythe's blank face to the lid and waited. She unsnapped the side hasps, and opened it.

For a second, Alan was back at the crash site. The smoke in his nostrils, the exhaustion in his mind, the fear and shock of it all, coupled with the rifleman's dread of those two awful words . . .

Friendly Fire.

He actually gasped and felt himself physically recoil from what he was looking at, but as the seconds passed and the room stayed still and silent, he overcame his first response and leaned in closer.

It was a jointed manikin, child size, but with over-large eyes, slits for ears, mouth, and nostrils, its pale skin shining slightly in the hard light of the SCIF. Unbidden, he reached out a cautious hand and touched the creature's chest. It felt almost slick and spongy, like a Nerf ball coated in latex.

"What the hell is this?" he breathed.

"Just wanted to put your mind at rest," said Kenyon.

"We've been carrying them since the forties," said Forsythe. "Useful bit of misdirection if we lose something we don't want people to know about. A rancher gets to it before we do, looks inside . . . Suddenly all he can remember, all he can talk about is little green—well, *gray*—men from Mars. He barely takes any notice of the craft itself, and not very many people are gonna take him seriously." She smiled in a way that was almost pitying. "It's about the cheapest way of keeping things quiet we've come up with."

"Wait," said Alan, his mind reeling, "so what we saw in the downed sphere was . . ."

"One of these little guys, yes," said Forsythe. "Some of them blink, and their chests rise and fall like they're breathing. Amazing what four double-A batteries will power these days, isn't it?"

Alan stared at her, not knowing what to say.

"Come on now, Alan," said Kenyon. "Can't be that big a surprise to you, not considering the alternative."

Kenyon flashed a grin around the room and several of the scientists chuckled pleasantly.

"It's a prop," said Alan to no one in particular, his eyes back on the diminutive "alien."

"Right from its birth, the CIA has been in the movie business," said Kenyon. "Well, thank you Captain Forsythe, I think Mr. Young found that most instructive. Now, if we can return to our conversation about reality which—I'm sure you'll agree—now has a slightly different cast to it. We were talking about why you came back."

Alan sat down again, but his eyes tracked to the yellow metal crate as the Air Force officer closed it up. He had never taken LSD, but this, he thought, was what it must feel like to emerge from a particularly strange trip. The world reordered itself, the logic of normality clicking familiarly into place. After the initial disorientation, it was surprisingly comforting.

"Mr. Young," said Kenyon, pausing till he had Alan's full attention. "You were saying you came back because you found ordinary life uninspiring. That's it? That's why you're here with us again?"

"Does there need to be anything else?"

"Not if there wasn't," said Kenyon, smiling. It was a broad, welcome-back smile but it didn't quite reach his cool blue eyes, and Alan thought there was still a question there.

"Nothing comes to mind," said Alan.

He wasn't sure why he was prevaricating. He hadn't intended to. There were specific reasons he had come back and it was no good pretending otherwise. But the prospect of saying it all out loud . . .

Kenyon laid his pen down and sat back in his chair, his eyes on Alan's. He didn't speak for a long time.

"So?" said Alan, at last, uneasy under Kenyon's pointed gaze. "Now what?"

"Well," said Kenyon, reaching into the briefcase and pulling out a well-thumbed paperback, a thriller by David Morrell. "I thought I might read."

"What?"

"You don't mind, do you?" said Kenyon, opening the book and finding his place. He glanced at the scientists and intelligence officers on his side of the table as if asking them the same question, and they responded with cautious acquiescence. They didn't know what he was playing at, but were prepared to go along.

"I thought you brought me hear to brief me, or debrief me or something," said Alan.

"Oh!" said Kenyon, as if greatly surprised. "You want to talk? Sure. Go ahead. Say whatever you like for as long as you like. It won't bother me. The moment you want to start telling us the truth, you let me know, and I'll start listening."

And he started to read.

For a moment, Alan just stared at him, then switched his gaze to the rest of the team. The counter intelligence officer stared him down, motionless, but the lady in the lab coat gave him a slightly uncertain smile. The two men exchanged quick glances, then turned to their laptops and started tapping keys. Alan's gaze returned to the Group Chief, who studiously ignored him even as Alan frowned. Kenyon sighed noisily, moistening his thumb with his tongue and carefully turning a page.

"This is crazy," said Alan.

Kenyon ignored him.

"Can I go back to my quarters?"

"No," said Kenyon, not looking up from his book.

Alan pushed away from the table and glared at him, but the other man did not respond. The counter intelligence officer stiffened as if she was going to leap to her feet and draw her side arm.

"Okay," said Alan, at last. "Something happened. Two things. Happy?"

"Ecstatic," said Kenyon, dog-earing his page and closing the book. "Why don't you tell us about it."

"It was nothing really," said Alan. "Probably mostly in my imagination."

Kenyon didn't react. He had set the book carefully between them, ready to pick it up again if Alan's answer disappointed. He waited. Alan clasped and unclasped his hands, sighed again, then, wishing the other observers were not there, blurted, "The salt shaker moved. Okay? Along the table. And then when we were driving back, a truck nearly hit us but sort of bounced off without touching our vehicle."

Kenyon smiled a satisfied, reptilian smile and picked up his pen again.

"There now," he said. "That wasn't too hard, was it? Let's deal with each incident in turn. The salt shaker. Tell me about it." He leaned forward a fraction, his cool eyes burning into Alan's as the people around him readied pens and keyboards to take notes. "Tell me everything in minute detail. I want colors, smells, details, however irrelevant you think them. I want to be able to paint a picture of each moment so vividly, and with such perfect clarity that anyone who was present at the incident would recognize it immediately. I want photorealism in words."

So, feeling slightly ridiculous, Alan told them, fielding question after question. Who was where. What the table was made of. What they were talking about. At what moment the salt shaker moved. How fast it moved. In what direction. And on, and on. Then the same with the almost-road-accident. How fast they were going. What they were talking about. What he could see as the pickup came close . . .

It seemed to take an age, but there was no clock in the room so he couldn't be sure. Kenyon pushed him for details he hadn't realized he had remembered, tiny specifics that had only come back to him under the agent's relentless prompting. At long last, with the other observers still sitting in silence, the Group Chief sat back and looked Alan over.

"That's it?" he asked.

"Jesus, what more is there to say?" Alan returned. He respected thoroughness but he hadn't really wanted to say any of this to begin with, and he had now been forced to unpack two fractional seconds till the recounting had lasted a thousand times longer than the original moments. "The salt shaker moved. The truck moved. That's it."

Kenyon tipped his head toward his left shoulder and made a skeptical face at the woman in the lab coat. She did not respond.

"What?" said Alan. "I swear I've told you everything."

"I believe you," said Kenyon. "But you talk about these two events as if they were quite separate and unrelated."

"They were."

"No," said Kenyon. "They weren't. They were linked. Also, you phrase your description the same way every time."

"What do you mean?"

"*The salt shaker moved. The truck moved.*"

"So?"

"You're hiding from the truth even as you tell it."

"What's that supposed to mean?" Alan demanded. After all the minute detail he was still getting grief?

Kenyon leaned in and lowered his voice, speaking slowly and clearly.

"What about, *you* moved the salt shaker? *You* moved the truck?"

Alan said nothing and, after a moment, Kenyon pressed the point.

"That, after all, is why you came back. You're still dodging the fact of the thing in your mind, which is almost ironic, because it was your mind that was doing the moving. These weren't two isolated incidents. They were connected by you, Alan. *You* are what made them happen."

"There were other people there," said Alan.

"Who wanted the salt?"

"What?"

"You wanted the salt. The salt came to you. That is not coincidence. And I'm pretty sure you didn't want to be in a head-on collision with a pickup truck."

"Barry didn't either," said Alan, holding on to what was left of his defiance.

"No doubt," said Kenyon. "And he saw it happening a moment before it did. But it was you who prevented it. You know you did."

"I don't . . ."

"You do, but we won't make any progress until you accept that and move beyond it."

Alan froze, openmouthed.

"Progress?" he said. "Toward what?"

"Toward unlocking your potential, Alan."

"I don't understand."

"This place," said Kenyon. "Everything you saw in Afghanistan and everything you've seen since. You didn't think it was just about *space ships*, did you?"

He said those two words with a quiver of amusement that was almost a sneer. Alan didn't know what to say and opted to stay silent. He felt as he had the first time he had flown the triangle, when up and down had become meaningless and he had realized that everything he thought was solid, reliable, and true was suddenly in flux. He glanced at the faces on either side of Kenyon, but they were being even more carefully neutral than before.

"This . . . potential of mine," he said, speaking the word with difficulty. "What do you mean?"

"That remains to be seen," said the agent, relaxing for the first time since the interview began. "I honestly don't know, though I'm sure you suspect some of it already."

"Piloting that craft changed me," said Alan, admitting it to himself for the first time.

The idea had been smoldering somewhere deep in his consciousness for a week now but he had kept his eyes averted from its glow for fear that acknowledging the truth of it would mean he was no longer the person he had been. For all the exciting possibilities he might imagine now in his future, it was impossible not to feel a pang of sadness about no longer being simply Alan Young, football player, friend, Marine, and pilot. If he was to grow, to change, he was also bound to lose something of himself in the process.

"Did you know that would happen?" he asked. "You knew I'd be back here. Did you know I had committed to something I didn't understand the moment I set foot in that ship?"

He was angry, which was unexpected. It was sudden and pure, and though he didn't raise his voice, Kenyon sensed it and, for once, seemed momentarily abashed. He turned to his right and the woman in the lab coat spoke, her voice level, the speech, he sensed, prepared.

"We couldn't know for sure," she said. "And in the heat of the battle, the loss of our other ships . . . You had to go up in the disk. The craft in question had not been flown by anyone before, you recall, so no. We couldn't have known for sure."

"But you suspected."

The woman hesitated, her mouth open, her eyes flicking to Kenyon, who intervened.

"It was a possibility," he said.

"And the pilot of the other ship? The sphere I shot down."

"You are wondering if it was another undisclosed vessel of ours," said Kenyon. "It was not."

"Even though it had one of those . . . things inside," he said, his eyes flashing to the yellow crate.

"Even so," said Kenyon evenly.

"Whose was it?"

"I think we should stay focused on you," said Kenyon.

Alan's eyes narrowed.

"Of course," he said, with a snort of muted laughter. "What was I thinking: coming back here for answers!"

"You'll get your answers," said Kenyon. "Some of them, at least. In time. But you need to begin with yourself."

"Fine," said Alan. "Then tell me. I didn't mean to do the things I did with the stupid salt shaker and the pickup. So why did I? How did I?"

"The answer to both questions," said Kenyon, "is the same. How did you do it? Why did you do it? Because, Alan, as my colleagues will attest, you are gifted."

MORAT
Somewhere north of Taraz, Kazakhstan

T HE MAN IN THE BLACK SUIT WHO WAS SITTING QUIETLY IN
the corner had his head down, but Morat still felt like he
was being watched. Ignoring him, he opened the fridge
and took out some prepackaged prosciutto and some sliced
Swiss cheese, which he arranged on a couple of slices of rye
bread with a sliver of onion and a carefully washed lettuce
leaf. He set a can of cold but uninspiring Russian beer beside
his plate and sat down to eat.

He could feel the man in the corner's eyes on him, but when
Morat turned in his chair and asked "Do you mind not doing
that?" the man had his head down again. He was sitting sloppily,
like a discarded dummy, and did not respond to Morat's remark.

Whatever.

Morat took a long draught of his beer—which was fine
so long as you didn't let it sit long enough to get anywhere

near room temperature—and took a bite of his sandwich. It crunched more than he had expected, and he hesitated in his chewing. When he swallowed he felt something moving in his throat, as if he had bitten into something alive.

Gagging, he leapt to his feet and made for the sink below the mirror, spitting. Bits of meat and cheese came up, but nothing untoward, and for a second he thought he had imagined the strange sensation in his mouth. It occurred to him to explain his behavior to the man in the dark suit, but he wasn't there anymore, and now that Morat came to think of it, it didn't make any sense that he had ever been there at all. He frowned, considering the empty chair in the corner, then returned to his sandwich, peeling back the top slice of bread and studying the contents warily.

Nothing but what he had put there.

He closed it, but as he picked it up to take another bite, he was distracted by a curious chittering noise that seemed to fade in and out, a strange and liquid clicking like you might make with your tongue against the roof of your mouth. It disappeared almost as quickly as it had come, but as he took another bite of the sandwich it came back, louder this time. Morat turned, his mouth full, and the man in the corner was back, still somehow watching him despite having his head down, and the noise seemed to be coming from him.

"What are you doing?" Morat demanded. He had to swallow to speak, and moments after doing so he felt it again, the squirming in his gullet. He looked back at the sandwich and now there could be no mistake. It was alive with pale, fat grubs, writhing blindly.

He stumbled over to the sink, retching till his sides ached, but when he looked up into the mirror he found the man in the suit was standing beside him, his head still bowed, and there was something strange about Morat's own eyes. He leaned into the mirror as the horror spiked, and saw that in each of his eyes was a cluster of hundreds of smaller eyes, black and shining, iridescent as the eyes of a fly.

Morat sat up, screaming and rubbing his face.

He was lying on his back on his own bed. There was no suited man, no sandwich infestation, and when he leapt to his feet and blundered over to the wall sink and mirror, his eyes looked perfectly normal. He drank from the tap, then splashed water on his face and considered himself closely. He was breathing hard and his heart was racing, but the nightmare was fading fast.

With a long, slow sigh, he returned to the bed and dropped onto it. He needed to get his head together before he was summoned, so he didn't lie back down. He perched on the edge, naked except for his shorts, feeling his racing pulse, and managed a rueful chuckle at his own expense.

You'd think, he told himself, *that after all you've seen, all you've done, nothing would scare you, but here you are . . .*

The chittering noise stopped him. It was coming from under the bed. He leaned hurriedly down to look under, and there was the suited man, curled up like a fetus, except that where his face should be there was only the tangle of eyes and a great black beak of a mouth surrounded by hairy tentacles. Before Morat could cry out, they reached for him, some feeling, some grabbing whatever they could find with tiny hook-like claws. The claws caught in his hair, his skin. They pulled him down and under the bed, the awful black beak-like maw opening wide to receive him . . .

He woke for real this time, a juddering, panicky surge that almost lifted him out of bed. A hand was shaking him by the shoulder, and as Morat's eyes tried to make sense of what looked like normality, the hand's owner—a uniformed sentry—spoke.

"Come on, Mr. Morat. You're late."

Morat glanced wildly around, taking in the alarm clock he had somehow slept through, and the rest of his room. Then he was nodding and muttering apologies, saying he had to take a shower before dressing.

Wash the dreams away.

A HALF HOUR LATER HE WAS IN A SMALLER ROOM IN ANOTHER part of the base, but his lateness had meant that his handlers had skipped the pre-exercise briefing.

"Maybe for the best anyway," said Rasmussen. "No point clouding your mind with expectations."

"Expectations?" Morat parroted. He still felt a little off kilter and he deeply disliked not knowing what was going on.

"Take a seat," said Narantuyaa. She was wearing a business suit with a slim skirt today. It muted what Morat had considered her warrior bearing, but softened her not in the slightest.

The seat she indicated was plush and canted into a permanent and inviting recline, but it faced the wall. Morat scowled at it, then turned back to where the two of them sat at a table with a laptop behind the chair's headrest.

"Doesn't seem very social," he said.

"Just sit down, Mr. Morat," said Narantuyaa in a voice iced with mountaintop air.

He did so. It felt like going to see the doctor, but stranger, since he couldn't see them.

"Tip your head back," said Narantuyaa. "Get comfortable. We want to see how you respond to the Ganzfeld technique. I'm going to set these over your eyes."

She loomed briefly into view with what looked like a ping-pong ball that had been split in two, one half in each hand.

"Can you tell me what's going on, please?" asked Morat, shielding his face before she could reach for his eyes.

"Nothing painful, I assure you," said Rasmussen. "We just want to cut out some of your sensory input. We'll also ask you to wear these headphones. White noise."

"And I'm supposed to do what, exactly?"

"Nothing for a while," said Narantuyaa.

"How long?" asked Morat. He was tired, but the prospect of falling asleep again—of dreaming—filled him with sudden alarm.

"Thirty minutes," she replied. "After that I will touch your hand once. You will stay as you are, but you will periodically announce whatever images come to mind."

"What do you mean?"

"Just as I say," said Narantuyaa, frostier still.

"Is this a test?" asked Morat.

"Consider it a routine training exercise," said Rasmussen. "Miss Narantuyaa will be silently considering a number of different images and sending them to you."

"Sending?" said Morat, sitting up again and pivoting in the chair so he could see them. This was starting to sound like bullshit.

"Consider it a radio transmission," said Rasmussen, "or as if you are logging on to a Wi-Fi network."

"Except that the network is neurological," said Narantuyaa. "Mental."

"You mean *psychic*?" asked Morat, not bothering to keep the scorn out of his voice.

"That is as good a term as any," said Narantuyaa. "The broadcast works telepathically. Psychically. Yes."

"Oh come on," said Morat. "Don't you have better things for me to do? I'm an agent, a pilot . . ."

"Mechanical exercises," said Narantuyaa, matching his note of disdain. "One day soon such roles will be taken by robots and computer systems."

"But magic is for the real people?" snapped Morat.

"No one said it was magic," said Rasmussen.

"Clairvoyance, then," said Morat. "Remote viewing. I thought everyone abandoned this as a nonstarter decades ago."

"It suited the CIA's agenda to say so," said Rasmussen.

"You've got to be kidding . . ." Morat began, but Narantuyaa cut him off.

"If Mr. Morat is unwilling to conduct this simple and harmless task," she said to Rasmussen, lowering her voice slightly, but not troubling to keep Morat from hearing, "we should send him back to his quarters, though I think we should then have a conversation about his continued usefulness to the program."

Clever. Obvious, clumsy, but clever nonetheless.

"It's fine," said Morat, swinging back around and laying his head onto the rest. "Whatever. Let's get on with it. Not sure why you need me for this instead of some uniformed grunt, but okay. If we're going to waste each other's time it may as well be doing the exercise rather than discussing it."

Narantuyaa's response was rasped to Rasmussen.

"I hardly think his attitude conducive to . . ."

"I said it's fine," said Morat, speaking over her. "I'll do it. I'll try. I'll be good. Throw me whatever pitch you've got and I'll catch it whether it's in the dirt, over the plate, or out and away."

"Out and away?" asked Narantuyaa, her steely tone faltering.

"Baseball metaphor," said Rasmussen. "Just give it your best shot, Mr. Morat. You might not see why, but it's important."

"Okay," said Morat. "Like I said: whatever."

He was pushing his luck, but he was irritated at having his time wasted like this. After all he had done for them. It was

113

insulting. Still, the tone of his *whatever* caught Rasmussen and he became a statue, hard and focused, his eyes fixed on Morat till he became self-conscious.

"Sorry," he muttered. "Go ahead."

"You want to know why we are doing these tests with you," said Rasmussen, "rather than with some—as you put it—uniformed grunt? Because you are best suited to it."

"I've never felt a psychic premonition in my life," said Morat.

"That you are aware of," said Narantuyaa. "Though I suspect that may be changing."

"Meaning what?" asked Morat, oscillating between resentment and unease. He didn't like the surety in her face.

"The craft you have been flying," said Rasmussen. "The technology. We think there might be . . . side effects."

"Like what?" asked Morat, his anxiety mounting.

"Good things," said Rasmussen. "Positive things. An enhancement of your sensory abilities."

"Because of the arrowhead?" said Morat. "I haven't felt . . ."

"It's cumulative," said Rasmussen. "We don't fully understand it yet."

"But it's safe, right?"

"Of course," said Narantuyaa with ill-concealed disdain. "But these tests will help us figure out the nature of any as yet unforeseen effects."

Morat frowned, not entirely sure he liked the sound of this, but at another steely glare from Narantuyaa, he lay back in the seat again.

"Work on clearing your mind," said Rasmussen. "The less consciously you are thinking, the better this is likely to work."

Morat considered saying something snappy in return about how it was tough to do that after hearing phrases like "unforeseen effects," but there was no point. He did his best to shrug out of the uncertainty and took refuge in his previous defiant skepticism.

It was all nonsense. Of course it was.

But if they wanted him to go through this farce, fine. It was their money. When it was done, he might have to reevaluate his work here, start looking for ways to extricate himself from whatever sad, desperate nonsense the remnants of the Consortium were trying to pursue here, but for now it was best to lie low. He had been on the losing side before. There was no shame in that. But he wasn't a loser, and this stuff—telepathy, clairvoyance—was surely the stuff of losers.

"Clear my mind," he said, growing still as Narantuyaa once more loomed over his head, the halved table-tennis ball at the ready. She met his eyes briefly, unreadably, then covered them with the egg-like hemispheres. "On it."

Next came the headphones. He half-raised his hands to adjust them, but she pushed them down.

"Keep still," she said.

"Do I keep my eyes open or closed?" he asked, as close to motionless as he could manage while speaking.

"As you wish," she replied. "We are adjusting the light in the room now."

There was a click, and the pale glow he could see through the ping-pong balls was replaced by something dimmer and redder, like the light in an old photographic darkroom. Then the headphones turned on and his brain was awash with what sounded like the sound of surf on a pebbled beach, except that it was constant and unmarked by wave or rhythm.

"I just lie here?" he asked, too loudly over the white noise.

No one responded. Or if they did, he didn't hear them. So he lay there. Waiting. Not sleeping.

And, after a while, as his irritation and sense of absurdity faded, as he got better at forgetting that he was being watched, it was almost peaceful. There were, after all, harder ways to make money than lying in a glorified recliner with your eyes shut. But Morat had spent too much time in real danger to give himself over to the experience entirely. He had trained for the disorientation of flight in advanced aircraft, like the arrowhead, in sensory deprivation tanks. That was as close to what he was doing now as he had come, but no one then had asked him to turn his thoughts off, to become neutrally receptive.

In his head he paced the hallways of the base's lower level, probing for ways to slip away, though he suspected a straight break-out was not a viable option. Sooner or later they'd put him back in his arrowhead. They needed him there. They'd lost too many other pilots. They'd give him a flight mission, and when they did . . .

Maybe the money would be better in Nevada. He'd get a rough reception, but the United States had a history of turning enemies into friends if they thought they would be useful, especially where space was concerned. The Americans could say what they liked about the Nazis, but they wouldn't have made it to the moon without them.

He needed a couple of hours in the gym. That would clear his head better than lying here like some debutante getting some kind of damned spa treatment . . .

He jumped slightly at the feel of the pressure on his hand. *Narantuyaa's touch, cool and strong.*

Had it really been a half hour already? It hadn't felt like it, and for a moment he worried that he'd fallen asleep. But he was sure he would have remembered the dreams.

Okay. Half hour up. Now what? He thought vaguely. I lie here and wait to see the Eiffel Tower?

"Eiffel Tower," he said aloud. His voice sounded distant and echoey in his earphones. He suppressed the urge to grin and wondered mischievously if he should just dream up a list of BS things to call out periodically. Keep them on their toes . . . He sensed no response from anyone in the room and wondered vaguely what kinds of things they would be trying to project. He had a vague memory of seeing a test like this on TV where they'd used geometrical shapes as the baseline test targets: squares, circles, a wavy series of three lines together that looked like water. That seemed the kind of thing.

"Star," he said, at random and, a minute later, "Circle."

Because a possibility had occurred to him. Laughable as all this was, if he bombed it completely, they might move on to some other test subject and leave him to do something else. That might be retaking his seat in the cockpit of his beloved arrowhead triangle, or it might be something else entirely, something he'd enjoy a good deal less.

"Triangle," he volunteered.

Too many shapes, he thought. He was getting into a rut.

"A rutted road," he added. "A field of cows."

And so it went on. After about a half hour they stopped him, their faces unreadable, neither Rasmussen nor Narantuyaa giving anything away as to how well they thought he'd done, so that Morat began to worry he'd been so disappointing that he wouldn't get another chance. More tests meant more time, more opportunities to make his exit before they deemed him of no further use . . .

"Give us a moment to lay out some sample images," said Rasmussen, clicking the track pad of the laptop as he cued up what turned out to be a slide show of symbols and pictures. When he was done he invited Morat to join them at the table. "We'll scroll through these images and you can flag whichever of them you think you may have seen or sensed during the test. Some of these Ms. Narantuyaa was thinking about, some we're just adding as a control. She only actually focused on about a quarter of the images we're going to show you, so a lot will feel irrelevant, even if you performed particularly well. When you've seen them all individually, you can consider all the pictures as a grid and make your selections."

Morat tried to look serious, as if he was genuinely interested in seeing how he had fared. Narantuyaa eyed him with cool skepticism. She wasn't buying his sudden engagement with the test, but Rasmussen was unreadable. He tapped a button and the images came up on the screen, one at a time, each one sliding into the next after a second or two. First came Mount Rushmore, then an African lion, a waterfall, and a patch of brilliant but otherwise featureless blue sky. Morat shifted in his chair, wondering if he had miscalculated.

"Take your time," said Rasmussen. "If anything looks familiar . . ."

"That one," said Morat, stabbing his finger at a photograph of a rusty red bucket.

"You never said bucket," remarked Narantuyaa, one eyebrow arching.

"I didn't see it exactly in those terms but . . ."

"Just watch the images," said Rasmussen. "You can make your decisions when we're through them all."

Iceberg. Banana. Maple leaf. Some kind of Asian temple . . .

Morat licked his lips. He should have taken this more seriously. He was going to get thrown out on his ass or worse . . .

"Wait," he said suddenly. The image on the screen showed a dirt road. Down the right-hand side ran a deep, water-filled wheel rut. "That! I said rutted road. Remember? I saw that."

He looked up, hoping his relief looked simply like delight, and he found Narantuyaa watching him cagily. Unconvinced. He couldn't blame her. He'd gotten lucky on one picture. Anything else he claimed would require some verbal gymnastics to connect the image he claimed to have seen to whatever nonsense he'd said.

And then the next picture slid into place. It was beautifully lit, a gorgeous Parisian scene dominated by . . .

"The Eiffel Tower," said Morat.

His eyes narrowed and his voice sounded not so much gleeful as it was uncertain, even confused. He looked up first at Rasmussen, then at Narantuyaa as they watched him, their faces carefully, deliberately blank.

"I think that's enough for today," said Rasmussen, his voice neutral. "I suggest you get some exercise. We will return to this tomorrow, but I have a field operation I would like you to attend to at the end of the week, and I want you at your peak fitness. There's has been rather too much sitting around of late."

"That's true," said Morat, still looking at the Eiffel Tower image till Narantuyaa snapped the laptop closed pointedly and gave him a probing stare. "It will be good to get in the arrowhead again."

"Who said anything about the arrowhead?" said Narantuyaa. "This is strictly a land-based mission."

Morat hesitated, then nodded.

"Okay," he said. "What have you in mind?"

Rasmussen turned the computer to face him, made a couple of clicks on the track pad, and rotated it once more. The image was divided into two pictures of the same black woman: one a smiling headshot in a frizzy gold wig, the other a surveillance image of the woman walking down a city street in winter clothes.

"Timika Mars," said Rasmussen. "I take it you've heard the name?"

"Of course," said Morat, settling into the empty seat at the table and studying the image. "I read all the reports that are sent to me."

"Have you met her?"

"Never."

"She became closely associated with Miss Quinn," said Narantuyaa.

"After my dealings with Quinn concluded," said Morat. "I've never actually set eyes on her."

"What about this man?" asked Rasmussen, pulling up another image, this one from what looked like a company website. It was labeled "Nicholas Tan, Assistant Professor." He was young, Asian, in black-rimmed spectacles that looked almost ironic.

But not quite.

Morat shook his head.

"Who is he?"

"Archaeologist based in Reno," said Rasmussen. "Specialist in the ancient Near East and, if what we're finding online is right, Atlantis."

Morat's eyebrows rose but he said nothing.

"We don't have the eyes on the ground or the resources we did," Rasmussen continued, "but it seems Miss Mars booked a flight to Crete. Dr. Tan went with her."

"You think there's another tablet?" asked Morat, his pulse quickening, all his previous doubts and prevarications splitting and cracking like an overripe chrysalis. "An artifact?"

"It's possible," said Rasmussen, "though I don't know where they are getting their lead."

"Stern's notebook?"

"Pointing to Crete?" said Rasmussen doubtfully. "If such an object had been dug up there, we'd know about it."

"Maybe it's still in the ground."

"Then how would they know where to look?" asked Rasmussen. "It's probably a wild goose chase, but we should look into it. If such an item is indeed in the vicinity, it is essential that we recover it. And if it's not . . . well, Miss Mars really should answer for the various inconveniences she has inflicted upon our organization, wouldn't you say?"

Morat smiled his faintly feline smile. He missed being up in the sky, soaring like a god with the kind of power at his fingertips most pilots could only dream of, but this, the simple clarity of it, this appealed to him on a visceral level.

"Absolutely," he said.

His blood was suddenly rushing like a waterfall and as the idea tightened his focus he felt every muscle and sinew stir with anticipation. It was a good thing he was going to the gym, or he would have to find some other outlet for what he thought of as his creative energy, and that was always messy.

13

ПICHOLAS
Пear Fotinos, Crete

NICHOLAS TAN'S EYES WENT FROM THE IMAGE TIMIKA had given him of the Ugaritic tablet to his hand-scrawled transliteration of the text into English consonant clusters and back, then checked to see what the Watson and Wyatt handbook to the language said about homonyms in a translation gloss:

> Although the sequence *bkm* looks like the particle *bk*, 'thereupon', this is impossible here as such particles are never postpositive: they always come first in the clause (RENFROE 1992, 58). Instead, here *km* means 'hill, mound' (as proposed by ARTUN, 1968, 291) and it is preceded by the preposition *b* (as part of the syntagm *'ly+b* 'to climb.')

Obviously, he thought miserably, shoving the book aside and sinking onto his bed feeling stupid and defeated. He was out of his depth, and not just with the nonsensical half translation he had cobbled thus far. This whole trip was a fiasco. One that might cost him his job. Maybe even his career.

He could almost hear Ted Jarret, his mentor back in the Reno anthropology department, intoning all the reasons why a junior faculty member needed to make significant steps toward the most important publications of his life in the first two years of employment. If there was no clear and measurable promise there at third-year review, he might not get a tenure bid, and being ejected then boded badly for getting a position elsewhere. The new, corporate training program that was twenty-first century American academia was hiring business and management faculty left and right, but Middle Eastern archaeologists were somewhat lower on the totem pole. Student enrollment in disciplines that were both difficult and not clearly vocational were plummeting, and as faculty like Jarret rode off into the sunset of retirement, they weren't being replaced. Departments were shrinking and combining; administrative and financial support was vanishing at the same rate that upper administration positions were ballooning in order to fill the make-work, spread-sheet-filling quotas demanded by boards of regents and trustees whose background was almost exclusively business rather than education.

Nicholas Tan, he thought bleakly, *with unerring and familiar cluelessness, you have committed to American higher education at precisely the moment of its grand unraveling.*

Overdramatic, perhaps, but not by much. The short version was that he was blowing the summer in which he needed to be most productive as a publishing scholar on a fool's errand that would leave him with nothing more than a suntan. Classes would restart in the fall, and between teaching, grading, and the constantly mounting service work of committees and department meetings, he would be playing catch-up for the rest of the academic year. The even shorter version, then, was that he was screwed.

He had known it the moment he had seen the dig site. Foolishly—and he couldn't believe he hadn't pressed for specifics before he had signed on to this little trip down the professional drain—he had assumed that there was something other than the Mars woman's mysteriously attained coordinates to direct their dig, preferably the incomplete excavation of a known, if minor, Minoan house or tomb. But there was nothing. The land was so rugged and wild, so untouched for decades at the very least that it could barely be called a field, and it was spotted with ancient trees and falling-down buildings of zero historical interest. One was a tiny ruined church, another looked like it had been a goat pen. There was absolutely nothing to suggest a reason for digging there, and to cover the entire region would take, conservatively, years.

And that was with a full team. But, needless to say, they didn't have a full team. They had Mars, who barely knew which end to hold a trowel; Nicholas himself—an academic more comfortable behind a desk in an air-conditioned office, with only a handful of real-world dig credits under his belt; and a surly female graduate student called Desma who had clearly been assigned to them because none of the local faculty wanted her on their pet projects.

Screwed was an understatement.

He had begun in the right spirit. While the graduate student performed soil analysis tests, he spent the first couple of days pacing the uneven ground with a theodolite and a laser measure, preparing a full topographical map of the site, but

Timika had watched him, her hands shading her eyes from the bright sun, periodically checking her watch. Midway through the third day he found her randomly swinging a pick ax into the ground over by the ruined church.

"Stop!" he had called. "What are you doing?"

"What are *you* doing more like?" she shot back. "Not much, it seems to me. We came to dig, so I'm digging."

"We have to document conditions before we start!" he protested. "If we don't, none of our findings will have any weight."

She made a face.

"Have any *weight*?" she echoed. "What the hell does that even mean?"

"It means that archaeology is a science and has to be conducted scientifically if we want other scientists to take us seriously."

"So your Syrian goatherd who stumbled on Ugarit in the 1920s was a scientist, was he?" Timika shot back. He knew he should never have told her that story. "Everyone ignored all the cool shit he found because he had gone in without doing a *topographical survey*?"

"Of course not!" he said, marching over to her. "But we're probably not going to find a complex of royal palaces, gold artifacts, and ancient language tablets. If this is anything like most archaeological work, we're going to find a few pottery shards, some discarded animal bones and maybe the masonry foundations of a building."

"So?"

"So what those things are and what they mean is going to be determined in part by how and where we find them. We need to measure the stratification of the earth inch by inch so that we know whether the bit of ceramic you stumble upon has been in the ground for ten years or a thousand. Otherwise we go home with a treasure trove of ancient Minoan soda bottle caps!"

She glared at him in hot, sweating silence, then said "Fine," dropped the pick, and walked back to the tarpaulin-covered lean-to they had set up as a field lab for preliminary cleaning and tagging of artifacts. He watched her go, but felt no sense of victory. He understood her frustration and disappointment all too well.

They had taken rooms in the nearest village, in a half-refurbished building divided into small and basic apartments that the university had leased on their behalf. Each had its own dwarfish kitchen, living room, bedroom, and bathroom. Each was furnished with the same simple pine furniture and ceramic tiled floors. Each came with its own sour-smelling toilet and assortment of desiccated insects in the cupboards. It was fine, mostly, though the rooms managed to feel both cramped and empty at the same time, and they took whatever personality they had from whoever was staying in them, which wasn't good news for either Nicholas or Timika, who brought their own little black clouds in with them from the site, like cartoon characters.

He wasn't sure how much longer he could do this. In his heart he knew they would find nothing. That there was nothing to find. His only hope was that something in the method would generate a conference paper or minor publication, and that meant sticking as closely as possible to protocol, however slow that made things.

But the topographical survey told him nothing definitive about the lay of the land that might indicate places where there once had been structures, and after four days, when they were as ready as they would ever be, he still felt like he was picking where to dig pretty much at random. In the end, and after a consultation with Desma, who had mostly shrugged and pointed vaguely, he had chosen to focus on the highest piece of ground in the field. It could hardly be called a true tell, and was certainly not large enough for any kind of fortification, but it was a ridge-like mound that ran between the ruined church and what had been an olive grove. It rose no more than four feet above the standard gradient, and most of it was more like two feet higher than the surrounding ground. The entire area was no larger than the square footage of his tiny apartment, but it would have to do.

When the area had been photographed, and divided into three-meter squares with string attached to stakes, and the whole carefully plotted onto a landscape schematic on his laptop, they positioned the plastic storage bins for anything they might uncover and laid out the brushes, trowels, and larger tools. On the sixth day after they arrived, and with Timika positively steaming with impatience, they began to dig.

Of course, *dig* was something of a euphemism. First, they cleared the squares of litter, obviously modern refuse, weeds, and undergrowth, none of which felt much like excavation to Timika.

"If I'd known we were going to be gardening I'd have brought the Roundup," she remarked.

"No chemical herbicides," said Nicholas absently, not looking up from the tan-colored dirt he was clearing. "Mustn't contaminate the site any more than is absolutely necessary."

"So the backhoe I ordered ain't gonna work?" she shot back. Nicholas started to stand up straight, caught the bleak grin that flashed across her face, and conceded the joke. "Relax, Dr. Tan. I'm not an archaeologist but I'm also not a complete moron," Tamika said.

"Got it," replied Nicholas. "Okay. Let's give this top surface a rake to see if it snags anything from underneath, and then we can start clearing the earth."

"With?" said Timika, eyeing the nearest pick.

"I'd like to start with a test shaft in this corner," said Nicholas. "See if we hit any large or shaped masonry. If we don't, we can use the picks."

"And till then?"

Nicholas tossed her a hand trowel.

"Oh hell no," she said. "You want me to dig up this entire field with an ice-cream scoop?"

"Just the trial trench," said Nicholas. "Desma, could you show her?"

The Greek girl rolled her eyes and dropped into a squat, scraping away the top soil with the trowel. "This way we don't damage anything in the ground," she observed.

"Maybe I should just blow on the dirt," said Timika.

"Very hilarious," said Desma. "Here. You try."

Timika took the trowel, glared at Nicholas and then froze, staring at a patch of scraggy shrub a dozen yards away.

"What?" he asked.

Timika continued to stare, then blinked and shook her head.

"Nothing," she said. "I thought I saw . . . Nothing."

He gave her a quizzical frown but she turned away and set to work.

It got hot fast. The site was virtually shadeless and the sun climbed high in the clear Aegean sky and hung there. By lunchtime the temperature was in the upper eighties and rising. Nicholas insisted they stopped for water breaks every half hour or so, but it was clear they wouldn't get much done in the afternoons. They would have to start rising before dawn and end the work day at lunchtime.

Timika was going to love that.

She had, he had to admit, buried her frustration as best she could and had put a brave face on things, but whatever she thought she had been coming to, it hadn't been this. She was a city girl through and through, and he doubted she'd ever spent this much summer time outside air conditioning, and considerably less digging in the dirt. Nicholas had only been to New York once for a job interview he didn't get, and his memory of the closeness and the heat of the summer, the scale of the buildings all seemingly designed to make you feel insignificant, had driven him close to insane. He had been secretly relieved not to get the job and hadn't returned to the city since. That was Timika's space, her comfort zone, so he couldn't blame her for feeling traumatized by a work environment as different as this.

She had brought the right clothes, or almost the right clothes, having consulted with him and various supply shops before they left the States: safari shirt, shorts, and hiking boots. But she wore them like she had been press-ganged into a photo shoot or had put them on as a joke, and couldn't wait to get out of them. He didn't get the impression that she was unduly preoccupied by her appearance, but she kept checking her fingernails unhappily and scowling at the sweat stains on her clothes. Desma, the dark, wiry graduate student, seemed pleased by this. She wore dirt like a badge of honor even when she wasn't emerging from the site, and her familiarity with the work seemed to compensate for her lack of interest in it. The two women had not exactly hit it off.

And they had found, of course, nothing. It was slow work and they felt like ants removing the earth one grain at a time, but still, he had hoped the exploratory trench would tell them something. It hadn't, so he'd moved two squares over and started another. It was early days yet, but the nervous ripple he felt in his guts from time to time registered the question he was trying not to consciously raise: How long could he do this without results before he started seriously considering abandoning the enterprise as lost, and fleeing back to Reno? One week? Two? Much more than that and he really would have blown the precious summer before classes restarted.

"I think we should stop for the day," he said.

"Oh, thank God," said Timika, dropping her trowel and settling onto her haunches. "I gotta lie down. And eat something. And shower. Not necessarily in that order."

"What time tomorrow?" asked Desma.

"I think we should look to start at six," said Nicholas.

"Six!" Timika shrieked.

"Okay," said Desma, slouching toward the end of the road, where her car was parked.

"Six?" Timika repeated. "In the *morning?*"

Nicholas began his explanation about the heat and the number of hours they needed to get in on the site but Timika waved him silent. She knew. She just didn't like it.

"So this is archaeology, huh?" she said, considering the baking field with a jaundiced eye. "I think I prefer the Indiana Jones version."

"This one has fewer Nazis," said Nicholas.

"Those guys," she said, rolling her eyes knowingly. "They're always cropping up." Nicholas gave her a bemused look but she shook it off and smiled to show she was kidding. "So, Dr. Tan, what do we do with the rest of the day?"

"Get cleaned up, get something to eat. I need to do some more work on that translation. And some research on the closest sites in case that helps me figure out what we should be looking for. Then an early night. You?"

"Some calls I want to make. E-mails to send. But the early night sounds good. Want to go get a late afternoon dinner?"

So far they had been foraging for themselves, hoarding bits of bread, cheese, and fruit picked up at a store in the village.

"At a restaurant, you mean?" said Nicholas.

"I think we have the budget," said Timika.

"Deal," said Nicholas, genuinely pleased. "What shall we eat?"

"Er, I'm gonna go out on a limb and suggest Greek food."

"Huh," said Nicholas. "Greek food. Not sure I've ever had that."

"Are you serious?"

"Yeah, actually. Unless it's something I just don't think of as, you know, *Greek*."

"Gyros, moussaka, tzatziki . . . Any of this ringing any bells?" asked Timika, caught between disbelief and amusement.

Nicholas shook his head.

"We've been here a week!"

"I brought some granola bars, and there were some bits of things in the fridge . . ."

"Let's just go find a restaurant," she concluded.

Nicholas grinned. "Say, 4:30?" he said.

"Sounds good."

ONCE HE WAS CLEANED UP HE SPENT THE EARLY AFTERNOON staring at his translation. It seemed, like a lot of ancient inscriptions, to suffer from what an old professor of his had called "braglist syndrome." Many of the exquisite Egyptian tomb hieroglyphs the layman thought so cool were no more than catalogues of things won, achieved, or presented to the deceased. Elsewhere the lists detailed territory taken in battle or offerings made to satisfy assorted deities. Structurally, Timika's tablet—the origins of which she was still being vague about—seemed to fit the template, but whereas such carvings were usually crammed with the contents of the list, here the rhetorical frame seemed oddly scant on detail. To make matters worse, the grammar of things being given to the gods was back to front, so that while offerings to the deity were referenced, the meat of the exchange was missing. The range of what might be given *by* the gods was pretty limited: rain, crops, victory in battle, some newly discovered resource like gold. Nicholas was used to such things. This was different.

He considered the script, a mixture of lines and triangles grouped into units and etched with a V-shaped chisel so that the triangulation registered three-dimensionally in the stone. Some of the indentations looked like little staircases, and in parts the light on the tablet made it hard to read the directional lay of the triangle, but Nicholas was convinced that the translation problem was down to neither Timika's photographic limitations nor his own skill.

The tablet was just odd. That wasn't a very scientific conclusion, but it was the one that pushed most at the back of his mind. Though it was clearly and classically Ugaritic in many respects, albeit an earlier, simpler form than most, there was something strange about it that he couldn't quite put his finger on, and that was without the odd metal trim at the edge of the stone.

Nicholas held up a pale-blue collared shirt in front of himself and considered his reflection in the mirror, unsure how to dress for his evening meal with Timika. She was technically his boss, he supposed, but she clearly didn't think of herself like that, so maybe he needn't look so formal. No tie for sure. Or jacket, because it was hot as blazes out. But a T-shirt didn't seem right either.

So this, he decided. *Top two buttons unfastened, sleeves rolled up.*

He heard the droning hum of the bicycle whine from the kitchen as it spun, and smiled slightly to himself.

Jeans or khakis? he wondered. He wished he could stay in shorts but they made him self-conscious when he wasn't working in them, and they didn't work with the collared shirt.

The bicycle wheel went up a notch in pitch and lessened. Clearly she was making progress. He walked toward the sound, still holding the shirt.

"Ma," he said, as he entered the kitchen. "What do you think of this shirt? Too stiff?"

She was wearing light cotton trousers with a pattern of brown leaves, and her oil-stained, smocklike work shirt. The bicycle was upside down in the middle of the floor, sitting on its saddle and handlebars while the old woman critically watched the front wheel spin.

She turned, wrench in hand, and smiled at him, but when she opened her mouth to speak, no sound came out.

"What?" he said. "I can't hear you."

Again his mother moved her mouth, chuckling to herself, he thought, though he couldn't be sure, but all he could hear was the thin whoosh of the spinning wheel.

"Can you stop that thing for a second?" he said. "I can't hear you."

But the wheel seemed to get faster, louder, though no one was spinning it, and the look on his mother's face was placid, benign, but unhelpful.

"Seriously, ma," said Nicholas. "I can't hear you. How are we supposed to talk when you're always working?"

Again her mouth moved, but while he was sure there were words in there somewhere, he could not make them out, and suddenly his mild irritation turned into frustrated misery.

"Mom!" he said. "Tell me! I can't make out what you are saying."

He was unreasonably sad, distraught, but that, he remembered, was because his mother was dead.

The shock woke him. Or that was how his brain made sense of the shift.

He was not in the dim little kitchen of the Alhambra apartment where he had grown up, and into which his mother's bicycle repair business so frequently spilled. He was in Greece. Crete. In a bright, clean, modern kitchen that came with his rented bedroom. There was no bike, no tools and, of course, no sign of his mother.

But Nicholas was upright, still clutching the blue shirt to his chest. He hadn't dropped off while lying on his bed, or even while sitting with a book in his hands. He had been in his room, and then he had come through here and she had appeared.

No. He had come through because of the familiar sound of the bicycle wheel.

So he had been dreaming as he stood in front of the mirror.

Which made no sense.

He draped the shirt over the back of a chair and went into the bathroom, where he splashed water on his face, then rubbed the droplets away with a towel, kneading the muscles of his cheeks. For a long moment he considered his face in the mirror.

Hallucinating? he wondered. *Bit young for that, Nicholas.*

Just tired. Stressed.

Which was no explanation at all. Not for something that felt so utterly real. Normal, even.

What did it mean?

He felt perfectly fine and levelheaded. But then he also had felt that way during the dream, or whatever it had been. Would he know if he had been drugged? He felt sure he would have some sense that something was a little off.

Tangerine trees and marmalade skies?

Maybe.

But he felt absolutely himself.

Then put it another way, he considered. *What did* she *mean?*

How could he know? He hadn't heard anything that had come out of her mouth. She had just been . . . herself. It was as if he had walked in on her as she worked, as he might have done ten years earlier. The pleasure of that idea, the joy of seeing her again, if only for a moment, overwhelmed all other more rational concerns. Against all the odds he found himself smiling, even as his eyes filled with tears. It had been exactly like that, like stepping into the past, or rather folding the past into the present. He had seen her, and maybe that was all there was to it. It was a gift, a wholly unexpected moment of connection with something he thought lost forever. It was strange. Impossible, in fact. But unless other things happened, things that sent him to the hospital asking for brain scans in search of tumors and other horrors, he would take it as no more than that: a gift.

He was still turning the vision over in his head as he joined Timika outside. He was wearing the blue shirt, as if his mother had indeed recommended it, and felt curiously buoyant, though he resolved to say nothing of the matter to anyone. Ever. It had been a moment, a capsule of something lost that he had back in his head now, like a snow globe, small and precious.

"You okay?" asked Timika.

"Yeah," he said, meaning it. "Fine."

They wandered into the village to a promising-looking taverna where they could sit outside under a canopy of grapevines. Though the place didn't get many tourists there was an English menu with pictures, and Nicholas was pleasantly surprised to find that the food didn't seem overly foreign. He ordered skewered lamb kebabs with crisp, golden fries and a side salad that was ripe with chunks of salty white cheese and musky black olives.

"Good, huh?" said Timika, setting down the pita bread sandwich thing she was eating and wiping her mouth.

"Really good," Nicholas agreed, grinning. "The trip might not be wasted after all."

"One-point-eight million dollars to discover that you like Greek food?" said Timika. "I think we might need more than that." She hesitated, catching something in his face. "You don't think we will, do you?"

He raised a hand while he finished chewing, stalling a fraction longer so he could phrase a diplomatic reply, but she saw right through him, and he just shrugged.

"Why not?" she pressed.

"Well, there's never been any excavation on the site before," he said, "and that means no folk memories, no grave robbers, no goatherds stumbling on bits of gold, no signs that the local buildings were made from pilfered stone taken from ancient structures. If there is something down there, no one has thought about it for a very long time."

"But there still could be, right?" said Timika, taking one of his fries. "These are really good," she added.

"Anything is possible," he answered, pushing the plate of fries toward her so she could share.

"But not likely."

He sighed.

"There's nothing on the surface," he said. "You might expect to find a few pot shards scattered on the top, bits of things stirred up by animals, say, but so far . . ."

He let the sentence hang, watching her face for signs of disappointment. He knew she hated the digging, the meticulousness of it, the slow, backbreaking work, the heat, but he also sensed that she'd put up with it to find . . . whatever it is she thought she might find. But to go through all that for nothing?

"Who knows?" he said. "Maybe we'll sink a few more trenches and, if we don't find anything on the mound itself, we'll open up a few more squares in other parts of the territory. Get a more random sampling."

She nodded, but he could tell she saw through his attempt to be upbeat.

"I've been working on the translation some more," he said, changing the subject and instantly realizing it wasn't going to make her feel any better.

"Yeah? How's it going?"

"Well," he said, "it's a bit weird, to be honest. It's set up like a typical tablet detailing impressive offerings made to the gods, but it seems sort of backwards and unspecific. The pronouns don't work. It's like . . . well, it's like the inscription *itself* is the offering. Which is crazy. And even though it was carved by people for the gods, the grammatical phrasing makes it feel like it's actually the other way around."

As soon as the words were out of his mouth, something snapped into place in his mind, and he saw the rightness of what he had stumbled on. His fork hovered forgotten in the air and his eyes lost focus.

"It's like the tablet is saying that it wasn't made by man for the gods, but *by* the gods *for* man, and that it's a kind of gift. I'd say that the stone itself represents a sort of pact, I guess, but the phrasing suggests it's more than that. It's not just a promise of divine favor. It *is* that favor. The stone is the gift."

"How could that be?" asked Timika. "What would it mean?"

Nicholas came back to himself, caught between certainty and a new befuddlement.

"I have no clue," he said. "Sometimes the fact of the message is all it means. Like, when a stranger asks how you're doing when you catch their eye in the street. It's not a real question so much as it is a greeting, a sign that they mean you no harm. Or a birthday card from someone you love."

"An ancient stone tablet is a birthday card?"

"Not literally, no. I mean, it means more than it seems to. It's a gesture. The words are less important than the fact of the message," said Nicholas, thinking of the bicycle in the kitchen, its wheel spinning. "Sometimes, especially when there's a strong relationship in play, words don't matter so much. It's the connection that counts."

"I don't think I understand," said Timika.

"No," said Nicholas. "Neither do I. Not yet."

DEPUTY DEWEY LARSON
2014, Forty-Seven Miles from Cedar Rapids, Iowa

DEPUTY DEWEY LARSON CHECKED HIS GPS AND PULLED the departmental Dodge Charger over onto the grass verge. For a moment he sat there, enjoying the blast of the AC before getting out into the heat of a full-bore-honest-to-God Iowa summer. He was out of his jurisdiction here in Jackson County and, not knowing the farm in question, was unsure how to proceed. He had been told to keep his contact with Sanderson, the former sheriff, quiet, so he didn't want trouble from whoever owned the land screaming about their right to privacy. He looked for a path that took him not up to the clapboard house but to the field beyond and set off walking nice and slow, his hat brim shielding his already burned neck from the worst of the sun. He slipped on his big aviator-style sunglasses in the hope that they would make his scanning of the land and buildings less conspicuous.

There was a barn with a little gantry windmill, both in need of a little love, but the parcel of land was bigger than he had first thought, and some of the machinery pulled into the yard behind the house was green and shiny. Maybe the place was doing okay after all, and Larson wondered if he should be able to tell if the corn produced here was for feed or ethanol. Harvest was still a few weeks away, but the plants were tall and yellowing on top, though the stalks and leaves were a vibrant, waxy green. It was, Larson had to admit, and in spite of the heat, beautiful.

Joe Sanderson was some five or six hundred yards away standing on what looked like a box in the middle of the adjacent field. He was a big man, a little more rounded in the shoulder than he had been, his hair thinning on top and a pair of glasses perched on the end of his nose. He was standing, slightly hunched, his hands on his hips, rotating slowly on the spot, surveying the crop around him. As Larson approached, Sanderson took out his phone, squinted at it, then started taking pictures.

From ground level it was hard to see exactly what the pattern of bent and cleared stalks revealed, but it was clearly symmetrical, even geometric, and looked, Larson had to admit, impressive. As he walked into the field, he made out a long curved trough cut cleanly through the corn, probably the arc of a circle, with spokes running toward some other feature close to where the former sheriff was standing, fumbling with his phone.

"Goddamn thing," he announced, as Larson approached. "Why do we fool with these damn things? Give me a decent 35 millimeter and film." He paused to give the deputy a sidelong look. "Hey Dewey," he said. "Come to reel me back in?"

"No, sir," said Larson, striding up as he removed his sunglasses and slid them into his shirt pocket.

"Sir, is it?" Sanderson mumbled. "Must be worse than I thought. You looking to bust Josh Harrup for killing all Jimbo Styles's cows?"

"Not sure yet."

"I figured," said Sanderson with another grin.

Larson grinned and extended his hand. The old man took it in a grip firm enough to banish the aura of frailty and managed a return smirk.

"How've you been?" asked Larson.

"Oh, you know. Can't complain."

"Keeping busy, I see."

Sanderson shot him a look at that, a hard, almost accusatory stare, though it lasted only a second before the smile knocked the corners off.

"Oh, you know me," he said, returning his gaze to the field.

"Yep. I guess I do at that, Joe. So what's going on here?" he said, trying to sound casual, flippant. "Aliens leaving us messages again?"

"Nope," said Sanderson, taking another picture.

"No?"

"No."

"So what are you doing?"

"Documenting. Collecting evidence."

"Of what?"

Sanderson shrugged and grinned.

"A fake, and not a very good one at that," he said. "High school kids, probably."

"You can tell?"

"I can tell that someone rode around here on an ATV trailing a couple of planks to knock the stalks down, but you wouldn't need to be Sherlock Goddamned Holmes to see that, would you?"

Larson blinked and looked down, his eyes studying the ground. He felt, unaccountably, a bit stupid.

"So if it's obviously a fake, what are you doing here?"

"Well," said the old sheriff, climbing down off the plastic crate he had been standing on and sitting down on it, "I didn't know it was fake till I got here."

"How long did it take you to realize it wasn't real?" asked Larson, not sure what he meant by *real* in this context.

"Oh, three maybe four seconds," said Sanderson, shooting him a mischievous grin. "I'm getting old."

"You ever seen a real one?" asked Larson, again pushing past the troublesome word *real* without looking at it too closely.

"Can't say that I have."

Larson breathed. He didn't know why, but the answer relieved him.

"Then, if you spotted it was a fake right away," he said, "why are you still out here?"

"Partly because I have to gather what evidence I can. There's some significant damage to crops here and whoever did it should pay for it."

"What's the other part?"

"I was waiting for you," he said, that same twinkle in his eyes, though it shifted in an instant and he got to his feet again, gazing back toward the road. "Or maybe for him."

Another car had parked beside the green and gold-striped Charger. It was black, and the man who was climbing out and heading toward them wore a suit to match. Larson nearly asked if this was the owner of the farm but knew better.

"You're popular today," he remarked instead.

"Funny how that goes, ain't it?" said Sanderson.

"You know him?"

Another smile, tighter this time, weighted with lots of things he wasn't going to say, then simply,

"Oh yeah, I know him."

Larson considered the man in the black suit as he made his way through the field toward them, then looked back at Sanderson with a question in his face.

"Yeah," said Sanderson. "That's him. The guy from state who took over the case last time."

"Last time?" asked Larson, suddenly wary of revealing why he had come.

"The last time we had dead cattle and missing people," said Sanderson, giving him a level stare. Larson just looked, and then the man in black was in earshot, one hand raised in silent greeting.

He was about Sanderson's age, early sixties, maybe, gaunt in the face but pouchy around the waistline. He had cool, watery blue eyes, intelligent but also somehow amused.

"Joe," he said simply, nodding at Sanderson, who nodded back. "Deputy Larson." Larson's name was on his shirt but he felt sure the man had already known it. He turned to address the stranger but the man stopped him with a gesture. "You can leave us, deputy. Your case was closed twenty minutes ago. Mr. "Jimbo" Styles was found alive and well, if a little disoriented, up near Hazel Green, just off Highway 13 heading north on foot. He isn't sure how he got there or where he was trying to go, and he's in bad need of a shower and a decent meal or three, but otherwise he's fine."

He spoke in easy, measured tones, like one of the newscasters on TV, one of the good ones who almost made you forget they were reading from a teleprompter. Larson forced himself to respond.

"What does he say about the night Josh Harrup was injured, the night the cattle died?"

"Mr. Styles has no recollection of that evening," said the man in black. "Seems he left the area that evening, though he can't remember why. He never saw Harrup and didn't know about his herd till he was picked up by highway patrol. He'll be fine, and he'll be compensated for the loss of his beef."

"And the case?" Larson persisted. Sanderson was watching them, saying nothing, showing neither outrage nor surprise.

"What case?" said the man from state.

"The cattle mutilation!" said Larson. "Jimbo's disappearance!"

"In the absence of evidence of any criminal activity, the matter will be handled at the state level by the department of agriculture. Mr. Styles has agreed not to press charges against Mr. Harrup and . . ."

"How could he decide that if he was *disoriented*?" asked Larson.

"It's done, deputy Larson."

"This is massive overreach by the state government," said Larson. "You can't sweep away evidence of . . . whatever this is . . . just because it might make people poke into things you don't want them to know about!"

"Actually," said the man in black. "We can. And believe me when I say that it's for your own good."

"I'm gonna call the sheriff."

"You do that. But I'll tell you now, he's gonna say exactly what I just told you."

Larson opened his mouth to respond, but Sanderson reached out and touched him on the wrist.

"Get in your car, Dewey," he said. "It was good to see you."

The deputy stood there, baffled and fuming, but finally did as he was told, trudging through the corn back to the

144

road, muttering to himself as he walked. For three whole minutes the two older men did not speak. Then the man in black turned to the former sheriff and said, "Speaking of. Let's us go for a drive."

Sanderson gave him a wary look.

"How far?" he asked.

"Does it matter?"

"Maybe."

"You know the great thing about retirement, Joe, is that you have all this time on your hands."

"I'm guessing you're not retired."

"I wish. Come on. Let's get in the car."

He took a step away but Sanderson stayed where he was.

"Give me one good reason why I should," he said.

The man in black toed the ground thoughtfully, then grinned.

"You should come," he said. "There's something you are going to want to see."

THEY DROVE FOR FIVE AND HALF HOURS, MOVING roughly northwest over the state line into Minnesota and on, all farms and forest and a scattering of lakes. There were no major cities to crowd the horizon, and the landscape was wide and flat on each side of the highway. Joe Sanderson sat in the passenger seat saying little, gazing out of the window and wondering vaguely and without fear if this was the last afternoon of his life.

It seemed at least possible, despite his driver's genial frankness.

The man from state. That's what Joe had always called him. When they had first met half a lifetime ago, the man had introduced himself as Art Grunel, pronounced the

French way with the emphasis on the last syllable, but Joe had quickly decided that wasn't his real name.

At first during the drive they chatted in a desultory way about nothing: the Bears and the Vikings a little, more about baseball and the Cards in particular, then about the weather and the vagaries of climate change and what it might do to the agricultural economy, and then nothing at all as they got within forty miles of the South Dakota border. They had eaten quickly and without a lot of chat at a Wendy's back in Mason City, but Grunel—or whatever his name was—seemed keen to press on, so that had only been a fifteen-minute break. They stopped again at a gas station on I-90 so that Joe could pee, and he had the wild idea of flagging someone down and telling them to call the cops because he was being abducted. He caught Grunel's eye as the man from state picked a Slim Jim off a rack and saw him hesitate as if reading Joe's mind. In the end Grunel just shrugged.

Your call, he seemed to be saying.

Joe got back in the car.

"What happens next?" he asked, as they hit the road again.

"Like I said," replied the man from state. "Something I want you to see."

"Then?"

Grunel gave him a look.

"Then I put you on a Greyhound back to Iowa."

"For real?"

"Why not?"

"Seems . . . I don't know. Generous? Unlikely?" Joe tried.

"You're not going to disappear, Joe."

Joe looked out of the window, saying nothing. It was getting late, but the long summer day seemed to roll on forever over the wheat and corn fields. And then, without warning, they were off the main road and following a rutted dirt trail that climbed a low granite bluff to what Joe could only describe as a checkpoint: a man in a suit matching Grunel's standing by the road with a phone and a clipboard. He stooped to the driver's side window as the car rolled to a halt, but merely looked at Grunel and at Joe before silently waving them through. The man's suit bulged over his shoulder holster. Joe shifted in his seat.

"You guys aren't big on communication, are you?" he said as they pulled away.

"What is there to say?" said Grunel. "Everyone is so into talking. Texting. Social media. Whatever. Constantly telling the world what you are feeling, what you had for breakfast, broadcasting every half-baked idea that occurs to you twenty-four hours a day. For what? For who? We've forgotten the value of silence."

Joe looked at the driver, his lean face brushed with the golden light of the lowering sun.

"You think you can keep all this quiet?" he asked, though he didn't yet know exactly what *this* referred to.

"Done it before."

"Kind of," said Joe. "The world has changed. There's no secrets anymore."

Grunel made a noncommittal noise.

"Your Iowa case is going quiet," he remarked. "Josh Harrup knows that if he says nothing he'll evade charges of trespass and other possible violations up to and including attempted murder. Jimbo Styles has signed away his right to speak on the matter in return for some healthy compensation for his dead herd. Sheriff Burnhardt knows which side his bread is buttered on too. Even your loyal deputy will keep his mouth shut once the case is officially closed. He has his career to think about."

"And me? What's to stop me taking this to the FBI, the CIA, right now?" asked Sanderson.

"You know what."

"Because they already know," Sanderson said for him.

"Some," said the other, "yes."

"The papers then. I could go to the press: conspiracy to conceal serious crimes, maybe even threats to national security . . ."

"They don't want to hear it," said the driver, killing the engine and letting the car idle to a halt. "No one does. They think they do, but deep down, they aren't ready. They wouldn't believe you anyway, and even if they did, you'd just be another fruit loop pointing at the sky. This country can't tell truth from fiction anymore. You know that."

"Maybe I'll take the chance."

"I don't think you will."

"Yeah?" said Sanderson. "Why's that?"

Grunel shouldered open his door and climbed out, then stood by the car, waiting. Sanderson joined him. After the long drive the old man's joints were stiff and aching. The man from state waited, then walked up a track through a stand of pines and some thick, irregular shrubs, leading the way over the rocky outcrop till they could look out over the golden wheat fields below. In the late afternoon light they looked brushed with amber and fire. Sanderson gasped.

Etched into the crop was a complex pattern of interlocking wheels and cog-like dials of various sizes, vast and ornate. It was intricate, elegant. Breathtaking.

"Is that . . . ?" Sanderson began.

"One of four that appeared on the same night last week," said Grunel. "We can go down and look at the field up close but I'll tell you now what we're going to find: no evidence of physical violence done to the wheat, such as we might see if it had been executed by people with boards or vehicles. These stalks are bent at the midsection, not at ground level. We'll detect lingering signs of microwave radiation and unusual magnetic fields. The plants will show new growth nodes, apparently formed very fast, altering the growth habit of the plant as it incorporated the larger design. Some of the stalks are even braided together, again not manually or mechanically—which would leave signs of stress or breakage—but evenly and organically. The wheat isn't dead or damaged, but thriving, albeit in an entirely novel and apparently unnatural developmental configuration. All signs point to a phenomenon that has simultaneously altered the core structures of the plant along the lines of the larger design while generating a massive growth surge. The crop has been guided and fueled, but it has, in real terms, grown the patterns of the circle itself."

Sanderson stared, wide-eyed, feeling a curious stirring of emotion. It felt like joy, but his eyes swam and for a moment he could not speak. At last he fought for some measure of resistance to the spectacle.

"I could still talk," he said. "Maybe not to the newspapers, but there are websites that live for this stuff."

"And most of them are stuffed with garbage, equal parts wish fulfillment and paranoia, as you well know."

"So?"

"So that's not you. Sheriff Joe Sanderson might have been a truth hound, but he was also a public servant and I don't believe he would do anything to put people at risk."

"Telling the world what's out there puts people at risk?"

"It might."

"From you and the people you work for?"

Grunel shook his head.

"Look at this," he said, nodding again to the filigree artistry in the wheat. "Stunning, isn't it? It's intelligent creativity, and it contains a message, for us, even if it's one we struggle to comprehend."

"So?" said Sanderson again.

"Did those cattle pastures feel like this?"

Sanderson gave him a sharp look.

"What do you mean?"

"I look at this and I feel peace. I feel like something is watching over us. It might not understand who we are, what we are, but it wants to reach out to us, to offer us something remarkable, and it does so in this indirect and sophisticated way, like the fractals of a snowflake. Does this feel like the Styles farm, which drove Josh Harrup to blow his foot off and Jimbo Styles to run mad with a panic so acute it has wiped the incident from his brain entirely? Does it feel like the nightmare that sent Emily Swainson wandering blindly in the woods, her mind so totally blown that she couldn't figure out how to get out or keep herself alive? Do the horrors of that night feel the same as this? All that clinical savagery, the meticulous barbarism of their invisible knife work: was it driven by the same sense of purpose as this?"

"What are you saying?" asked Joe Sanderson, turning to face him, feeling the urgency in the other man. "That the cattle mutilations and the crop circles are coming from similar but different sources with different agendas?"

"Different agendas, different plans, a wholly different sense of who we are and what we are worth," said Grunel, his eyes intense, his voice low. "We don't know for sure, but that's what we think, yes, and until we know where we stand with them—both of them, whatever they are and wherever they come from—we need to be very careful what we say. I'll drive you to the nearest bus station now, or put you in a hotel for the night if you'd prefer, but then you'll go home, you'll enjoy your retirement and you'll say nothing, because I think you understand that talking will only accelerate whatever is coming, and we—as a people, maybe as a planet—need to be ready."

Sanderson considered the man for a moment, then nodded once. Grunel smiled at last, the first real smile he had given all day.

"Thanks," he said. "I knew I could trust you. I'm so glad I don't have to kill you. Kidding," he added at the look on Sanderson's face.

"You said there is a message in the crop circles," said Sanderson. "In this one. Can you read it?"

"Not sure. We have some very smart people trying various decryption techniques, drawing on their shapes and their geometrical relationship to each other, but all they have managed to generate so far is a string of numbers, and we don't know if we are even close to reading them right. Our team can't decide if they are supposed to be some kind of formula or mathematical sequence. In fact, they look exactly like coordinates, but that doesn't seem to make much sense."

"Where to?"

"Well, if they *are* coordinates, let's just say they point to somewhere well outside our jurisdiction."

"Yeah?"

The man from state shrugged, half embarrassed by what he was about to say, sure that it was wrong and meant nothing.

"They seem to pinpoint a spot on an island close to Greece."

"*Greece?*"

"Specifically, Crete."

JENNIFER
Hampshire, England

"**K**IDNAPPED?" SHE SAID, AGHAST. "THAT'S NOT possible. No one ever said . . . Kidnapped?"

"I'm afraid so," said Deacon. He looked grave; his face and voice had a weight to them she had not seen even when he told her that her father had died. He got up suddenly, moved to a cabinet above the model railway layout, and opened it. He brought out a bottle of Scotch and two glasses, which he put down heavily on the end table by his chair. It struck her as strange that he hadn't asked permission, doubly so when he poured her a hefty measure without asking and brought it to her. She took it and cradled it in both hands, smelling the heady vapors, her eyes wide, her mind in a stiff fog.

"How?" she managed at last.

"Your parents had guests. A dinner party. Your mother put you down to sleep in your cot."

"Which room?" She didn't know why it mattered, but she wanted to know.

"Your room. The one you still use."

"What happened?"

Deacon shook his head.

"We never found out for sure," he said. "They looked in on you after the guests had left and the cot was empty. No note. No explanation. You couldn't have climbed out so we knew right away . . ." He hesitated, his mind miles away, seeing it all again. "We questioned the servants but no one had seen anything. We didn't even know how the kidnappers had got in. Your father was always pretty security conscious and the doors were kept locked as a matter of course."

"What did the police say?"

Deacon frowned.

"The police weren't called," he said.

"What? Why not?"

"I really don't know," he replied. "You asked when your father became secretive? It began that night. Your mother was distraught, hysterical. Of course. Who wouldn't be? But your father . . . He was more scared than distressed. Terrified, I'd say. But he was insistent. No police. No one beyond the staff should know."

Jennifer stared at him.

"My mother went along with that?"

"Not at first. She was . . . *wild*. Like someone I'd never seen before. Howling mad. Grief and anger and . . . I don't know. It was terrifying. She snatched up the phone but he took it from her. Your father was not a violent man. Ever. But that night . . . I wondered what he might be capable of."

Jennifer couldn't process what she was hearing. None of this squared with her parents as she had known them. She shook her head in disbelief, slowly at first, but then with certainty.

"No," she said. "This can't be right. You must have misunderstood or misremembered. Or you're lying."

Deacon recoiled fractionally at that, but he maintained his dignity.

"I almost wish I was," he said. "Your father told me to leave them. Search the house. He needed to talk to his wife. I had never been afraid to leave him alone with her before but I don't mind telling you, I didn't want to go. He told me to. Said I'd lose my position if I waited another second." Again, the long look back into memory, the strain in his face, and the fractional shrug. "So I went. I searched the house again, but quickly. I was back in the nursery in under fifteen minutes."

"And?"

"It was totally different. Your mother, who had been shrieking like a banshee and bouncing off the walls was just sitting there, meek and quiet. She barely even looked at me when I came back in. To be frank, it was scary. She didn't seem frightened of your father and there was no sign of . . . that he had hurt her. She just sat there. And he was as close to normal as was possible. Composed, like he was going back into a contentious boardroom but had a plan. I asked him what he wanted me to do, and he said 'Nothing. Wait.' So I did."

Jenifer had crept to the edge of her chair and she was now perched there, watching him with a kind of fascinated dread.

"Two days I waited and nothing happened. Your mother barely came down, but your father insisted that everything else went on as normal. So it did. I waited for the phone call, the ransom demand or whatever, but if it came, I never heard it. Your father went on long walks around the grounds and gardens which were, in those days, even more extensive than they are now. He always went alone. He took no phone and never asked if anyone had called. Didn't even check the mail more regularly than usual. It was possible he met people out there in the woods or in one of the farmhouses, but he told me not to follow him or ask questions, so I didn't.

"And then on the third day, you were back. Your mother heard you crying and went into the nursery, found you back in the crib as if you'd never been away. You were clean, not obviously hungry or sick. It was all very peculiar."

"What did they say to you?"

"Your mother said nothing. Ever. It was like she locked it away in her head. Sometimes when she looked at you I thought I saw it in her eyes, the fear, the wild, animal fear . . . But your father just said the *matter was closed* and he expected not to hear mention of it ever again. I asked him how he had sorted it all out, but he just said it was done and I wasn't to speak of it. In fact," Deacon continued, and now he looked genuinely upset, "he came up to me, very close, and said that if I ever disclosed what had happened, I would be fired and he would see that I didn't get hired in a comparable position again." The words felt like quotation, and Jennifer knew that moment had lived in Deacon's mind ever since. His voice shook as the sentence ended and he had to blink and clear his throat before he could add, "When I said I didn't understand, he said something—a quote from Shakespeare, I think—about how there were all kinds of things I didn't understand, and left it at that."

"Shakespeare?"

"He called me Horatio," said Deacon, with a half smile.

The line came to her in an instant.

"*There are more things in heaven and earth, Horatio, than are dreamt of in your philosophy,*" said Jennifer automatically. Deacon's eyebrows raised.

"Yes," he said. "Exactly."

"Sounds like Dad," said Jennifer with a half smile. Her father had been one of those old-fashioned businessmen who had believed he should be "cultured" as well as rich.

Those were the days.

"Anyway," said Deacon, "I assume money changed hands, but I never saw any irregularities in the accounts and could find nothing missing. Your father was a good husband, a good father, and a good man, but those three days changed him in ways I couldn't understand. It was unnerving, but once it was done—save for those little secrecies he started keeping—he was the same person as he had been before. A week later you wouldn't have known it had happened, and his love for you never wavered for a second. I know you struggle with that, given your ups and downs with him, but I can tell you it's true. It never wavered. Not till the day he died."

For a long moment the two of them sat in silence, Jennifer tasting the whisky and trying to make sense of all she had been told.

She couldn't. It was as simple as that. She believed Deacon, she trusted him, but it sounded impossible: a story about people she'd never met. Still, it made a kind of sense in one area and one area alone.

"You think Maynard were involved?" she said. "Or the people who became Maynard later?"

"I don't know," said Deacon. "But if your father was coerced into dealings which were less savory than his customary business practice, I'd look very closely at those few days. Perhaps the ransom had nothing to do with money. Perhaps it was about favors, or influence, or promises of future support. If Maynard was involved in things as bad as you have implied—and I thank you for the lack of specifics since I prefer to keep my memory of your father as it is in my head—it would take some terrible scare, some unspeakable threat. Taking you would provide just such a threat, particularly if Mr. Quinn thought they could do it again."

Jennifer became very still, the rim of the glass pressing softly against her lower lip as the thought took hold in her mind and spread like blood in water. All this time she had been wondering what could have made her father do the things he had done and now she saw the answer.

She was responsible. Not directly, of course, but still. What was the one thing Edward Quinn had so wanted that he would violate all his other ethics to get it? Her safety. All her life, while she had sparred with him and thumbed her nose at his gifts, his wealth, his conventionality, she had been his Achilles heel . . .

"Where did he go walking?" she asked.

"What?"

"You said he walked in the grounds."

"All his life," said Deacon. "It was what he did in place of going to the gym. Sometimes he'd be gone hours. All around the formal gardens, of course, and the kitchen garden. He used to like cutting herbs for the cook when he was eating at home. But most of the fields around the house are still part of the property and are only leased to the local farmers. And the copse. Not much north of the house, but on the south side it's all the land bordered by the stream, including what we used to call the fairy ring. Why?"

"I feel like a walk."

"It's getting late."

"I'll take a flashlight, but I doubt I'll need it. Memory is a powerful map."

▼　　▼　　▼

THE FAIRY RING WAS IN A WILD MEADOW SURROUNDED ON three sides by what Deacon had called the copse, a ragged patch of woodland that was all that remained of the forest that had covered much of the area into the Middle Ages. According to family lore the owners of the original manor house had felled and sold off the timber to pay for construction costs in the early seventeenth century, and some of the roof work and much of the paneling in the library had come from those very trees. The fairy ring, amazingly, was almost as old, a circle of little mushrooms about a hundred feet across. The grass within the fungal border was a shade darker than that outside, and the perfect roundness of the thing had, in ancient times, been read as a sign of its magical properties: a place where the forest elves came to dance.

As a girl she had loved the idea and had often kept watch for the tiny, butterfly-winged sprites she had seen in Victorian children's books and in a famous series of photographs taken by two young girls. In fact, of course, though the girls swore to the truth of the pictures for decades, they confessed late in life that the images had been staged using little figures cut out from books. The science of how fairy rings were formed was well known and, later in life, she had read about it, always with a slight sense of disappointment.

Still, she had loved the place when she was little, however much her father had cautioned her about straying so far from the house, and she loved it still. It was quiet and peaceful. Even the local sheep and cows stayed away, though rabbits cropped the grass within the circle from time to time, and that was good too. She had always been a little afraid of the cows, with their big liquid eyes, by the sheer bulk of them, which might crush you without them so much as noticing. But she liked to watch the rabbits.

She went there now and sat on the old bench—or *an* old bench; the original had probably been replaced several times—and considered the darkening meadow and the woods beyond. Without the magic she had believed in as a child, the quietness of the place held a tinge of melancholy, and she wondered again what it meant for her to be here now that her father was dead. Would she continue to live here, rattling around in the old place out of a sense of . . . what? Love? Duty? Tradition? The madness of the weeks after her father had died had seemed so full of life and peril that she had barely had chance to wonder what would become of her when it was all over.

And it was, she thought. Over. Mostly. Now she was just the lady with the money who paid for things while other people, people with real expertise and talent, did the actual work.

The questions lingered. Had her father come down here, sat on this bench, and waited for whoever held the leash of her kidnappers? What promises had he made in exchange for her return, and how might she find out? Unless he was lying—which she didn't believe—Deacon, the one true archive of her past, of the house and the family within it, knew nothing.

She felt suddenly alone and, without thinking, as if planning the conversation might persuade her not to have it, she took out her phone and called Timika.

The American picked up right away and didn't sound surprised to hear from her. They were, Jennifer supposed, in a kind of business together, even if neither of them understood exactly what that business was, so it made a sort of sense that the woman supplying the funding would get in touch to see how things were going. Timika talked easily about setting up the dig site despite being clearly dissatisfied with the conditions and their prospects for success, and Jennifer found herself pleased to sit and listen as the sun vanished behind the copse and the fairy ring slipped steadily into darkness. It had been a long time since Jennifer had a friend, and though she knew the word was almost certainly wrong—given how short a time she had spent with Timika and how their continued relationship hinged on Jennifer's wealth and a shared preoccupation—it fit the American as well as it fit anyone else in her life.

"Nicholas made some progress on the inscription," said Timika. She repeated what the archaeologist had told her over dinner almost word for word in case there was some nuance in the description that might touch off an idea or a memory in Jennifer. There wasn't, and the conversation moved on while Jennifer wondered vaguely in what way a carved hunk of stone could be a gift from the gods.

"Nicholas's cool," said Timika. "Took him a while to warm up, and I think he's freaking a bit about our not finding anything, but yeah, he's cool. Don't let me get started on *Desma*, though. If she gives me that 'why you not know how to do this?' look one more time, I'm about to get seriously stabby. Oh, speaking of which, I called Dion again . . ."

Jennifer laughed quietly. Maybe *friend* wasn't overstating the case so much after all. She listened while Timika railed on her *former* boyfriend, who had just announced that he was moving out of their Mt. Kisco apartment and therefore wouldn't be contributing to the last month's rent.

"You believe that clown?" said Timika, outraged. "Suggested I either pay the whole amount myself or come put my stuff in storage before they throw my ass out. I swear to God if I could have reached through the phone, I would have taken hold of his . . ."

"What about Barry?" asked Jennifer, a teasing lilt to her voice. "Have you spoken to him since you got to Crete?"

"Maybe," said Timika. "Why do you ask?"

"Just curious," said Jennifer, grinning.

"You're quite the little detective aren't you, Miss Marple?"

"Oh, thank you very *much*!"

"What? It was a compliment!"

"Miss Marple was like ninety years old!"

"Yeah?" said Timika. "I just figured she was English. I get y'all confused."

"You're feeling feisty," said Jennifer.

"I am now," Timika replied, and Jennifer could hear her smile. "I guess I needed a chat. You should come to Crete. It's pretty nice when you're not digging in the dirt for no reason."

"And no trouble? No problems?"

"You mean, like people snooping around, shooting at us, shit like that?"

"Shit like that."

"Nah. It's quiet. To a fault, you might say. I think we're clear. I take it you pulled the plug on Maynard?"

"Insofar as I could. There've been a lot of arrests, frozen assets and such, but I'll bet some slipped through. Watch your back, okay?"

"Yeah, you too." Timika hesitated, and for a moment it seemed as if Jennifer could hear the miles between them, the air over forests and long stretches of road, the distant churning of blue sea. "There was one thing."

Jennifer waited, but when Timika let the remark hang, pressed her.

"What?" she said.

"Well, I know this is going to sound dumb, but when we were on the plane, I looked out the window. Don't think I'm crazy, okay?"

"Okay."

"Well, I could have sworn there was something on the wing."

"Something?"

"Something alive."

Jennifer frowned but was silent for only a second. They'd seen a lot of strange stuff in the last few weeks and Timika was obviously confiding in her in ways that probably tied her stomach in knots.

"What did it look like?"

"Well, it was dark outside but . . . I don't know. Kind of like a big bug, but crossed with a kid, maybe. It had stick arms and legs with little claws. Like the branches of trees. And its face was blue."

This time Jennifer's silence was longer. She just didn't know what to say.

"Okay," she managed. "And what did it do?"

"Sort of crawled along the wing and looked at me. Like it could see me and didn't care. It smirked."

"Smirked?"

"I know," said Timika. "It's nuts. I probably dreamed the whole thing, but it didn't feel like a dream, you know? I just had to tell somebody. I kind of thought I saw it again the other day. At the dig. In a bush. I couldn't see properly because the thing is mostly sticks itself."

"But it had a blue face?"

"Yeah, but the body was like . . . I don't know, like it was part of a tree or something. A raggedy bundle of twigs come to life. Like I said, I know it's dumb . . ."

Raggedy.

The word touched something in Jennifer's mind. A memory, perhaps, and she shuddered. She tried to focus on it, to draw it into the light, but it wouldn't come and a part of her, she was troubled to find, was relieved.

"No," she said, her voice distant, dreamy. "It's not dumb."

"It means something to you?" asked Timika, her voice stressed and hopeful.

"Maybe," said Jennifer. "I'm not sure."

And that was about it. They promised to talk again soon, using the same untraceable prepaid cell phones, and hung up, but in spite of hearing about Timika's odd sighting on the plane Jennifer found her spirits lifted considerably, and her mind had moved away from her absent father and the strange circumstances of her childhood kidnapping.

Even so, the darkness was suddenly close to complete, and when she stood up the fairy ring looked unsettlingly ominous, like the outline of a great mouth in the earth. She hesitated, and as she did so she caught the fractional movement of a shape just inside the tree line beyond the grass circle. It was too big for one of the roe or fallow deer that occasionally strayed through the grounds, and its movement lacked animal grace. In an instant, her heart suddenly thumping, she was sure that it was a person, and that he or she had been still, watching her across the fairy ring.

Listening, perhaps . . .

Fumblingly, she pulled out the flashlight she hadn't thought she would need and snapped it on. Its beam didn't reach the woods but the light made her feel better. She considered calling out, demanding who was there and trespassing on her land, but neither the role nor the confidence suited her and she wanted merely to get away. There was, after all, no reason to assume sinister intent. It was probably just a local farmer hunting a stray sheep who had stopped to smoke or take a pull on a flask . . .

And yet.

Plausible though such a scenario felt to her brain, she couldn't shake the sense of something more ominous, and between the childhood legends of the place and the sudden, creeping dark, Jennifer wanted only to be gone. She didn't want to turn her back on whoever was out there to return to the house, and when she did it was with a sense of strange, dreamlike dread, so that in her haste to get away she stumbled on a tree root, and gashed her knee. Once on the path, she directed her flashlight down and abandoned the pretense at walking, breaking into a jog as she cleared the stile leading into the formal gardens, and running all the way up the gravel path to the house.

TIMIKA
Near Fotinos, Crete

AS SOON AS SHE HUNG UP TIMIKA WAS CONSCIOUS THAT she'd dodged Jennifer's leading question about Barry. She'd admitted to talking to him, and then run in the opposite direction, and not just from the idea of confiding in someone she barely knew. She was running from the idea itself.

Barry Regis.

She smiled to herself and wondered. She had spoken to him twice since they parted company, both times casual, low key, though she had updated him on the status of her non-relationship with Dion and she was pretty sure he had picked up the implied signal. She wasn't sure where that left her though, and not only because they were a couple thousand miles apart at the moment. He was military, stationed in Nevada, while she would eventually go home to New York. She had known him for no more than a few weeks, and had spent only a handful of days in his actual presence. It wasn't much on which to build a long-distance relationship.

But he had called her before he and Alan had reached the base to recount the oddity of the near-collision, the way Alan had seemed to prevent it and the way Barry had, in his words, *seen it happen right before it did.* Alan said it was something to do with the craft he had been flying, but Barry hadn't flown any such craft, and he had been no nearer to the downed ships than she had. Timika felt entirely herself, and had experienced nothing like the flash of precognition Barry had described apart from the momentary impression of the raggedy thing on the plane, which had surely been just a mirage brought on by exhaustion.

The debunker in her said Barry had imagined his experience of precognition, or misremembered it. Events get confused in the adrenaline of a near-death experience, in which category a head-on collision would certainly qualify. Still. It felt odd to her, and she couldn't get it out of her mind. Barry said he and Alan had been arguing about nothing when the pickup came at them, a nonsense quarrel about the strangeness of two boyhood buddies being assigned to the same place. Timika knew nothing of the military and she had considered this a pretty unremarkable coincidence until Barry raised it.

Now she wondered.

She had been trying to make small talk: just hanging out on the phone, getting to know him in the most cautious and self-protective way she knew. But the reporter in her had turned that into probing, albeit gently, harmlessly, asking questions about his past, his schooling, his early friendship with Alan back in Monroe, North Carolina. Both high achievers academically and physically, both nonetheless at odds with their parents, both recruited to the Marines early with promises of success in whichever branch of the Corps suited them. They had been the golden boys of their graduating class, and Monroe was just small enough that their career choice seemed natural, something to be proud of, rather than brushed aside for careers in finance or law.

"Even had the same pediatrician," she remarked.

"What?" Barry had said. "No, I don't think we did."

"You said you saw the doc with the weak R. The guy who called you *Bawwy*. That wasn't when you were kids?"

"Oh, yeah. Dr. Vespasian. But he wasn't our pediatrician. He was a specialist I saw from time to time. I had some issues."

"Yeah?"

"When I was a kid," said Barry. "I have a genetic condition. A couple, actually. Beta thalassemia combined with hemoglobin E. One from each parent. Not the best combo."

"Wow," said Timika. "Sounds rough."

"Kind of like sickle cell."

"I figured. But you're so healthy! In the army and all."

"Marines. Was."

"Right. Sorry."

"Yeah, lots of blood work as a kid but it turns out I had enough fetal hemoglobin to keep ticking over, else I'd have been on transfusions constantly, and that really would have killed my military career. I'm fine. Gotta say, we made fun of Dr. Vespasian, but the man knew his stuff."

"Wait, Alan had the same thing?"

Timika didn't know much about the diseases he was talking about, but she knew that sickle cell was much more common in African Americans.

"What? No. He had something else. He'd get fevers from time to time. But it was also a blood thing, so he'd see Vespasian too when the doctor was in town."

"No wonder you two bonded."

"Yeah," he said. "So tell me about *your* childhood."

And she had, partly to change the subject, partly because he had cooed the question in a way that said he really wanted to know, and that was a turn-on she wasn't used to . . .

Still. The previous conversation had lodged in her gut afterward, and when her mind was wandering over the details in a pleased, dreamy sort of way, it snagged on Dr. Vespasian like he was a hangnail. In a mad moment she had considered calling Barry's family to ask . . . what? How best to scare off a potentially interesting man by behaving like a stalker?

Fortunately the mood had passed, even if it did niggle at her, like an itch she wanted to scratch. But she was too busy scratching the very real itches of caustic weeds and a blazing sun that beat down on her as she dug in the dirt of the excavation site like a foraging gopher. Finding nothing. From time to time she'd look up and watch the others, but no one was feeling especially chatty as they plodded pointlessly on. It was no wonder her mind kept straying to Barry.

And Alan. Unrelated childhood ailments that required seeing the same specialist but nevertheless allowed them to star on the same football team? Something stirred in the back of her mind, a familiar reporter instinct feeling for the areas where a story felt patched or incomplete. It was probably nothing . . .

Like the blue-faced stick man you told Jennifer about, she thought ruefully. Maybe she was coming down with something.

When they finished work for the day at lunchtime, she waited for Desma to slouch off to her car and then asked Nicholas if she could have a word in the thin shade of the sorting tent.

"What's up?" he asked, though she thought there was something disingenuous in his smile. He knew what was coming.

"I'm useless here," said Timika. "You know it and I know it. Desma sure as hell knows it." Nicholas started to shake his head but she overruled him. "Yes, I am. And that's okay. I have no qualifications in this area so I'm basically just muscle and not particularly skilled muscle at that. Muscle can be replaced. We have money. The university lent us Desma as part of her work-study or whatever they call it, but we could also just hire a couple of strong backs to help with the ground clearance. Make sure they understand that they work for you, and pay them as day laborers. I can set up the account so that you can use it. I trust you."

"Wait," said Nicholas. He had been nodding thoughtfully till now but was suddenly alert and wary. "Where will you be?"

"Well, that's the thing," said Timika. "You don't need me here. Not till you find something, which could take days or weeks . . ."

"Or never," said Nicholas, admitting his fear.

"That too," she answered. "But my standing over you, pushing a wheelbarrow around from time to time or busting my ass with a spade . . . It's not helping. Not really. Not compared to what you could get out of a couple of paid workers."

"While you do what?"

"You said you had a friend you could trust who might help you with that translation."

"At UNC Charlotte, yes," he said. "But you wouldn't let me send it to her."

"How about I take it?" she said.

"Fly back to the States just to hand-deliver a photograph of an ancient tablet?"

"There's other stuff I need to do back home," she replied. "I can fly to New York via Charlotte. Take a few days to make sure my business hasn't burned to the ground, and come back. A week, tops. Sooner if you find something."

He nodded again, then cocked his head and gave her a puzzled look.

"What's going on?" he asked. "There's something you're not telling me. Maybe a lot."

Timika chewed on her lower lip.

"There is," she said, at last. "And I will tell you. Eventually. I swear. It's nothing illegal, unethical, or immoral. I swear that too."

She let the words hang in the hot air between them and he gave her a searching look, then sat back on the bench and nodded once.

"Okay," he said.

"For real?"

"I believe you," he said.

Timika was overwhelmed by a wave of sudden and surprised gratitude, but all she said was, "Thanks."

"When will you go?" asked Nicholas.

"Let me look at flights this afternoon. See what's available."

THE FLIGHT TO CHARLOTTE WENT VIA ROME, BUT IT WAS A considerably shorter trip than the outbound journey had been, and she was able to get a seat for the following day. Two days later she'd go on to New York.

Should be time enough.

For what, she hadn't completely decided, but she called Marvin, her tech guy, ostensibly to give him a heads-up about her return but also to ask him a favor.

"Just a couple of quiet background checks," she said. "Nothing that will raise red flags, yeah? I just want some basic info on a couple of guys."

"Sure," said *Debunktion*'s resident pot-smoking hacker. "What are you looking for?"

"Not certain," she said. "Things that smell weird. Oddities. Coincidences. Early medical records if you can access them discreetly."

"O . . . kay," said Marvin, not sure he was getting it. "What are their names?"

"Major Alan Young and Sergeant Barry Regis, both former Marines from Monroe, North Carolina, now CIA. And see if you can turn up anything on a Dr. Vespasian who treated them both when they were kids."

He pressed her for why she was checking them out, but she couldn't tell him.

"Call it a hunch," she said. "I'm setting up a new Gmail address now. Send me anything you find through that in twenty-four hours, whether you think you have anything or not."

He agreed. She gave him the address and hung up, her insides squirming. It didn't sit right, and though she had intended to call Barry before leaving, she found the prospect of talking to him without telling him what she was doing made her feel sick. She lay awake for an hour, twice considering calling Marvin back, telling him not to bother. But she didn't.

She rose early the next day to say goodbye to Nicholas, promising to be back soon, sooner if he needed her to be, then took a cab to the airport, kicking herself for how little of the island she'd seen. Nicholas had promised to show her around Knossos, the ancient center of the Minoan civilization and legendary home to the bull-headed Minotaur. She suddenly regretted her decision to leave with so little accomplished.

When you get back you'll do more. Promise?

She promised herself, reflecting dimly on how rare it was for her to be a real tourist. She'd always said she wasn't interested in travel or didn't have the time, but looking back now, and comparing her life to Jennifer's, which had been dotted with almost constant long-haul flights to every corner of the world, she realized it wasn't about lack of time or interest. It was about money. Plain and simple. She'd been working since college, just trying to keep her head above water as she carved out a minor career as a journalist and website manager. Maybe it was time that stopped and she got to do some things for herself.

The first leg of the journey was easy. Rome got more chaotic, and the US security check was, predictably, miserable, but once she was on board and could immerse herself in the lightest, dumbest movies she could find on the plane's in-flight system, she was fine. It was a slow crawl back across the Atlantic, but it was also daylight all the way, so that while she arrived tired, she didn't have that crippling sense of a lost night's sleep. And there were no blue-faced stick fingers clinging to the fuselage, which she considered a bonus. Forty minutes after touchdown, she was renting a Ford Focus at Charlotte Douglas and heading to her uptown hotel.

She showered as soon as she'd checked in, and had gotten into bed when she remembered to check her newly established e-mail. There was a single message from Marvin. It read "Call me."

The sleepiness that had been threatening to smother her and had forced her to be doubly careful as she navigated the unfamiliar city's traffic slid off her like fine sand. It took her phone a second to reconnect to the US network, and she stared at its cycling icon impatiently before placing the call.

"Hey," she said, as Marvin's permanently groggy voice answered. "It's me. What you got?"

"Well, it all checks out, kinda," said Marvin. "Monroe isn't exactly huge. In the eighties, which is when your guys were growing up there, the population was in the low twenty thousands. A few of the local hospital staff had visiting privileges but serviced a number of clinics and hospitals in the area, traveling around for non-emergent procedures and scheduled appointments. I guess your Doctor Vespasian, a hematologist, was one of those."

"Why do you say it checks out *kinda*?" asked Timika.

"Well, Monroe is pretty close to Charlotte," said Marvin. "Most unusual cases would have been sent there. Not sure why a specialist would travel to Monroe specially."

Timika waggled her head, unconvinced.

"Seems plausible to me," she said. "Kind of like making house calls, right? If there were multiple patients in one area . . ."

"Yeah, but here's the thing," Marvin responded. "It didn't take much pressing to find your two guys' medical records. It was easy, in fact. Barry Regis had . . ." There was a pause while Marvin found the reference and read the unfamiliar words back: "Beta thalassemia combined with hemoglobin E."

"I know," said Timika. This was starting to feel like a blind alley and, suddenly exhausted, she didn't know why she had bothered asking Marvin to poke around in the first place.

"But your other guy, Alan Young, had periodic fever syndrome."

"I know that too."

"Well they are pretty different conditions," said Marvin. "Yes, they both have blood issues, but it seems odd that they'd be considered similar enough that a hematologist would come specifically to see them and only them."

"Only them?"

"Yeah. I've looked through the records of the hospital and can't find any reference to this Dr. Vespasian."

"Huh," said Timika. "You got an explanation?"

"Not exactly, but I was wondering how these two guys got cleared for military service. I mean, these are potentially serious conditions."

"Yeah, but it turned out they weren't as serious as they first thought," said Timika, remembering what Barry had said. "Something to do with fetal hemoglobin in Barry's case."

"Maybe so," said Marvin. "And maybe not."

"I don't know, man," said Timika wearily. "I think you're grasping at straws on this one." For a man who spent his life helping Timika debunk conspiracy theories, Marvin was quite prone to a joining of the dots that often seemed less guided by evidence than it was by a desire to find a really cool picture at the end, one that reinforced Marvin's gut suspicion that nothing was as it seemed and the government was out to get you.

"Well, there's one more thing."

Good old Marvin, never a dog to let a good bone go unchewed.

"Shoot."

"I've searched every hospital and private practice in North Carolina from 1987 to '92. There's no Dr. Vespasian on record anywhere. If he was making house calls, he was coming from a long way away."

Timika scowled thoughtfully as the familiar journalistic instinct stirred out of its slumber, ears pricked.

"Huh," she said. "Okay. Not sure what to do with that."

"Me neither," he admitted.

"Keep looking, will you? Neighboring states first."

"Sure thing, boss."

"You have their home addresses?" asked Timika, cutting to the stuff she could actually use.

"Yeah," said Marvin again. He sounded a little disappointed reeling them off, as if he had hoped to generate a more stimulating lead.

"Thanks, Marvin," said Timika. "That's really helpful. Honest."

She hung up and considered the phone in her hands dreamily. Maybe this wouldn't be a wasted trip after all. The thought should have made her feel better, but she got into bed with her mind unsettled, so that for all her exhaustion it was almost two hours before she found sleep.

But sleep she did, and mostly soundly. Shortly after dawn she began dreaming of long, brown rats, such as she sometimes saw in the Canal Street 1 subway station, their fur slick, and eyes hard and bright as glass, and woke squirming in her bed. Whether it was the jet lag or the fear of slipping back into the same dream, she found she couldn't go back to sleep and decided to get an early breakfast.

She had been eating pretty healthily in Crete and, for that matter, in Nevada, but the biscuits and gravy at the hotel's buffet couldn't be passed up. She wasn't sure when she'd get lunch, so it made a kind of sense to fill up now. She went easy on the bacon and eggs, added some fruit with a sense of virtue that was positively saintly, and drank about a gallon of coffee. The biscuits and gravy were absolutely worth the price of admission.

Timika hadn't decided what to do about Nicholas's contact at the university. For all his self-doubt, her instinct said he had the translation under control, and that the text read strangely because it was, well, strange. She was doubtful that a second set of linguist eyes would resolve the oddity of the tablet, and had to balance any possible benefits with the risk of bringing another person inside the secret. Nicholas had been prepared to accept Timika's non-account of the stone's origins because he wanted an excuse to dig in Crete. Other archaeologists might not be so easily charmed into silence . . .

Timika threaded the white Ford Focus through the traffic of morning rush hour, onto the frantic, baffling loop that was Interstate 277, and then headed southeast on 74 into Union County. The minimal web surfing she had done over breakfast had told her that this was Jesse Helms country and, only a half century earlier, had been one of the strongholds of the KKK. She rolled her shoulders and pushed the accelerator a little harder, teeth tight together, eyes focused. With Charlotte receding behind her, the road became a straight, divided four-lane highway whose median, thanks to occasional construction, showed where the grass had been peeled back to reveal the hard red clay beneath. As she got closer to the town, the highway was flanked by sprawling low-rise buildings, home improvement stores, and car dealerships, all relishing the south's greatest gift: space. She doubted any of the development had been here in the sixties.

It was turning into a hot, bright day, and even with the AC cranked Timika could feel the humidity in ways she never had in Crete. The blacktop and concrete shimmered in it. Alan had grown up in the Hillsdale region of the town, across the highway from a strip mall featuring a Belk department store and a Planet Fitness and, as if for balance, a Pizza Hut. She kept driving. She could stop by this area on the way back to Charlotte.

The old town center was closer to what she had expected, complete with its fifties Americana main street, public library, and red brick courthouse ornamented with pale trim and a white clock tower. Once not too very long ago it had looked out beyond the roofs of the town to tobacco fields and the slaves who worked there, the tower shining in the sun, a beacon to . . . what? Law? Justice?

Yeah, thought Timika. *Right.*

The home where Barry Regis had grown up was a small, brick affair on the east side of town whose well-tended yard was surrounded by a chain-link fence. The steps were concrete but the paintwork on the old-fashioned window trim was well maintained, the paint a bold aquamarine that shone cheerfully in the morning light. It was almost exactly the color of the sea in Crete. She rang the bell and stepped back so as not to crowd the doorway. She could hear a studio audience clapping on the TV indoors.

The inside door was pulled open, but the screen door stayed closed. An elderly black woman in what Timika thought of as a checkered housecoat loomed vaguely through the mesh.

"You selling or preaching?" she asked, her voice balanced so it was impossible to guess the right answer.

"Neither, Ma'am," said Timika. "I'm a journalist doing a feature on local kids who joined the army."

"Marines," said Mrs. Regis.

"Right," said Timika. "Sorry. I was wondering if I could have a few moments of your time to talk about your son Barry."

"A few moments, huh?" said Mrs. Regis, still unreadable. "Well, I'm not sure I got that many moments to spare, but okay. You want a drink or something? I'd offer you some sweet tea but I can't stand the stuff. A Coke or something?"

"I'm fine, thank you, Mrs. Regis."

"Grace. Mrs. Regis was my momma."

"Timika," said Timika extending her hand.

The old woman took it in a strong, callused grip and squeezed it, her eyes giving her a frank once-over.

Apparently gaining approval, Timika was shown into a sitting room in which lace figured prominently. There was a single small window heavily shaded with slightly outmoded swag curtains reducing the light in the room to a soft, honey-colored glow. There was an upright piano in the corner and a lamp whose base was a sugar-sweet shepherdess dancer. It looked like an heirloom.

"So, you want to hear about Barry, huh?" said Mrs. Regis, moving a magazine from a lumpy chair so that Timika could sit. She was older than Timika had expected, or seemed it. Late sixties, maybe. If not for the handshake Timika would have thought her frail. "He's a good boy. Always was. Most of the time. This is him right here."

She reached for a silver-framed photograph of her son in uniform. He looked perhaps ten years younger than he was now.

"Good-looking guy," Timika remarked, honestly.

"Like his daddy," said Grace Regis. "Rest his soul."

It hadn't occurred to Timika that Barry's father might be dead, and she was momentarily taken off guard. How had she not asked him that?

The realization made her reassess the house and garden. If she kept it all going by herself, she couldn't be as frail as she seemed. Grace nodded to another picture of a still younger Barry, also uniformed, standing beside an older black man in almost identical blues.

"Your husband was in the Marines too?" asked Timika.

"Semper Fi," said Grace, nodding and smiling proudly. "So," she added, "what do you need to know?"

"Oh, just general background really," said Timika, rallying and pulling out a notebook and pen. "I believe he was friends with another Marine from close by, name of Alan Young?"

"That's right," said Grace. "They were never apart."

"How did they meet?"

"In school," said Grace. "Same class."

"I heard they met in a hospital?" said Timika. She said it as neutrally as she could, and there was a smile in the question, like she was fishing for some heartwarming detail for a feel-good story, but something in Grace's manner changed. She stiffened very slightly and hesitated before speaking.

"No," she said, shaking her head as if casting her mind back. "I don't believe so. Barry was a very healthy boy."

"I thought he had a combination of blood disorders that required treatment when he was small?"

Again, the momentary hesitation and then a smile.

"Oh that," said Grace. "Yes. Turned out to be nothing."

"That must have been a relief."

"It was a long time ago. I don't really recall."

"But it might have been quite debilitating, right?"

"I didn't know. Never been in the hospital a day in my life myself so I didn't understand that stuff. Not even when Barry was born. Had him right there in the back room. Midwife arrived and I was done."

Timika blinked, suddenly sure she was being snowed.

"What did Dr. Vespasian tell you?" she asked.

The hesitation was longer this time, and the look that flashed through the old woman's face had a note of alarm.

"I don't recall anyone of that name," she said. "Of course, it was a long time ago."

"Yes, it was. Perhaps if you looked through some records from his treatment it would come back to you," Timika pressed. "You have documents about that here?"

"Who did you say you worked for?"

"It's just a local feature," said Timika.

"For the *Monroe Sentinel*?"

"Yeah," said Timika, unthinking.

The old woman smiled, and though her eyes gave nothing away, Timika knew she'd screwed up.

"That's not the name of the local paper, is it?" she said.

Grace reached over and pulled something from the magazine stack that she laid on the coffee table, face up. Its masthead read *Monroe Enquirer Journal*.

"I'll see myself out," said Timika.

"Might be best that you do," said Grace, getting creakily to her feet.

Timika wasn't sure which of them was more uneasy.

She got into the rented Focus without looking back, but she could feel the older woman's eyes on her all the way.

Now what?

Grace Regis was, for whatever reason, on her guard, though Timika had no idea what that would mean. Maybe the old woman would call someone, but who? Barry? Timika shuddered at the thought. Or Alan's parents? If so, they'd be ready for her when she arrived with her questions. Or someone else entirely?

Something was going on. She didn't know what, and maybe it was something that had finished a long time ago, but there was a secret here. She could smell it.

ALAN
Area 51/Dreamland

ALAN SPENT THE FIRST FULL DAY BACK AT THE BASE IN A series of fitness and medical tests. He had a complete physical examination, spent a half hour on a treadmill wired up to an electrocardiogram, aced a series of vision tests, had his dental work reviewed, met with a rail-thin nutritionist and then with a counselor who discussed his sleep patterns and stress levels. Every test was conducted by people he had never seen before who called him Alan or Mr. Young—not Major—and introduced themselves only by job title. He was given a lunch break in the middle, and was invited to play on a Wii U sports game at the end of the day. When he said he'd rather just go chill in his quarters, he was told by a slightly sheepish Air Force staff sergeant that the computer games were part of his assessment; hand-eye coordination and the like. Alan sighed, and spent an hour playing ZombiU while the Air Force officer—whose name badge read Reynolds—tried not to look like he was charged with keeping score.

Then Barry arrived, similarly escorted, and they managed to have a kind of fun with a series of older Wii Sports and Sports Resort games that allowed them to spar with each other—literally in some cases—while talking trash and trying to ignore the hovering officers. It was like having a chaperoned play date.

But when it was done, it was really done, and they went to dinner with a sense of normality reasserting itself even though, as soon as the food arrived, Barry pushed the salt shaker slowly and deliberately across to Alan's side of the table.

"Wouldn't want you causing an international incident," he remarked dryly.

"You've been planning that line all day, haven't you?" said Alan, giving his friend a rueful grin.

"Since yesterday," said Barry. "I was afraid they'd never let us eat us together and I wouldn't get to use it."

"Guess you can die happy."

"It's a load off my mind, I can tell you."

"And with a mind like yours, you can't afford much heavy lifting," said Alan.

Barry grinned, then lowered his voice.

"You're closer to the truth than you think," he said. "I don't know if it's being back here, or what happened on the road or what, but I've been having the weirdest dreams."

"Yeah?"

"Yeah," said Barry, cutting a piece of meat and considering it critically before shoving it into his mouth on his fork. "And not just dreams. Weird thoughts that just come into my head."

"Yeah? Like what?"

"Well . . . this is going to sound weird."

"Then you've come to the right party."

"Okay," said Barry. "Like . . . You remember when Dave McIntyre got married and we went out to that strip club for his bachelor party?"

"Man, that was a long time ago," said Alan. "But yeah. When we were at Cherry Point. He kept drinking some big pink cocktail in a glass like a goldfish bowl. Till he fell over and couldn't get up."

"That's right!" said Barry. "Okay, so there was a stripper that night. Blond girl. Had some weird Christmas elf thing going . . ."

"Candy Cane," said Alan, amazed by the memory.

"Exactly! Glad I'm not the only one who remembers."

"She was something," said Alan. Strip clubs weren't his thing so, having only been to two or three in his life, he actually remembered the evening pretty well.

"Okay, so here's the weird part," said Barry, leaning in and lowering his voice again.

Alan waited as his friend glanced around. Finally Barry said, "I saw her yesterday."

"What?"

"I saw her. Here. On the base."

"Must have just been someone who looked like her," said Alan.

"No," said Barry, shaking his head emphatically. "I mean I saw her. In full costume. Pink bodice. Fishnets with bows. The whole bit."

"I don't understand," said Alan.

"I came out of my quarters, and she was just standing there. Sucking a goddamned lollipop. Said '*Hi there, Barry,*' like she'd been expecting me. Then she offers me the lollipop and says '*Fancy a lick?*'"

"You're kidding."

"Deadly serious."

He looked it too. All the laughter had gone and he looked spooked.

"That's nuts," said Alan.

"I know."

"I mean, that was years ago. She wouldn't look the same. She certainly wouldn't be dressed like . . ."

"I know," said Barry again, more emphatically this time.

Alan frowned and said nothing for several seconds, then just shrugged.

"I don't know what to tell you, man," he said. "Maybe someone's messing with you."

"Not you?"

"Hell, no," said Alan. Barry considered him, then nodded.

"If you find out who is," Barry said, "tell them to knock it off, okay? I mean, it's funny and all, and nothing bad has happened so . . . no harm, no foul, right? But yeah. Make 'em stop. We have enough weirdness here without that kind of malarkey."

"You really think you saw her?"

"Swear to God."

"That's pretty weird."

"You're telling me."

Alan nodded, then changed the subject, at which Barry relaxed visibly. They compared notes as to how they had spent their day, but that didn't take long since they'd both undergone the same battery of tests. But there was one thing on Alan's mind and he couldn't finish his meal without bringing it up, though he wasn't sure how much he was supposed to say.

"They show you the crate?" he asked.

"What?"

"The yellow crate," said Alan, watching his friend's face carefully.

Barry gave him a baffled look, then his eyes widened with realization.

"Oh the *crate*!" he said. "Yeah. That was pretty wild, huh?"

"Or the opposite," said Alan. "I was kind of disappointed."

Barry gave a chuff of knowing laughter and nodded.

"Assuming it's real," he said.

"Course it was real," said Alan. "I touched it. Felt sort of squidgy but it was, I don't know, plastic and rubber. Man-made."

"Well sure, what they showed us was fake: a doll," said Barry, as if this didn't completely satisfy him. "But that's not to say . . ."

"Oh, come on," said Alan, sitting back.

"I'm just saying, if they wanted to cover their tracks, and knew what we'd seen, this is how'd they do it."

"But they told us! This is how they cover the tech!"

"Yes, *they told us*. I'm just saying I'm not sure."

"Are you serious?"

"When you catch someone lying to you over and over and then they come to you and say *okay, I wasn't telling the truth before, but this time, I swear to God* . . ."

"You think that's what's going on?" Alan said, a mocking smile spreading over his face. "Occam's razor, my friend. The simplest explanation is the most likely."

"And you reckon that carrying fake alien dummies around just in case is the simplest explanation?"

"Simpler than there being actual aliens," said Alan.

"Says the man who flies UFOs out of Area 51 for a living."

"I'll give you that," said Alan. "But those are things I can understand, including the secrecy. And when they showed me what was inside the crate, everything made a little bit more sense."

"Understandable," said Barry. "We all want the world to make sense."

Alan nodded thoughtfully, conscious that neither of them had actually conceded their position.

"Candy Cane notwithstanding," he said.

Barry rolled his eyes.

"No shit," he said.

"What do you make of all these tests we're being put through?" Alan asked.

"Feels like we're being prepped for something," said Barry. Alan nodded.

"Guess we'll find out in the morning."

"If you passed," said Barry. "I think you've been getting a bit soft with all that barbecue and off-duty beer. I mean, it's not like sitting in a cockpit was that taxing in the first place . . ."

And they were off, the usual good-humored ribbing, in-jokes and shared anecdotes that said things really were back to a brand of normal they had shared for a very long time. They laughed, they finished each other's sentences, they anticipated punchlines and recalled past glories, sliding in and out of memory, so that Alan found himself wanting to say how glad he was that Barry had come back with him to make the strangeness feel somehow do-able. He didn't, of course. That wasn't how they talked. But he felt it, and when he slapped Barry's muscular shoulder as they separated for their respective quarters, he thought his friend sensed it and shared the feeling. He went to bed that night feeling that returning to the base had been the right decision after all, and then worried if Barry had been right, that they were being kept together to make each other comfortable, stable even, in preparation for some new assignment.

The question stayed with Alan through breakfast the following day and into a morning of tests conducted by the Air Force scientist who had been present at his debriefing, assisted by a young male tech who ran the systems from his laptop. The

scientist was Dr. Imelda Hayes, mid-forties, pale and bespecta-
cled with sharp blue eyes and a no-nonsense manner. She was
trim, strong looking, probably a runner . . .

"Your task is a simple one, Mr. Young," she said, businesslike, as he took a seat in a small, dimly lit room that felt
oddly like a recording studio. There were what he took to
be baffles on the walls, irregular padding in black foam that
looked like egg packaging. The floor was carpeted and the
door surrounded by a rubber sealant, so that the chamber
had a curious dead sound, and he could hear nothing beyond
those four walls. There was a single desk, behind which Hayes
sat, a large flat screen on one wall, and a device resembling an
analog weighing scale on a stand directly beneath the screen.
The scale featured a red needle in the center of the display,
currently registering zero pounds, zero ounces. As she spoke,
Hayes reached over and, fingers splayed and crablike, put a
little pressure on the top of the scale, making the dial beneath
it spin till it registered a weight of three and a half pounds.
"I'd like you to move the dial using only your mind."

Alan blinked. He had sensed something like this was
coming, but he still found it hard to believe.

"Do you think I can?" he asked.

"What I think is irrelevant," said Hayes. "I'm merely here
to observe and maintain a controlled environment for the
experiment." She nodded to the tech, who had been setting
up a video camera on a tripod in the corner. He tapped a button and, as a red light on the camera came on, stepped away.
"Focus on the scale, please," Hayes said.

Grudgingly, Alan turned, adjusted his chair and stared at
the scale. He could feel the tech's breathless silence. After a
minute or so, Alan looked back to Hayes.

"I can't," he said. "I don't know how to."

"Just try."

"I said, I don't know how to."

"Focus on the scale. Imagine pushing down on it. See the movement of the dial."

Alan frowned, tried, gave up.

"I can't," he said.

"Try closing your eyes."

He did. But when he opened his eyes again there was no sign that the dial had moved.

Hayes made a note.

"Perhaps you'd like to try with a digital device. Perhaps you will visualize it differently."

"Okay," said Alan, trying to sound game.

The analog scale was replaced with another, smaller one with a greenish LED display on the front. It looked like it was designed for measuring recipe ingredients. Numbers flashed briefly as the setup was completed. The tech stepped back, as if he was completing some kind of ceremony. Hayes gave him a professional smile and then nodded at Alan.

"In your own time," she said.

Alan considered the scale. He stared at the numbers, willing them to change, imagining their flickering square-sided digits transforming from zero to three, to eight, but nothing happened. He tried again, leaning forward in his chair, straining with his mind, reaching for the scale, feeling the muscles of his neck and jaw tauten with the effort.

Nothing.

He sat back, flicked a sideways look at Hayes, then went back to the scale, this time focusing not on the numbers themselves but on the pressure pad on the top, trying to make it seem as if some invisible hand in his mind was pushing steadily down. He felt his actual fingers pressing against each other as he visualized the effort, but nothing happened. After another minute or two, he sat back and shook his head.

"I can't do it," he said. "I'm sorry."

"Not to worry," said Hayes, still matter-of-fact. "Let's try another measure."

With another nod, she set the tech to removing the scale and replacing it with a carefully positioned glass marble about the size of a golf ball. It took him a moment to get it perfectly seated, and it was clear that the slightest pressure or wind would send it rolling off the stand.

"Try to nudge the sphere into motion," said Hayes.

Again, Alan leaned into his concentration, imagining the slow roll of the marble, the feather touch it would take to make that happen. But the glass ball did not move. Conscious of being watched, feeling his failure and wondering if they would now doubt all he had said about what had happened, Alan's thoughts became hotter, more irritated. He saw the salt shaker in the marble, saw the stand as the restaurant's table-top, and snapped his hand open as if the sphere would not simply roll off the stand but shoot into his hand.

Nothing happened.

Next he tried not so much nudging the marble as shoving it, throwing it, propelling it right through the wall, a bullet of his own angry making . . .

It did not move, and at last he threw up his hands.

"I'm sorry," he said.

"Let's try a little stimulus," said Hayes. Another nod to the tech, who stepped up close to Alan's seat with a pair of headphones ready to go. Alan's failure so far had obviously been anticipated. Which didn't make it feel any better.

"What I told you before, about what happened in the diner, I mean, it was all true. I don't know how I did it but . . ."

"Let's focus on the test in hand, shall we," said Hayes, like a teacher talking over a student who was making excuses she'd heard a thousand times before. "Forget the restaurant. Move the sphere."

And then there was noise in his ears, music first, New Agey synthesizers and wind chimes, not really a tune but pleasant enough. He listened absently and refocused on the marble for what seemed like minutes, before the sound shifted abruptly to pounding hard rock with a shrieking guitar solo and driving back beat. Metallica? Iron Maiden? Something like that. It was louder than was comfortable and he winced, his eyes flicking away from the marble for a second. When he found it again, it had not moved. And now there was something else in the music, bangs that were off rhythm, like distant mortar fire. The explosions got louder and more insistent, till they drowned out the music, and somewhere from far away he thought he could hear screaming. In the same moment, the flat screen above the stand came to life and he saw a jumbled collage of images racing into each other, the chaos of a stampeding mob, the snapping jaws of a shark, knife blades, fire and the carnage of battle, bodies with awful, unspeakable wounds, some of them children, a bright amber light in the sky . . .

Alan snatched the headphones from his head, and turned his anger on Hayes.

"What the hell kind of manipulative bullshit is this?" he demanded. His heart was racing. Sweat was beading on his forehead. The marble had not moved. "You want me to move this?" he snapped. He reached across and swiped at the table with his hand, sending what Hayes called the glass sphere shooting across the room and bouncing on the carpet and under the desk. "There," he said. "Happy?"

Hayes' chilly calm seemed to ruffle for a moment. Her eyes tightened and a crease scored her forehead, but then she recovered her professional serenity.

"Time for a break," I think. "Mr. Montague will direct you to the restroom. I'll get you some water."

She smiled like a plaster saint, then left the room before Alan had a chance to say that he didn't need any damned water *or* the restroom. He went anyway, just to get out of the room, and stood in the restroom staring himself down in the mirror. He muttered irritably to himself, then took a series of long, deep breaths, glanced at his reflection once more, and returned to the test chamber.

Suck it up, he told himself as he re-opened the door.

Alan sampled the chilled plastic bottle which awaited him on his return, though he sniffed it pointedly first. He wouldn't put anything past her, including drugging his drink. For her part, Hayes managed not to roll her eyes at his suspicion, and moved on to the next test.

While Alan had been in the restroom, the stand with the marble had been replaced by a child's plastic track with a toy car sitting on it, a free-running little jeep, bright pink with a hot-rod engine. She didn't need to tell him what he was supposed to do.

He couldn't do it.

He gave it his best shot, then something more resentful, and finally a listless, bored, defeated effort, but none of them made any difference. In keeping with the pre-K feel of the tests, Montague, the tech, then set up a dozen dominoes on end: tip one and they would all fall in a long, satisfying rush . . .

He couldn't do that either, with or without the headphones. He flatly refused to sit through more of the video montage. An hour passed, two, and Alan had showed no telekinetic ability whatsoever. As far as the tests were concerned, he was just a regular guy who had probably romanticized the sudden shift of a restaurant dining table, and then imagined that an accident averted by a sleepy pickup driver had something to do with his own blind panic . . .

"Time for lunch, I think," said Hayes. She pushed a button on her desk and lowered her face toward the speaker an inch or so. "Can you send Mr. Young's escort, please. We're done for the morning."

"You mean there'll be more this afternoon?" said Alan, wearily.

"We have to test your ability," she said.

"You mean my story," said Alan.

"Has anyone on the team disputed your testimony so far?" asked Hayes, neither apologetic nor offended.

"No," said Alan grudgingly.

"Then let's not get ahead of ourselves, shall we?" she replied.

Alan nodded vaguely and looked away.

His escort to lunch turned out to be Reynolds, the Staff Sergeant who had overseen his video games the night before.

"This way, please, Mr. Young," he said, indicating the long hallway. They stepped out of the soundproofed lab and the door snapped shut behind them as they paced the corridor. "You having a good day today, sir?" asked Reynolds in his bluff, formal way.

"Not especially, Staff Sergeant," said Alan.

"I'm sorry to hear that, sir," said Reynolds. "I hope the day improves for you. Some good offerings for lunch today at least."

He would have said more, but the air was torn apart by a sudden screeching wail. Red lights mounted up by the ceiling that Alan hadn't noticed before suddenly came on, bright enough to send the hallway flickering crimson as they flashed rapidly.

"What the . . . ?" Reynolds began. He turned on his heel and took Alan forcibly by the crook of his arm. "Let's get you back to the lab," he said. Alan couldn't help but notice the way the younger man's free hand dropped to the holstered Sig P320 at his waist.

"What is that?" Alan asked as they walked. "An intruder alarm?"

But Reynolds didn't answer. He was spinning in response to something he had heard or felt behind him. Alan glanced back and saw a man in a mask and dark combat fatigues rounding the corner, the barrel of his black machine pistol leading the way.

Reynolds didn't hesitate. He stepped toward the gunman, drawing his sidearm and raising it as Alan, who was unarmed, shrank back.

"Drop your weapon!" shouted Reynolds, but it was too late. There was a deafening series of pops and the brilliant flashes of the machine pistol's muzzle, and Reynolds went down face first. The P320 pistol flew out of his hand and tumbled halfway along the hall to where the gunman was still coming, his weapon aimed squarely at Alan.

There was nowhere to run. The corridor behind him was featureless for thirty yards: no cover of any kind. The masked man's eyes raked him, his arms taut. Alan actually saw the movement of his trigger finger before the gun fired.

Reynolds' pistol was a good five yards away. He couldn't possibly reach it before . . .

And then, almost without warning, the P320 had spun on the ground, lifted and flown as if snapped on an invisible strap directly into Alan's waiting hand.

He barely even had to aim.

18

MORAT
Rethymno, Crete

THE NAME ON THE CARD READ ERNESTO MORETTI, INTERPOL Works of Art division, Customs liaison. The picture—ruggedly good looking, vaguely Mediterranean, mid-thirties—belonged to the man who had recently been known as Jean-Christophe Morat. He slid the ID out of his wallet and across the desk, face up, then followed it with a printout with another face, this one cut from Nicholas Tan's university website.

"I'm looking for this man," he said in passable Greek. "An American. He's been associated with several excavations in Greece, Italy, Egypt, and Israel. I need to ask him some questions."

"Is he in some kind of trouble?" asked the woman.

Bingo, thought Morat. He'd asked the same questions and shown the same picture at five different places since he arrived on Crete two days earlier, a mixture of museums, dig sites, and universities. All he'd received were blank looks and occasional flashes of curiosity akin to rubbernecking as you pass a road accident. This was different.

The woman, the only person he had been able to track down in the Rethymno archaeology department, looked immediately anxious. Her eyes had widened and her face had colored. She didn't just recognize Tan; she felt responsible for him. He pretended not to notice.

"As I say, I just want to ask him some questions."

"About what?"

The woman looked scared, breathless.

"A number of artifacts have gone missing from their host institutions," he said, still smiling, picking his words with care as if being careful not to leap to conclusions. "Objects resembling them and lacking verifiable documentation as to point of origin, previous transaction, and so forth, have recently turned up on the American black market."

"What kind of artifacts?" she asked. The plate on her open office door said her name was Professor Elina Nerantzi. A real agent wouldn't answer that, of course, but Morat had done his homework and knew that responding would help. He put his attaché case on her desk and opened it just wide enough to slide out a loose-leaf binder of page-protected images, all carefully numbered and captioned with their provenance and the date of their disappearance. There were Cycladic figures, black and red Greek amphora and kylixes, fragments of slightly misshapen gold jewelry, marble statues from a variety of periods, and a bronze dagger, its blade inlaid with intricately depicted animals.

Miss Nerantzi gasped and put a hand to her mouth as if to hide it. The other hand fluttered unsteadily, so she put it firmly out of sight. He decided to give her the easy way out.

"Anyway," he said, flipping the book shut. "If you come across this man . . . you have my card." He gave her a short, professional and—most important—final smile and turned on his heel. He was out of her office and down the hall in a matter of seconds, deliberately not waiting for her to call him back. If she did, there would be more cat and mouse, more evasions and anxieties and testings of faith and loyalty. None of that interested him. He didn't want to know what she thought or believed, and he certainly didn't want to have to win her over. Better that he left her alone to lead him to Tan and—crucially—to Timika Mars, possibly to Jennifer Quinn too, with whom he had unfinished business.

He didn't loiter downstairs, but went straight to his car and circled the almost deserted lot until he was pretty sure which vehicle belonged to Nerantzi. The powder-blue Renault was a dead giveaway. He hopped out, clicked the magnetic GPS tracker against the body just below the rear bumper and returned to his car, which was stiflingly hot and smelled of near-molten plastic. Forty-five minutes later he had checked into a room at the nearby Hotel Artemis, from which he periodically consulted the app on his phone to see if the professor's car had moved.

It was good to be out of Kazakhstan, away from all the damn testing and the vultures who ran them. He had hoped he would be flying again, but this was almost as good, and the fact that they had come to him reinforced his sense that they knew they needed him. It was that fact more than any other that had made Morat put aside the thought of making a break for it the moment he was turned loose. Need was good, because when it was real it was also expensive. The more they depended upon him, the more he could wring money out of them like blood from a butcher's apron.

Morat had been quietly wealthy for a long time now, and he knew that had changed him. He had become a connoisseur of so many things, a gourmand, an enthusiast. Wealth took hobbies and elevated them, turned them into passions. It allowed the most extravagantly absurd of indulgence and earned no more rebuke than a wry smile at the spender's eccentricity. Actually, it was more than that. Spending more on a meal than most people did on a month's rent, spending more on a car than most people did on a house, these things made you special. They confirmed in others a sense of your taste and sophistication, as if you were some kind of ethereal and mystic wonder. No one ever thought of it as being merely a matter of the grubby notes and coins that changed hands with almost miserable predictability.

Morat knew this, and knew also that he had to keep his little extravagances to himself. He knew how to indulge himself without attracting attention. He hadn't grown up with money, so he had spent much of his life counting it, worrying about it. It was nice not to. It was nice to order the bottle, the watch, the girl he wanted on a whim and never have to worry for a split second if he could afford it. No wonder the rich were different from ordinary people. No wonder they had confidence and determination. They had grown accustomed to equating desire and its achievement with the swipe of a credit card.

This made them gods on earth.

The idea amused him and, to celebrate it, he ordered caviar and champagne to the room, those being the kinds of things the rich ordered, and amused himself still further by taking no more than a few sips and still fewer bites before pushing it all aside and calling the front desk to have the detritus removed. It was worth it to see the look on the face of the maid who came to clean up when she asked if the food and drink had not been to his liking.

"It was delicious," he told her, smiling at the way he intrigued and impressed her. "I just decided I wasn't that hungry."

When she was gone, he checked his phone and smiled to himself again. Nerantzi was moving.

He didn't go hightailing it after the little Renault yet. He had already turned up her home address in a rudimentary web search, so he knew from a cursory glance at the tracker that she wasn't heading there. She was going to see Mr. Tan. He was sure of it, but there was no need to risk spooking her by chasing her car through the streets like they were in a Bond movie. It always paid to be patient and deliberate. Things with the Quinn woman had only gone off the rails when he'd been rushed into impulsive choices . . .

That said, of course, this whole expedition was an impulse, as was his decision to begin today, before the rest of the team arrived. Rasmussen would hit the roof if he knew, but if Morat could wrap things up tidily by himself, that would send a nice, concise message as to his indispensableness. Resources were shorter than they had been before the Quinn fiasco. Proving he was worth any four agents they chose to send would go some way to securing his future.

Morat went down to the lobby, bestowed his most debonair smile on the concierge, and went out to the gravel parking lot where he had left his rented BMW, slipping on sunglasses as he stepped out into the hot afternoon light. He opened the door and gave it a second before climbing in. It smelled of baking leather and vinyl.

He checked the pistol in his glove box. It had been purchased for him in advance with bitcoin through some Internet back alley, and left in a shoebox behind a pharmacy in Heraklion with a hundred rounds of ammunition. The gun was secondhand but in decent shape, the serial number filed off, which meant it probably had an interesting history. It was something else Rasmussen would have disapproved of, a pistol Morat had never used but always wanted to, a Soviet-era

PSS: squat, ugly in a bald, utilitarian kind of way, but—by all accounts—almost completely silent. Its effective range was less than thirty yards, but only an idiot would get into a pistol fight over distances greater than that anyway. It was a small price to pay for an almost noiseless weapon. Morat checked the box-like magazine with its six 7.62mm rounds, keen to try it out.

He checked the display on his phone, noting that Professor Nerantzi's Renault seemed to have stopped a mile or so north of a tiny hamlet in the foothills south of the city, then replaced the pistol in the glove box.

It was turning into an interesting day.

PETER GREENWOOD
Hull, England, June 19, 1801

IN THE EAST RIDING OF YORKSHIRE, SITTING ON THE FLAT northern bank of the Humber where it flows down and out into the bleak North Sea, sat Kingston-upon-Hull or, more commonly and simply, Hull. Home to some 27,000 souls at this dawning of the nineteenth century, the town had been there since at least the late twelfth, beginning as a port for the local abbey, before evolving into a fishing and market town trading with Scotland and the lands to the east, Holland and Germany, Norway and Denmark. Screened by the Pennines, the north English climate was a little milder there than in the Lancastrian west, and the vaulted roof of Holy Trinity church enjoyed a little more sunshine than its counterparts in Liverpool and Manchester; this June day had been a case in point, a fine, clear afternoon when, from high ground, you could see straight down the river to Grimsby.

Peter Greenwood had slept through most of the day, knowing that he wanted to be putting his boat in the water in time to catch the early morning tide. He now sat amidships in the vessel he owned with his brother Michael, thumbing through the nets for tears before painstakingly doing one last check on the sealant around the well smack. They might be at sea for as long as a fortnight and the well smack—a watertight hold dotted with augured holes at various heights below the water line to let the brine pass through—was essential for keeping their catch alive. It was an expensive addition to the trawler, but one that would pay for itself if properly maintained.

And the sea didn't take them.

Peter didn't think much about that. This was what they had inherited, and though it was hard, it was not just how they made a living. It was how they lived. That it might also be how they died was not worth dwelling on. They were good, God-fearing folk. What else was there to wonder at?

He did not speak as his brother joined him. A nod was all they needed. They had made these preparations too many times to need to discuss them. While Peter finished checking the nets, Michael went through the well smack's slatted trunks, which would hold the plaice and halibut they would—God willing—catch in the next two weeks. The nets were fine but not so fine that they would trap the sprats and other small stuff the law did not allow. Old Bob Jenkins had been caught selling undersized plaice and dab and when he couldn't pay the twenty-shilling fine had been soundly whipped and given ten days' hard labor. Even with such punitive measures in place, Peter had a hunch that the sea's bounty was drying up and that it was their fault. They had to sail farther for longer to bring in the same catch, pushing deeper into waters off the coast of Iceland, where the Grimsby cod fleets fished with line and hook.

Inland a church clock struck the midnight hour and Peter stretched, rolling his head on his neck. They would have to leave soon and then, for all the emptiness of the sea, they would be cramped in the little boat for two long weeks . . .

Michael stood up suddenly, gazing across the river to the southwest.

"What in the name of all that's holy is that?" he muttered.

It was as long a sentence as Michael had uttered in Peter's presence in many a long while, so Peter set the nets down and rose to join him.

His brother's eyes were fixed on a speck of light that was the color of a gas lamp, soft and blue but strong considering the distance of the thing. It hung low in the sky like Venus, but as Peter watched it seemed to get closer and swelled palpably so that, within a minute or two, it was as large and bright as the moon, and possessing a similar kind of radiance. As it neared, and it did indeed seem to be moving, its perfect circle was revealed to be divided across the center line by a horizontal black bar. That made it unlike anything Peter had ever seen in the night sky before.

"What do you think it is?" he muttered, not taking his eyes off the phenomenon that was now so bright and clear that the Humber beneath it sparkled with its frosty glow, and the rooftops of the town looked bright and bluish, as when the snow came. Michael said nothing, but shook his head, gazing up in mute wonder. Somewhere along the street that ran along the harbor a door creaked open and Peter could hear voices raised in questioning astonishment, though he did not turn to see who was speaking because, at that moment, the unearthly sphere seemed suddenly to divide into several parts. He counted seven new orbs of fiery light hanging in a balanced cluster like so many torches or some great heavenly candelabra. Whatever it was, this was no planet, no simple comet.

"Great Lord above," muttered Michael to himself.

Even as the words were out of his mouth, the lights all vanished and the night was suddenly black again. But only for a few moments. Their eyes had barely adjusted to the darkness when the light returned, single again, another brilliant moonlike sphere more dazzling than the first. Peter looked at his brother momentarily, and was struck by how the boat and everything on it seemed to pulse with the cool radiance in the sky, every detail of the deck, its ropes and mooring cleats bright as day but cast in the ethereal blue of the lights, so that the little trawler became a ghost vessel out of ancient sailors' yarns.

Peter stood transfixed for several minutes, absorbing the pearly transfiguration of his boat, the pebbles of the wave-washed shore and the gray stone of the wharf, but then the light altered and he looked up again. The ambient circle had divided once more, this time into five distinct spheres. These too seemed to float above the town, and he had the strange impression that they were watchful and thinking, though what such things could think he could not imagine. He was pondering this vaguely, feeling like a saint of old, confronted by the glory of God, when the lights became a scattering of stars that faded, at last, to nothing.

Normality returned with the striking of the clock to mark the first hour of morning, and dimly aware that the voices behind him were now many, Peter turned to see the doors and windows of the town open like eyes and mouths, the people of Hull spilling out to share their awe and confusion. Yet, there was something else in the air. Peter felt it when he met his brother's eyes and when he watched the growing assembly, united as they were by the oddity of the experience, and by its curious serenity. They should have been afraid, he thought, struck with terror by the possibility of some imminent celestial calamity, but they were not. They felt only a kind of shared peace, and they basked in it as the town had basked in the unusual lights that had so visited them.

They did not sail that morning. At a loss to make sense out of their experience, they decided to wait to see if something else would happen the next night.

It did not. The marvel—which was reported in the *Hull Packet* and the *Northampton Mercury*, and was picked up nationally over the next few days—was much discussed, but did not repeat itself. Some said it had been a comet, but Peter had seen enough of the night sky to doubt such an explanation, and over time he heard that even the astronomers in London and the universities had disputed such a claim, saying it did not square with the accounts as reported in the papers.

Michael assigned it a sign from God, and he was not alone in doing so, though no one could be sure what the sign was supposed to mean, a problem that made it, to Peter's mind, unlikely. Surely the Lord God would be clearer if he wanted to give a message to mankind? Peter did not say as much, however. He was a man of few words and he spent them wisely. What he had seen stayed with him but he spoke of it rarely, and as time passed with no repeat of the sighting, the incident faded from popular memory like the lights themselves which, their shifting glories done, had melted into the thick Yorkshire darkness of ordinary times.

JENNIFER
Hampshire, England

JENNIFER WAS STANDING ON THE EDGE OF THE FAIRY circle. It was, she thought, a little smaller than it had been, but then so was she, so it was hard to tell. She was maybe ten, her hair gathered back in a ponytail, and a dainty basket of wildflowers clutched in her little hands. She was wearing a red-and-black plaid dress and white tights with the neat patent leather shoes she had so loved because she could see her face in them if she squatted down and looked really hard.

Actually, only half of the basket was full of flowers. The other half had bunches of thyme and rosemary clipped with nail scissors, and a few pungent leaves of sage, gathered as requested by the cook. Her father had taught her which were which a few months ago, and her weekly trip to the kitchen garden had become a Saturday morning ritual.

"Don't take them all, mind," said the cook. "Got to leave plenty to fill in what's cut."

As if she didn't know. The cook—whose real name was Margery—was a good cook but an annoying person, always explaining things long after Jenny had understood them. Every time Jenny took rosemary to her, Margery told her to smell it and make sure it was right, because rosemary looked like yew, which was poisonous and got planted in churchyards so that the sheep and rabbits wouldn't go in. Why the cook thought sheep and rabbits could tell the difference between yew and rosemary but Jenny couldn't, she never said.

It was the cook who had warned her to stay out of the fairy ring. She'd said it with a little twinkling smile and a glance at the housemaid to show she didn't really mean it, that it was the kind of joke grown-ups played on kids who didn't know what was real and what wasn't.

"That's where the fairies dance in the moonlight," said the cook. "But if you step into the circle they'll whisk you off to fairyland and not bring you back."

"Aren't fairies very small?" Jenny had demanded, distrustful as ever.

"They can be, but they can also be as big as you or me, and they're magical, so if they want to take you, you're charmed and can't stop them."

"Magic isn't real," said Jenny.

She only said it to prove the cook wrong, and hated the sound of the words as soon as they were out. In truth, she didn't completely believe her own hard-nosed realism. She had almost given up on magic, but still held out a little hope. She knew grown-ups didn't believe in such things, but the prospect of a world without magic made her feel sad and, strangely, miserably, old. Sometimes she wanted nothing more than to be eight again, when she knew less. She hated the way the cook's talking down to her made her grow up faster just to prove she could.

So she still came down to the fairy ring with an ear open for the tinkle of tiny bells and the fluting of the invisible pipes that made the elven music, even though that meant walking through the cow pasture. She got through as quickly as she could, avoiding the big, considering eyes of the cows. Her ten-year-old self knew the fairies wouldn't come, knew they couldn't because they weren't real, but she wanted to believe otherwise for just a little longer and would risk being watched by the cows just on the off chance.

She wasn't sure why it was supposed to be so bad to be taken by the fairies. Their world would be glorious. She had seen pictures in books, fairies riding on the backs of bumblebees and swallows, fairies with gleaming butterfly wings singing and dancing so lightly that they floated above the grass, fairies in royal coaches like beautiful ladies at a masked ball . . . If it wasn't for the goblins she would run away to join them in a heartbeat.

Jenny wasn't clear whether goblins were also a kind of fairy, but they weren't beautiful and elegant. They were rough and ugly and beady-eyed, all teeth and clothes and scratchy insect hair, or bundles of sticks with eyes, like Raggety, the scary imp thing in her *Rupert the Bear* book. She skipped through that story as she did the goblin pictures, closing her eyes sometimes as she turned the pages to get to the paintings of the fairy court. But she thought that maybe the goblins and the fairies weren't as different as their appearances suggested. After all, while the fairy world was gorgeous and the goblin world was a darksome hole rank with dirt and maggoty carrion, they both stole children. Everyone knew that. So maybe it was best not to wish to be taken, in case the wrong sort got you.

But there they were, the tiny floating lights that glimmered on and off in the dusk of the fairy ring, dancing, calling, and now little Jenny was even smaller than she had been, so small that she did not know herself, let alone the place, and all was a great, confused blur of sound and color. There was a great golden glow at the heart of the ring and around it were creatures like bees, buzzing evenly, and they were gold too. The lights were as big as she was now, bigger, and shone so bright that she could see that where the fairy ring had been all grass and mushrooms and trees, this was a room, a nursery, and she was peering up through the wooden rails of her crib as the light blossomed into something else entirely, something that filled the room like sound. Little Jenny, tiny Jenny, was so light now that she floated, drifting into the fairy dance and out of the world, though she could hear no music, no laughter, and the chittering sounds that filled her ears were surely and terribly goblin . . .

Jennifer sat up abruptly in bed, her heart racing. It had been a dream, and yet it had not been like a dream. More like memory, if confused and abstract and nonsensical. She blinked and put on the bedside light for comfort, her gaze moving over the familiar furniture, looming for anything out of place, looking for strangeness, for . . .

goblins

. . . any sign of what might have troubled her sleep or awoken her.

Even so, something of the dream lingered, a distant humming drone like the buzzing of wasps, and with it came the fleeting image of a pair of gold bees balanced harmoniously on either side of a sparkling circle that might have been the center of a sunflower. She blinked, and the sound receded.

But then the dream connected to something else and she got up and crossed the room to the shelves where her oldest

208

children's books sat, and pulled out the *Rupert* annual she had so loved as a kid. The stories were weird, trippy in an *Alice in Wonderland* way, the adventures of the bear in his sweater and checked trousers told in rhyming couplets, the world often fusing a prewar ideal of rural England with a storybook China. Endearing, but very odd. She flipped hurriedly through, feeling the old unease as she hit on the one story that had made her queasy and given her nightmares, and there it was.

Raggety.

A creature of sticks, but vaguely anthropomorphic too. It wore clothes but had no clear body mass and seemed to hover, insect-like, though it had no wings. Its face was blue.

A raggedy thing, Timika had called the creature she had seen through the window of the plane. But surely *Rupert the Bear* was distinctly, uniquely British? It certainly felt that way. So what was Jennifer's childhood nightmare doing in Timika's head?

What indeed?

Jennifer picked up her phone and used it to snap a picture of the image. She was hunting for Timika's e-mail address when Deacon knocked, pushing the matter out of her head.

With something like relief, she dressed and moved on to more concrete matters concerning her father's various enterprises and the stocks and other assets that came with them. It had been days but she was still extricating herself from some of his less savory investments, many of them tied to what had been Maynard, and not all of that could be done with a few clicks of her mouse. There were formalities to go through, he said warningly, documents to sign in the presence of witnesses.

"Sounds like I'm getting married," she remarked sourly.

"More like divorced in most cases," said Deacon, "but yes, the analogy is apt."

Jennifer considered him, waiting for the other shoe to drop, and Deacon cleared his throat uncomfortably.

"You are telling me we have to go into London, aren't you?" she said at last.

"I will have the car at the door in forty-five minutes," he said with an apologetic smile.

Jennifer sighed.

"Fine," she said. "But you have to do the driving yourself. I don't want handing off to some nervous footman who will be so terrified of Her Royal Spoiledness that he'll plow us into the first tree we pass and kill us both. Didn't think I knew they called me that, did you?" she added with an arch smile.

"I'm sure it is a term of endearment," said Deacon.

"Seems unlikely," said Jennifer.

"Well, I haven't heard it used for many a year," said Deacon loyally. "And it was never deserved."

"It was," said Jennifer, looking up and meeting his eyes levelly. "Kind of wish it wasn't, but there you go. I can't change what was, only what will be."

"A most healthy attitude, if I may say so, Miss. Do you mind my enquiring why you particularly want me to drive you, apart from my expert handling of the vehicle, of course."

"Of course."

"Perhaps you would like a little coaching en route about the various accounts and businesses from which we will be separating the Quinn estate?"

"Partly that," said Jennifer, grinning.

"And the other part?"

"I want to hear more about my childhood kidnapping," she said.

Deacon's smile stalled a little like a small plane that lost altitude as its engine sputtered through some minor mechanical inconvenience and then attained level flight once more.

"Very good, Miss," he said.

JENNIFER FELT NO MORE CONVINCING IN A BUSINESS SUIT than she had that day in the Maynard Consortium board-room, but this time the thought did not worry her unduly. She wasn't trying to convince anyone of anything. Or impress them. If they thought she looked about to try scratching the suit off before their very eyes they wouldn't be far wrong, and she didn't much care who knew it. It felt constraining and stiff, and she wanted to slough it off like snake skin, or like an insect emerging from its chrysalis prison.

Yes, she thought, struck by the peculiar rightness of the image. *That.*

She gazed out of the car window and watched London's familiar patchwork of drab suburbs grow up around them before the sheer moneyed grandeur of the City crowded in on her. They passed a bus stop whose sheltering wall panel displayed what looked like a blaze of gold that reminded her of the bees in her dream, but by the time she had turned to see what it really was, they had driven past it.

"I don't know what else I can tell you about your disap-pearance as an infant," said Deacon from the driver's seat. "I didn't have your father's ear in those days as I did later. I've told you all I know."

"Who did have his ear?" Jennifer asked.

"No one," he said. "Your mother, I suppose, though not—I fear—in this case. Perhaps there were people at work but at home . . ." He shook his head, frowning at the traffic. "Yes," he muttered to the car in front, "the light *is* green, you may now proceed." He rolled his eyes, seeming to have for-gotten Jennifer's presence entirely, then frowned and said sud-denly, "There was the cook. She had worked for his mother and he felt oddly comfortable with her. He liked to watch her work. The servants often commented on finding him whiling away the hours in the corner of the kitchen while she baked. I don't think they talked much, and it seems unlikely that he would have confided in her, but perhaps she picked up something I didn't."

"The cook?" said Jennifer, incredulous. "You don't mean old Margery? That frightful busybody!"

"Margery Cullen," said Deacon. "Retired now, of course."

"Years ago, no? I don't think she was here when I came home from university."

"Maybe for a little while, but not for long, no. She must be close to eighty now."

"If she's still alive," said Jennifer, watching the bankers in their slim suits and pink ties walking briskly to their meetings, talking on their phones as they slipped under the shadow of St. Paul's heading for Threadneedle Street. She and Deacon were nearly there now and she found she was navigating by her sense of where the Thames was.

"Oh, she's still alive," said Deacon. "I saw her at your father's funeral."

"She came back?" asked Jennifer, touched. "Did she have to come far?"

Deacon laughed.

"Hardly," he said. "Your father wanted to keep her on hand so she could help cater for special occasions, or so he said. I don't think he ever actually employed her again after she retired, but the white lie—if that was what it was—sopped the old woman's pride."

"Her pride. Why? What might she have otherwise been too proud to accept?"

"A cottage," said Deacon. "One of the few left still in control of the estate. She lives a hundred yards from the copse on the far side of the fairy ring."

Jennifer stared at him. She didn't know why, but the revelation sent a chill running through her, like ice water had been dripped down her spine. She remembered the figure she had glimpsed in the woods the night before, and the dream she had in which the cook had made a fleeting appearance.

It was coincidence. Of course it was. But she shifted in her seat and when they pulled up and parked she was, for the first time in her life, almost relieved to leave her thoughts behind in order to concentrate on a business meeting.

It was almost five hours before they were back in the car, and Jennifer felt utterly spent. It wasn't merely the bewildering business jargon and double-speak, or the mind-numbing tedium. Every meeting had been frigidly adversarial with batteries of lawyers on both sides citing precedent and referencing footnotes as they navigated contracts to say what Jennifer could and could not do with her father's money. It felt like something between chess and single combat, and it was laced with a level of personal acrimony Jennifer hadn't been prepared for.

"It's a lot of money," Deacon had said with a shrug after one particularly unpleasant exchange with a CEO who had come within a hair's breadth of threatening her. "You can't blame them for being upset. Your father's investments kept some of these companies solvent. Without them . . ." He paused to take in Jennifer's battered mood and changed tack. "But it serves them right."

"Yes!" said Jennifer with passion. "You know what these people were invested in? If their products were manufactured in countries with any kind of meaningful child labor laws their manufacturing costs would go through the roof! The average wage of these kids for their fourteen hours . . ."

"Which is why we no longer do business with them," said Deacon, cutting her off almost as deftly as he had slid the

Jaguar into traffic. "You have just had a miserable day, but it is over and I suggest you put it out of your mind."

"They said I was a disgrace to my father," said Jennifer quietly. If she hadn't been so tired, so worn down, she would never have voiced the thought but Deacon was right. It had been a long day. "Practically all of them, one way or another, said the same thing."

"Which only shows how little they knew Edward Quinn," said Deacon. "Your father made his mistakes, but I feel sure he would be cheering you on every step of the way."

Jennifer smiled gratefully, then turned to look out of the window. It was still light in central London and the streets seemed as packed as ever. There were tourists everywhere, billboards advertising West End shows, taxis . . . She watched absently, tipping her head back, closing her eyes, and blowing the day out in a long, slow breath. She was sick of thinking about money. It started to feel like that was all she was, a loaded bank account.

However much she knew other people would kill to be in her position financially, she was sick of it, sick of being nothing more than the key to a vault . . .

"You know what I want?" she said, realization dawning. "A really good Indian. I could absolutely murder a proper curry. The kind of chicken Madras that sears your mouth and makes you drink rubbish beer by the keg, served with naan bread and chutneys and . . ."

She stopped suddenly, staring out of the window as a double-decker bus passed, red and glossy and striped with a long yellow advertisement for something at the British Museum. A pair of bees on opposite sides of a bright circle. And it wasn't yellow. It was gold.

"Miss Jennifer?" said Deacon, picking up on her stunned silence. "Are you all right?"

"I'm . . . What's that?" she asked, pointing.

"The bus?"

"What does that banner thing on the side say? Pull up alongside it."

Deacon frowned and checked his mirrors. The Jaguar was pinned in its lane.

"I'm not sure we can catch it," he said. "Does it matter?"

"Yes," said Jennifer, not knowing why. "It really does."

Deacon gave her a quick look, read her face, and set the car in motion, turn signals blinking. He waved apologetically, getting horns and fingers anyway, but he edged into a space and the Jaguar leapt forward. Two hundred yards later they were riding the bus's shoulder and Jennifer, her window open, was craning to look out and up. Another few seconds and at last she could see it, the oddly familiar image: stylized gold bees clinging to a disk.

She could almost hear them buzzing.

The advertisement read *Treasures of Minoan Crete, a special exhibition from the National Archaeological Museum in Heraklion*. It was over-stamped with the austere lettering of the British Museum logo.

"What time is it?" she asked, still staring at the bus.

"Half past three," said Deacon, half turned toward her, his voice doubtful, even concerned. "Why?"

"Make a right up here," she said. "It should still be open."

TIMIKA
Monroe, North Carolina

TIMIKA SAT IN THE HOSPITAL'S PARKING LOT AND considered her options. She could probably get access to some hospital scrubs inside without too much difficulty simply by visiting the laundry or a locker room, but she wouldn't get far without a name badge complete with the kind of code that could be read by a computer scanner. Everyone had those these days, and people were a lot more protective of confidential medical records than they used to be. She had considered asking Marvin to try to hack the system, but she expected their firewalls would be pretty good and didn't want to get him into trouble if things went wrong.

Better to use the old-fashioned way.

Which was what? In her case, it was usually bluff and bluster, but while she could talk her way past a lot of minor protocol issues, even a few professional ethics, she couldn't see herself convincing someone to break the law. And if truth were told, however much she was sure Barry's mother had lied to him, she still felt awkward about prying through his private medical history.

Maybe she was going about this the wrong way. Medical records would be fiercely protected, but what about personnel? Come at it not through the patients but through the doc who treated them? She liked that approach better: she was lost when it came to matters of medicine, but local admin she could handle. She checked her reflection, glad that she had dressed professionally this morning. You never knew when things like that might give her the edge she needed, especially when you were a black woman in Jesse Helms country.

She pulled out her phone, typed the name of the hospital into the search engine, and added "Human Resources." The screen filled with corporate PR blather about *optimum health-care providers* and *serving the community through the placement of the right people in the right positions.* Below this was a series of addresses, all tagged with the name of the parent company: Batria. Timika executed two more searches and then returned to the HR page. Batria was, apparently, an Atlanta-based operation with a string of hospitals, clinics, and specialty practices dotted all over the southeast. Alongside Novant and Atrium, they employed the vast majority of the state's health professionals. She studied the addresses, selected a couple whose home pages she reviewed, and got out of the car.

The performance began with the way she slammed the car door and moved with hasty purpose to the main entrance, pressing the phone to her ear and talking quickly to some imaginary person on the other end.

"No," she said, as an elderly white lady in a wheelchair was pushed toward her by a weary-looking woman who might have been her daughter. "Check the P-7s and update the I-96s. I want to see those records no later than tomorrow lunchtime and earlier if you can make it. I need some review time before the section admin meeting at three tomorrow."

The security guard and receptionist both ignored her, which she took as a win. She pretended to pause in her conversation and mouthed "HR?" at the latter who pointed to an elevator and raised three fingers. Timika gave her a thumbs-up and kept walking, making up more forms and job titles, which she spouted into the phone as she went.

She had the elevator to herself, so she took a break from the improv set she was doing with the phone and organized her thoughts. As she reached the third floor and the doors slid apart, she began the second act.

There were two staff on duty at the counter. Timika hesitated, still chatting into the phone, dropping the names of people at the various local offices that she had pulled from their websites.

"Yes," she said. "I'm here now. Tell Mr. Simmons I'll have it cleared up right away, assuming their records are complete . . . Yes. Probably just an oversight, but we can't move forward with their clearance till this is cleared up . . . No, we'd have to shut down the hospital's entire electronic medical records system . . . Hours, at the very least. Maybe days. Yes, I realize that would be disastrous. That's why I came myself. Yes. Yes. Okay. I'll call you back as soon as I know."

She put the phone away and turned her most brilliant smile on the receptionists who, she was pleased to see, had just exchanged an anxious look.

"Hi," she said. "I'm sorry to bother you. My name is Shauna Dupont. I'm from the Mooresville office. We've run into an anomaly in your records and we need to get it resolved as soon as is humanly possible."

Timika pretended to be fumbling in her purse for her ID, looking puzzled when she didn't find it right away, and resolving not to bother.

"Sure," said the first receptionist, a middle-aged black woman wearing a kind of huge glasses on a chain around her neck that Timika hadn't seen for at least a decade. Her name badge read K. Stevens. The other receptionist, white and skinny, seemed glad not to be involved, and in truth Timika had chosen her colleague on purpose. She got more immediate sympathy—and credibility—from black people, though she felt a little guilty about exploiting that now. "What kind of anomaly?"

"Ancient history, I'm afraid," said Timika. "A doctor who practiced here in the late eighties but doesn't exist in our records at head office. I'm assuming it was a glitch in the data transfer but we have to make sure."

"What's the name of the doctor?" asked Stevens, waking up her computer.

"Vespasian," said Timika. "V-E-S-P . . ."

The receptionist cut her off.

"I got it," she said. "Yes, I see him. Visiting credentials. But . . . Huh. I see what you mean."

"Problem?" said Timika, suddenly tense.

"Well . . . I don't know. Look at this, Vi." The white woman rolled her chair over a couple of feet and leaned across, her face sharpening. "See, there he is. He's not listed as being on staff, which is fine, but his case files are all empty."

Vi grunted with disapproval.

"You tried looking him up by badge number?" she suggested. Timika wasn't sure if her blather about holding up their records clearance had the women spooked or if they were offended by the implication of failure, but they both looked unhappy.

"Yeah, see?" said the other. "Nothing."

"Do you have contact information for him or his employer, practice, or hospital?" Timika ventured. "Maybe we could clear it up by speaking to whoever sent him."

"Let me pull his personnel records," said Stevens. She tapped at her keyboard, pulling up other screens Timika could not see. "Huh," she said again. "That's weird. It's all blank. Completely empty."

Again Vi leaned across, disbelieving, but her colleague was apparently right.

"Can you check his original employment file?" suggested Timika. "Maybe there are references or . . ."

"Hold on," said Stevens. More clicking and typing, more dissatisfied puzzlement. "No. This isn't right. See?" she said to Vi. "Not even a social or date of birth."

So there *was* something about Vespasian. Her instincts had been right. Clearly at a kind of stalemate, the two receptionists stared unhappily at the computer screen.

"Better check with the super," said Vi.

Timika's defenses came hurriedly on line.

"Super?" she said warily.

"Our supervisor, Mr. Hardy," said Stevens. "He knows the system best. Was probably working here back then. Hold on. I'll call him."

Timika vacillated, not sure she wanted the inquiry to go beyond these two women, but Stevens had already picked up the phone and dialed a number.

"Mr. Hardy?" she said. "Hey. Yeah, we're trying to track down a doctor who used to work here but wasn't on staff. Name of Vespasian. Captain. Hematologist. Came in from Tysons Corner, Virginia, but that's all we have. No case files, no contact info . . ." She went quiet for a moment and her forehead puckered into lines of thought as her eyes came up to Timika's. "I'm sorry," she said, "who did you say you were again?"

"Shauna Dupont," said Timika, her sense of alarm mounting. The receptionist's manner had altered subtly but unmistakably.

The receptionist repeated the name and then, with a curious air of deliberation, put the phone down. When she spoke again she seemed evasive, her eyes down so that even Vi gave her a quizzical look.

"Just take a seat over there, Ms. Dupont," she said, nodding to a pair of institutional-looking armchairs. "Mr. Hardy will be right with you."

Timika nodded and managed a smile, but though she turned toward the chairs she walked right past them, out through the glass doors and along the hall to the elevator, her footsteps getting faster as she walked, her eyes fixed on the way out ahead. As she neared the elevator she saw one of the hospital's uniformed security guards talking furtively into his collar radio, and took a hard left down a hallway signposted to the cardiac unit.

Might prove handy, she thought bleakly, feeling her heart beating hard in her chest.

She was moving just this side of a flat-out run, but she might be a grieving relative rushing to someone's bedside. She went past the cardiac unit—its waiting area not significantly different from the HR office, all pastel shades and bland, cheery furniture—and made a right where she saw an exit sign. Going through a simple metal door with a locking bar put her in a utilitarian stairwell. She went down two flights of steps, listening for the signs of pursuit but—guessing that the lobby might be watched—took one more flight down.

If the stairway had been plain, the basement area looked like a parking garage. The walls were bare concrete and the ceiling was strung with ducts and cables looped through girders furred with spray insulation. She was disoriented, but had a suspicion that she was walking toward the back of the building where, she hoped, she might find an unwatched loading dock or ambulance bay. Her car was parked at the front, but the hospital staff wouldn't know that, not if she got out before they could review any security footage, and she felt sure that walking around the outside of the building was safer than going through the main doors.

She passed through a series of janitorial storage units, one with a service elevator, and she marveled at how much a hospital looked like a hotel when seen from the right perspective.

Short stay, she thought bleakly, *and not everyone checks out except, you know, by "checking out"* . . .

Her mind was racing as if to keep pace with her heart, throwing out nonsense so that she wouldn't think about what would happen if she got caught. She was pretty sure she'd been in worse trouble, and no hospital security guard was going to shoot her for asking awkward questions, but she didn't want to have to explain herself to the police.

Or to the military.

That wasn't nonsense. Not quite. The possibility had been ghosting through her brain ever since the receptionist had referred to the mysterious Dr. Vespasian as *Captain*.

Vespasian might not have been affiliated with the military, of course, but if he had been it would make sense that he had been assigned a military rank in addition to his M.D., and captain sounded about right. As to whether there was anything to be wrung from Tysons Corner, Virginia, that was something she'd set Marvin on.

Assuming you aren't in a police cell by nightfall.

She made another right, starting to feel maddeningly, alarmingly turned around in the hospital's basement no-man's-land. She had seen no one since coming down. It felt stuffy and ignored. Or secret. Maybe little Barry and Alan had been brought to some private room down here . . .

Bawwy and Awan. My favowite patients.

She had to get out of here.

From some way over on her left came the echoing clang of a heavy door, followed by brisk footsteps. She caught a snatch of conversation. Male voices. Then more footsteps.

They were hunting her. She could feel it.

Timika made another turn, glancing over her shoulder to see if she could see them, and backed suddenly into something unyielding. The footsteps were closer, louder, and she had run into a wall in some miserable damn cul-de-sac . . .

She turned in exasperation but found that the wall was, in fact, a door. The warning sign across the central bar said that the door locked automatically, but did not say it was alarmed. She pushed it.

The parking lot was a blaze of flat, bright sunlight, and after the dim concrete hallways of the basement, Timika squinted against it. It did not slow her, however, and she was quickly out and hunting for her rental, orienting herself as she walked. She had come out of the building's western side, not the rear. The upside of that was that she didn't have as far to walk, but she realized almost too late that she had just crossed into the field of vision of anyone watching from the front entrance.

There was someone. A young black officer, his hand pressed to his radio. He happened to be facing away from her.

Timika dropped hurriedly behind a silver Camry, then loped low as she could get to the first vehicle she could see with a bit more height: a green minivan with a family of stick figures on the rear window. Even in her present anxious mood Timika managed to roll her eyes.

She waited there, watching the security guard through the van's tinted windows. Her little white Ford was one bay over and three cars down. A young woman in powder-blue scrubs was sauntering up to the main entrance. She was cute in an All-American kind of way. Timika timed her run.

As the young nurse neared the front doors, the security guard, with the kind of masculine predictability that Timika could have diagramed, turned to smile at the young woman, muttered something, and pushed the door open. By the time the nurse was inside and the guard was watching the sway of her ass appreciatively, Timika was up against the side of her car, pulling the door open from a half-crouch, and sliding awkwardly into the driver's seat.

She composed herself, closed the door quietly, and fished her shades from the glove box. She turned the engine over and the car came to life in virtual silence, without the roaring and smoke-pumping drama that had heralded the start of any journey in Dion's crappy little Corolla. The memory gave her a pang of remorse and she resolved to call him, if only to pay for the car which, last she heard, was sitting in a police impound lot in rural Pennsylvania.

She checked her mirrors and screamed.

There was something in the back of the car. It had long, black, spidery limbs that tapered to nothing, but branched at the knees and elbows so that in spite of its striped red shirt, it looked like an animated thicket of sticks. Its face was blue gray and pointed, sprouting twigs like whiskers. It seemed to hover as if weightless, and its dark, hard eyes were full of gleeful malice.

Timika snatched her sunglasses from her head with one hand and reached for the car door handle with the other, desperate to get away. But as she was in the act of doing so, the creature—if a tangle of woody stalks with a face merited the name—vanished.

For a long moment, Timika sat, staring at the rearview mirror, then, reluctantly, she turned in her seat and examined the back seat properly. There was nothing there, nor any sign that there had been.

Moments later, sitting low in the seat, Timika was guiding the Focus away from the hospital, checking her rearview mirror for any sign that the guard on the door had spotted her. She edged out of the parking lot and sped away into traffic, unsure what exactly she had learned, but confident that she had gotten away clean, even if the strange apparition in the car had stolen her sense of triumph.

Trying to process the bizarre vision got her nowhere. She felt a visceral revulsion and sense of horror, though what it meant, what it had actually been, Timika couldn't say. But this wasn't the first time she had seen it, and it was getting harder to pretend it wasn't significant.

She was back on the road to Charlotte before her phone rang.

"Miss Mars?"

Timika stiffened. It was a woman's voice, but its formality made her doubt the perfection of her escape.

"Who's this?" she said.

"This is Elina Nerantzi, from Crete?"

"Oh!" said Timika, surprise and relief washing over her. "Hi. Is everything okay?"

"I am not sure."

Timika hesitated.

"What's up?" she asked, instantly on her guard.

"I sent you an e-mail but you didn't respond, and since the matter might be urgent . . ."

"Yeah," said Timika, "it's been busy. Sorry. I didn't see it."

"I thought I should follow up," said the Greek woman. "A man has been here asking questions about your colleague,

Mr. Tan?" Every sentence ended in an upward inflection as if she was asking a question.

"What man? What kind of questions?"

"He says he is Interpol and that he needs to speak to Dr. Tan about some missing antiquities?"

"Missing from where? He only just started digging!"

"From other places where he was worked before. Italy, for one."

"That doesn't sound right," said Timika. "Maybe he has made a mistake."

"I thought that but . . ."

Her voice trailed off. Timika overtook a motorcyclist carefully then said, "But what?"

"He is wearing a very nice suit for a policeman."

Timika felt suddenly cold with dread and, without warning, she thought of the strange, raggedy bundle of sticks with a face she had glimpsed in the back of her car.

"Hold on," she said. "I'm pulling over."

She hit the turn signal, pulled into the front lot of a Burger King, and parked.

"Okay," she said. "You have a name for this guy?"

"Said he was Ernesto Moretti, from Interpol's division of art and customs."

"What does he look like?"

"You have access to your e-mail now? I sent a picture."

"Hold on."

Timika pulled up her e-mail and scrolled through the recent messages till she saw the one with Greek characters in the "from" address. She opened the attachment, but the picture came up slowly. It was grainy. Judging by the high, wide-angle vantage it was probably taken from a security camera feed. It showed a good-looking man in a dark suit with one of those designer stubble beards that made everyone look like they were trying to impersonate the late George Michael. Timika squinted and started to shake her head, saying "I don't think . . ." but then something in the eyes struck her, and distant corner of her memory chimed. Weeks ago, the first night she met Jennifer, they had been about to enter some diner by the highway in the middle of the Nevada desert. Jennifer had looked through the window and freaked.

There had been three men inside. They had turned out to be Barry, Alan, and another man Jennifer then knew as Letrange but who everyone else called . . .

The name spilled out of her like a curse.

"Morat."

NICHOLAS
Near Fotinos, Crete

IT HAD TURNED INTO A QUITE REMARKABLE DAY.

Nicholas had arrived at the site before the sun was up because he hadn't yet hired a replacement for Timika and didn't want to get too far behind schedule. That was a bleak sort of joke at his own expense: there was no schedule, no purpose, just poking in the barren dirt until they ran out of money or interest and he would slink back to Reno, his tail firmly between his legs and his job very much on the line. But however bleak the outlook, Nicholas was at heart an optimist, a good thing for an archaeologist who lived in the expectation of things past discovered in a future that may begin at any moment. He would keep going, harder than ever, until the weight of reality was too much for his optimist foundation, and the whole mess came crashing around his ears.

So he dug. And as he did so, the very thing that had frustrated him so far—the total absence of any kind of archaeological findings—took a slightly different and more perplexing cast. Though the largest of the Greek islands, Crete was just not that big—a little over a hundred miles long and only about thirty at its widest point—and given that the place had been continually inhabited for multiple millennia you'd expect all but the most inaccessible mountain areas inland to be thoroughly layered with evidence of human occupation. The dig site was at the end of an inconvenient dirt road, but was only a mile from a real village and less than thirty from major settlements. It was mostly flat, was in sight of the sea, and was well screened by higher ground to the south, all of which meant that the ruined church and tumbled-down goat pen should be only the most obvious parts of an almost unbroken line of constant habitation.

But they had found nothing. Normally the ground clearance alone would accumulate bins of fractured masonry and ceramic shards from various periods turned up, reused, and discarded over the years. The dig he had worked near Jerusalem as a graduate student had a virtual carpet of Byzantine pot shards just a few inches under the surface, and sometimes you'd see them just lying in the grass, little brownish pieces etched with a three-line decorative band, their shattered edges smoothed by fifteen centuries. Since their interests had been Bronze Age, they had dug right past such "modern" remains, and though most of them were bagged and collected, he doubted they were ever studied or displayed, and a lot were left right where they were.

So the Fotinos site was odd. There should have been Byzantine remains here too, and Ottoman, and Venetian, Roman, Classical Greek, and Mycenaean as well as Minoan.

Interesting or not; valuable—financially or academically—or not; there ought to be five thousand years' worth of accumulated crap around the field, and the fact that there wasn't said that he was either the worst and unluckiest archaeologist in the world, or that the place had been cleaned up.

But if so, when and by whom? There was no record of any formal excavation of this site anywhere in Greek archaeological records. He had looked, and he had double-checked with Professor Nerantzi. One of the reasons he was being allowed to come out here to conduct a largely unsupervised dig was because no one in the past had thought the place worthy of attention.

And now that he thought about it, that too was odd. So he began another exploratory trench as the sun started to rise over the glittering waters of the Aegean, allowing him to turn off his battery lamp and focus on the gentle swing of his mattock, biting beneath the roots of the surface weeds and turning over the dry, dusty clods of earth. As he worked, he thought of the moment he had walked into the kitchen of his little borrowed apartment in the village and found his mother repairing a bicycle. He wasn't trying to analyze the moment or what might have happened to his mind to trigger it, but replaying it in his head as he might replay a favorite song, focusing on its details, reveling in it, grateful for the fact of its existence.

He didn't look up when he heard the car's engine, or the clunk of its door, only straightening up as he saw Desma in jean shorts and a red tank top slouching her way toward him across the field. He raised one hand in greeting, though he knew to expect little in the way of pleasantries from her, and went back to work, swinging the mattock gently, meticulously. It made the soft thunk as its bit cut through the soil, then he worked it out, turned the dirt over and pushed it aside, made another cut an inch or two below the first, repeated the whole process, then made another, and another.

He heard the distinct chink of metal on stone and paused. The ground had been—again—almost oddly free of rubble. He cleared the dirt away and made another cut, even more tentative this time, and once again found something hard and immovable. He pulled a brush from his belt loop and dusted the sandy gray earth away. The stone he had hit was pale and flat on top. He squatted down and used a combination of hand trowel and brush to clear more dirt away, cutting a few more inches down the side of the stone. He found the crack that marked the base of the block, but something pale glinted hard below it, and when he worked the soil free—working fast now, his heart beginning to race—he realized it was another stone. It had roughly the same dimensions as the one that sat on top of it. It could be chance natural placement, of course, a couple of stray rocks that had wound up on top of each other, or it could be . . .

A wall.

The words came to him in a breathless rush. He stared, blinked the sweat from around his eyes, and called to Desma, who was sauntering between tool bins under the tarpaulin lean-to.

"Bring the camera!" he shouted. He thought she frowned and nodded, though it was hard to tell at this distance, but he was pretty sure she hadn't sensed his mood. He should probably stop, wait for her, document the process thoroughly, but it was still—he reminded himself—probably nothing, and besides, he wanted to know, and he didn't want to wait.

He moved the mattock to the end of the exposed stone and started working his way down. Two stones on top of each other might be coincidence, but if they were aligned with more . . .

He made three small cuts, cleared the debris, and looked. The two rocks—or as he was already thinking of them, *blocks*, stones that had been selected, even roughly shaped by a mason—abutted two more.

"Desma!" he yelled, his eyes alight. "Camera! Now!"

This time she heard the urgency in his voice, saw it in his body language, and she came at an awkward trot. She didn't ask what the big deal was. In fact, while she looked confused, there was something else in her face that he hadn't seen before: a spark, a kindled inner excitement that flared as she looked down into the exploratory trench. Then she was raising the camera, snapping pictures and muttering to herself in excited Greek. Then she gazed at him, her face almost unrecognizable with a joy so sheer and naked that it was almost embarrassing to look at. But then he felt it too, and seeing it in her made him surer in his conviction. It still might be nothing, the remains of an animal pen from a hundred years ago . . .

But. In his gut he knew it wasn't, and as time passed, his certainty built.

Two hours later Nicholas was pretty sure what they were looking at. There would be tests, slow and painstaking, but in his heart he knew what those tests would eventually say. He'd read about sites just like this. The stacked stones went only four or five deep—no more than a couple of feet— before hitting bedrock, but they were indeed part of a wall that traced a slow curve. It might be weeks before they knew for sure, but if his hunch was right, they were looking at a circular foundation whose walls were mostly natural stone mortared together with clay. They were looking at a Minoan tholos tomb, what were sometimes called beehives because of their roughly conical tops, and it had been there 3,500, even 4,500 years.

It was extraordinary. There were, of course, other such tombs on the island, but even if it was empty, it was a major find. In the space of a few hours his career had turned entirely around.

There were still lots of questions, not least of which was how quickly they could uncover the rest of the tomb without risking damage to the site or anything contained within it, and how soon they could expand the excavation. Minoan tombs were frequently complexes. What they had just uncovered might be the tip of a substantial iceberg.

But the site's other oddities raised another question, this one cautionary. The lack of artifacts on the top surface despite the relative shallowness of the tomb foundation, and the softness of the largely rubble-less ground they had been digging through suggested that they weren't the first here. The site had surely been looted and filled in long ago. After all, Nicholas reminded himself, he had been directed here by someone else, someone who knew there was something worth looking for in the area. How would they know that, unless they'd already been here?

All of this meant that he should prepare himself to find nothing more than foundations, the stone traces of the *tholos*, but as he had told Timika, archaeology wasn't an Indiana Jones movie. He wasn't here for gold or the statues that tourists would coo over. He was here to learn and to contribute to the discipline. A looted tomb foundation would do that just fine.

Desma was transformed. Her belligerence and resentment had burned off, and beneath it she was young and vibrant and thrumming with excited rapture. She gabbled away constantly, sliding between English and Greek as if barely conscious of what she was saying or who she was talking to. She wanted to get help: local labor and whatever resources the university had kept to itself. They would still document, photograph, they would still proceed with professional caution, but they would get the core tomb uncovered in days, maybe even hours, instead of weeks or months . . .

Nicholas wasn't sure. He needed to speak to Timika but it was still early in the United States, and he wanted to be able to give her a clear picture of what was and wasn't here. When Desma said they could start with her brother and her uncle, both of whom had worked on archaeological digs before, Nicholas said okay. She drove to the village to call them, and they were there within forty minutes, arriving together in a little van from which they pulled spades and pickaxes and approached, grinning. They were big men, bearded and tanned to the color of old olive wood. The younger was Dimitri; the elder, Prokopius. Both had curly black hair, bright eyes, and big voices, so that Nicholas felt a little intimidated by them and kept his distance, except to thank them for their help and tell them where to dig. As he watched them work cheerfully, their spades cutting just a little more aggressively than he would, he wondered if he had already made a mistake. He needed to call Professor Nerantzi.

There was no cell phone signal at the site, but he was wary of leaving the dig unattended with these strangers here and, for a few minutes, he dithered. It was an old habit, one of the things he hated most about himself, and it left him feeling stupid and weak. Most of the truly decisive people he had met had either very sharp minds or were too stupid to see the consequences of their actions. Nicholas was just smart enough to see the consequences of his actions stacking up disastrously in the future like terrible actors waiting to come on stage. He couldn't leave the site in the control of people he didn't know. What if someone unearthed something important or

234

valuable and chose to pocket it? What if they damaged the site or planted something . . . ?

They almost certainly wouldn't, but that *almost* held him paralyzed on the horns of his dilemma . . .

And then, without warning, the matter was taken out of his hands.

Desma called his name. He wasn't sure he had ever heard her use it before. Now she yelled it twice, telling him to come. Fast. Beside her, Desma's uncle, shirtless now, was standing with a pickax in his hands, but he was motionless, staring down at the earth he had just broken up. Her brother had stepped back, his face troubled. Sensing the very disasters he had been worrying about, Nicholas ran over the uneven ground.

But it wasn't any calamity he had feared. Indeed, it wasn't something he could possibly have anticipated.

Lying against the foundation of the tomb wall was what Nicholas first took to be a ragged bundle. He had already knelt beside it before he realized he was looking at cloth, faded and threadbare, but cloth nonetheless, embroidered in parts, and casing something white, and rodlike.

Bone.

He snatched out his brush and swept the dirt away, realizing before he finished the action that what he was seeing was no ancient relic. Desma's uncle had been frozen in the act of removing a spadeful of dirt some eighteen inches from the thing that Nicholas was looking at, and as Nicholas sat back in bafflement, the big man completed the action, slowly and deliberately, lifting the clod of sand-colored earth from the floor of the ancient tomb. It came away cleanly in a solid chunk, and underneath it was more bone, more fabric. The pale rod encased in cloth that had first caught their attention was a human arm. The newly exposed bone was the upper half of a human skull turned up to the sky, and on its head was the moldering remnants of a cap with a peak and two badges.

Unlike the rest of the remains, the badges were barely even stained by the dirt. They were metal. The upper one was in the shape of a heraldic eagle, its wings spread in geometrically even balance, its claws holding a circle dominated by a swastika. The other showed, as if in parody of the bones beneath it, a skull turned slightly away from the viewer with a pair of long bones crossed behind it.

Nicholas stared but Desma's uncle, whose face was ashen, spoke in a low, dead voice.

"SS," he said.

The truth of it was immediately clear to Nicholas.

"Huh," he said, the strangeness of the thing making him oddly calm, like he was watching himself from a great height. "We just dug up a dead Nazi."

"Someone is here," said Desma.

Nicholas turned to look past the tent to where a familiar blue Renault was racing up the dirt road, spitting stones. Caught up in his own confused excitement, it took him a moment to make sense of the way the car didn't so much park as simply stop at a wild angle, the driver's door kicking open. Professor Nerantzi spilled out, shouting and waving as she did so with obvious alarm.

Nicholas felt momentarily irritated. He had so much to say, so much to lay out! They had found a previously unrecorded Minoan tomb! They'd found a member of Crete's Second World War occupation force! There was nothing she had to say, no administrative nonsense about rights or funding or *anything* that he would allow to trump this most remarkable of moments.

He strode toward her, beaming widely, telling her to be prepared to be astonished, talking over her till she was right in front of him, red-faced and babbling, not listening to him. He reached for her, intending to take her over to the grave site, silence her with the evidence of her own eyes, but she shrugged his hand away.

"Shut up!" shouted Professor Nerantzi, her eyes shining. "Just stop talking and listen. There is a man on his way now. You need to go."

"What?" said Nicholas, still smiling through his bafflement. "What are you talking about?"

"There is a man coming to kill you. You need to run. Now."

23

BRADLEY SCOTTALINE
Buenos Aires, Argentina. November 3, 1947.

RADLEY SCOTTALINE, FORMERLY OF THE NATIONAL Intelligence Authority but reassigned to the newly minted Central Intelligence Agency on its formation two months earlier, opened his hotel room window to check the outside air temperature. He breathed the night in and pursed his lips, a sign only his most intimate coworkers knew meant satisfaction. A balmy sixty-eight degrees, or as near as made no difference. He had worried that the Argentine summer would be oppressive, that the nights would be sticky like they'd been in North Carolina when he'd been stationed there. He didn't like removing his suit jacket or sweating through his shirt.

Scottaline was lean and compact still, though it was almost two decades since the bare-knuckle boxing days of his twenties in Queens, before his Marine enlistment. He'd been tough then, he knew, but it was a superficial toughness, all physical fitness and a wild-eyed ferocity that scared his opponents almost as much as did his infamous upper cut. He'd drawn heavily on such things throughout boot camp and the nightmare that was the Guadalcanal campaign, and the latter had forged in him a mental toughness that had granted him an almost Zen-like calm under pressure. He needed that now far more than his ability to punch or block. It had been a strange year in which he had learned of new threats far more menacing than the Japanese bayonets and machine gun nests that had kept him awake through the tail end of the war. He had been told of these things because his superiors knew he would listen, and nod, and ask only the questions whose answers would directly assist him in getting the job done, and then he would say nothing. Ever.

It was a useful skill, silence, and one that would come in handy today. Scottaline strapped on his custom-made shoulder holster, inserted the newly cleaned High Standard HDM pistol with its long, built-in suppressor, and shrugged into his suit jacket. He buttoned it, checking the line of the fabric in his hotel room mirror, and, when satisfied that the bulge of the gun was minimal, picked up his briefcase and stepped outside.

The hotel was only a couple of blocks from the Casa Rosada, the presidential palace, from the balcony of which Perón and his movie star wife liked to wow the masses. Scottaline, who spoke passable, if poorly accented, Spanish, had watched the newsreels and was, as in so many things, unmoved. The wife, who called herself Evita, had recently gotten back from a European tour during which she had conducted herself more like a queen than anyone in the royal households she had visited. It was, he thought, no wonder the United States was watching skeptically, wary of the administration's leftist agenda and its economic expansion.

Scottaline had no real interest in politics. Some of his colleagues were obsessed with the reds at home and abroad—real and imaginary—but he knew that there were more perils in the world than communism. Hell, till a couple of years ago, the Russians had been their allies against the Nazis and the Japanese. The world had changed since the end of the war, though not, perhaps, as completely as people thought, and Perón and his cronies were hedging their bets. Which was, in a way, why Scottaline was here with his suit and his gun.

He walked to the Alvear Palace Hotel, keeping to the shadows without really planning to, circled the property once, taking in its Old World elegance without being in any way affected by it, and let himself in through an unguarded rear entrance. He checked his wristwatch: almost three in the morning. He knew his target's schedule to the minute. On the third floor he paused in the stairwell while a bellhop brought luggage into a gated elevator; then he moved with his customary no-nonsense deliberation down the hallway to room 17. He used the key he'd had duplicated the day before, supplied by an obliging maid for more money than she made in a month, and let himself in.

The room was quite grand by hotel standards, with a separate sitting room complete with writing desk. Quietly, efficiently, Scottaline checked that the suite was deserted, disconnected the wire to the panic button on the night stand, then took his seat at the desk with the lights out and waited.

Mueller arrived, on schedule, twenty minutes later.

Scottaline kept very still and silent, listening to the turn of the lock and the creak of the door, heard the man's sigh as he closed it behind him. Funny, he thought, how often he had heard just that sound from men entering hotel rooms alone, as if they had been some different public person until just that moment, and now relaxed into their private self.

A mistake, of course, though Scottaline was not here as an assassin. Not this time. He stayed where he was in the shadows, listening to the man as he ducked into the bathroom to urinate, then came out into the suite proper, loosening his tie and tossing his jacket onto the bed. Only then, moving merely a single finger, did Scottaline announce his presence by turning on the desk lamp.

Mueller spun, his face a mask of outrage, but the fear showing through in his eyes. In passable Spanish he demanded to know who Scottaline was and what he was doing there, but the CIA man waved the questions away and told him, in good, solid German, to sit down.

Now the outrage was gone, and Mueller was all caution and dread, his eyes flicking to the panic button. Scottaline pretended not to notice, watching the man's face as he inched along the bed and tried to look casual as he stretched toward it. If Scottaline had had much of a sense of humor, it might have struck him as funny.

"Mr. Mueller," he said, at last. "I represent the United States government. I have a proposal for you."

Mueller blinked, and his face seemed to positively ripple with the ideas chasing each other through his head. At the same time, his fake-casual reach toward the panic button stalled.

Smart, thought Scottaline, unsurprised. *He's weighing his options.*

"What do you want?" asked Mueller, switching to English but still trying to look affronted, like this might all be some absurd mistake.

"I'm here to offer you a job," said Scottaline. "A good job. And while the product would be going to different places, overseen by different people, and in pursuit of a slightly different mission, you'd be doing pretty much what you're doing now."

"I am a salesman," said Mueller. "My name is Gustav Prinz, I work for a car manufacturer here in . . ."

"No," said Scottaline. He spoke so flatly and with absolute, even bored, confidence, that Mueller hesitated, and in that moment Scottaline reached into the open briefcase and drew out a sheaf of papers. He consulted the top page and, with the same weary exasperation, read aloud. "Klaus Mueller, late of the V-2 rocket program, SS number 549 . . ."

"That's not me," said Mueller, panic in his voice, his face pale. "You have the wrong man."

"Right, you're Gustav Prinz and you build automobiles till three in the morning. That's quite a shift. Come now, Mr. Mueller. Let us not waste each other's time." As he spoke, he angled the lamp very slightly, so that the light revealed the long-barreled semiautomatic on the desk beside him. Again, Mueller's eyes flashed to the panic button, though the calculation was different now, more desperate.

Would help come in time?

"I already disconnected it," said Scottaline, nodding at the button. It was an act of kindness. No point letting the man wrestle with an option he didn't really have. "You have two choices. You leave with me, quietly, and are collected by a private car that will be at the back door in precisely seventeen minutes, a car that will take us directly to the airport. Or . . . well, better not dwell on that," he said, his eyes dropping to the pistol in a way that eloquently conveyed the reluctance but also the ruthlessness with which he would use the weapon if Mueller proved recalcitrant. The German was a big man for a scientist, fit-looking, but a fight would not go his way, even without the gun, and if he was half as smart as top brass thought him, he'd have figured that out all by himself.

"Why?" Mueller asked.

It was probably at least partly a stalling tactic, but there was genuine curiosity in his eyes. Perhaps it was vanity, a need to hear how valuable the United States thought him, Scottaline thought. Clever people were often like that, particularly if they worked outside the glow of public acclaim. He thought vaguely of Eva Perón, perfectly coiffed and dressed to the nines, waving from the balcony, half movie star, half saint, her adoring, worshipful subjects gazing up in rapture.

Funny, he thought again, *the things people want.*

Again, he reached into the briefcase and drew out a single eight-by-ten glossy black-and-white photograph. He pushed it across the desk face up and watched Mueller's face.

"One of yours?" Scottaline asked. "I mean, when I say *yours*, I mean . . . Well, you know."

The picture showed a ragged disk-shaped object about the size of one of the automobiles Mueller claimed to build. Its final form had to be guessed at because so much of the craft was stripped away, and most of what remained was twisted wreckage. It looked like it had been photographed under bright lights on the concrete floor of what might have been a warehouse or hangar. It was stamped "Top Secret," dated four months earlier and labeled simply "Roswell, New Mexico."

Mueller blinked but said nothing, his mind racing, his options few. Scottaline felt the presence of the stationary pistol exactly eight inches from his right hand, felt it burning into Mueller's consciousness as he weighed his next move.

"Why seventeen minutes?" he asked.

It was the first, the only surprise of the night so far, and Scottaline felt his lips purse in his version of a smile.

"What do you mean?" he asked.

"If you were going to kill me, why wait so long for the car to arrive? Clean up?"

Scottaline shook his head.

"Shoot and leave," he replied simply. "Better that way."

"So," said Mueller, almost calmed by this, as if they were debating the merits of an equation. "Why seventeen minutes?"

"Because I want you to come willingly. Because there are things you should know that will make you come, even if I put the gun away."

"What things?" asked Mueller, licking his lips. He was very still now, watchful as a lizard.

"You didn't just bring technical expertise with you to Argentina, did you?" said Scottaline. "You people with your *automobiles*. Nazis."

"I am not now and never was . . ."

"Yeah, no doubt, but the people you work for were and are, so let's not split hairs. My point is, our eggheads have been going over this little craft, its remote control systems, its means of propulsion, its flight characteristics, and they think that for all your skill with missiles and jets and shit, that you had help."

Mueller's eyes widened now. He was terrified. Partly he sensed Scottaline's change in mood, felt his implacable menace, but it was more than that, and Scottaline would have been prepared to bet all he had that the German was at least as afraid of his friends as he was of him. Mueller opened his mouth to deny or question, but the words wouldn't come, and when Scottaline just nodded and gave him a silencing gesture with his left hand, he shut up and sat there, sweat beading on his forehead, though the room was cool.

"I'm not going to say who that help came from," said Scottaline. "That's beyond my pay grade, and yours too, I suspect. But I will say this. You aren't the only ones getting help, and I think you'll find that our respective helpers don't like each other very much." He sat back to let this sink in, then began again, breezier this time, giving the man a break. "Let me tell you a story," he said. "You know, while you think. When I was a kid, my Uncle Jimmy had a bit of a farm in New Jersey. Beautiful place. I used to visit and play in the fields. It was another world to me. I was a city kid."

Mueller looked baffled, but he said nothing, giving Scottaline the floor to tell his story.

"But one of the things they had on the farm that we also had in the city," Scottaline continued, "was rats. Big ones. Nasty things. Now, my Uncle Jimmy had no truck with rats. They got into the produce and the animal feed, spread disease, destroyed half the produce of a corn field once, and contaminated what they didn't eat. Can't have that. So my Uncle Jimmy, he finds where they live. There were burrows, complexes of little tunnels in the bank of a creek that irrigated the land. Uncle Jimmy brings in twelve Yorkshire terriers. You know the ones?"

"Yes, "said Mueller, still wary. "I know."

"Little dogs, yeah? Cute, but fierce, pound for pound. Anyway, Uncle Jimmy sets them on the rats. They're little, see, so they can get into the burrows and chase the rats down. Of course, as soon as the rats realize what's going on, they start popping out of emergency holes like the place is on fire, and Uncle Jimmy and me are ready with spades, smacking them on the heads as they come up." Scottaline slammed the desktop with his open hand three times, and Mueller jumped. "Pop, pop, pop! Just like that. And the terriers come out, blood in their mouths, dragging the dead rats out, crazed by the taste of it, you know, so that as soon as they have pulled one out, they dove back in for more. Eighty-seven rats, we killed that day. Counted them myself. Cleared them out, end of problem."

"Why are you telling me this?" asked Mueller.

"'Coz that's only half the story," said Scottaline. "When we were done, my Uncle Jimmy turns the spade on the terriers. No nonsense. Pop, pop, pop. Just like he had done with the rats. Well, I was just a kid. I cried, begged him not to kill them. But he said, 'Work's done. Don't need 'em no more.' And that was that. I ran away while he did it, but he never apologized, never explained. To him, you see, the terriers were just tools. Like the spade. He brought them in to get rid of the rats, and once the rats were gone, he had no use for them."

"I don't understand," said Mueller, blanched and sweating. "You think I'm a rat?"

"No," said Scottaline, his lips pursed. "Or if you are, so am I. I think you and me, all of us in this world, are either rats or terriers, victims or hunters. And we fight tooth and nail because being a rat means that the terriers are the enemy and being a terrier means that the rats are the enemy. But here's the thing. Even if we're not the rats, we're still just tools. We're rats or terriers, but we're not the farmer, see? We kill the rats, and we think we'll be rewarded or something, but then along comes Uncle Jimmy. We're just tools. And when we're done, the spade is waiting for us."

Mueller blinked and his tongue flashed uneasily over his dry lips.

"You had help," said Scottaline again. "But you only got that help because Uncle Jimmy wanted to put the terriers to the throats of the rats."

"And if I come with you?"

"You'll still be a dog," said Scottaline. "But maybe, just maybe, when the farmer comes back with his spade, when he figures we've helped all we can and he has no further use for us, he'll find that what he thought was a terrier was actually a puppy, a baby version of something much bigger, see? A wolfhound, maybe. A mastiff. And while Uncle Jimmy wasn't looking, that puppy has grown up. Maybe that hound will never be big and mean enough to take the spade away, but you never know. He might have a fighting chance."

Mueller stared, then nodded and looked at his watch.

"Give me five minutes to pack," he said.

ALAN
Area 51/Dreamland, Nevada

ALAN SAW THE MASKED GUNMAN'S EYES WIDEN IN astonishment, but he was already thumbing off the safety and squeezing the trigger of Reynolds' Sig P320. It clicked.

Alan stared, aghast, pulling the trigger again and again, but the gun did not fire.

But that was not the only strangeness. The masked man was putting his weapon down and raising his hands, and Reynolds, who had been lying motionless on the hallway floor, was stirring and getting to his feet. Alan heard the snap of the door down the hallway and turned, the useless pistol still raised, to see Dr. Hayes and Montague, the tech, emerging and looking satisfied. Alan turned wildly back to the gunman, who had now removed his mask and who, seeing the continued shock in Alan's face as Reynolds got to his feet and gave him an apologetic look, said simply "Blanks."

Reynolds actually grinned and offered his hand, which Alan shook before he understood what he was doing.

"Wow," said Reynolds, suddenly less a staff sergeant and more a twelve-year-old boy meeting a rock star. "That was wicked cool."

Hayes touched her ear and said, "Disable alarm. All clear," then nodded up at a monitor camera by the flashing light and said, "That, Mr. Young, was more like it."

ALAN DIDN'T BOTHER TO HIDE HIS ANGER, BUT HAYES WAS unrepentant.

"You had already demonstrated that you saw any attempts to stress your system as manipulative fakery," she said. "Your gift wouldn't respond because you knew the circumstances were inconsequential. I needed to see what would happen if that changed. I'm sorry if you feel misled . . ."

"*If* I feel mislead?" said Alan, still smoldering.

"I misled you," said Hayes, owning the phrase but not apologizing for it, "but it was necessary."

"Really?"

"Of course it was. We had only your word, your impression to go on. Now we have proof." She hit a remote, and the whole scene in the hallway played itself out in black and white on the wall-mounted flat screen. "Interesting, isn't it? You can see it in your face. It's not so much thought as it is *need.*"

Her manner, so scientific and yet so genuine, stole his anger. He watched the tape, then settled into a chair, put his hands to his face, and blew a long sigh into them like a pitcher on a cold night.

"I still don't understand how it's possible," he said.

"Me neither," said Hayes, shooting him a sudden smile that made her look like a completely different person and took ten years off her. "Cool, huh? Watch this, right . . . *here*." On the flat screen the gun spun on the ground and then flew directly into Alan's hand. "Ho-ly shit," she added, transfixed.

"Okay," said Alan, "but you must have some idea. I mean, why research something you don't think is possible?"

"I know it's possible because I've seen it, and before this little demonstration I've heard of it many times. The fact that we don't understand something doesn't mean it isn't real. We have theories to explain the phenomena, but they are rudimentary, exploratory and complicated."

"Try me," said Alan. "Until I have some way of explaining what just happened out there I'm going to feel like a freak."

"Okay," said Hayes, sitting at the table and giving him a thoughtful look. "We're used to thinking of two distinct areas of experience: science, which describes the physical world, and metaphysics, which describes whatever is outside that, if there is anything. Metaphysics speaks to things that are essential to the lives of many people—questions of being and purpose, identity, religion, spirituality, and the pursuit of meaning—but such things are largely derided by the scientific community, not least because the proponents of metaphysics are often themselves hostile to science. 'Did God make the world?' is a metaphysical consideration, not a scientific one, and the insistence that God *did* make the world will generally be perceived as an antiscientific premise, unless the nature of that *making* is so nuanced as to be rendered almost metaphorical."

Alan shifted in his seat.

"Okay," he said, "but what does this have to do with me?"

"Belief in psychokinesis—the ability of the mind to influence the physical world, say a firearm," she said, nodding at the flat screen's endless loop of footage, "is generally considered a debased form of metaphysics: a kind of mysticism which, in the absence of respectable religious tradition to back it up, is easily dismissed as pseudoscientific fantasy. But there are various brands of pre-scientific mysticism that put mind over matter, seeing the power of consciousness itself as a way to affect the world—faith healing, say, or levitation. The concept of energy fields connecting all things is ancient wisdom in matters of religion. Think of the notion of *chi* or *ki* in various east Asian cultures: the life force that binds things together and sustains them."

"You sound like Yoda," said Alan.

Hayes smiled.

"True," she said, "and *Star Wars* certainly borrowed some ideas about the force from China, Japan, and other neighboring regions. But what if it isn't the stuff of space opera fantasy? What if we stopped viewing these ideas in the contemptuous terms of antiscience and the primitive? What if we were able to assimilate both positions as compatible within an expanded notion of physics, a unified theory, if you like, which recognizes that the metaphysical concerns of the human mind— including its so-called paranormal capacities—can coexist harmoniously in a strictly scientific notion of the universe?"

Alan suspected the question was rhetorical but he couldn't resist saying, "And is that likely to happen any time soon?"

"Have you ever heard of zero-point energy?" asked Hayes.

Alan shook his head.

"It's also called ground state energy," said Hayes. "According to quantum mechanics, it's an all-pervasive energetic field that is random, ambient, and fluctuating. What's interesting about zero-point energy is that it that exists even in so-called empty space. So instead of thinking of the universe as a collection of isolated particles, we have to view the universe as made up of continuous fields, the quanta and fermions of matter fields and the quanta and bosons of force fields."

"Okay, doc," said Alan, "you're losing me now."

"And I didn't even get to the uncertainty principle yet," said Hayes with another grin. "I'll spare you. Simply put, the idea means that everything is connected, not by matter, but still by physics, all things and their absence being linked by energy. The question then becomes not whether such random fluctuations might influence matter, since they evidently do, but how we view such metaphysical concepts as thought and consciousness. The mind clearly functions in physical terms— if someone cuts out pieces of your brain, your thinking is going to be affected." She smirked to show she was joking, but did not wait to proceed. "But what if the converse is also true, that the activity of the mind can affect the physical, since the mind's activity must necessarily interact with that zero-point energy connecting all things? In quantum terms the phenomenon is more than plausible, and the truly scientific approach is not to dismiss it as pre-scientific magical wish fulfillment, but to seek proof of its activity and analyze how it functions."

"I'm guessing we're not there yet," said Alan.

"Depends what you mean by *we*," said Hayes with another twinkling smile. "The scientific community as a whole, no. But one of the perks of doing research in secret is that your reputation doesn't depend on your being able to convince other people of what is clearly true. There is something wonderfully empirical about a place like this, Mr. Young. If something works, I don't have to know for certain why it works before we can use it. Think of the various flying machines you have piloted since you came to us . . ."

She caught herself the moment the words were out of her mouth, the shock of her error registering in the widening of her eyes and the rush of color to her cheeks.

"Wait," said Alan. "What? You're saying we don't under-stand how the Locust and the disk craft actually fly?"

Hayes shook her head vigorously, one hand gesturing vaguely. She looked flustered.

"Now, Mr. Young," she said, "You are putting words in my mouth. That's obviously not what I meant. Let's take a break for now, and we'll return to your psychokinesis exercise later. Right. I think we've made a lot of progress. Well done."

She rose as she babbled and managed to leave the room without ever making direct eye contact. For several minutes Alan just sat there, then left the room with no clear idea where he was going.

Not that it mattered. Unless he went outside—which would get him in serious trouble if he went without an escort—the corridors were all the same, long straight blank white walls set with white-noise speakers, and institutional carpet broken by occasional doors, the hallway turning in on itself like the passages of a maze. After a few minutes he found himself genuinely disoriented, and when he rounded the next corner he found it dead-ended in nothing.

Cursing softly under his breath, Alan retraced his steps, turned a corner, but found a T-junction he didn't remember seeing before. He went left, noting how the usually ubiqui-tous numbered doors had all vanished. Now he was just in corridors. The next turn brought him to another cul-de-sac and, muttering his frustration at the idiocy of the layout, he turned around again. But at the next corner the corridor ahead seemed to stretch on for miles, marked by unmarked and identical junctions every few yards.

This is nuts.

He paused, turning around, trying to make sense of where he was going, or where he had been, and as he did so, he heard the growl of something large and animal coming from one of the corridors ahead. He hesitated, disbelieving, then peered around the corner.

There was nothing there, but even as he stared the sound came again.

From the white-noise speaker? Or from somewhere out of sight?

It sounded louder this time, a rasping breathing that was almost a snarl.

"You really should find your way out," said a voice behind him.

He turned to find a black girl, a ballerina, maybe ten years old, looking at him. She was wearing a green tutu and cream-colored ballet shoes laced in a crisscross pattern up her shins.

"What?" he said. "Who are you?"

"My name is Gretta," said the girl. "I am the most elegant dancer in the world."

"What are you doing here?"

"Saving your life," said the girl matter-of-factly.

Alan stared, but the girl pivoted gracefully on her toes and walked away from him.

"Quick!" she remarked over her shoulder. "It's coming."

She rounded the corner into another corridor and, baffled, Alan blundered after her.

But when he got to the corner, the corridor was empty and there was no sign that the girl had ever been there. As he looked about, he heard it again, heavy, bestial breathing and lumbering footsteps.

Suddenly certain that he did not want to be caught there with whatever was coming, Alan turned on his heel and ran blindly down the closest hallway. The walls now were not plain white, but were decorated with the massive insignia of a two-headed ax, executed like a regimental badge in red and black. Having never seen it before, Alan was tempted to stop and consider it, but the animal noises seemed to be getting closer and, his heart in his mouth, he sped up, rounded another corner and almost collided with Dr. Imelda Hayes.

She gave him a puzzled look, processing the alarm in his face, the sweat on his brow. Alan, who realized immediately that the sounds of the great beast had disappeared completely, as had the strange ax-head symbols, hesitated, feeling stupid.

"Everything all right, Mr. Young?" said Hayes.

Alan glanced over his shoulder, but everything seemed normal. The hallway was just a hallway, not some baffling corner of a maze, the walls were white, the animal sounds gone. There was no sign of the ballerina.

"Yes," he said. "I'm fine. Could use a little water, is all."

Hayes gave him another curious look, but said "I'm sure that can be arranged," and led him back toward the testing room via the drinks machine. Alan said nothing, his mind full of what he had just experienced.

Or thought you experienced.

He thought of Barry's talk about Candy Cane, the stripper who had appeared to him on the base. They really ought to talk about this stuff.

"You sure you're okay?" asked Hayes. "I realize all this psych stuff is strange for a hardheaded military man like you, but it really is rather wonderful, and I'm sure you'll get used to it in time."

"Right," said Alan, trying to look serious rather than surprised and uncomfortable. It was better she thought he was a little freaked about his newfound abilities than the idea that he was having psychotic episodes in the hallways. "Yes. Just takes a little getting used to."

"I'm sure," she said, smiling.

But if Hayes thought that the excitement with the fake shooter would transform Alan's performance in the psychokinetic testing room, she was to be sorely disappointed. Over the next two days he went through the same set of tests with the scale, the marble, and the toy car to no avail. On the third day they tried—perversely to Alan's mind—to have him try to shift larger, heavier objects. The marble became a bowling ball, a twenty-pound dumbbell was added to the scale, and in a last and clearly desperate effort, the toy car was replaced by a real one, an Air Force Humvee that was sitting in neutral in an otherwise empty hangar. After the incident with the gun in the hallway, Alan had at last escaped the sense of stupidity, embarrassment, and failure that the tests had generated, but being videoed while staring at an immobile vehicle brought it all right back.

Over dinner with Barry that night, Alan came to a conclusion.

"I'm going to tell them," he said. "The tests are a waste of time. I'm not going to do them any more."

"Aren't they trying to give you more control of your ability?" asked Barry, putting his knife and fork down and pulling a fistful of candy from his pocket, which he spread on the table between them.

"Yeah, but they're not!" said Alan, helping himself to a Jolly Rancher. "If these were training exercises I'd be fine with them. But training implies getting slowly better, right? Taking a half second off your time, or lifting an extra three pounds. But these aren't doing that at all. I've made zero progress. They still feel like they are trying to see whether I can do something—even though they know I can—rather than helping me to do it better."

"Maybe they don't know how to do that."

"Okay, but how is that my problem? I'm wasting my time. I'm gonna tell them."

"That you want to do what instead?"

"Fly," said Alan. "I'm a pilot, remember? All this other stuff is just . . . getting in the way."

"There are lots of pilots, Alan. Not many of them can move bits of the world around with their brain."

"Well neither can I, apparently, unless I think my life is in danger."

"I know you like salt," said Barry, nodding at the shaker, as he unwrapped his third candy in under a minute, "but I think you might be overstating how much you need it."

"Yeah, yeah," said Alan. "You know what I mean. Apparently I have an ability. But I can't control it and nothing they have done so far suggests they know how to help me with that."

"So . . . what? You are about to quit so that you can spend the next three years meditating in some Kathmandu temple till you are at one with the universe?"

Alan had told Barry the way Hayes had discussed a bridge between the scientific and the paranormal. He shook his head meditatively.

"I just want to fly," he said. "Let the other stuff look after itself. I haven't left the ground in almost a month. I'm ready."

It had never occurred to him before that he *needed* to fly, to feel the separation of the ground beneath his aircraft, but he saw it now. Whatever else he was, Alan had found his natural element in the air, and being earthbound like this made him feel like a penned animal that dreamed of open spaces. In the Locust he had found still greater freedoms, and in the disk he had flown only once those freedoms had stretched till he had become a creature of air and spirit. Keeping him trapped on the ground, trapped in those little testing booths, a man of stone and clay, was more than imprisonment. It was torture.

"I don't know if any of the craft are serviceable yet," said Barry. "We lost a lot, and those that came back or were recovered took a lot of damage. Maybe they'll let you use the simulator. Keep your hand in."

Alan shook his head. After actual flying, the simulator felt like the psi-tests, lacking the urgency he felt he needed. He wanted to fly, not to pretend to.

"Maybe I should go back to the Marines," he mused. "At least then I could get back in a Harrier."

"I'm not sure that's an option, man," said Barry, popping another Jolly Rancher in his mouth and crunching it so loudly that Alan feared for his teeth. "I don't think this is the kind of gig you walk away from and go back to whatever your life was before."

Alan looked at him unwrapping another candy and nodded.

No, he thought. *Probably not.*

"What's with the candy?" he asked.

"I have no idea," said Barry stickily. "It's like an obsession. Started a couple of days ago. A craving, I guess you'd call it."

"Didn't know you had a sweet tooth."

"I don't. It's the damnedest thing. It's in my head all the time. Candy. I don't even really like it."

"Just trying to get in good with Candy Cane," said Alan, grinning. Barry winced and looked down. "What? Don't tell me you've seen her again?"

"Twice," said Barry. "Once as I was leaving the range, once in my quarters."

Alan whistled, still smirking, but Barry shook his head.

"It's not like that," he said earnestly, like it was important that Alan understood. "It's not a sex thing. I don't get it. I mean, she looks the same. Full stripper gear and all. There was even a pole."

"Like . . . *a pole?*"

"Yeah. In my quarters. She did this school-girly routine thing with the pole, and the lollipop. But it wasn't . . . It didn't make me . . . I just wanted candy!"

Alan peered at him. For a second he almost confessed his earlier confusion in the hallways when he had felt lost and in the presence of some large animal, the appearance of the strange ballerina, but he couldn't put it into words.

"You, my friend, need some serious down time," he said, adding half to himself, "We both do."

Coward, he reprimanded himself.

"No kidding," said Barry. He looked embarrassed, then pushed the heap of candy and wrappers away from him just as his phone rang. He checked the number.

"I have to take this," he said, getting up and away from the table, turning away and speaking quietly into the phone so that Alan watched him quizzically for a moment. It was unlike his friend to be secretive. But then it was unlike him to see imaginary strippers and cram his face with candy too.

And at least he told you about his visions. You can call people out for being secretive after you've told them about Gretta, the ballerina in the hallway.

An hour later, the blacked-out bus that normally returned him to his quarters took a different route from the usual. The road surface felt wrong and the journey was at least ten minutes longer than normal, so that Alan's wary anticipation had a chance to build. At one point they came to a halt and sat there, engine idling, then pulled forward slowly, carefully. When the bus stopped and the door opened, Alan found they had driven right into a familiar hangar, vast and featureless but flanked with control stations and observation decks.

They were in the Papoose Lake, S-4 facility.

Kenyon was waiting for him, flanked by techs in coveralls. At the far end was a great shutter that closed off another hangar in which Alan had first glimpsed the disk craft he had dubbed the sport model, but his eyes did not linger there.

They focused, with a quickening of his pulse on three black triangular craft: Locusts. Two of them were obscured with tool-cluttered work platforms and gantries. Cables and pressure hoses snaked over them, and one of them showed crumpled damage to the paneling below the cockpit while the finish had an erratic blue-black iridescence such as you get on a knife blade after it has been heated over a flame.

But the third.

The third had been pulled clear of the others. There were no laboring engineers with hard hats and blowtorches ministering to it. There were no panels hanging open like surgical wounds, exposing the vessel's innards, no blemishes on its pristine aerodynamic angles.

The third was ready to fly.

"Think you could log a few flight hours, Major?" asked Kenyon.

Alan dragged his hungry eyes off the ship and nodded.

"Where am I going?" he asked.

"Does it matter?" Kenyon replied with a knowing smile.

"No, sir," said Alan, smiling back. "It really doesn't."

25

MORAT
Near Fotinos, Crete

MORAT WASN'T A FAN OF DRIVING IN GREECE. THE MAIN highways were fine, but the back roads, the narrow avenues through towns, the sudden traffic circles, the chaos of central squares, and the random parking all got on his nerves. He set the professor's parked car as his destination and let the GPS handle the navigation so he could concentrate on not getting hit by some clown in a Škoda. Beyond the reaches of the town it got easier, if slower, and at one point there were actual goats in the road, but he felt controlled, like a virtuoso musician about to step out on stage safe in the knowledge that he had done all the practice he needed and could play every note beautifully in his sleep.

He was wearing a slim-fitting charcoal Caraceni suit and a white shirt without a tie, the sleek BMW's sartorial equivalent, both of which were indulgences that might attract attention, but that was okay. The job wouldn't take long, and if he had to ditch his look he had ragged jeans and T-shirts ready to go. If everyone was looking for a suave business type in a sports car, the scraggly beach bum on the bus got a pass. With luck he'd be on a flight to the mainland within a couple of hours.

Nicholas Tan's connection to the Mars woman still wasn't clear to him, but he was confident he could clear up that mystery before cleanup. Morat had found no sign of any link between them before they suddenly planned a trip together, and that almost certainly meant she'd hired Tan, or rather Quinn had, and the Mars woman was serving as facilitator. That was good. It meant that it wouldn't take much to break whatever minimal loyalty Tan felt toward them. Morat might not even have to kill him, but that seemed optimistic. Besides, he had that new gun to try out.

The only fly in the ointment was how little intel he'd been given about what he was looking for. He hadn't been able to decide if Rasmussen had just been playing his cards close to the vest, or if his employers didn't really know what was going on either, and he sure as hell wasn't about to wait for the rest of the team to arrive.

Guess you'll just have to find out for yourself.

Which was absolutely do-able.

When he spotted Nerantzi's blue Renault at the end of the road ahead, he slowed to a halt, then reversed down the hill twenty yards out of sight. He took the gun from the glove box and slipped it into his waistband under the suit jacket, putting a dozen spare rounds in his pockets, just in case, and got out. The heat was dry and oppressive, and he considered ditching his suit coat, but vanity won out. He popped the trunk and opened an attaché case containing a white drone quadcopter and its remote. He switched on the batteries in both, set the copter on the roof of the car, and pushed the throttle on the controller till the little rotors were spinning fast enough to raise the drone straight up. He flicked on its nose camera and a moment later an aerial image of the car receding as the drone climbed appeared on the handset.

He adjusted the handling a little, checked its balance, and looked up. It was already high, high enough that you probably wouldn't see it even if you were looking, and from here it was completely silent. He sent it speeding toward where the professor had parked, taking in the rugged area and looking for movement.

What the hell were they doing out here?

And then he saw them. Five people in an open area, some of the ground marked into squares, parts of the greenish undergrowth cut away, showing the sand-colored earth beneath.

Well, look at that.

They really were digging. There was no doubt about it. Mars had brought Tan over here and he was actually excavating, but for what? Morat knew that part of the reason why they had wanted Jerzy Stern's notebook was because he had laid breadcrumbs not just to information but to a thing that had been hidden in the Nevada desert, and Morat had guessed enough to know that his esteemed Maynard colleagues had failed to recover it. He had asked Rasmussen about it and the older man had just scowled and said it was "An object of great antiquity and considerable interest."

Which meant next to nothing, and at the time he had dismissed it as deliberate Maynard spookiness, misinformation of some sort, an area in which they had considerable experience and expertise. But now he wondered.

An object of great antiquity.

And here was Timika's little Asian lackey digging away . . .

Morat brought the drone directly overhead, then tried zooming in. He knew which was Nerantzi and thought he recognized Nicholas Tan, though it was impossible to be sure from above, but he had no idea who the other three were. One was a female in a red shirt. Not Mars. The other two were men.

That changed things.

They were huddled together, seemingly engaged in some animated conversation. Maybe Nerantzi was calling Tan on his supposed misdeeds, telling him she knew everything because she'd already met with Interpol. He'd deny it, but she'd expect him to, so that was okay. So long as they didn't get to talk for too long . . .

But then, quite suddenly they weren't talking at all; they were moving back toward the parked vehicles. It wasn't clear if they were fighting or what. They were moving toward him, but the group was diffuse, hard to read . . .

They were leaving.

Morat felt a tightening in his gut. After a long and leisurely pursuit, he suddenly saw his window of opportunity closing in a hurry. This was supposed to be recon, an opportunity to ask some leading questions, particularly about their little impromptu dig back there, but now . . . Now he wasn't sure and it felt like the situation was dissolving fast. They looked . . . what? Hurried, for sure. Anxious? Scared? It was hard to say, but it was certain that they wouldn't be there much longer, and if he wasn't careful they would walk right into him.

He hit the return command on the drone, set the remote down, and began walking purposefully up the hill, still not sure what his play would be. He drew the pistol and held it down against his thigh, switching on a pleasant smile. Smiles were like IDs, badges, police shields: they disarmed. They made you hesitate. You might see the gun, but for a second the other evidence seemed to override it.

A lot could happen in a second.

He rounded the corner as the five people reached their cars. Nerantzi saw him coming, and though he smiled and even raised his free hand in a cheery half wave, she turned back toward the others screaming, her face mad with terror.

"He's here!"

So she knew. He didn't have time to wonder how. But it changed everything. He kept walking, his pistol hand rising. He fired once at her—a tiny snapping sound a fraction of the volume of a champagne cork—and the passenger side window of the little Renault exploded. She dropped behind the car, though he wasn't certain he'd hit her. He reminded himself to conserve ammunition and not shoot at extreme range.

He liked the gun though. There was next no recoil, and the shot had been so quiet that the others looked more confused than scared. They weren't sure what had just happened. He kept walking, knowing they couldn't read his eyes behind his sunglasses as he assessed the threat level. The younger man looked Greek. He was fit, maybe eighteen or nineteen, and he was carrying a spade which, in about three seconds, might become lethal. Morat took two long strides toward him, pointed the PSS and squeezed the trigger.

Again the gun snapped but there was no muzzle flash, no rush of gas, smoke, or flame. The boy dropped, his T-shirt blossoming red over his breastbone. The woman in red started screaming hysterically, and now the bigger, older guy was rushing at Morat, his face dark and distorted with rage. He had something small in his hand, some kind of tool . . .

Morat fired once, catching him lower than he'd meant, but doing enough damage to neutralize the threat. The man crumpled, holding his gut, and Morat strode past him, kicking the tool—some kind of hand ax—safely out of reach, his eyes scanning for Tan.

There was no sign of him. The field itself had precious little cover, but there was an open-sided tent with a kind of workbench, and a couple of half-collapsed buildings. One was little more than a couple of waist-high walls and a lot of rubble. The other looked to have been a tiny church with a barrel tower, its top third fallen away. Morat turned and scanned the disorderly gravel patch that they were using as a parking lot but could see only the two men on the ground and the girl in red, who was crouching over them and shrieking. Tan could be back there, he supposed, but it was unlikely. Morat would have seen him as he walked. He must have come back this way . . .

He checked the tent, but there was nowhere to hide there, and he was already moving to the low walls of the abandoned animal pen, the PSS held out in front of him. Tan wasn't there, and now, as he calculated the distance to the ruined church, one of the cars at the end of the road fired noisily up.

The blue Renault. The Greek professor was apparently alive and looking to make her escape as the other woman attempted to bundle the wounded man into the back. There was still no sign of Tan, but Morat knew he didn't want witnesses fleeing the scene. Irritated, he gave up his search and turned back toward the cars. He would find the Asian guy after he had made sure of these others.

He fired as he walked, punching a hole in the Renault's trunk as it tried to turn into the road, even with the girl still attempting to manhandle the older man into the back. They were screaming warnings and orders in Greek. He kept walking, pistol raised. His shot hit the older man in the back, which would probably do for him, but the next went wide, and now the gun was empty.

He kept walking as he sprang the box magazine out, pulled another half dozen rounds from his pocket and thumbed them one at a time into the mag, finally slamming it into the grip with the heel of his hand. With any other pistol he wouldn't have even had to look, but he'd never worked with the PSS before, and his feet faltered as his eyes dropped to the weapon. When it was fully loaded and ready he looked up to find the girl in the red shirt almost on top of him and cutting wildly with the hand ax.

He fired rather than protecting himself, but he was off balance; the shot only grazed the woman's shoulder even as her swing with the ax found his. It hit hard, and for a second the pain was blinding, but there was no spray of blood, and as he shrank back, his gun hand clutched against the wound, he knew he'd avoided the blade's sharp edge. He had been lucky.

But he might not be next time, so he had to stop her from doing it again.

She wasn't thinking. She was just desperate with grief and fear and blood lust, all of which he could sidestep—literally, as it happened. She lunged with the ax but he pivoted once, stepping into her charge, and pulled the trigger of the odd, noiseless little pistol. She was inches away and staring into his face as her eyes registered first shock, then nothing at all.

She sagged to the ground at his feet and Morat stepped over her.

He fired twice more at the Renault and the rear window burst, but the car was pulling fast away, its rear passenger side door flapping wildly. Knowing he was beyond the range of the little handgun, he sent another two shots after it, suddenly irritated by the undramatic sound of the thing, and was unsurprised to see the car keep going. He didn't think he'd even hit it. There was only one upside to the mess, and that was that he was pretty sure Nerantzi was alone in the front. He would have seen if Tan had managed to get into the back.

Which meant he was still here.

Morat covered the remaining ground to where the vehicles were parked, stooping to look beneath them as well as peering through their windows. The two men were as close to dead as made no difference. No concerns there. But there was no sign of the Asian, and that meant he had somehow managed to run back through the site unseen. Morat scanned the area around the low rise where they had been digging and beyond to the ruined church. He had to be in there or hiding behind it.

Morat reloaded the PSS's damned six-shot magazine. The gun—perfect though it may be for dropping someone in a crowded place where you could get in close and then step away before anyone realized what had happened—was wrong for the job at hand, and he had been a fool to choose it. Giving his card to the Nerantzi woman had been a mistake too. He had no idea how she had seen through his cover so rapidly and completely, and he knew he was going to get an earful from Rasmussen if he didn't deal with her very quickly indeed, but Tan was the prime target. At least the archaeologist was now alone, so Morat might get some answers from him in the moments before he killed him.

But he had to find him first.

Pistol held in front of him, Morat began, for the first time since he had arrived in Crete, to run. Almost immediately he felt the rush of the hunt, all his previous frustrations turning into a hot and vengeful determination to find Nicholas Tan and deal with him. Morat knew nothing of the man, but he had been made to feel clumsy and stupid, and to a man like Morat, humiliation of that kind was a personal affront, and it worked on him like hatred. When the day began Morat had thought it possible that he could get what he needed without killing Tan. That was no longer an option. As his feet pounded the dusty ground he remembered vaguely telling himself only a few days before that he killed when he had to, but didn't enjoy it. Feeling the rush of hot, vengeful anger now as he ran, the eagerness and exhilaration that trailed it like the tail of a comet, he knew that had been a lie.

NICHOLAS
Near Fotinos, Crete

NICHOLAS WAS ALMOST BLIND WITH FEAR AND HORROR. Nothing made any sense. He had barely seen the man in the suit before the first shot, and he might not have even noticed that if it hadn't been for the glass of the car window breaking. He had never heard a gun before. He figured they'd be like in the movies, like cannons. This had been little more than a click.

A click that killed a man. Probably two, he couldn't be sure. He had seen them go down and he had run.

It was surreal, dreamlike, the elegant man in the dark suit and shades strolling around, his little toy gun that had barely made a sound but left bloody holes in the men Nicholas had been working alongside only minutes before . . .

And Desma. The girl who had been transformed by their find, all her surliness mutating into shared joy and excitement . . .

He couldn't think of that. Not yet.

He had run away from the gunman, away from the nightmare, thoughtlessly, unseeing, back into the field, weaving around the few dwarf olive trees and ducking into the shade of the little chapel.

There was nowhere else to go.

The ancient door was ajar but the stone threshold was weedy and thick with dirt. Nicholas ducked inside, and found himself in a dim hallway with cracked terracotta tile on the floor, and white unevenly plastered walls, much of which had fallen away, revealing thin irregular bricks behind. To his right was what he assumed was called the sanctuary, a tiny white-plastered nave no more than twenty feet long with a vaulted roof, open to the sky in places, and narrow glassless window high up in the walls. The body of the chapel was heaped with ancient, moldering chairs. At the far end was a stepped altar on a wooden platform floor with a stone lattice screen, surmounted by a gilded dome, the paint chipped and fading. He might crouch hidden there for a moment behind the remains of the screen, but it would be only a moment: two steps onto the wooden platform and the killer would see him. Up on one of the window ledges something stirred and Nicholas spun, panicked, as a dove or pigeon rose into the air with a noisy beating of wings, exiting through a gap in the rafters.

There was nowhere to hide in here, and no way out if the gunman came between him and the door.

Across from the main entrance was a tight staircase going up into the little tower. Nicholas had seen enough to know there wouldn't be much up there, but he could think of nothing else. All he wanted to do was get away, to retreat, like a kid going under the bedclothes as if that would keep the monsters out . . .

He crossed the hall and started up the narrow spiral. There was no rail anymore but the steps were not much broader than his shoulders. The tower, like the rest of the church, seemed to have been built at a quarter scale, more a model than a real place where people came to worship.

It was only twenty stairs to the top. There had once been a belfry here, but it was gone and the tower's cupola had long since collapsed. The wall at the top of the stairwell was just high enough to hide him, but the rest had crumbled away, as had most of the floor, whose joists were bare and riddled with wormholes. Only the center where the bell had hung looked solid and sturdy still. It had been built out of one of the chapel's main buttresses to hold the weight of the brick assembly between which the bell had hung. That might give him a little cover, but reaching it meant a long step, almost a leap, over rotten floorboards. Nicholas pressed himself against the most complete fragment of wall and shifted carefully, listening to the thudding of his heart, till he could just about see down and across the excavation field without showing more than an inch or two of his face.

The blue Renault belonging to Professor Nerantzi was speeding away. There were bodies at the end of the road—Desma's brother and uncle, both motionless; Desma herself on the edge of the field, still and face up. The man had shot her at point-blank range so it was delusional to hope she might still be alive, but until this moment Nicholas had held on to the possibility like it was the thread that might lead him out of the labyrinth. Looking at her now, the angle of her body, the blood pooling darkly in the dry earth beneath her, he knew she was gone, and the thread broke. For a split second he saw her again in his mind's eye, her usually morose and resentful face split by rapture as she realized what they had unearthed in the field below him, and then his attention was on the gunman again.

He was looking at the cars, looking *around* the cars, looking *for* him. The man had given up chasing the blue Renault. Safe in the assumption that Professor Nerantzi was surely speeding to safety, a little voice in Nicholas's head whispered to the man with the pistol, "Go that way. Walk to your car. Go back down the road. Get out of here before the police arrive . . ."

But the killer didn't go. He turned to look across the field, his eyes unreadable behind the shades, and then he was coming, walking purposefully toward the church, breaking into a steady, purposeful run. Nicholas shrank back against the wall, fighting down a breathless sob.

There was nowhere to go. If he went down now, he'd probably meet the gunman in the doorway. So what was he to do?

Stupid. Stupid.

He shouldn't have come up here. Shouldn't have entered the church at all. He should have just run, lost himself in the trees, kept going till he found a farmhouse . . .

This poor hiding place on the tower would afford him no more than a few seconds of freedom. Then what? Fight? Nicholas had never thrown a punch in his life. Even if he had, the killer had a gun . . .

He could hear him now, his footsteps on the hard ground slowing as he reached the church door. He'd lead with the gun, checking behind the jamb like they did in the police shows, moving quickly, pistol already aimed and ready. He would be inching into the tiny chapel now, scanning the heaped bits of furniture for someone who had snuck in among it.

Maybe he should have done that. If he'd been spotted down there, he would die, but maybe he would have gone unnoticed. Whereas up here, there was literally nowhere to hide. Nicholas's only advantage, he figured, was his location.

Maybe he could kick at the man's face as he came up the tower . . .

But the assassin would be ready for that. He would catch his foot, twist it, pull him down, putting two bullets in his belly in the process . . .

Maybe he should just wait for the guy to start exploring the church, then jump from the tower and run. It was only twenty feet. Not enough to kill him. But, he thought, that was more than enough to sprain or break his ankle, leave him crawling as the gunman came out to find him . . .

Perhaps the other side of the tower would be easier to climb down. He reached out a cautious foot, but he felt the wooden beam give significantly before he had put his full weight on it. He snatched his foot away, but not before the rotten timber cracked and collapsed as if he'd dropped a cannonball on it.

In the church below a new shaft of sunlight would be picking out the motes and splinters of the useless timber as they fell, in case the noise had not been enough to give his position away . . .

He was dead. There was nowhere to go. Nothing to be done. The man in the church below had already shown himself to be ruthless and professional, a stone-cold killer who—for reasons Nicholas couldn't possibly guess—had come to destroy him.

The sheer baffling absurdity, the pure ridiculousness of the situation hit him like the booming of the church's long absent bell. He was going to die without any clue as to why. He had come here in some vague search for Atlantis, for tenure, and—he suddenly realized—to spite his idiot colleague Jarret, who thought he should be writing about fucking Ming dynasty China or some damn thing . . .

It was almost funny.

But it also made him suddenly angrier than he could remember being.

Nicholas Tan looked up at the remains of the assembly from which the bell had hung, wishing wildly that it still had been there and he could have set it ringing in alarm, though he doubted there was anyone but the killer to hear and come running. It was as if the universe had conspired to give him no options at all, and that idea, the injustice of it, stoked his anger. Suddenly Nicholas was furious, and with the wild conviction that comes to you when you have nothing else to lose, he balled his fists to fight.

The bell had swung between two towers of bricks, pulled presumably by a rope that went through the floor to the little vestibule below, pivoting back and forth from an iron bar. The bell and ropes were gone, but the bar, orange and pocked with rust, but solid and thick as his thumb, was still there.

Maybe if he could get it out . . .

He had to step out across the treacherous wooden beams to the brick base of the belfry assembly, an unnerving and desperate stride that left him clinging to the surviving brick structure with his left arm while his right reached for the iron rod and tried to work it free. It was rusted in place. A shorter bar that was welded to one end of the rod stuck out horizontal to the ground, like the half hilt of a sword, and ended in a loop where the rope had been attached. Nicholas grabbed it and pulled, hoping the extra torque would loosen it. He felt the metal give fractionally, but it didn't come free.

Footsteps echoed on the tower steps. He was coming. Slowly and deliberately as death itself, the gunman was climbing the stairs.

Nicholas was a trapped rat. A gasp that was almost a sob broke from him as he pulled on the iron bar. It did not move. He shook it to no avail, listening to the gritty scrape of shoes in the stairwell. He let go of the brick stack with his left arm, seizing the iron loop with both hands and pulling on it till his entire body weight was hanging from it.

With a metallic groan, it broke free of its rusty mooring without warning, turning abruptly till it pointed straight down, and in that instant Nicholas felt himself falling. For a moment his feet fought for purchase on the brick collar surrounding the belfry, and then he was safe and dragging the iron rod from its housing like he was unsheathing a claymore.

He turned to the top of the spiral staircase in time to see the short black barrel of the pistol leading the killer up. He shrunk behind the brick stack of the belfry, hefting the iron rod, unsure whether the stinging in his eyes was sweat or tears, and hesitated.

He heard his attacker reach the top steps, and bent lower. The belfry structure was only just head height. Nicholas listened, his mind piling fury on top of fear till he was seething with it. He forced himself to wait, left hand gripping the corner of the brick stack, feet inching apart for balance on the circle of bricks around the belfry, right hand taut with the weight of the iron bar, gripped below the angled bracket with the loop. He held it behind him like he was drawing back the string of a longbow, his body stiffening with exertion and anticipation.

And then he moved.

He lunged around the belfry assembly toward the stairwell, still holding on with the fingers of his left hand, but stretching out, reaching with the poker-like weapon in a single downward slashing motion. He couldn't see his target till he had already begun his attack, and he saw too late that the assassin was still in the spiral. The sweep of the iron bar was too short to reach his head, but it caught his gun hand in the instant the pistol fired.

Brick exploded in a hail of sharp, hard flecks inches from Nicholas's face, but the shot went wide, and then the gun was out of his grip. The man in the shades clutched at his hand, then reached behind him as Nicholas gathered to swing again and came up with a blade, cruel-looking and bright in the sun. He lunged with it, and Nicholas, panicking that his plan hadn't worked first time, ducked back behind the belfry.

He had lost his moment of advantage.

The killer's gun had skittered across the floor and was lodged in a hole in the ruined floor of the tower, inches from falling, but he had looked more than comfortable with the knife in his hand. He would close fast, get inside Nicholas's swing like he was hugging him, and he would bury the blade in his heart up to the handle . . .

With no other option, Nicholas lunged out again, swung again, but the suited man knew he was coming. He ducked, raised his left arm to deflect the iron bar, and stepped into the attack exactly as Nicholas knew he would.

The knife stabbed once.

Nicholas doubled up, anticipating the pain, but in that instant the floor opened up like a trapdoor. The killer's knife thrust had been expertly balanced with a single step toward him, the kind of step that would give the stabbing all the force it needed, but the weight was more than the ancient joists could bear.

In a crash of dust and fragments, the floor gave way and the killer went down through the tower.

After the explosion of noise and action there was a sudden, uncanny silence as Nicholas clung to what was left of the belfry, barely able to believe he was still alive and unharmed. He looked through the hole to where the man had landed on the hard floor of the vestibule. He was, for the moment, still.

Nicholas looked around, spotted the gun where it lay half suspended in the remains of the wooden boards, and reached for it with the tip of the metal rod. A second later he realized the obvious truth—that he was as likely to dislodge it as hook it, and if it fell, he would basically be rearming the man who had brought it to kill him. He left it where it was.

The body below still hadn't moved, but Nicholas doubted the man was dead, and that made going down the narrow stairs more than a little unnerving.

But it's that or stay here till he wakes and comes back up . . .

Put like that there was no logical argument to make and Nicholas needed all the logic he could get right now. He made the half jump across to the stairs, took a breath, and descended the tight spiral, the iron bar held in front of him like a blazing torch.

For an agonizing moment he was on the spiral, unable to see the body, whether the killer was coming to, getting to his feet . . .

And then Nicholas was down and running.

At the bottom he did not even check the body. The terror of being close to him again was too much. He turned and fled out of the church and across the field toward the road, running hard.

The bodies were still there. Somehow that was a surprise, and he felt the horror of their deaths again, even as he kept running past them and onto the dirt road. He didn't know where the keys to the truck were and he wasn't about to hunt for them. He ran past the parked vehicles and on toward the main road. He would be at the closest village in minutes . . .

In fact, he never made it that far. Professor Nerantzi had raised the alarm before she had come to warn him, and Nicholas rounded the first bend in the road to see a white car with a blue stripe, lights flashing, siren blaring, as it sped toward him. There was at least one more behind it.

Nicholas stepped to the side of the road, nodding, pointing and shouting incoherently, all his composure and deliberation melting away at the blessed opportunity to turn things over to someone better qualified to deal with it. As one car kept going toward the site, the other slowed and an officer climbed out, talking calmly into his radio.

"He's still there," Nicholas babbled. "In the church. And get an ambulance!"

"Someone is hurt?" asked the cop.

"Three," said Nicholas, almost collapsing under the truth of it. "Dead, I think. Three people."

And as the officer's face changed and he began barking into his radio with none of his previous professional detachment, Nicholas sank into a crouch on the edge of the road and buried his face in his hands.

He was still there a half hour later, by which time the road was crammed with police and emergency vehicles, their lights cycling so that even under the bright Cretan sun the world seemed to flicker as if he was trapped in a dream.

Professor Nerantzi was sitting beside him, saying nothing. She had returned with one of the police cars, her arm bandaged where it had been cut by the shattered glass of her car window. She had been made small by shock and grief. Prokopius, the elder of the two men who had been working the site with him—Desma's uncle, he reminded himself— had been stabilized and would probably recover, but Dimitri, her brother, had been whisked away to emergency surgery, and his chances looked bleak. Desma, who Nicholas had just started to get to know but who had been a student of Professor Nerantzi's for two years, had been pronounced dead at the scene.

At the scene was one of those cop show phrases that Nicholas's mind had produced to try to explain the madness around him. It only increased the aura of unreality.

The police had found no one in the church. They had located the gun and impounded the car he had used, but the man himself had walked away, apparently cutting through the ragged fields and olive groves northeast of the site. The police thought he wouldn't get far, said they had a search team already assembled and at work. A few minutes later a helicopter buzzed the steep hillside in low, wandering loops. They'd find him soon enough. They were confident of that.

Nicholas nodded vaguely, picturing the killer's cool, professional efficiency as he went about his business. When Professor Nerantzi leaned against him, he put an arm around her shoulders, secretly relieved that she did not seem to think him to blame for what had happened.

"Crete is not a large island," she said. "He's on foot and hurt. They will catch him."

Once more Nicholas nodded but said nothing, turning away so she would not see the doubt in his eyes.

HENRY "HANK" BABISH
Johnston Island, July 9, 1962

ENRY "HANK" BABISH CHECKED HIS CONSOLE AND
crossed his fingers under the desk. There was just over
a minute till launch. He risked a look toward Doolan,
but his superior was focused entirely on the readout in
front of him, which was probably as well. It was too late to
argue now, and besides, Babish had been making his feelings well known for months. He was now in the curious
position of hoping to be wrong.

Babish had been assigned to Operation Hardtack at the
Pacific Proving Grounds on Enewetak Island four years
earlier, some thirteen hundred miles east of their base for
today's operation, and had been present for the Yucca test as
well. The purpose of the highly classified experiment was to
examine the effects of detonating a thermonuclear device.

A bomb, in other words.

Back then they had used a helium balloon to get the thing aloft, releasing it from the deck of an aircraft carrier after they'd figured out that the movement of the ship could counter the effects of the high winds that tended to shred the balloon when the bomb was launched from solid ground. The Yucca test effectively initiated a new subset of Hardtack, operation Fishbowl, in which the bombs were all exploded at high altitude. Yucca was a 1.7-kiloton device rigged with various fail-safes, including a system triggered on contact with seawater, which would destroy the electrical components inside before the nuclear weapon could be armed, and another guaranteeing that the device would sink rather than floating on the ocean surface. Babish remembered laughing about that with the engineers, making some crack about making damn sure the Russkies didn't snatch up their high school science project before they had got it working.

Science project. Jesus.

But that was how it had felt. A bit of a game, a competition. One played for very high stakes, of course, but still, from his perspective, a challenge and, if he was being absolutely honest, kind of fun. He remembered the growing sense of anticipation during the three and a half hours of the balloon's ascent, and the way their excitement had been blown away not by the explosion itself, but by the shock wave that hit the carrier three minutes and sixteen seconds later.

But the tests had continued. Next had been Operations Teak and Orange, bigger bombs launched by Redstone missile from the Marshall Islands, where Babish was now, explosions that could be seen lighting the sky from Hawaii, almost a thousand miles away. They began as a yellow fireball turning through orange to red as they expanded, and from their center rose a great cloud that lingered for almost half an hour. But it wasn't just the light that gave the tests away. Long-range communication all over the Pacific was disrupted and commercial aircraft lost contact with their ground controllers.

This stemmed from what the British called "radio-flash," an electromagnetic pulse generating current and voltage surges. Babish had seen the effects overwhelm the oscilloscope during the Yucca test and had been arguing ever since that the scale of the pulse generated by the bombs was far in excess of anything they had anticipated. Moreover, the readings were significantly different from the results found in low-altitude tests, in matters of both charge and polarization. Babish had said so till he was blue in the face, but Doolan had dismissed the effects as an anomaly of wave propagation.

Now they were trying again. Operation Starfish Prime, it was called, and the bomb was now 1.44 *megatons*, almost a thousand times more powerful than the Yucca device.

In thirty-eight seconds.

Babish checked his instruments. This was the third attempt to launch the test bomb by way of the Thor rocket. The first, code-named Bluegill, had been blown up in flight on June 2 when radar lost its fix on the vehicle, though it later turned out that the missile had never veered off course. On June 19 the second, Starfish, had run into difficulties a minute after takeoff, when the engine ceased firing and the rocket began breaking apart. The missile and warhead were blown up, and the debris fell all over Johnston Island and in the surrounding waters, contaminating some of it with plutonium.

It was no wonder he was nervous.

Nineteen seconds.

He shifted fractionally in his seat, pressing the headphones to his ears with one hand, eyes fixed on the display in front of him.

Twelve, eleven, ten . . .

Out on the launchpad, the great rocket smoked with expectation. For all the measured, military tones of the voices around him, you could cut the atmosphere with a knife.

Six, five four . . .

The base of the missile lit up the night, a bright, flat flare leaking out and taking shape as the rocket rose and the gantry up the side leaned away with almost casual precision. A murmur of relief rolled through the control room as the rocket began its ten-minute climb, but there were no cheers, not yet. Babish chewed his nails absently, watching, listening for signs of disaster.

For a long time, nothing happened. Then, at an altitude of some 680 miles, the missile slowed, hung for a moment in the exosphere, turned, and began to fall.

Another long, watchful silence followed as everyone in the installation prepared for the detonation.

It came as the missile plummeted through the thermosphere at a height of 250 miles above the earth, thirteen minutes, forty-one seconds since launch, generating a brilliant and momentary white flash directly over the island base. Those observing at windows watched through heavily smoked goggles, but the flash vanished as quickly as it had come, being replaced by a smoldering red disc that crowded the sky. From its heart came an expanding rush of red and white light that blossomed like thrown streamers over the next half minute or so. Within a few more minutes, the red glow had faded to nothing, and there was no sign in the sky that anything at all remarkable had just happened. The entire event took place in total silence.

It was quickly clear to Babish, however, that he had been right. The electromagnetic pulse was staggering in magnitude, blowing past all the equipment designed to measure and analyze it.

"Woah," he said.

Amidst the cheering that had finally broken out, Doolan looked over at Babish and caught his expression.

"What?" said his supervisor, wariness breaking through his smile.

"The EMP is off the charts," said Babish. "Massive."

Doolan moved fast, half vaulting the back of his chair to see what Babish was seeing.

"You're recording all this?" he asked.

"With what? Everything is blown out."

"There are monitors that went up with the rocket."

"They'll be in no better shape than what we have here."

"Will people notice?"

"We've lost all radio communication," said Babish, snatching off his headset. "I've no idea how far this will go, but don't be surprised if you get reports of blown telephone and microwave links as far away as Hawaii."

"That's nine hundred miles!"

"Yeah," said Babish. "I know where it is." He was managing not to say *I told you so*, but it wasn't easy. "Not just radio communications either. I'll bet you're going to see blown streetlights, burglar alarms set off, power grids disrupted . . ."

"No," said Doolan, but it wasn't an argument so much as a plea, and it sounded desperate. "This was a top-secret test."

"I think the huge flash in the sky might have tipped people off."

"Well, obviously, they know what we're doing out here, but they need a sense of security. I don't want Hawaii to start feeling like it's the next Hiroshima. Streetlights? You're serious."

"As a heart attack," said Babish.

Babish's phone rang.

"Well, said Doolan, "something's working."

"Double-shielded wiring," said Babish, reaching for the receiver. "Hello?" The voice on the other end of the line was staticky and inconsistent. "Say again," said Babish, putting a hand over his free ear. "I can't hear you."

The speaker was repeating his message over and over. "This is Major William Keen, Naval Space Surveillance System in Dahlgren, Virginia. Repeat. This is the Naval Space Surveillance . . ."

"Yes, I got you," said Babish. "Sorry about that, Major Keen. We're having some technical issues here, but I can hear you."

"Yeah, we're having some issues too," said the voice, unamused. "Like we think your little experiment just fried a low Earth orbit satellite or two."

Babish didn't know what to say. For a second there was only dead air on the line and Doolan looking terrified three inches from his face.

"You have good data on that, sir?" asked Babish.

"Six receiving stations and a network of Baker-Nunn cameras," said Keen, "not to mention some very pissed-off Brits. Sounds like pretty good data to me. And that's only minutes after your little science experiment."

The phrase, coming as it did right out of Babish's own thoughts, knocked him off balance, but he recovered.

"Sorry to hear that, Major. I'm sure that if your equipment has suffered any negative effects they will be quickly remedied. We think there was a larger than anticipated electromagnetic pulse, which may disrupt some radio and electrical systems, but it should pass, with a reboot if necessary. No other actions on our part should cause further disruption to your systems."

Doolan nodded encouragingly. That was the right tone to take.

"It's not all our systems," said Keen. "Like I said, at least one was a British satellite but there's also . . . Hold on." The line went staticky again, but this time it sounded less like radio interference and more like someone holding the receiver against his shirt while he talked to someone else. When Keen came back on he sounded different; rattled. "Yes," he said. "So. We may have a problem."

Babish, already still and tight in his chair, stiffened further.

"What's that, sir?" he managed.

"It seems . . ." Again, the pause, the uneasy, uncertain note in the voice. "It seems like that electromagnetic pulse has done more than stop some satellites from transmitting. Our sensors suggest that one of them is coming down. Now."

"What?" gasped Babish. "Where?"

"Not clear," said Keen, his voice tight.

"How is that possible? You knew where it was."

"Not exactly," said Keen. "It wasn't actually on our radar till it began to drop. We don't know where it was. We don't know *whose* it was or what it was doing. To tell you the truth"—never had Hank Babish heard a composed military man so clearly out of his depth and off script—"we have no idea what the hell it is or was. We just know it's coming down."

28

JENNIFER
London, England

I T HAD BEEN YEARS SINCE JENNIFER HAD SET FOOT IN THE British Museum. At least a decade, she thought, and probably longer. She knew she had visited as a girl on some school trip or other but in later years her political earnestness had rather gotten in the way of her enjoyment of a place she had been fond of referring darkly to as *The Imperial Treasure Trove: Gallery 1, Stuff We Nicked. Gallery 2, More Stuff We Nicked. Gallery 3, Stuff We Grabbed When No One Was Looking. Gallery 4, Stuff We Took While Everyone Was Looking But Couldn't Stop Us* . . .

And so on.

She smiled a little ruefully at the thought, but her younger self wasn't far wrong. The imposing Classical façade of steps and columns and the intricate frieze set into the pediment made it look like you were entering a temple, though what exactly was being worshipped therein was unclear.

Empire, said Jennifer's younger self. *Victorian Britain at its most rapacious, hoarding the artifacts and cultural properties of whoever it colonized.*

The whole world seemed represented, and key parts of the collection had been the subject of legal bids for restitution: the Rosetta Stone, for instance, by Egypt, a series of bronzes demanded by Nigeria, thousands of manuscripts and paintings claimed by China and, most infamously, the so-called Elgin marbles, pilfered from the Acropolis in Athens in the early nineteenth century and clutched fiercely to the imperial breast in memory of former potencies ever since . . .

But all this she had thought before. What she now felt as she climbed those steps and made her five-pound donation was something far less clear, images and impressions without logic or organization, and all touched with the coppery taste of adrenaline. Her excitement was confused and edged with something like fear as she thought of the image on the bus, the golden sphere with the bees so like the image she had been dreaming about.

None of this made sense.

She didn't know why she was there, why she felt it was so important, so essential, that she saw that exhibition.

Deacon was looking for somewhere to park, so she was alone with the crowds, though at this time there weren't many still queuing to get in. She followed the signs to the special Minoan exhibition and filed in, her eyes sliding over the cases of terracotta figurines of bare-breasted women holding snakes in each hand, the vivid frescoes of dolphins and ringlet-haired men vaulting over bulls, focused and moving swiftly, rudely through the throng as if drawn to the little glass box that contained the original of the poster image she had seen on the side of the bus. It pulled her like a magnet vibrating in her mind.

The thing itself was small and exquisitely made, a pendant a few inches across molded in gold and worked with filigree: a pair of bees, their segmented abdomens touching, their legs gripping the intricate circle in the center, their heads together, large insect eyes ringed with tiny spheres. Their wings spread out behind them like heraldic emblems and from each a rod wrapped in fine wire suspended a circle, matched by a third, which hung from the point where the tips of their abdomens—right where their stingers would be—made contact. Above their heads was a tiny spherical cage containing a ball of gold.

It was approximately 3,600 years old.

And it sang to her.

In fact it hummed in her ears as if the bees were alive and buzzing, and Jennifer stood in awe before it, lost in its age and the strangeness of its familiarity. She put both hands on the heavy glass of the case, and as she did so she felt a pulse of something like energy pass through her. It tipped her head back and she gasped, sucking in air as she felt the power of the thing.

The room swam and her eyelids fluttered, then closed. In her head she saw the bees, heard the swelling sound like a swarm all around her, and then there was light, a patch of clear blue sky framed by a ragged hole. She was looking up, and as the image cleared she saw what she felt sure were the broken edges of something brown and gray that might have been wood, and above that the uneven, broken fragments of a plastered wall now reduced to a ruined crag.

A moldering stone tower.

Again she gasped for breath, but then the pain hit her. It slammed into her shoulders and all down her right side. Her right elbow shrieked with it, and the base of her spine groaned with a deep and powerful agony so that she cried out where she lay on the hard, stony ground, and could not get up.

"Excuse me, Miss?"

She gritted her teeth against the pain but it coursed through her back like molten steel, and try as she might she could not move. There was only the sky up there, above the shattered church tower and the hole in the floor through which she had fallen.

"Miss? Please take your hands off the case."

Through the buzzing of the golden bees she heard the voice drifting nonsensically into her head, but she could not make sense of it. She had to put all her strength into getting up, getting out of this place before they found her . . .

The hand on her shoulder startled her back to the museum. A discreetly uniformed woman was standing next to her looking stern. Her hands were on Jennifer's arm.

Jennifer was not on her back. There was no sky above her, no fractured church tower.

She was in the British Museum where she had come with Deacon to see . . .

"I'm sorry," she said, vaguely, taking her hands off the cool glass of the case. It contained an ancient piece of gold jewelry. Nothing more. The sound in her head had gone, and she suddenly did not know why she had come, or what she had hoped to achieve, though the strangeness of what had just happened to her vibrated throughout her body. She shifted, testing to see if the pain had really gone, and flashed her eyes to the ceiling, as if half expecting to see the tower and the sky above . . .

"I'm sorry," she muttered again, stepping back, her baffled eyes sliding between the exhibit and the docent who had reprimanded her.

"Are you all right, Miss?" asked the woman, the hardness in her face turning into something else. "Would you like to sit down?"

Jennifer shook her head.

"No," she muttered, stepping away from the display case, suddenly uneasy and wanting to be gone. "I just . . . No. Thank you."

And then she was walking out as fast as she could, keen to put as much distance between herself and the peculiar artifact as possible.

▼　　▼　　▼

SHE DIDN'T TELL DEACON WHAT HAD HAPPENED, NOT BECAUSE she was being secretive, but because she didn't understand it. When she tried to line up the words in her head they made no sense at all. Combined with her obvious distress, they made it sound like she had suffered some kind of psychotic episode.

So she said nothing.

Deacon, ever the diplomat, accepted her bland assurances that she was fine and drove her home in silence, turning on the radio to catch the football results as they hit the highway. Jennifer said nothing all the way home, then thanked him for driving and his help in the meetings. Then, saying she had a headache, she excused herself for the evening.

Jennifer lay on her bed for an hour, her eyes closed. When her cell phone rang she considered ignoring it, but when she saw who was calling, she knew she had to answer.

"Hi," said Elina Nerantzi. She sounded somehow older and impossibly far away. Worse, she sounded broken.

Jennifer sat quickly up, all the fog in her mind burning off as panic gripped her.

"What's happened?" she asked.

Elina told her about the fake Interpol man who Timika had called Morat, about the dead student and her family members who were in intensive care, speaking haltingly, seeking for the words and the strength to say them. Jennifer sat motionless on the edge of the bed, listening, tears of grief and horror running down her face. She had never met Elina Nerantzi, the girl Morat had killed, or the brother and uncle he had sent to the hospital, but what did that matter? Jennifer had set up the dig, had financed it. It might not be her fault exactly, she told herself, but it clearly wouldn't have happened if not for her. When Elina hung up, Jennifer held the phone absently, staring at nothing, still lost in the tragedy of the thing, and then she wept properly, loud, ugly sobs that racked her body and turned from grief to rage and back.

This is your fault, she accused herself. *You sprinkled your money and walked away while the people who did the actual work died.*

It was minutes later, as she turned over all Elina had said, that she thought back to the image of the killer falling through the floor of a church tower and how he had lain there, wounded, but somehow escaped before the police could come and arrest him.

Blue sky through the ragged hole in the wood. The pain of lying there on the hard ground . . .

Her sobs stopped abruptly. She moved to the basin in the bathroom and washed, then stared at her stunned face in the mirror, half expecting to see him, suave and cruel, staring back at her from the reflection.

What is happening to me? she wondered. *And, worse, what use am I if I can't stop it?*

▼   ▼   ▼

SHE ATE VERY LITTLE AT DINNER, BUT HAD THE GOOD SENSE not to drink. She didn't need anything else that would make her feel less than wholly stable. When the maid came to collect her plates, she apologized for how little progress she had made on the lasagna and salad.

"It was very good," she said. "I just have no appetite. Would you ask cook to cover it and leave it in the fridge for me? I may be hungrier later."

The maid, Carrie Ward, a girl from the village whose mother had also been employed by the family, smiled sympathetically and said "Certainly, Miss."

"Carrie," said Jennifer. "You remember old Margery Cullen, used to cook for us?"

"I know who she is, Miss, but she was before my time."

"Do you know where she lives now?"

"In one of the estate cottages, I think, yes? Not sure which one. Mr. Deacon would know."

"Let's leave Mr. Deacon out of it, if you don't mind," said Jennifer, not wanting to stir Deacon's constant worry for her.

"I could call me mam?" said the maid, hovering at the door with Jennifer's plates in her hands.

Jennifer hesitated. It had been a strange day. Perhaps this was a way to bring in some form of rationality. It was probably a blind alley, but the attempt to learn more about her childhood disappearance and what it had done to her father felt somehow both relevant to and more manageable than the current strangeness and horror of what had happened in Crete.

"Thank you, Carrie," said Jennifer. "That would be very kind of you."

Except that it wasn't kind so much as it was a servant obeying the command of her employer, a command robed as a request to save everyone's blushes.

The idea bothered her and made her wonder, not for the first time, what she was if you took away her money, her status.

Your father's money. His status.

Which made it worse. She hadn't even earned it herself. She had inherited it all, all the while fighting with him, complaining, dressing up in fashionable causes, always secure in the knowledge that his money, the very money she railed against, would get her out of trouble. In the last weeks she had gone through some remarkable experiences, but she was still the lady up at the big house, still pulling the financial strings while other people did the work.

And paid the price.

After the maid had left, Jennifer sat where she was, sipping from her water glass and thinking back over the events in the museum, trying to determine how much of it she had imagined, and why.

Blue sky, and pain and the broken stone of the tower . . .

Ten minutes later, Carrie returned with a folded sheet of the house notepaper her father had consistently ordered long after everyone stopped writing letters by hand. On it was written, in Carrie's childish hand, 14 Cross Lane. There was a phone number as well, but Jennifer instinctively decided not to use it. She wanted to see the woman's face when she arrived unexpected at her door . . .

There it was again, that sense of impulses, ideas, desires that made no clear sense. Jennifer wasn't entirely sure why she wanted to see the old woman again. Her brain said that the old cook might be able to offer more insight into her kidnapping that Deacon couldn't, but there was something else, something less fully formed in her head, a vague impression that pressed compulsively on her mind as the golden bee image had, but of which she could make no sense.

It was time Jennifer stood up and did something. Not pay someone else to do it for her. She should do something herself.

Taking her flashlight, a small, lightweight thing with a bluish LED beam, Jennifer put on sturdy shoes and stepped out into the night. It was cooler than she had expected, the early summer heat dying quickly with sunset in that distinctly English way, but she did not need a jacket, and set out down the stone steps and along the gravel path through the formal gardens with a sense of resolution, of bringing order to an unsettling and distressing day.

Her father had possessed what she had occasionally derided in her unforgiving youth as bourgeois tastes when it came to art. The gardens, though generally dark with carefully crafted yew shrubs, were dotted with pale statues modeled on classical originals: Artemis and the stag, Actaeon, Apollo and his bow, Poseidon with his trident rising from a pool. As she had put aside some of her angry rebellion, they had come to feel at least familiar, if not the height of artistic sophistication her father saw in them, but now the Greek themes reminded her of what had happened on Crete, of the dangers she had thought were past.

She passed through the trellised walkway, which was hung with fragrant wisteria, crossed the path that wound to the east and back to the house via the walled protection of the kitchen garden, and continued down to the perimeter wall and the lodge, where the gardener, Grimes, lived with his wife. Then on down the lane through the pasture, where she paused to pick a path that would keep her away from the cows, which stood in unconcerned knots around the field. One of them gazed at her with its big eyes, chewing absently, and she felt the old childish shudder of unease at the look, blank and soulful at the same time, like there was something inside the beast looking out.

Don't be stupid, she told herself. *It's just a cow.*

Still, she kept her route circuitous, avoiding the animals' eyes, and almost ran the last few yards to the stile when she could see that the way was clear. Then she took the path alongside the woods, which nearly surrounded the fairy ring, and on past the old village cross and right along the lane of detached cottages to number 14.

There were no streetlights here, and without the flashlight Jennifer would have struggled to find her way safely, even though the darkness was not yet as thick as it would be in an hour. In winter, when the days were markedly shorter, it would be brutally dark, particularly for old people, and Jennifer marveled that her father had never thought to get lights installed. The cottages themselves looked old—late eighteenth century, perhaps—if well maintained, their stone thresholds bowed smooth with wear. They had bay windows with lace curtains, and some sort of creeper like ivy that mantled the south-facing walls. In daylight it was probably picturesque, but at night it gave the houses a wild, overgrown look, as if they had been abandoned years ago.

Jennifer felt suddenly uneasy, not sure why she had come or what she was going to say when the little door with its leaded window in the top half opened, and she stood with her fist raised to knock, but still. The cottage was quite dark.

Maybe there was no one home. Jennifer could walk back the way she had come, all the way to her cozy bedroom, safe in the knowledge that she had tried and been thwarted . . .

A breeze ruffled the ivy so that the house seemed to breathe in its sleep.

Jennifer lifted the discolored brass knocker and rapped it twice on the striking plate, waited a few seconds, then—as if to prove something to herself—did it again. She waited just long enough to pretend that she had done all she could, and had begun to turn back down the path when a light came on in the downstairs bay and she heard the distinct shuffling of feet in a narrow, echoing hall.

29

TIMIKA
Charlotte, North Carolina

HER BREATHING SHALLOW WITH AGITATION, TIMIKA CALLED Jennifer but the phone went to voice mail. For a long moment she sat in the Burger King parking lot staring at her cell, then stowed it and steered back out into the Charlotte traffic. Forty minutes later she was back in her hotel room which, judging by the perfect, tight sheets, had just been cleaned. She slipped off her jacket and let the air conditioning play over her arms as she paced, chewing her nails, and redialing Elina, getting only an answering machine message in cheery Greek. She asked for an update, trying not to sound desperate, and hung up.

If Morat was in Crete, then things were far from over. Nicholas and the others there were in real danger, and Timika's own movements had clearly been tracked. Far from the spent force they had assumed it was, Maynard was alive and kicking, and the secret organization's intel gathering was as good as ever. Suddenly the pristine hotel room with its crisp sheets felt as clinical as the hospital she had just left and twice as isolated. She had checked in under her own name, used her own credit card. If they wanted to get to her, nothing would be easier . . .

She considered calling Barry, but knew she would sound jumpy, hysterical. And what was he supposed to do from Nevada? Plus, she'd have to explain why she was in Charlotte, and that wasn't a conversation she was ready to have with him. So she called Marvin instead.

She began with her investigation into Barry and Alan's medical past, knowing that she was doing so in order not to sound too freaked out, asking him about the mystery doctor.

"Captain Vespasian," she said. "A hematologist from Tysons Corner, Virginia."

"Yeah, Charlotte is a real long way to go to see two patients," Marvin remarked. "And there's something else . . ."

"Hey, Marvin?" she said, cutting him off, all her previous composed determination evaporating. She could hear him typing in the background. It didn't matter if she sounded jumpy. She had to tell him. "Listen," she added, trying to sound breezy, "I think there may be something going on in Crete. Might be nothing, but I just got word that the hit man—Morat—was seen there. If that's right, his people may have a better idea of what we are doing than I thought." She swallowed. It was impossible not to feel like she had made a massive error of judgment. "The authorities there have been alerted but if they are still interested in me too . . ."

"They will know where you are," said Marvin, all his stoner goofiness vanishing in a second.

"What should I do?"

"Get out of your hotel. Make a reservation for a different hotel somewhere else. Buy a ticket to that city on your credit card, then go somewhere else."

"What about this phone? It's a burner so I figured it would be safe . . ."

"They'll be watching the phones of anyone you might call. This number is okay because only you and Audrey know I have it but if you've called anyone else . . ."

"I did," she replied, feeling stupid again.

"So they'll have your number even if they can't actually hear what you are saying. Dump it and get another. Don't call anyone unless you absolutely have to. Get cash from the nearest ATM, lots of it, and don't use your cards again till you're safe. Is the US government involved?"

"The government?"

"Can you trust the police, the military?"

"I'm not sure," she said. "I think so but Maynard has a lot of reach. And their people are lethal. I couldn't be sure that they wouldn't get to me even in police custody. Better that no one knows where I am."

"That's not easily done these days, Timika," said Marvin. "Not if they can get access to surveillance systems, traffic cameras . . ."

"Okay," she said, cutting him off. She was getting more spooked, not less. "Okay. Is your e-mail still safe?"

"The protected account, yes. But write to it from a new address every time and don't use your real name in any of the sign-up processes. If I don't hear from you . . ."

His voice trailed off.

"Marvin?" said Timika. "You still there?"

"Yeah," he said, his tone dreamy again.

"What is it?"

"Tysons Corner, Virginia," he said. "I was hunting around while we talked."

"And?"

"Well, it might be nothing but I see a Captain Vespasian in the Air Force who was listed as resident in Tyson's Corner."

"Barry and Alan were both Marines. So were their families. Why would they be seeing an Air Force doc from out of state?"

"I don't know," he conceded. "Do either of them show symptoms of their conditions?"

"Not that I've seen, but I don't know how they would manifest."

"Sure," said Marvin. "But it's weird, right? Health issues serious enough to get them looked at by a DOD doctor as kids but no symptoms and no interruption to their military careers as adults? Also, I looked into those conditions you described. That's what I was going to tell you before. The firewall on these old digitized medical records ain't what it should be."

"What did you find, Marvin?"

"Right, so you said Barry has beta thalassemia from one parent and hemoglobin E from the other."

"Yes."

"Well, here's the thing; neither parent was ever treated or—so far as I can see, diagnosed—with either condition. I checked their records. Some arthritis late in life, statins for cholesterol for Barry's father, a hysterectomy for his mum five years after Barry was born. Nothing else worth noting."

"You think there was nothing wrong with them?"

"I can't say for sure because their records are sealed tighter than a duck's ass. Can't get near them."

"Okay," said Timika, not sure what to do with this, but getting the same prickle of anxiety she had felt before. Something wasn't right.

One more thing," said Marvin, "then you should go. In 2009 Tysons Corner, Virginia, became home to the SAIC: Science Applications International Corporation."

"Which is what?"

"Not entirely clear," said Marvin. "It's part think tank, part R & D corporation emphasizing information technology, with fingers in various military pies including intelligence and engineering. They, and the related Leidos Corporation, have contracts with the NSA, Homeland Security, the works. Billions of dollars' worth. They recently absorbed Lockheed Martin's Information Systems and Global Solutions business. Heavy stuff, Timika. Seriously heavy stuff. According to this document I'm reading now, SAIC adopted a matrix operating model in which different service lines collaborate to serve a given contract."

"What the hell does that mean?"

"One-stop shopping for the military and intelligence services. They do it all: physical tech, personnel, information systems and intelligence gathering, connections all the way up the chain of command. You'd better hope these folks are on your side."

"But when Barry and Alan were kids it would have been different, right?"

"Yeah," said Marvin in a voice that implied only kind of. "These places tend to stay in the DOD family. Whatever it was then, I'll bet it involved intelligence and technology, probably experimental."

Timika frowned, then nodded to herself.

"You got a picture of this Vespasian character?" she asked.

"Not yet, but I'll send it to you the moment I do."

"Thanks, Marvin."

"Absolutely," he said, still concerned. "Stay safe."

SHE FOLLOWED HIS ADVICE TO THE LETTER, FIRST BOOKING A flight to Miami even as she examined where Charlotte's minimal Amtrak links would get her. D.C. looked like the best bet, though after Marvin's warnings about government-implicated corporations it was impossible not to feel like that was walking into the lion's den. To make matters worse, she had already missed the morning train and the next one didn't leave till a quarter of two in the morning. That meant she had time to kill. She drew eight hundred dollars in cash from the ATM on the corner—which practically emptied the account—checked out of the hotel, and drove to the airport. There she returned the car, then hopped a CATS bus back into the city, paying cash for her ticket and figuring she would get off as soon as the tower blocks of what she took to be the Bank of America and Wachovia buildings looked close enough to walk to.

She had just gotten out when she got the call from Jennifer with the news from Crete. It took a moment to make sense of what she was being told.

Desma dead, and two others in critical condition, one with near-fatal wounds. Hastily finding a bench away from the prying eyes of security cameras, Timika sat down with her hands over her face and wept.

IT WAS TOO HOT JUST TO SIT THERE. AFTER A HALF HOUR staring at nothing, Timika completed her journey on foot and ducked into the Founders Hall shops in the Bank of America building. There she found an electronics store, purchased a replacement phone, and texted the new number to Jennifer, Marvin, and Barry before breaking the old one with the heel of her shoe and dropping it in the trash. Then she found a table at the back of an Italian restaurant and settled in to kill as much of the late afternoon as she could. As she sat there, pushing her food around her plate, she considered her next move, wondering if she should ride the train all the way to New York. At least she knew people there and might lie low for a while, crashing on friends' couches if she didn't feel safe going back to her apartment. But then she thought of the people whose lives she had already put on the line and decided against it. From here on, she'd tell no one anything unless she absolutely had to, and wouldn't involve a single person if it might put them at risk.

How could we have been so stupid to think that cutting Maynard's purse strings made them a tame snake?

When the mall closed at six she walked down the street to a bar stuffed with bankers and did her best to look simultaneously off-putting and inconspicuous, while drinking ginger ale and ordering a vinegary pulled pork sandwich. When that too got ready to close she had the harried girl at the door call her a cab for the airport, giving her name as Janice.

She had just killed nearly ten hours, doing nothing. What had been happening in Greece in that time she couldn't begin to imagine, though her mind strayed back to the awful possibilities constantly, and it was only by focusing on her own potential danger that she was able to stay alert. She waited in the shadowy doorway of the bar till the cab pulled up, double-checked the interior to make sure there were no other passengers within, and ducked hurriedly inside. Only when they were moving did she say that she actually wanted the railway station, not the airport.

"Girl say airport," said the driver unhappily. He was a black man with a distinctly African accent.

"Must have misheard me," said Timika. "Is it a problem?"

The driver checked her expression in his rearview mirror and, if he had been considering making a big deal of the change, thought better of it.

"No problem," he said. "Just shorter ride."

Timika pulled two twenties from her purse and shoved them through the grill. The driver took them wordlessly and smiled at her, though the smile read her mood and faded.

"You okay, lady?" he asked.

Timika nodded, but did not trust herself to speak.

WHEN THEY REACHED THE STATION SHE MOMENTARILY panicked, thinking that she had misread the timetable, the place was so dark and quiet. Even so, she didn't want to spend a lot of time standing visibly on the platform, and timed her ticket purchase as late as she dared before taking her single bag and half running to get aboard before the coaches started to roll out. The train was subdued, with a lot of empty seats. She found one by the window facing forward and with no one next to her, though there was a middle-aged white woman in a black business suit across the aisle; business woman or, she supposed vaguely, a lobbyist.

As they pulled out, she pressed her face to the glass but saw no one on the platform who looked like they might be hunting for her. At last she sat back, letting some of the tension and anxiety slip from her shoulders, though she found her mind full of the Greek student, Desma, who had wandered blindly into Timika's life and was now dead because of it.

"You okay, hon?"

The business woman was tapping her on the arm and offering a Kleenex across the aisle.

Timika stared, blinked, and took the tissue, pressing it to her face.

"Yes," she lied. "Thank you."

The woman hesitated for a second, then decided—mercifully—to leave it at that. She drew out a paperback novel, and Timika, grateful, turned back to the window. She sat

305

like that, as the lights were turned down and the overhead announcer confirmed that they were en route to the nation's capital, which they would reach in a little under nine hours. Timika sat very still as the voice counted off the stations they would stop at, but it had been a long and difficult day, and with the welcoming dark swallowing her up, and the rhythmic rattling of the wheels on the rails, she gave herself over to an uneasy sleep. She dreamed of corridors with strange symbols on the walls, of insects buzzing behind doors and, predictably, of a surreal cartoon creature of sticks and thorns, its blue face full of malice.

She woke briefly in High Point to find the woman across the aisle gone, but could see next to nothing out of the windows once the train had eased out of the station beyond an uneven line of wooded hills occasionally dotted with the distant lights of gas stations and street lamps. Then nothing. She closed her eyes again, and woke next as they were leaving Richmond, Virginia. She sipped from the water bottle she had bought with her ticket, then slept again, dreaming of the hot Cretan sun and digging in the dirt till she found the faces of people she knew, and one that was blue, spiteful and framed with twigs. She woke with a start, conscious that the door into the carriage had just slid closed.

She felt a thrill of danger like the scent of blood on the air, or the heat coming from the door of a burning room. For a moment she hesitated, smelling, tasting the uncanny chemical rush in her mind, her body coming to attention as some ancient animal instinct took over.

Maybe it was just the dream. Or maybe the dream danger meant something real was coming . . .

Moments before she had been asleep, but now she sat up, wide awake, pulling the station list toward her to see how far into the journey they were, trying to make sense of her sudden alarm. The train was stopped, the platform outside bright but empty and she could see no sign. She felt sure that the Richmond stop had been recent. She scanned the list, her breath catching as she read the name of the next stop just as the train rocked forward and began to pull away once more: Quantico.

Her mind raced. She sensed people moving on the train at both ends of the coach. Had they just boarded? As she looked around, the name of the place rang in her head like a strange and unsettling chime.

Quantico.

Which meant what?

The word echoed from a dozen TV shows but she wasn't sure how. She snatched up her phone and typed the word into the search engine. It wheeled for a moment, then led her to a Wikipedia page. She read hungrily, and with mounting panic. Quantico was home to a Marine Corps base, but that was, in turn, home to the presidential helicopter squadron, the DEA training academy, the FBI, the Army and Navy Criminal Investigation Units, and the Air Force Office of Special Investigations. Population of the town was listed at only 480. But a lot of people had just gotten aboard. She could sense that too.

They were looking for her.

The train was still moving very slowly, the engine still gathering its creaking strength before the inertia took over, and now she saw the Quantico sign on the platform as it slid past.

Talk about the lion's den . . .

She looked behind her. Someone was coming along the coach with a blue-white flashlight, which he shone into the seats as he passed. Not a ticket inspector. She saw no insignia, no name badge. He was a big, square-shouldered guy in a trim suit, and in the dim security lights that never went completely out, she could see the way he touched the side of his head, like he was talking into an earpiece.

She had seen that movement before. Back at The Hollows, the weird retirement home where she had found Katarina Lundergrass. She had thought then what she thought now: government agents.

He was still five or six rows back. She considered throwing herself on the floor and lying still beneath the seats, but the footrests made it impossible. She had no choice but to move.

She gathered her strength and propelled herself up and into the aisle in one surge of motion, walking lightly but quickly toward the front of the train. The man with the flashlight saw her a moment later. She felt his light fix on her back, but she kept walking, catching the spike in the urgency of his voice. The train was still moving slowly, still leaving the lighted platform behind them. If she could make it to the end of the coach, she might risk opening a door, jumping down . . .

Another door opened ahead. Another light. This one hit her in the face.

She kept going, banking on brute force and surprise, elbowing past with as much righteous indignation as she could muster. For a half second it seemed to work, the man slumping sideways as she caught him off balance and barreled past, but then the doors ahead of her opened and a third flashlight stopped her in her tracks.

"Timika Mars," roared a voice. "Federal agents! Get down on the ground! Now! Hands behind your head."

Even in the darkness, even blinded by the glare, she sensed the mouth of the pistol trained on her, felt its hunger. She hesitated, half turning, but the other one was closing too.

"On the ground!" bellowed the voice.

There was nowhere to run.

ALAN
Area 51/Papoose Lake, Nevada

I T WAS LIKE SEEING AN OLD FRIEND. THE ASTRA-TR3B
Locust welcomed him aboard, its familiar echoes as he
climbed in greeting him, its Martin-Baker cockpit seat a
firm handshake. He was home.

"Major," said Carl Hastings, nodding.

"Not any more. Call me Alan."

Hastings was to be his copilot. They had never flown in the
same craft together before, but knew each other by sight and
reputation, and had both flown in the last great battle in the
skies over Nevada, though Hastings had taken fire and been
forced to come down in the Badlands of North Dakota. The
CIA had promptly thrown its customary net of secrecy over the
area citing a downed satellite containing radioactive material,
but it was hardly a perfect outing, and Hastings had returned
to Dreamland sound in body but angry and humiliated.

He was a tall man, tanned, with straight black hair and a slightly hooked nose that gave him an aquiline face, so that he always looked like he was standing on his dignity. Not a lot of warmth there. Alan thought he might have some Native American blood in him, but there was nothing about his clothes or manner to support that. He was also a damn fine pilot, though it was impossible not to feel that returning to the two-seater was taking a step backward, and he wondered which of them was considered not quite ready to go solo.

Maybe both.

Couldn't really blame them for that. Their last excursion had been rough, to say the least. The only other pilot who had made it home that night had been Rodriguez, who was still laid up in hospital, and even if he'd been fit the agency didn't have enough operable craft for all of them. No wonder they were being cautious.

Alan's orders had been to take the lead until told otherwise, though he still didn't know where he was going. He buckled himself into his five-point harness and looked around as the last of the crew disembarked, noting with bleak amusement that the last thing they had stowed, securing it with restraining straps under part of the console, was a yellow crate. It was closed, but unlocked, presumably so it would pop open should they crash, ejecting its little alien manikins to amaze and baffle whoever found the wreckage . . .

Hastings caught him looking at it and shot him a sharp and knowing grin that was almost an eye roll: *quite the job we have here, huh?*

Alan matched the look and began the preflight check, touching the standby mode, which brought the comm and nav systems online, then setting the home preset. He spoke into his headset, scanning the window that ran all the way around the triangle's central bulge so that he could see the rear fins by glancing over his shoulder.

"This is Magnus01, checking all systems, over."

Magnus was the squadron name, a new handle for the refurbished craft which had emerged from the Nevada battle. Alan's personal call-sign was still Phoenix, but as commanding officer of the new flight, he would talk to ATC as Magnus01. It occurred to him that this was almost certainly the same two-seater he had flown with Morat. The thought gave him pause.

He felt the thrust control lever in his right armrest and cupped his left hand over the red directional control sphere on his left.

"This is Flight Control," answered the radio. "You're green for departure, Magnus01. Let's get you outside."

"Roger that, Flight Control. Kick the tires and light the fires."

In front of them, the hangar doors slid aside. A pair of rotating red lights illuminated on either side, and with a few touches of his controls, Alan set the Locust rolling slowly out into the desert night. The ground crew watched him out under bright artificial lights, waving their paddles until the Locust was clear of the hangar and the proximity lamps went off.

Alan checked Hastings, who was scrolling through their system readouts on a tablet. Feeling Alan's eyes on him he turned and nodded, replacing the tablet in its console housing with a snap.

"Ready to start getting some mission parameters now, Flight Control," said Alan.

"Roger that, Magnus01. Transmitting initial target coordinates now. Your instructions are to engage maximum covert ops muting systems before commencing your mission. Once in place you are to record and communicate any anomalous readings matching those you will find in your mission log database. Confirm comprehension of directive please, Magnus01. Over."

He wasn't sure why they had been told nothing of the mission until boarding, and while these kinds of security measures were the rule rather than the exception, it was impossible not to think that this renewed caution all connected to Morat's treachery. Still, it would be nice to get a look at the script before you had to walk into the scene . . .

"Got it, Flight Control," said Alan. "Copilot is reviewing anomalous signal profile now. Over."

There was a long moment of silence while Hastings cycled through the description in his mission briefing. He tapped the console and the coordinates locked into the nav system.

"Control, this is Magnus02," said Hastings, whose personal call sign was, for reasons Alan had never heard, Firmware. "Destination logged. Flight plan prepared. Over."

"Roger that, Magnus02. You are cleared for takeoff."

"Control, this is Magnus01," said Alan. "Activating flight systems."

He touched the blinking amber square on the console in front of him and it changed into a solid green light. Instantly he felt it, that remarkable transformation that he had so missed, as the craft that had been something of the earth became subtly different, shifting into something of air and space. He felt the craft's bewildering weightlessness, and knew that though anyone outside would not see the difference, the slender undercarriage that seemed to be holding the triangle up was now no more than a stage magician's prop, something whose purpose was entirely illusory. Whip it away and the Locust would just sit there in the air. He remembered Hayes's offhand remark about how they didn't really understand the technology of the craft they flew, and he bit his lip.

Alan pushed the thrust lever, and almost noiselessly—generating no more than a faint background hum—the craft rose vertically, buoyed up on a cushion of nothing at all. Conscious of Hastings beside him, he didn't speak, but he had to fight down the impulse to gasp, as if something he had dreamed about had turned out to be true. He had flown the craft many times before, but it would never cease to amaze him.

"Setting the auto transit mode . . ." Hastings began, but Alan cut him off.

"It's been a while since I was in one of these things," he said. "Mind if I take it manually?"

"Be my guest," said Hastings.

Alan cupped the trackball with his left and pivoted the ship to face its new coordinates, angling it up as he pushed the thrust lever and the velocity scale leapt into life. As ever, the Locust turned and climbed so effortlessly that it seemed that all normal laws of physics had been suspended. Alan felt no inertia, no G-force, no drag or strain as the great triangle knifed through the air. It was like being an angel, a god, and Alan remembered what Kenyon had said about the divinities of ancient Greece, riding across the sky in their flaming, impossible chariots . . .

"What makes you think they ever left?"

Alan had half expected they'd be bound for Russia or some former Soviet satellite state, but their course took them south and slightly east, down along the western coast of Mexico and Guatemala toward Panama and Colombia. Once they had climbed to almost sixty thousand feet they disabled their usual detection countermeasures and increased velocity to a heart-stopping Mach 6, close to X-15 speeds, but with none of the G-force or other stresses on the aircraft or, for that matter, the pilot. They cruised at that extraordinary speed for almost an hour, before slowing to Mach 1 and re-engaging countermeasures—per their flight plan—as they descended over Bolivia and came to rest some forty miles east of Esquel, deep in Argentine Patagonia, at a height of only eight thousand feet above sea level, and only six thousand above the ground.

"What's down there?" muttered Hastings.

"Got me," said Alan. They were just on the leeward side of the long spine of the continent that was the Andes. It was wild, rugged, and sparsely populated country, softly lit by a waning gibbous moon. "I'd say not a whole hell of a lot, but I doubt they'd send us this low without a good reason. Let's see what we can find."

He toggled through his comm link options.

"Flight Control, this is Magnus01," he said. "Come in, please. Over."

"Reading you, Magnus01. Go ahead. Over."

"We're in position and enabling tracking systems as per pre-set instructions. Over."

"Roger that, Magnus01. Maintain your position and let us know if something pops. Over."

Hastings pulled up a new screen on the console and tapped a sequence of control panels, which brought a collage of data streaming across the display in colored bands: radio, radar, UV, infrared, and some form of chromatography Alan had never seen before.

"You know what we're looking for?" asked Hastings, off the main comm link.

"No clue," said Alan. "Condors?"

"Guanaco," suggested Hastings.

Alan gave him a look.

"What's that?"

"Kind of llama," said Hastings. He grinned unexpectedly and Alan found himself warming to the man.

"Good to know," he said, then toggled the comm system over so he could talk to home base. "Flight control, this is Magnus01. You should be getting data now. Over."

There was a momentary pause, then the voice came over his headset.

"We have it, Magnus01. Over."

They waited in the Locust's unnatural stillness, but nothing happened.

"We're all set, Magnus," said Flight Control. "Commence surveillance pattern Zeta Four, keeping your speed to between one hundred and one hundred and fifty knots. Over."

Alan frowned. The pattern was like tracing a net, spreading out from the starting point in a series of geometrical zigzags to cover a large area. He had been taught to use it in search of debris or a downed airman and it generally meant that mission command had only the vaguest of ideas as to where the target might be. After the thrill of getting back aboard the Locust and putting it through its paces, it was a bit of a come-down to find they were performing so rudimentary an exercise. He didn't even need to make the adjustments himself. He input the Zeta Four plotting system into the console and the triangle adjusted its flight pattern and began the maneuver.

He felt Hastings' eyes on him and shrugged, not bothering to mask his disappointment.

"Life in the fast lane," said Hastings dryly.

"Just about to lose my mind," Alan confirmed.

Hastings nodded, then thumbed his comm off, so that Flight Control wouldn't hear whatever he was about to say. Alan turned to him, sensing something was coming. Both had the visors of their helmets raised.

"Morat killed Hatcher?" asked Hastings without preamble.

"That's how it looked," said Alan, after the briefest of pauses.

315

"Then got away."

"I tried real hard to make sure that didn't happen," said Alan, feeling suddenly wary, defensive. On the console in front of him the data continued to scroll across the screen, fluttering a little, but showing nothing beyond normal background noise.

"But he got away," said Hastings.

"You know he did," said Alan, eying his copilot levelly. "Something on your mind, Carl?"

"Just wondering. Morat trained you, right?"

"Partly," said Alan, eyes still on the lines of colored numbers and graph data. "I'd been flying for years . . ."

"But not in one of these."

"So?"

"You must have felt some allegiance to him. Loyalty, right? Even friendship."

"Until the moment he killed another man to whom I owed loyalty and friendship, yeah, maybe. So what? The moment that happened, I knew what he was and I went after him."

"But you didn't get him."

"And so far as I recall, Carl, neither did you."

"My mind was clear on the matter though."

"So was mine," said Alan. His knuckles were white with the strain of keeping his composure. "You're obviously not going to drop this any time soon, so I suggest we shelve the conversation for now and pick it up again when we're on the ground. Maybe over a beer. Whaddayasay?"

He managed to sound both friendly and forceful so that Hastings couldn't misread his anger or his refusal to back down.

"That sounds like a great idea," said Hastings. "I lost some real friends that day . . ."

"And you think that's my fault?"

"Did you know Steve Jackson?"

"Only by sight."

"He was a good guy." Hastings' voice was deliberately casual, like they were at some backyard cookout chatting about people who had moved out of the neighborhood, but Alan sensed the strength of the copilot's feelings.

"Like I said, Carl," he replied, "wait till we're on the ground."

"Over a beer."

"You know, I think the beer may be off the table," said Alan, steely again. He flicked the comm signal and said into his mic, "Still nothing. You reading all this data, control? Over."

"We see it, Magnus. Adjust the algorithm to raise the UV mix by twenty percent and expand the radar sweep by fifty miles. Over."

"Sure thing," said Alan, half turning to Hastings and giving him a nod of instruction.

Hastings received the command with a resentful glower, then pushed a pair of sliders on the monitor's display. Something beeped. On the map display between the main consoles a yellow light had appeared.

For a second they both just looked at it.

"Flight Control, this is Magnus02. We have a new contact," said Hastings.

"We see it, Magnus02. Hold your position and orient the craft to the south-southeast, nose depressed twenty degrees below horizon."

Alan made the adjustments by hand, rolling the ball delicately in his left hand and locking the new angle in place. The data on the screen responded accordingly.

"That's not a ground target," he said, almost to himself.

"Switching to optical simulator," said Hastings. He touched the controls and the map was suddenly overlaid by a series of trace outlines made up of the digitally projected colors of the various feeds. They described a long cylindrical object suspended at an angle directly ahead of them. An amber alarm light began to pulse.

"We have company, Flight Control," said Alan. "Approximately two miles dead ahead. Contact is shrouded but giving off enough data that we have a fix. Appears to be artificial, some three hundred feet long and roughly cigarshaped. Physical dimensions resemble a dirigible or airship, but the surface is deflecting radar."

"Sensors are conflicted as to whether the object is solid," added Hastings. "Except that's not quite it. It's more like they can't decide if it's really there. Like it doesn't clearly inhabit conventional space."

Alan glanced at him, but Hastings was right. The image on the screen was shifting on and off though the background remained constant, portions of it alternately flickering in and out of existence. Suddenly all of Alan's exhilaration of being back in the sky was replaced by something tense and alert, as if his body had caught some scent in the air that sent adrenaline pumping through his body. They were not alone in this strange world of impossible craft, and that was, as it should be, terrifying. He forced himself to get a grip on his emotions.

"Object is not presently in motion," he said, "but registers as maintaining a position two thousand feet above the ground. I see no sign of a tether, restraint, or apparatus responsible for keeping it in place. The object seems to be free-floating. No conventional heat source indicates a propulsion system."

"Hold your position, Magnus01," said Flight Control. "Keep that data streaming. Do you have visual contact?"

Alan stared through the window into the Argentine night. The craft should be out there somewhere. His eyes were good, and at a little less than two miles away, he would expect to be able to see something unless the ship was operating without running lights of any kind. Even then he'd guess there was just enough moonlight to pick up a foreign object.

"Negative, Flight Control," he said. "Sky looks empty, but it is pretty dark out there."

"Let me see if I can firm up that image," said Hastings. He tweaked the sensor controls, and the display shimmered, some of the translucency vanishing as the Locust's computers made sense of what they were scanning. The object seemed to become denser, harder, its lines clearer. There were no lights on the object that they could see, but what had seemed to be a uniform cylindrical shape was suddenly pocked and segmented so that its surface looked paneled.

There was a long, breathless pause, and then the light, which had been blinking yellow, softly turned into a hard and vivid red. In the same instant an alarm rang out in the Locust's cockpit, shrill and unnerving.

The cause was immediately apparent. The cylinder on their display was rotating along its axis and pivoting so that one end faced the triangle.

"It's moving," said Hastings. "Flight Control, this is Magnus02, the object is coming about. Repeat: the object is coming about. It knows we're here and it's coming right for us."

"Confirm that please, Magnus01."

"That's confirmed, Flight Control," said Alan. "Contact seems to be responding to our presence. Request immediate instructions."

"Roger that, Magnus01," said Flight Control. "Run."

"I'm sorry," Aland began. "Didn't quite copy that . . ."

"Disable scan and return to base, all countermeasures engaged," said Flight Control over the radio. "Maximum velocity. Get home, Magnus01. Do it now."

MORAT
Near Fotinos, Crete

H<small>E HAD BEEN AWAKE WHEN</small> T<small>AN CAME DOWN FROM THE</small> tower. Only just. But he had been at least momentarily awake. He could hear the man moving, could almost feel his terror. But Morat hadn't been able to move, and had been cycling in and out of consciousness, unable to process what had happened or what he should do next. At times the drowsy confusion seemed to fall away and then Morat wondered if he had shattered his spine in the fall, that he would have to lie there, paralyzed, until the Asian came back with the cops, or—spurred by anger and vengeance—with the gun.

It would be, perhaps, no more than he deserved. Not because he had killed innocent people. No one was innocent in Morat's book. Not really. If he deserved to die it was because he had been stupid and impetuous. He had been so keen to prove his usefulness, his indispensability, to Rasmussen and Maynard generally that he had pressed ahead before the rest of the team could gather. He had opted to take care of things single-handedly, assuming—wrongly as it turned out—that a couple of unsuspecting civilians would be an easy target.

They should have been. He had eliminated considerably tougher targets with ease over the years. But he had rushed things. He had been smug. Even the choice of weapon had been a mistake made out of whimsy. He should have picked up a CZ 83, a Sig P232, or a Beretta 87, the one with the long target barrel he could thread for a silencer. Still the best-looking 22 he'd ever handled. He could almost feel the weight of it in his pocket that first night in Prague all those years ago, the tang of cat piss in the alley, the chill metal of the Beretta in his hand. He had almost gone with the Walther P22, but had chosen the Beretta instead because of its classic styling . . .

It was almost a litany, the familiar names of the guns moving through his mind as he lay there like the words of an old prayer learned in childhood, sliding in and out of consciousness, gazing up at the blue of the sky through the fractured tower.

Prayers, he thought, dimly. *Church.*

It had been a long time since he had been in a church. But he was in one now. In Greece. He remembered the mission, the dig site. Nicholas Tan and all that had unraveled, and somewhere in his head a distant bell began to ring. It began like a phone in another room, something intended for someone else, but then it swelled, got closer, became shriller, more insistent, like a fire alarm, and he realized slowly that it was for him. And it was less like a bell and more like a buzzing, a vibrating insect hum that spoke of stings and clawed feet and—for reasons he couldn't quite figure out—a blue face with beady, cartoon eyes full of malevolence.

He blinked the image away and focused on what it meant. He guessed at that, but it was a solid instinct, like when you feel someone is watching you. It was telling him he had to get out of there. He had to move, to stand up. Now.

He tried shifting muscle by muscle, testing the pressure of his limbs against the stone-like tiles beneath him, exploring for discomfort, for lack of function, testing to see where he might be broken. The pain woke fast, breaking out all over him but registering sharpest in his left elbow and hip. He managed to get a hand to the back of his head and found it came away slick and red. He was surely concussed, and that meant he couldn't trust his senses as to how long he had been here.

You need to move. Now.

It was the first coherent thought he'd had since coming to, and he felt its urgency like a train bearing down on him. It started to fade, but he seized it and held on, forcing himself to deal with the facts, all that had gone wrong, all that might yet go worse.

Get up.

He tried to roll onto his chest so he could push himself to his feet, but the first attempt stalled. He felt drunk, absurd, so that he almost laughed at himself through the pain, like he was watching from above, looking down on his body as it struggled and flopped like a fish on the ground. Dying.

Get up.

He tried again, groaning as he shoved himself over and up, his left arm shrilling with agony. He got into position like he was doing push-ups, but the wounded arm had no strength in it, and he collapsed painfully on his face. Pulling his left arm down and close to his chest, he pushed with his right, rolling onto his left side. The wounded—broken?— arm felt like it was burning, but he completed the movement, drew his legs up, and rocked up and onto his knees.

For a moment he stayed like that, kneeling, gazing into the nave of the ruined chapel as he waited for the strength to stand up. There was the remains of a fractured stone screen and an altar at the far end on a wooden platform and the shadow of a crucifix long since removed, but still visible as the shadow in the cracked white plaster.

Morat stood up.

There was only one doorway, and he did not trust himself to try climbing up and out of windows, so he hesitated in the shade of the threshold and looked out across the uneven, rubble-strewn field with its occasional stunted olive trees. He could see the roofs of the cars, the salmon-colored tarp of the lean-to the archaeologists had raised, and what looked like a body on the ground. The girl he had shot. The others would be where the field met the road and where the cars were parked, but he could not see them. There was no sign of Tan. He might be hiding, or even just sitting behind one of the vehicles. Or he might have gone. It was impossible to say.

Morat hesitated, not wanting to go out there in the bright hot sun, rolling his shoulders and pivoting fractionally at the waist, mapping the pain, the damage to his body. He would not be able to run, not for a while. Nor climb. And his thoughts were not as clear as they should be.

But he had to go. The blue-faced insect man had told him that.

He risked one more appraising look at the field and decided, stepping out as quickly as he could. He stooped as far as his back would let him, and doubled back around the church tower, hugging the wall to stay in what minimal shade the structure afforded. He didn't know what was on the other side of the church. He should, but he had rushed the recon, and that sloppiness was about to make his life a lot harder.

He couldn't head back the way he had come. Not that the ridiculously flashy car would be of any help to him now. Perhaps if he could find a vehicle on the street . . .

The thought had barely registered when another decision was made for him. Distant but clear came the sound of police sirens approaching from the northwest. That meant the village and the road were now out of the question. He forced his mind to focus. Murder happened everywhere, but he was pretty sure that hired international hit men killing locals would earn him some serious press coverage in a place like Crete.

He had to avoid people. Here, that meant heading into the mountains. Much of them would surely be wild, rugged, and pocked with places to hide. If he could find somewhere to rest, at least until he was physically well enough to move more efficiently . . .

He skulked across the field to a low wall made of heaped fieldstone. It looked untended, forgotten even, and in parts it was only a couple of feet high. He climbed painfully over and then doubled back along it, following the rise of the ground, staying just far enough back to not be visible from the dig site.

They would have dogs. Not right away, but soon. That would need thinking about. For now, he just had to put as much distance between himself and the place of the attack—the place of his failure—as possible. He felt for the backup piece in his ankle holster: a five-shot .38 revolver. No suppressor. It was still there. His phone, however, which he had stowed in his back pocket, had shattered in the fall. For now, at least, he was on his own.

There were more ruined buildings back here, the remains perhaps, of a farm. The largest and most intact, which might have once been a barn, had moldering doors pushed shut. It was too close to the church to use as a hiding place, but he dragged one of the doors half open in the hope of slowing down his pursuers. The ground was hard, and where possible he made sure his feet fell on stones or in dense weeds where they would leave no prints. He checked his arms and legs for open wounds. It would be hard enough to stay ahead of any tracker dogs without leaving a blood trail, impossible with it.

He was grazed and badly bruised. His left leg throbbed with each step and his arm pained him even when he wasn't trying to use it, but there were no nasty cuts, and he felt his head clearing. But the island was small, and in spite of the seemingly wild terrain, major cities were not far away. They could have dogs here in an hour. A helicopter in less. He had to get as far from the site as he could, but he needed to find cover quickly.

He moved through the desolate farmyard following the rise of the land. Ahead, perhaps five miles away, the mountains rose steeply and craggily over the foothills. If he could make it that far . . .

At the brow of the incline he came upon a gravel road that skirted the hill to the north, running west to lower ground and a distant village marked with rooftops and a church tower, and east, in a slow meandering route up and around the hill. Morat knew that tracker dogs fastened on to the scent of clothes and skin cells, and that—countless movies notwithstanding—crossing a river or the like wouldn't help, and could actually intensify his scent. The weakest link of a tracking team were the handlers, whose pace and decisions determined the speed of the pursuit. His best asset was speed and rugged terrain, though whether his body could handle either was another question entirely.

He crossed the road at as close to a sprint as he could manage, and scrambled up the steep rocky embankment on the other side. It smelled of heat and dry herbs. Oregano maybe. Thyme. He kept going up, intermittently running and climbing, feeling dangerously exposed on the barren hill-side. He had been rested and in peak fitness before the day began, but his left leg was slowing him down.

Push through it. The first half hour is key.

The longer he could stay away from the inevitable pursuit, the harder it would be for them to track him, particularly if he got a break from the universe.

Rain.

It was unlikely at this time of year on Crete, but his chances were better the higher he got.

So he staggered on, clawing his way over rocky outcrops and weedy, dusty ground. Here and there were scattered cedars and pines, the occasional wild olive, and where possible he used their shade to screen his ascent from the land below. The church was out of sight and he realized that he could no longer hear the sirens. It was too much to hope that he had gotten too far away to hear them. They had probably just silenced them on reaching the site.

Which meant they were securing the scene now. Any moment, the order for the hunt would be given.

He kept going. It had been ten minutes since he had left the church and he was still climbing. His heart was starting to hammer and his legs were getting wobbly, but he had no choice but to keep moving as fast and hard as he could. If he could outlast the daylight, he could rest somewhere . . .

The idea was like cool water. It refreshed and invigorated him, gave him focus. Higher still he climbed, and then he was at a road again, the same one as before, probably. Following it was tempting. Its ascent was gradual and smooth.

No.

They would drive this way, he knew. The dogs would come loping along, measured and determined. The steeper route was his only hope.

So he crossed the road once more, and now the gradient was steeper, harder. After five more minutes he felt an eerie calm descending on him, as the hot afternoon silenced even the birds, and after another ten he felt sure that he was leaving behind land that had never been lived on or farmed. It was too rocky, too difficult. It slowed him, but he pressed on regardless. In ancient times his escape might have been the stuff of legend . . .

He wasn't sure where that thought came from, and he pushed it away as stupid and complacent. He had real issues to focus on, not fanciful delusion, and for a moment he wondered if the concussion had been worse than he thought.

Or the dehydration.

He couldn't go on like this much longer without water. But stopping wasn't an option. The sweat ran in his eyes, stinging, but he clambered and staggered on until, without warning, he came over a ridge bristling with wind-bent pine trees, and found a long flat meadow of poppies and other wildflowers with what looked like an abandoned stone hut only a half mile or so away.

So his guess that the land up here had never been worked had been premature. Of course it had. There had been people here for millennia. They had eked a living out of every blasted inch of the ground. It was absurd to think he could reach true wilderness in only twenty-five minutes of running.

Hubris, he thought, vaguely, staggering through the grass and flowers. *That's what the old Greeks would have called it . . .*

Again the thought struck him as strange, foreign, and he brushed it away like a fly. The image of the fly, the sound of its buzzing, wouldn't leave him, however. He felt it thrumming through his head, like a swarm.

Strange . . .

But it wasn't just in his head. The sound was real. It was coming from the south, swelling as it moved through the air, and he was almost sure it wasn't an insect swarm.

Helicopter!

He found the word seconds before reaching the abandoned stone hut. He dived inside, rolling in to the only piece of the wall where there was a fragment of roof to hide him. He lay there in the fragrant herb-strewn grass for only a moment before the hum of the swarm became the unmistakable juddering whine of the chopper banking overhead. He lay quite still, feeling its shadow pass over the hut as it swept the hillside like a hunting eagle.

Morat realized he was holding his breath and he let it out, drawing deeply on the scented air as the helicopter passed over and on.

Safe. For now.

It would be back, perhaps soon, so he had to decide whether to stay where he was, or go farther, higher. The meadow had given him a break from the climbing, but the next phase would be the hardest, a steep and relentless scaling of the pale mountains that ran down the heart of the island.

But if he could get there, if he could make it across and up without being seen, his chances got exponentially better. He lay there, breathing, listening to the sound of the receding rotors as the helicopter dropped over the ridge and traced the road back toward the site. He had a few minutes at least, and the momentary rest had helped immeasurably. He drew himself into a crouch and got to his feet, pounding through the poppies, the long grass whipping at his legs as he sprinted for the steep rise ahead, which rose up like a cliff wall.

Morat was pretty sure he was leaving a trail, but there was nothing he could do about that, and he didn't even look back to see how badly the bent and broken grass stalks announced his passage. As the rock escarpment loomed ahead—a blank, unbroken expanse of jagged, pale stone broken only by occasional ledges and the hardiest of weather-blasted shrubs— he was suddenly struck by the certainty that he had made the wrong decision. It was going to take hours to make the climb. Even if his body would hold out that long, he would be frequently exposed, and not just to the helicopter. A police car on the road might pick him up with binoculars. A hiker might see him, a bird-watcher.

For the second time today, Morat had made a terrible mistake.

He should have gone down, not up, made for the villages and towns, blended in among the crowds of tourists and seasonal workers who flew in from the mainland. If he could survive the first hour it wouldn't have been too hard to become anonymous. Up here he was an anomaly, a stranger whose very presence was suspicious. He had no food or water and if anyone saw him, anyone at all, he was as good as caught.

He felt the weight of the five-shot revolver at his ankle. He would have to use it soon. One way or another that seemed inevitable.

Without even glancing around to see if he might have been seen he reached for a handhold in the rock, wincing at the heat of the stone and the worrying twinge in his left arm as he finally demanded some effort from it, and started to climb.

32

NICHOLAS
Near Fotinos, Crete

NICHOLAS WANTED TO GO HOME—NOT "HOME" IN THE little Greek village; *home*, Reno, the States—but the officer in charge said that was out of the question. No, he was told, he wasn't a suspect. And no, they would prefer not to involve the US consulate in a local police matter just yet, but yes, it was imperative that once his statement was taken—and retaken twice more—he stay around to help with their inquiries. He might even take a lead supervisory role in the clearing of the excavation site, which seemed relevant to the case and which apparently needed to be demarcated as a war grave.

But Nicholas's interest in the site, in *any* site, had blown away with the gun smoke. A girl had died. Others might still die. And though he did not understand why, it seemed certain that those deaths had something to do with his digging, even if the killer had really been hunting for Timika Mars, who wasn't even in the country anymore.

"Will she be coming back?" asked Nicholas, wearily.

"We are looking into that," said the Detective Inspector, a local man called Anastas. "We do not seem able to identify the sponsoring organization for your excavation."

"No," said Nicholas, wondering how he had become caught up in all this. "It's a private enterprise, I think."

"Seeking what?"

"What do you mean?"

"This private enterprise. Were they hoping to locate artifacts for sale on foreign markets?"

"What? No! They were just digging for the same reason all archaeologists dig. They were looking for . . . I don't know. Knowledge. Truth, I guess."

"Truth?" said Anastas, arching his eyebrows. He was a young man for his rank, only a few years older than Nicholas, but he had an air of knowing dignity that made Nicholas feel childish and irrelevant, his expertise and interests something that the detective would sneer at as soon as he had the opportunity.

"History," Nicholas clarified weakly. "Fact."

"But the history you found was rather not so old as you had thought," said Anastas.

"Well, we found an ancient Minoan tomb site, but it seems we weren't the first to find it."

"The German officer whose body you uncovered has what looks like a bullet wound in his head."

Nicholas blinked and frowned.

"Okay," he said. "I hadn't . . . I didn't get a good look at the bones."

"There is a bullet hole," said Anastas, reaching and touching Nicholas's temple with his fingertip. "Right here."

Nicholas pulled away half indignant, half revolted.

"So?" he said.

"I wondered if you had thoughts about that."

"Thoughts? Like what? The man has been dead for seventy years or more. What does that have to do with me?"

Anastas stared out over the rugged hillside and down over the rooftops of the village to the distant sparkle of the sea, and shrugged.

"You dug him up," he said.

"By chance," said Nicholas. "I happened to be digging in that spot."

"You happened to be there," said Anastas, nodding thoughtfully. "In a spot where a previously unknown ancient tomb was located. This is what you call a coincidence, no?"

"Yes," said Nicholas, wary now. The policeman's English was excellent, idiomatic even, but there were times when he seemed to play the bumbling foreigner for his own purposes. "Exactly. A coincidence."

"I wonder," said the detective. "Tell me again why you chose this place to dig."

"I didn't," said Nicholas. "I was given the coordinates by someone else."

"Miss Mars," agreed Anastas, checking his notebook. "Who is not an archaeologist, nor is she working for any known archaeological enterprise. Someone who refused to tell you both how she made the selection of this rather unpromising area for a dig and why she chose you to lead it. I see. Yes. It is all most interesting. I think you would be an excellent specialist as we uncover the rest of the tomb. In case we find anything older than the dead Nazi, you understand."

"Yes, but I really don't want to be involved in . . ."

"No," said Anastas, smiling and making a placating gesture as if he was doing Nicholas a favor. "Really. I insist."

Nicholas considered the policeman. He was lean, olive complexioned, unevenly shaved and rumpled in his slim suit, though his air of nonchalance made him somehow seem more sure of himself where Nicholas would, in the same state, have seemed less so.

"Am I a suspect?" he asked.

"Of what? Being shot at? You are—what is the phrase?—helping us with . . ."

"Your inquiries," Nicholas finished for him.

"Exactly so," said Anastas. "And you are digging, which is what you came here for. What you like. Maybe you will find something interesting."

"What about staff, resources? Clearing the whole tomb site is going to take some time."

"We have arranged to bring some more students from the university," said Anastas, adding when he saw Nicholas's face fall, "and I'll have two armed police here while you work, plus a forensics expert in case you come across anything which is less old than Minoan."

"Including World War II?"

"Including World War II. As well as being of interest to local historians, any bodies and personal effects need to be reported to the proper authorities. Families must be notified."

That curbed Nicholas's defiance. He nodded, humbled by the idea.

"Okay," he said.

"We will clear out the old church and use it as a place for equipment storage. We can add doors with locks and run some electric cable from the village. Give you a computer station there. The roof is not so good, but," he paused to consider the cloudless sky, "I do not think we need to worry about rain."

Anastas was as good as his word. Within the hour preparations had begun, and Nicholas was struck by the disconcerting idea that in other circumstances he would have been delighted to be suddenly handed such resources and manpower. But he needed a break before availing himself of it, and asked for it. Anastas hesitated fractionally but said, "Of course. I should have asked. I apologize."

Nicholas was escorted back to his room by a uniformed policewoman—attractive in a slightly hawkish way that made him feel tense, scrutinized. She wore a pistol in a shiny black belt holster and did not respond to his weary, apologetic smile. She stood somewhat impatiently just inside the front door of his rented rooms while he showered and changed, though what he was trying to wash away had more to do with memory than it did with dirt. He ate a sandwich without really tasting it, then returned to the hot police car and drove back to the site, which was now teeming with people. The bodies were all gone, the ground photographed and cleaned up. One young officer in a white body suit and latex gloves, which made him look like a hospital orderly, was collecting a series of numbered plastic tags that had been used to identify . . . what? Spent cartridge cases? Nicholas was only dimly aware how guns worked. Or maybe this was about blood spatter or footprints. Since Nicholas's experience of such things came from old episodes of *Castle* and *CSI*, he had no real idea.

There was no sign of Professor Nerantzi or of whatever students would be dragooned into replacing Desma, which came as something of a relief. He didn't want to meet their eyes, let alone explain what he was doing or why their help was wanted. With luck, everyone would leave him alone, taking care of all the real organization and administration of the work, leaving him to his trowel and his brush and his private thoughts. It felt stupid, pointless, but it was what he did, and he was in no mood to start trying to take charge and play the leader now.

He wasn't the only one working there, though he was alarmed to see that the two men in shirtsleeves, their police uniform jackets carefully folded up in what passed for shade under a scraggy olive tree just outside the grave circle, were wielding picks like they were mining for coal.

"No!" he called, hurrying over, and reaching for one of the picks. "No. You're not doing road work!" One of the policeman scowled, gave him an appraising look, and grudgingly hefted the pick handle toward him. Nicholas caught it and bent to the ground, shortening his grip on the handle and pecking at the ground with the bit. "Gently. Like this. You can't damage whatever might be just under . . ."

"Okay, okay," said the policeman. He extended a strong, open hand and Nicholas returned the pick. The cop bent over and mimicked him, chiseling away the earth like a woodpecker, rolling his eyes as he did so till his buddy smirked.

"Yes," said Nicholas, straightening up. "And keep the line precisely straight." The policeman gave his friend a blank look, and Nicholas made a slow, sweeping gesture with his index finger. "Straight."

"Okay," said the officer again, shrugging as if to say he would do as he was asked though he couldn't see the point . . .

It was going to be a long day.

It was, but by the end of it most of the top layer of soil in the tholos circle had been peeled carefully away by a team at times up to a dozen strong. They subbed in and out like football players, sheltering in the shade of the church and drinking from water bottles stored in a Styrofoam cooler. He would have the complete team tomorrow as well, but after that, he'd get only what the excavation seemed to justify in criminal rather than historical terms. Two men traded off with a metal detector. A liaison had been sent from the Greek army and he—an elderly man with a stiff, upright bearing—had booked a room in the village for the night, though he clearly intended to be on his way by the end of the following day.

However unified the team seemed when they got out there with their spades, they were actually divided by different agendas, three at the very least. Anastas and the police were investigating a crime scene for evidence that would help them catch a killer. The military man was trying to make sense of what had happened here in the 1940s, if only to close the book on a missing German officer. And Nicholas was looking for . . . What?

Atlantis, he thought, and grinned bleakly. *Idiot.*

The police combed the rest of the field, the street, and the abandoned rental car with a forensic team, but if they found anything crucial, no one told Nicholas. The military liaison, whose name was Patras, seemed to be having the most luck, albeit of a confusing sort. An hour into the communal dig a shout went up from the west side of the grave circle. One of the policeman had found what looked to be human bone. Progress slowed to an almost academic crawl as the gray earth was slowly picked away, revealing a complete skeleton to which scraps of long-decayed fabric clung. A half hour later, another was found. And in late afternoon, as the sun was just starting its descent, another.

Four bodies in total, two of which showed remnants of German military insignia. The clothing of the others was largely reduced to belts and boots, but tiny silver earrings next to the skull of one of the smaller skeletons suggested the person had been female. Beyond the bones themselves, there was no trace of human remains such as hair or fingernails, which came as a relief to Nicholas. Ancient bodies did not bother him. Modern ones did.

The forensic unit raised a white plastic tent on aluminum poles over the entire tholos site and brought in halogen lights run from generators, so that as the afternoon turned to evening the area glowed bright and hot like a movie set. The work, it was announced, would continue through the night. Rain was unlikely, but Anastas and Patras didn't want to risk the site's contamination. Nicholas was consulted, which is to say they notified him of their intentions. His thoughts on the matter were not requested, and he was told he could go back to his rooms. He would be notified of anything that fell in his jurisdiction.

Whatever that was.

And in truth he didn't want to leave. Partly he was fascinated by the process, by the sense of history—albeit comparatively recent history—unfolding in front of him. Partly he was keen to see what else might be found that would help explain his own presence and the interest of Timika Mars and the shadowy organization she represented. But mostly it was a dull unease edged with fear. He didn't want to go back to his rooms alone, even with a duty officer to keep watch such as Anastas had promised. He wanted to stay close to the halogen lamps, close to the police and the sense of disciplined order they brought to a place that, only hours before, had been a site of hellish chaos.

So he hovered on the edge of the grave circle just inside the clinical white tent flaps, being careful not to get in the way so they wouldn't have reason to kick him out. He grabbed a folding stool and sat, watching as the cameras flashed and the bodies were carefully bagged for removal to the lab.

"What are we looking at?" he asked Anastas as the last was carried out to the waiting ambulance and the tent had almost completely emptied of personnel.

"Looking at?" echoed the policeman, confused. He seemed drawn, close to exhaustion.

"Who were these people?" Nicholas tried.

Anastas shrugged.

"Difficult to say. There will be tests. Teeth. Jewelry. The German will probably be the easiest to identify. His military identification was on the body."

"Dog tags," said Nicholas, nodding.

Anastas gave him another puzzled look, then shrugged acceptance of the term.

"The other bodies look like civilians. Probably Greeks."

"What do you think happened here?"

Another shrug, but the policeman fished in his pocket for a clear plastic evidence bag on which a series of numbers had been written in black Sharpie. It contained four pieces of gray misshaped metal, each one no more in mass than a penny. Anastas smoothed the packet flat so that Nicholas could see them.

"Bullets?" he asked.

"Yes," said Anastas. "The people here were all shot."

"By each other?"

"No weapons were found. Their bodies were put together and buried, possibly by the same people who removed the guns. There is also burning of the soil here, here and here," he said pointing to three blackened circles in the earth that formed a triangular pattern inside the circle. "I thought perhaps they had tried to burn the bodies, but the forensic team says the bodies were not burned. Just the ground under them."

Nicholas scowled, bewildered.

"When the Nazis were in Crete," said Anastas, "they led several illegal excavations of ancient sites. They collected artifacts. Often they used slave labor: locals, prisoners of war. We think maybe this was such a place. Perhaps the slaves rebelled.

Killed the officer in charge and a guard, but were then killed themselves."

"And all buried together? Isn't that unusual?"

Anastas nodded.

"Yes. If a German officer was killed during an uprising, we would expect his body to be returned to Germany and there would be records. And reprisals. Unless it happened right at the end of the occupation. But it is also strange that locals would leave the bodies of their friends and relatives out here without moving them into local . . . what is the word? Places for the dead."

"Cemeteries."

"Cemeteries. Exactly. So it is strange. Someone covered the site but we do not know who or why, and neither the German army nor the local people seem to remember anything of what happened here. No one knew there was anything here or had ever been anything here. No one, that is, until you came."

Nicholas gaped at him but, in the face of Anastas' searching look, could think of nothing adequate to say in response.

HENRY "HANK" BABISH
Pacific Ocean, off the British Solomon Islands. July 15, 1962

I T WASN'T A SATELLITE. HANK BABISH WOULD SWEAR ON that, though no one was asking what he thought or saying much of anything. The official story hadn't wavered from the first version: that Starfish Prime had generated a massive electromagnetic pulse that had disabled a satellite and somehow caused it to fall out of orbit, but there was still no word on whose satellite it was, what it had been doing, or how the pulse might have actually caused it to slip out of its orbit. What *was* clear is that the US government very badly wanted it recovered, even if it was in a million pieces.

To Babish, that meant one of two things. The first option, the one most of his coworkers seemed to have signed on to, was that it was one of theirs, something so secret that it was imperative no part of it fell into enemy hands. However, he had talked to the intel guy from space monitoring—Major

Keen—right after the word came through, and he was pretty damn sure Keen hadn't known what it was. The obvious alternative was that it wasn't theirs at all, that it was Russian, but if so, why the internal secrecy? Babish was steaming across the Pacific at a high rate of knots, but if they were about to run into the Soviet navy looking to protect what remained of their hardware, the US force was in no position—legally or militarily—to take any kind of stand. Babish was the technical adviser on an unarmed research vessel, and their fire support came from a single Farragut-class destroyer, code-named the *Monahan* expressly for this mission, crewed by 21 officers and 357 enlisted men. It had some antisubmarine capacity but its main weapons were a bank of antiaircraft missiles and a single five-inch gun: more than enough for dealing with pirates and rebels, or to scare off Soviet missile boats, but if they had subs lurking and aircraft in the vicinity, that would be a very different story.

So Babish hoped his hunch was right, and that there was a third option regarding what had fallen out of the sky a week ago; that it wasn't a satellite, which would become the center of an international standoff loaded with Cold War tension. Of course, that raised the equally unsettling question as to what the EMP *had* knocked out of the air. A spy plane of the type the CIA kept denying they had? Some kind of pilotless drone of the sort he had heard whispered about as central to the Roswell fiasco a decade and a half earlier?

Or something else entirely?

The ship was equipped with cranes for gathering wreckage from the surface, and strainers for use below the water line. They had some hastily gathered dinghies, divers, and even a small submersible with a recovery arm, but they didn't know exactly what they were looking for, what shape it would be in when they found it, or how large an area it might be dispersed over. They had journeyed a thousand miles southeast at breakneck speed, pursuing rumor, third-hand witness accounts of falling debris, and a scattering of odd readings on radar and other detection systems, several of which had only just been restored after the damage done by the original EMP. Now they were in sight of the coast of the British Solomon Islands and were arcing northwest toward Papua New Guinea, on the sketchy evidence provided by weather monitors and those who scrutinized ocean currents and temperatures. More to the point, and in ways guaranteeing to give Babish nightmares, they were being trailed every step of the way by a Soviet research vessel that had been lurking, uninvited, off the Marshall Islands during the initial Starfish Prime test. Word was, there was another in the Samoan Islands, which was all too close to their apparent destination, and God alone knew what kinds of friends they might have skulking beneath the ocean surface.

Whatever else happens in the next few days, Babish thought, *the diplomats will be kept busy. Just thank God you're not in charge.*

It was warm and humid outside, though this was about as cool as the area got, and Babish was counting his blessings, spending as much time above decks as he could and trying not to ask questions. The captain's name was Merrill, a grizzled, red-faced veteran who, Babish suspected, had been sidelined to keep him out of the escalating mess that was Vietnam, something the Navy man apparently resented, though Babish—very much a scientist—couldn't for the life of him imagine why. What was clear was that Merrill wasn't in charge. He ran the ship and made sure it went where it was supposed to, but he did so under instruction from an older man called Bradley Scottaline. He was sixty-five if he was a day, probably older, and CIA, a hard, unreadable man who spoke little and had an odd quirk of pursing his lips instead of smiling. The word was that he had been part of the agency from its earliest days and he spoke a handful of languages with at least functional competency, suggesting he had moved around a lot. God alone knew what the man had done, and Babish figured he would prefer not to know. Looking at him was, he thought, like watching someone whose body was merely a kind of disguise, a simulation, while the real person inside was just a consciousness that made it move around.

It was an unsettling thought, and in his heart Babish suspected that some of his newfound love of being up on deck came from the fact that outside he couldn't get stuck in a room with Scottaline.

"Half man, half lizard," said Doolan after he met the CIA agent for the first time, an observation which, being both funny and true, was a first for Doolan. He was on board too, for which—stupidly—he blamed Babish, as if he was being punished for not listening to Babish's warnings about the possible damage done by the bomb's electromagnetic pulse. He kept to his bunk when not on duty but still seemed to suffer bouts of nausea though they had been at sea for the better part of a week.

Scottaline got regular coded briefings whose full contents he shared with no one, giving each member of the team—including the commander of the destroyer—no more than he thought they absolutely needed.

"The guy probably orders his breakfast with cypher sent to the cook in invisible ink," said Doolan. It was less funny, but was offered almost as an olive branch to Babish. Doolan was trying to bond. When Babish offered a weak smile, the other man lowered his walrus head and muttered conspiratorially. "What do you think this is about?"

Babish made an innocent face and shrugged.

"I just crunch the numbers," he said.

Doolan frowned, dissatisfied, then snapped his fingers.

"Something came for you," he said. "Radio transmission. Just cleared by the code operator. Classified."

"I don't have clearance for that," said Babish, staring at him warily.

"I told him. He said it went to Scottaline and you're to open it in his presence."

Babish blew out a long breath.

"Okay," he said.

"Don't look into his eyes," said Doolan. He made woo-woo noises and waggled his fingers, then grinned like a jackal.

Babish found Scottaline on the bridge, staring through the front window over the prow to the blue water beyond while the captain consulted with the radio operator. He was holding a large envelope sealed and stamped across the flap and, as Babish came in, he brandished it unsmilingly.

"For you," said Scottaline. "Tracking data collected from various sources. Need your expert eye to help determine which, if any, are relevant to our search. It goes without saying that the contents of this envelope are top secret."

Babish nodded, mute.

Scottaline glanced at the radio operator and added, "We'll take this outside, if you don't mind, Captain."

The bridge was cramped, and privacy anywhere on the research vessel was hard to come by, so the request was understandable, but Babish caught the way the florid-faced captain's mouth became a thin line, tight as the envelope's seal, as they stepped outside. They turned into the cargo loading bay and under an oilcloth awning, so that Babish had

the distinct impression that Scottaline wanted cover overhead, as if they might be the subject of aerial photography.
Jeez, this guy is paranoid.

Scottaline handed the envelope to him, a brisk, snapping gesture, during which those unblinking reptilian eyes
never left Babish's face. Babish slid his finger under the flap
and ripped it back inexpertly, mildly annoyed by the way
it tore. He took out a sheaf of printed papers with columns
of data gathered from monitoring stations, listening posts,
spy satellites, and surveillance aircraft all over the world.
They included radar, radio, infrared, sonar, and UV scans.
It was a mess, a collage of radically different types of information captured over several days and covering points all
around the globe.

"Well?" said Scottaline.

"It's going to take me hours to make sense of this," said
Babish. "Days, maybe."

"No," said Scottaline, as if Babish had asked him if it
was raining. "I need your gut impulse now."

"That's not possible! There's data of every conceivable
type in this document and the only thing it has in common
is the time stamp. You probably have readings on a hundred
different events here, and maybe a few bits of it are relevant
to what we're looking at." He stabbed at the first page with his
index finger. "This could be a radiation leak at a power plant.
This could be an unusually intense forest fire. This could be
a solar flare. Any number of these could be meteorites or . . ."

"Gut impulse," said Scottaline flatly, as if Babish hadn't
spoken. "Now, please."

Babish stared at him for a second, then shrugged. If
the guy wanted a thoroughly unscientific response, it was
his funeral. He considered the columns of numbers and
symbols.

"Well, the first thing I see," said Babish, his defiance turning to baffled curiosity, "is a correlation here between the British Jodrell Bank and the Goldstone Deep Space Communications radio telescopes, which seem to show a transmission originating outside our galaxy immediately after the Starfish Prime EMP . . ."

"That's not relevant," said Scottaline.

Babish stared at him.

"Did you hear what I just said? A transmission from *deep space!*"

"Yes," said Scottaline, unblinking. "We've known about that for years."

Babish opened his mouth, but could think of nothing to say. If it was anyone other than Scottaline he'd think he was being joked with. A question formed in his mind but Scottaline cut him off.

"Classified, remember," he said. "Forget you ever saw that."

"Yes, sir," said Babish meekly.

"What I need is point-of-impact information," said Scottaline, moving along as if the previous exchange had not taken place. "Where the object came down. Precisely where. And I need it now."

"We've been at sea for days," said Babish, who was tired of feeling stupid. "What's the rush?"

"The rush, Mr. Babish, is that we are about to experience a tense exchange of views with two former Soviet Chinese destroyers and, unless our sonar stations are on the blink, they are accompanied by a Romeo-class submarine. So you'll understand that we need to find what we are looking for with considerable haste and then get the hell out of these waters. So why don't you take another look at that list and give me something I can use."

34

JENNIFER
Hampshire, England

THE COTTAGE DOOR OPENED SLOWLY BUT THE PERSON who dragged it back did not wait to see who was there before walking back along the narrow, carpeted hall, so that Jennifer, who hadn't even seen her face clearly, hovered at the threshold, unsure if she was supposed to follow. It was, she was fairly sure, Margery Cullen, her father's former cook, older now, bent and spindly, wrapped in unseasonably warm clothes, but since she was basing her assessment entirely on the woman's receding back, it was hard to be sure.

"Hello?" she ventured. "Mrs. Cullen? I'm Jennifer. Miss Jennifer. From the big house."

That was what the locals had always called Steadings. Jennifer had grown to hate the phrase, but it tumbled out of her unbidden. The old woman didn't hesitate, hobbling away

347

through the gloomy hall, which was lit only by the amber glow of a table lamp.

"I know who you are, child," she muttered without looking around.

Jennifer had the uncanny sense that her visit had been expected. Feeling uneasily like a child in a fairy story, she stooped under the stone lintel of the cottage's low front door, and closed it behind her. The house was at least three hundred years old, probably remodeled from time to time though not extensively, and it was the opposite of the free flowing, spacious homes preferred in more recent days. It felt cramped and stuffy, its only windows small and divided into leaded diagonal panes. There was a staircase going up from the hallway, and a door on the left into the front room, but otherwise it was just a passage to the kitchen-*cum*-sitting room at the back. What the locals called a two-up two-down house: four rooms total plus a tiny bathroom upstairs. Jennifer hesitated, but when the old woman continued to move through to the kitchen without a word, she followed.

The floor was uneven and the flocked wallpapered walls bowed, the building having settled over the years like an old man slumping in an armchair. The hallway was lined with curious framed paintings of fairies riding dragonflies, their elegant carriages drawn by stag beetles, or dancing with gilded butterflies. They reminded her of the book she had had as a child, but though the figures were elegant, beautiful even, Jennifer found them creepy nonetheless. She stooped again to get into the kitchen and found herself on stone flags with a scrubbed wooden countertop and an ancient gas stove. To the left a pair of oddly delicate armchairs were arranged on either side of a dead fireplace whose soot-stained chimney breast was clearly in regular use. There was even a scuttle of coal by the hearth, though where the old woman bought coal these days, Jennifer had no idea.

Margery Cullen settled into one of the armchairs and sat quite still, only her shiny black eyes moving, fixed on Jennifer as she sat cautiously in what felt like over-sized dollhouse furniture. The old cook's hands, gnarled fingers laced together like rat tails, were pressed to her chest, her ankles primly together. Her facial expression was strange and unreadable, and Jennifer found herself getting more and more uncomfortable under those watchful, birdlike eyes.

Had the cook always been like this, eccentric and slightly creepy? Jennifer didn't think so. Maybe the woman had succumbed to some form of dementia in age.

I shouldn't have come here, she thought.

There was only a single lamp by the fire, and Jennifer guessed that for much of the year most of the light in the house came from the fireplace and the stovetop. Now, it was dark, the corners lost in shadow, and the woman's peculiar face lit from the mantelpiece so that the deep wrinkles and hollows of her cheeks became black and cavernous. Motionless as she was, it was like looking at a mummy in a museum. Jennifer remembered the gold bees in their case, but pushed the thought hastily away.

The cook said nothing, which was, itself, unsettling. They hadn't seen each other for years insofar as Jennifer could recall, though it was possible she had been in the crowd at her father's funeral and Jennifer had just not recognized her. Now they sat looking at each other, speechless until, embarrassed and keen to be gone, Jennifer said, "I expect you're wondering why I've come to see you."

Margery's face twitched slightly. It might have been some involuntary muscle spasm, but it seemed almost like a crooked smile, though it contained no pleasure. The woman said nothing.

SEKRET MACHINES

"I remember you from when I was little," Jennifer continued. "My father thought very highly of you."

The old woman's eyes narrowed slightly, but she gave the smallest nod of acknowledgment, which sent the shadows dancing.

"I thought perhaps that he confided in you," Jennifer persisted, her mouth dry. "When I was small, I mean." She hesitated, then added with careful emphasis, "When I was *very* small."

This time the woman's smile was unmistakable, though it was still hard and dry.

"When you were *gone*, you mean," she said at last. Her voice was as dry as her smile, cracked with more than age.

"Yes," said Jennifer, the hair on the back of her neck prickling. She didn't like the house or the woman who owned it and she wanted to be gone.

The woman leaned forward and again the light confused as much as it revealed, though her eyes glittered like beads of glass.

"You want to know where they took you," she said.

Jennifer swallowed.

"Well, first I want to know who they were," she said.

Again the smile as the woman sat back in her chair looking pleased with herself.

"He never told you," she observed. "All those years and he never said."

"Told me what?" Jennifer asked.

"Any of it," she said, sounding smug. "And you the lady of the big house."

"I know that they didn't ask for money," said Jennifer, defensively. "I know that my father felt in their debt from the day I was returned to him, and I think that debt shaped the rest of his life in ways he wished he could take back."

350

She had spoken stridently and for a moment the little room seemed to ring with her voice, but the old woman was not cowed. In fact her face hardened.

"You know nothing," she snarled.

"So tell me. My father is dead. I need to know what happened to him as well as to me. I think you can help me with those things."

Margery gave a long breath that might have been a sigh, and for a second her eyes flicked away from Jennifer, as if she was thinking something through. Jennifer watched her, but for a moment the closeness of the room became oppressive and it seemed almost like she was in the woman's head looking back at her own face through strange eyes that showed her in miniature many times over.

Compound eyes, Jennifer thought, mistily. *Insect eyes.*

She blinked and was herself again, watching the old woman, who was still sitting in silent thought. She looked almost sly.

"I know nothing of your father's business dealings," she said at last.

Jennifer sagged in her seat.

"I thought you knew what happened!" she said.

"I know some of what happened," said Margery. "Not all. No one but your father knew all."

"Do you know their names?"

"Names?" Margery echoed blankly, as if the word meant nothing to her.

"The names of the people who kidnapped me."

Margery's face wrinkled with confusion and something like disdain.

"They don't have names," she said.

"What do you mean? They never used their names or . . . ?"

"I mean they don't have names, not names we can know. We give them names to make them seem more like us—Oberon, Titania, Queen Mab—but they aren't real."

Jennifer shook her head as if trying to clear it. The words the old woman had spoken stirred vaguely in her memory, like things in deep water brought to the surface by some unseen current.

"Wait," she said. "I'm sorry, I don't understand. Those are . . . Shakespeare, right? *Midsummer Night's Dream* . . . They are fairy names."

The old woman put a crooked finger on her lips and shushed her with a slow and sibilant breath as Jennifer stared in disbelief. Somewhere in the kitchen, a trapped fly or wasp buzzed against a window. In the sudden silence, the insect seemed unnaturally loud. Reminded again of the golden bees in the museum, Jennifer felt her patience snap.

"I'm sorry," she managed to say, "what?"

"We do not speak the word without honoring them," the old woman whispered.

"What word? *Fairies?*"

Again the woman shushed her.

"You are saying I was abducted by fairies?" she said, all her frustration spilling out at once. Her father had died. Other men and women had died, in New York, in Nevada, in Crete, and this woman was giving her *fairies?*

You must be bloody joking.

"Great," she snapped. "Thanks. You know, if you didn't know anything, you could have just said so."

"The elven folk have always taken their changelings," said Margery undeterred. "Your father had to promise a great deal to get you back."

"Oh for fuck's sake," said Jennifer, getting stiffly to her feet. "I don't know if this is supposed to be funny, but my father gave you a house to live in for free. I would think you owed him more than nasty jokes at my expense."

"Your father knew better than to doubt the existence of the Fair Folk who have roamed the woods and meadows of this land since time immemorial!"

"Fair folk?" said Jennifer, not sure she could believe her ears.

"The beauteous elves of the land."

"Okay," said Jennifer. "I think I've heard enough. I'd thank you for your time but . . . You know," she added, feeling a spike of cruelty she felt the woman had earned, "I don't think I ever really did like you, even as a girl. I'll see myself out."

And so saying she turned on her heel and stalked out of the cluttered little chamber and into the narrow hallway. She was suddenly furious and didn't trust herself to stay in the house another minute. Maybe the old woman was actually delusional rather than merely in possession of a mean sense of humor, but right now Jennifer didn't care. She reached the front door, snapped the latch, opened it and strode out, slamming the door behind her as if that would spell out all the indignation she had not uttered.

Fucking elves and fairies. Jesus. What a colossal waste of time.

It was dark outside, darker still than it had been. She pulled the little flashlight from her pocket and switched it on, its tight bluish beam making the ivy shrouding the cottage leap into unnatural color. The street was utterly, eerily silent. Jennifer took two steps down the cottage pathway and stopped, suddenly missing her father as if he had died only the day before. She wasn't ready for the feeling and didn't understand why it had struck her with such force now.

Because that woman who he thought of as a friend does not deserve . . .

She couldn't finish the sentence. The thought wasn't rational or coherent any more than was the lunatic cook's talk of elves. Jennifer was tired and sad and lost. She felt responsible for what had happened in Crete and was trying to do something, anything, that would give her a sense of purpose and achievement to counter those feelings. It wasn't the old woman's fault. Not really. And if Margery really had succumbed to some form of dementia, Jennifer had just treated her horribly.

You know, I don't think I ever really did like you, even as a girl.

Jesus, what a thing to say.

She turned on the spot. She hadn't heard the door lock behind her and there was no sign of movement through the uneven leaded glass above the knocker. Margery was probably still in her armchair in the back sitting room. There was still time to apologize.

With a soft *plink*, her flashlight died. Jennifer looked at it, shook it slightly, turned it off, then on again, but it did not come back on. Before she could think further about it, however, the night was suddenly lit by rays of hard, white light that streamed from every aperture in the house. They cut through the night from the window in the door, from the keyhole and the cracks around the letterbox and the seams around the hinges. It was as if a bomb had gone off inside the cottage and they were trapped in the moment of the explosion before the blast of sound hit. Jennifer staggered back, shielding her eyes. The light came from every tiny window, even lancing straight up into the sky from the chimney, a fierce, silent radiance brilliant as the heart of a blast furnace.

And then, as suddenly as it had come, it vanished. The night was dark once more, and after the brilliance of the light, Jennifer could see nothing at all, even though her flashlight clicked quietly back on as if nothing had happened.

Somewhere in the distant woods a fox barked, shrill and hard, breaking the spell, and a moment later, without ever really deciding to do so, Jennifer was wrenching the cottage's front door open and barreling inside, shouting.

"Mrs. Cullen! Are you all right? Mrs. Cullen?"

Jennifer was down the hallway and into the back room in a few long strides, but the armchairs by the cold hearth were quite empty. There was no sign of the old cook in the kitchen or in the front room. Nor was she upstairs in either bedroom—one long disused—or the bathroom. The back door out of the kitchen was bolted from the inside, but Jennifer unfastened it anyway, going out back to a coal shed and outhouse where the old woman did her laundry, but there was neither sight nor sound that anyone had been there for hours, or even days.

Jennifer searched the downstairs again, knowing she would not find her, but compelled to do it anyway, and she began to notice that the curious paintings she had noticed on her way in—the delicate and colorfully whimsical images of elves and their insect servants—were represented in every room of the house. They looked Victorian, but far from being merely quirky and decorous, Jennifer saw a darkness in them. Indeed, the ones in the hallway were the sweetest, the most playful. The rest showed fairies whose features were aristocratically hard and scornful, and their insect mounts were frankly alarming, all stings and pincers and long, probing antennae. Jennifer found herself shuddering and scratching, as if half expecting to find one of them on her back or in her hair.

She called the old cook's name twice more, then blundered into the hallway in a haze of confused shock, and the only thing she was sure of as she moved toward the front door was that she needed to get out of that house.

TIMIKA
Quantico, Virginia

THEY DIDN'T HOOD HER OR SEDATE HER, BUT TIMIKA WAS cuffed, forcefully escorted off the train and bundled into the back of a black SUV. She was then driven through a couple of checkpoints and onto the Quantico base, which practically surrounded the railway station. She was too scared to process much of what she saw, though her eyes lingered on the sign outside the building in front of which they eventually pulled up: *FBI*.

The agent in the back with her saw her look.

"If you were a Marine, like the guys you've been poking into, this would be handled by NCIS, but since you're a civilian, we get you. Till we have the evidence to turn you over to Homeland Security, that is. Get out of the vehicle and stand by the door, please."

Timika did as she was told. It was far from clear what she was going to be charged with and what she should be doing to protect herself. At some point soon, she assumed, she would get to make a phone call, and was already considering who best to speak to. Dion was out. Talking to Barry would only get him in trouble. Jennifer had money but was neither in the country nor a US citizen, so Timika doubted she could do much in the short term to help. Marvin and Audrey might be her best bet . . .

Not ideal.

"This way, Miss Mars," said the agent. He was in his late twenties, Hispanic, looked like he worked out more than was strictly necessary. There were two more who had been riding up front, both in dark suits, flak jackets with name badges, and ball caps. They led her past more guards and desk officers into a nondescript interview room with a mirror on one wall, a camera mounted in the corner of wall and ceiling, and a digital recorder on the table.

It could have been one of a thousand city police stations.

Timika took her place at the table in an orange plastic chair and waited while papers were filled out and signed. She was told to stand so she could be photographed, and then another officer came in with a handheld machine to take her finger-prints. An older man in civilian clothes came with him and sat wordlessly in the corner looking at a closed manila folder.

"Right four fingers here," said the officer, indicating the glass screen.

"You can't make me do that," she said. "I haven't commit-ted a crime."

"Four fingers here, please, Miss," the officer repeated as if he hadn't heard her. "And we're going to need a blood sample."

"No way," said Timika. "That's unlawful search. Hell," she added, "it's assault."

"You are assisting us with our inquiries," said the officer. "Your compliance is requested."

"Shove your compliance," said Timika, feeling a little more sure of herself. "I know my rights."

The officer who had been riding in the front passenger seat smiled at her.

"I'm Agent Pivetti," he said. "I'm in charge of this stage of the procedure, or at least I will be until it's handed over to Homeland Security when, Miss Mars, you'll find your rights few and far between. I suggest you help us out."

"What am I being charged with?" she replied, still defiant.

"Attempting to access privileged information."

"I'm a reporter. I was following up on a lead."

"Misrepresenting your identity as you did so," said Pivetti, unruffled. "More to the point, you were recently involved in a shooting in New York, had run-ins with law enforcement in Nevada, and are the subject of an investigation on the Greek island of Crete for which an extradition order is pending. Any one of those incidents will give us the warrant we need to take fingerprints, blood samples, and anything else we want, so I suggest you go along with our requests before we stop asking nicely."

He was still easy, conversational, but Timika looked in his eyes and knew he wasn't bluffing. She nodded fractionally.

"Have a seat," said Pivetti. He gave the officer with the fingerprint device a look and he took her hand cautiously, like she was a dog that might snap at him. He scanned her fingers, then her thumb, then thanked her for her assistance. "Send the phlebotomist in, will you?" said Pivetti as the agent left. "So, Miss Mars," he said, sitting opposite her, "want to tell me what all this is about?"

"All what?" said Timika, still on her guard.

"To begin with, let's start with your attempt to get medical information on two former Marines, Alan Young and Barry

Regis, including an attempt to extract information from the latter's mother at her home yesterday morning."

So Mrs. Regis had reported her. Timika wasn't surprised but it pained her nonetheless. Barry would hear about it for sure, and while their fledgling relationship wasn't real high on her priority list right now, she felt herself deflate a little further.

"Do I get a lawyer?" she asked.

"If you feel you need one, sure."

The door to the room opened and an East Asian woman in scrubs entered with a blue plastic case, which she opened on the table. It was full of stoppered vials, tubes, and syringes. Timika frowned at Pivetti and used the business of rolling up her sleeve and offering her forearm to the phlebotomist to give herself a moment to think.

"Let me be clear, Miss Mars," said Pivetti. "So far you haven't clearly done anything we might want to see you prosecuted for, but you've set off a lot of alarm bells, and I think your best course of action is to tell us why you were doing what you were doing, who you were working with, and to what end. If what you say checks out, you'll be free to go, pending whatever the Justice Department agrees to with the Greeks. If it doesn't check out, or you refuse to cooperate, then our level of suspicion goes up dramatically and we—and the DOD—will start looking at you for involvement in some very bad stuff. Believe me when I say, you don't want that to happen."

She wondered if she might try to reverse the game, tell him she was not at liberty to discuss what she was working on, that she had recently signed a classified document to that effect. It was broadly true, and though it was just a smoke screen, it might buy her some time and sympathy, though that would evaporate in a hurry if the CIA opted to say they'd never heard of her.

What happens at Area 51, stays at Area 51, she thought with a grim smile. *It was like Vegas.*

Timika winced as the blood was drawn, her eyes sliding away from the needle and on to the older man in the corner, who was yet to speak.

"Who's your friend?" she asked Pivetti.

The question seemed to throw the agent momentarily, and he turned to the other man expectantly. He was in his late sixties, balding with shocks of white hair above his ears, his face slack, his eyes a muddy brown and wet-looking, so that he had something of the bloodhound about him. He was holding the folder in his lap as if someone might try to snatch it away.

"Let's say I'm an interested party," he said.

Except that he didn't say that exactly. He said *intewested.* Timika gasped, a giveaway she immediately regretted. His face tightened. He knew she had realized who he was.

"Doctor Vespasian, I presume," she said.

He smiled stiffly in acknowledgment but said nothing, so Pivetti took over.

"That's as good a place as any to begin," he said. "Can you explain your interest in the doctor's work?"

"Curiosity," said Timika. "His patients are friends of mine."

"Indeed?" said Pivetti. "And do you make a habit of checking the medical records of all your new friends?"

"Just the ones who are treated for conditions they don't have," she said. "You can't cure beta thalassemia combined with hemoglobin E."

"You make the symptoms manageable," said Vespasian.

"Maybe, but that doesn't wipe it from your blood," Timika shot back. "I've seen Barry Regis's medical records. He never had either condition." She was lying, but Vespasian didn't know that, and when his eyes flashed uncertainly to Pivetti she knew she had him. His grip on the folder on his knee tightened defensively. "So what were you doing, doc? Treating children for illnesses they didn't have?" She stared him down, then turned to Pivetti. "You sure you're interrogating the right suspect?"

"Doctor Vespasian's medical practice is not your concern," said Pivetti. He seemed unrattled, but that, she thought, might be an act. He was good at his job and wasn't about to give up the stratagem because his colleague couldn't play his part worth a damn. "Medical records are confidential. He doesn't have to defend his actions to you. You, however, have no right to access that information."

"We broke no laws," Vespasian interjected, red-faced. "We had the parents' consent."

Pivetti silenced him with a hand, clearly annoyed.

"None of that is pertinent to this inquiry," he said. "The question of wrongdoing lies squarely with Miss Mars, not what may or may not have been done twenty years prior."

But Timika's journalistic instincts were on fire now. She saw the concern beneath Vespasian's anger. There was something he was keen to keep hidden, which was probably why he was sitting in on this little chat in the first place.

"If you're not actually treating a condition," she said, "why would you need to see patients on a regular basis, and perform so many invasive procedures? That's what Barry told me—of his own free will, mind you. *He was always sticking us with needles, drawing blood, pumping us full of stuff.* So I start thinking, maybe it wasn't so much about treatment, and it was more about testing. Experimental, maybe. Using the military cover and promises to the family about the boys' future careers to do things the AMA might not look too favorably on."

"That's an outrageous accusation," Vespasian huffed. "How dare you . . . !"

"Perhaps you'd like to step outside, Doctor," said Pivetti, clearly nettled. "I'll check in with you later."

"I would prefer to stay," he said.

"Then I must ask you to let me, and me alone, address the prisoner," he said.

The doctor stiffened like a chastised child, looking suddenly surly and resentful, but then sat back and inclined his head under Pivetti's pointed glare.

"Now, Miss Mars," he said. "Where were we . . . ?"

The door opened again. Pivetti gritted his teeth as another agent, fresh-faced and earnest in ways that made him look like a Mormon missionary, stooped and whispered into his ear. There was a loaded pause; then Pivetti leaned back to stare at him.

"Here?" he said, incredulous.

The clean-cut agent nodded but he looked tense, even apologetic.

"Also . . ." he said, then recommenced his whispering. Pivetti's eyes narrowed as he listened.

"Okay," he said. "Excuse me a moment," said Pivetti to Timika. "Doc, you're with me."

It wasn't a request. Vespasian stared at him, but didn't argue, and as he rose he kept the folder flat to his stomach as if Timika might try to snatch it as he passed the table. As the door closed behind them, Timika rocked forward, her head in her hands and her mind racing.

This isn't what you thought it was, she told herself. *You aren't the one who should be afraid. They are.*

Vespasian for sure. She could almost smell it coming off him like smoke. He was desperate to know what she had learned.

Which is next to nothing, she reminded herself.

But he didn't know that. She had lied about seeing Barry's medical records and Vespasian had believed her. And he had panicked. Timika found herself wondering what would be best for her right now, to know everything or nothing. If Vespasian was afraid for what she might have uncovered, how would they deal with her? She had spent enough time around conspiracy theory crazies to know that a lot of people were quick to believe their government capable of all manner of expedient actions against their own citizens if they thought it in the national interest, but she had never been one of them. She didn't really know what people meant by "the government" when they whispered it like that. Not elected officials for sure. Some nebulous but somehow perfectly organized hive mind that acted with ruthless efficiency to protect its own interests?

Bullshit.

Large bureaucracies didn't work that efficiently, even if they had the Machiavellian intent. She had always thought so, and it was one of the torches that had lit the fires of *Debunktion* for years. She wasn't about to cave on that idea so easily. But what she couldn't imagine large bodies of people agreeing to was well within the grasp of a single individual looking to cover his own ass. Vespasian was spooked, either because he had done things he shouldn't, or because exposing him would expose other events or people above him. He might be as afraid of them as he was of her, maybe more so. If only they hadn't taken her phone when they booked her. She would dearly like to let a few people know exactly where she was and who she was with.

It felt like they were gone hours. At last Pivetti opened the door again, but he was still talking with the other agent and didn't come in right away. Framed in the open doorway, Timika could see Vespasian in earnest conversation with the phlebotomist in the corridor. He had a cardboard coffee cup in one hand and a sheet of paper in the other. He was staring at the sheet of paper, then looking at the Asian woman in undisguised bewilderment and disbelief. His eyes went back to the paper, and then he turned to stare at Timika through the open door. For a moment, they just gazed at each other. He didn't look nervous now. He looked alarmed, and if Timika had to express what she saw in words she would say that he was no longer afraid of what she might know. Now he was afraid of something else entirely.

The idea chilled her to the core.

The next instant he was barreling into the room, ignoring Pivetti and muscling up to the table. He slammed the sheet of paper facedown onto the tabletop so forcefully that he spilled his coffee, and stooped to get in her face, looking suddenly quite deranged.

"Who are you?" he demanded.

Timika angled to look past him to where Pivetti was hurrying in, looking both irritated and alarmed. He seized the doctor's arm and pulled him backward, and this time the coffee splashed across the table, soaking the sheet of paper Vespasian had put down and sticking it there in a brown, irregular pool. Pivetti muttered to Vespasian, propelling him back toward the door, but as Timika got defensively to her feet, trying to put some distance between herself and the crazed doctor, her eyes fell on the paper. The topmost surface was blank, but she could see something of what was printed on the other side bleeding through the coffee. A logo. Timika knew that distinctive interlocking spiral pattern. The double helix was unmistakable and appeared in the context of only one thing: DNA.

"Who are you?" spat Vespasian over Pivetti's shoulder. "*What* are you?"

ALAN
Argentine airspace

"GET OUT OF THERE NOW!" SAID FLIGHT CONTROL OVER the radio.

Alan didn't hesitate.

"Roger that," he said. Tearing his eyes from the display screen, he reached over and hit the Home preset button.

He waited for the uncanny blurring of the windows as the Locust leapt to maximum speed while it followed the on-board computer's continually updated emergency flight plan, but nothing happened. The button pulsed with menacing red light and a new alarm joined the chaos. He stared at it as a second message came up on the flight monitors.

Emergency Return System Inactive

Alan hit the system reset, then punched the button again, but got the same result.

"What the hell?" said Hastings. "Flight Control, we have . . ."

"We see," said the voice over the radio with the kind of studied calm that took a hell of a lot of training and experience. "Take her out manually. Maximum velocity."

Alan punched keys and pivoted the red track ball in his armrest. He had grown so used to the fluidity of the ship's movement, its disorienting lack of impact on the human senses even in the most extraordinary of maneuvers, that it took a second to realize that the ship hadn't responded to his inputs.

This is bad.

"Negative, Flight Control," said Alan with the same restrained deliberation as the flight controller. "Helm is not responding. Repeat: helm is not responding. We have neither directional control nor thrust. We're stuck here."

"Target in motion," said Hastings. "It's making right for us."

There was still no sign of it through the windows, which showed only the blue-black of the Argentine night. He stared hard, looking for the merest shimmer of moonlight on metal, the glow of a cockpit window, but there was nothing. He switched to auxiliary power and tried to restart the nav system but nothing happened. Suddenly the various control panel icons grayed out as every major system went off-line. Even the screen that had been showing the dirigible-like craft drifting steadily toward them went blank.

"We've lost our lock on the incoming ship," said Hastings. "Controls not responding!" he said. "I have nothing. Detection countermeasures are disengaged, along with all flight controls and sensors. Frankly, I'm not sure how we're staying up."

There was a moment of silence and a buzz of inaudible chatter over the radio as if furtive conversations were taking place off mic, then Flight Control was back.

"Weapons systems?" it asked.

Alan caught Hastings' eye. The copilot was scared. They both were, and with good reason.

Alan's fingers slid over the screen and pulled up the appropriate menu. While every other operations system was down, the weapons icon still glowed green.

"Weapons seem to be operational," said Hastings.

Even in the suppressed panic of the moment, that struck Alan as strange. But then the Locust's windows suddenly filled with the nose of the great cylindrical craft shimmering into dim reality in front of him, and everything else went out of his mind. On the display it had looked like an elongated oil drum, its sides segmented and marked with irregularities that could have been windows, sensors, or power ports. The ends had looked flat, but they were now revealed under the pale light of the moon to be rounded, like the tip of a bullet.

"Flight Control, we have visual confirmation," said Alan, holding on to protocol to help him keep it together. "Target is now visible approximately one hundred and fifty yards dead ahead. I'm guessing at that since no systems are functional save weapons. Flight Control? This is Magnus01, come in. Over. Come in Flight Control, this is Magnus01."

"There's nothing," said Hastings. "Comm's down. Everything's down." He tapped the weapons systems menu and an array of options filled the screen, all fully functional. Hastings shot Alan a look, his fingers hovering above the controls. "Munition recommendations?"

"Wait," said Alan.

"What? We have to knock them out of the sky before they wipe us out!"

"Just . . . wait!" said Alan, trying to align his thoughts.

"Our weapons are the only thing we have left!"

"Yes," said Alan. "Which makes no sense. If it was true, we'd be crashing."

"So they've interrupted our controls but not our systems," said Hastings, his voice urgent. "All the more reason to use what controls we still have to fight our way free."

Alan frowned. His eyes had slid back to the bullet-headed ship, which was staring them down through the window ahead. It had come to a complete stop several seconds ago and had not moved since. There were panels in the front and along the sides that shone like glass. They might have been windows, though he could see nothing beyond them. He felt, however, a presence: something careful, watching, waiting.

"You think they have the power to derail all our systems *except* our weapons?" he said. "That doesn't make sense."

"I don't care whether it makes sense or not!" said Hastings. "We have no choice. We have to protect the ship and ourselves. Choose a weapons system, or I will."

"Negative," said Alan. "I'm the mission commander on this flight and I say no."

"I strongly recommend . . ."

"Recommendation heard and declined," said Alan, not taking his eyes off the nose of the cigar-like craft. It was still motionless, hanging in the air in front of them, two impossible ships considering each other. He loved the Locust, but he suddenly wished he was in the disk he had flown that one night over Nevada and which was now battered, perhaps beyond repair, in some classified holding corner of Dreamland. Maybe in that they would have had a chance. "I hate to say it," he went on, "but we are technologically out-classed. If we attempt to fire I'm pretty sure we'll find those systems don't work either, but our intent may be the justification they need to bring us down."

"What are you talking about? The icons are lit. We could hit them with a burst of laser fire in under a second . . ."

"They've disabled every other control we have," said Alan. As the seconds ticked by, as Hastings got angrier and more desperate, Alan felt a curious calm that was almost reflective descending on him. He turned slowly to find Hastings glaring at him. The copilot was sweating, his jaw tense and his eyes wide. "Feel that," said Alan.

Hastings blinked in the unnatural silence, stunned by Alan's composure. He glanced quickly around as if hunting for something, then shook his head and said, "What?"

Alan closed his eyes as if listening.

"It feels like . . ." he began, waiting for the right word to present itself, "like a test."

"What are you talking about?"

"Shhh . . ." said Alan, his voice almost dreamy. His mind was full of possibilities, swirling like gray mist. "Listen. They are waiting to see what we'll do."

For a second there was quiet. It went on just long enough that Alan thought Hastings was listening to him, but then the copilot snapped.

"This is nuts," said Hastings. "If you won't shoot our way out of this, I will."

He lunged for the screen, selected a bank of laser cannons, slid the power meter to its maximum level, and pulled up the targeting computer.

Alan just sat there, watching as if he was replaying a scene from a movie he'd seen a hundred times before.

"Targeting system online and locked," said Hastings. The "fire" button was now red and ready. Hastings's hand hovered over it, but he still glanced at Alan for his approval.

"You don't think it's strange that the targeting system still works when we can't get their ship to register on our detectors anymore?" asked Alan.

"Must be a glitch in their defenses," said Hastings.

"I doubt it."

"I don't care," said Hastings. "It doesn't matter why we can still shoot them. It matters that we do it now."

"No," said Alan.

"I'm opening fire, Alan."

"No," said Alan again. "I'm overruling your advice."

"It's not advice, it's . . ." but he didn't bother to finish the sentence. He slammed his hand onto the console's fire button. Or very nearly.

A centimeter above the panel, his hand stopped, not of Hastings's own volition but because it had met some invisible force directly over the control screen. He stared, baffled, then tried again, pressing through whatever was between him and the fire button.

Without success.

Hastings felt the surface of the panel, or rather he felt the strange, invisible barrier immediately above the controls, then turned to Alan, whose eyes were open and watchful, though his face gave nothing away.

"What did you do?" said Hastings. "I don't . . . What are you?"

The question surprised Alan, made him turn suddenly to look Hastings in the eye. What he saw there was more than anger at being thwarted, more than alarm at their predicament. He saw fear. Not fear of the craft hanging in the night only yards away. Fear of the man sitting next to him.

The feeling unsettled him and, for a moment, Alan's composure, his cool certainty, melted away and he was suddenly terrified, as if he had never flown before and was sure they were about to go crashing to earth. He opened his mouth, but could not think of suitable words. He felt himself caught in a torrent of conflicting feelings: the impulse to offer sympathy and steadying explanations, the exactly contrary impulse to rage at Hastings, to berate him for his stupidity and disloyalty, but also the impulse to agree with the man's unmistakable terror of him. For a moment he wanted to leave his own body, flee from the strange pilot in his skin whom he did not know and who could do equally strange, impossible things.

Because that alone was clear to him. He had prevented Hastings from opening fire. Somehow. He had sealed off those controls as surely as if he had encased them in crystal, and he had done it with his mind. It hadn't been a quick, unthinking impulse as it had been when he snatched up the fallen pistol during Hayes's test, or when he had somehow punched the pickup truck away before it hit Barry's car in the desert. This had been different: calculated, planned even. He had guessed what Hastings was about to do and he had decided to prevent him. Before, when he had employed his new and troubling "gift" it had been like swiping desperately at the world, a ragged, unseeing punch thrown in some blind melee. This had been different. It had been precise—a scalpel incision, definite and meticulous. It had been a choice.

Hastings stared at him, but then his attention was drawn by a pulse of soft orange light through the windows. The nose of the cigar-craft had blossomed into a radiance like sunset that swelled till it filled the windows, growing bright and hot enough that it turned yellow-white, and the two men flinched away, shielding their eyes.

And then it was gone.

The light, and the craft.

They hung there in the Patagonian darkness alone, and as they stared, and peered through the windows for signs of the retreating ship, there was a sudden twittering and flickering of colored lights from their consoles as their computer systems all came back online.

The radio picked up midway through Flight Control's streaming panic.

". . . come in. Repeat, come in Magnus01, we have lost your signal. Repeat . . ."

"Flight Control, this is Magnus01," said Alan. "All systems are restored. Contact has withdrawn. Repeat, this is Magnus01. Systems are restored and contact has withdrawn. We're fine."

"Very glad to hear it, Magnus," said Flight Control. "You guys gave us a bit of a scare back here."

"Sorry about that, Flight Control," said Alan. "Everything is back to normal. Locking in home coordinates now. We're okay."

He felt Hastings' wary eyes on him as he spoke, and knew that what he had just said wasn't true, not really.

THEY HAD SAID LITTLE ON THE RETURN FLIGHT BUT ALAN had resolved to cover Hastings as best he could. The copilot's attempt to release munitions in defiance of the mission commander's order might be career ending and, if seen as mutinous, might result in jail time. Perhaps if they made it sound like they readied the weapons together but agreed not to fire them, it would all go away, though he knew that was asking for serious trouble if the truth ever got out. A few months ago he wouldn't have even considered concealing the truth of a mission during debriefing, and a sizable part of him still thought it a terrible and morally dubious idea, even if it kept a badly needed pilot flying.

But in the end, he hadn't had the chance to come to Hastings' defense. The moment they came down from the steps of the Locust on the Dreamland tarmac, Hastings approached the nearest duty officer, saluted, and presented his hands for cuffing.

"Carl Hastings reporting for voluntary confinement pending charges of gross insubordination before a superior officer," he said to the slightly bewildered soldier.

And that was any possibility of a covering action from Alan shot out of the skies. Maybe the guy was just getting out in front of something he knew he couldn't hide forever. Maybe there were cockpit voice recorders that would have exposed the whole thing within minutes of them touching down. Still, it felt oddly generous of Hastings to come so completely clean that Alan wouldn't have to cover anything. He tried to catch Hastings's eye to let him know the gesture was appreciated, that he'd help in any way he could, but his copilot was in full disciplinary mode and his eyes were locked unblinking on the middle distance.

After they had been debriefed, together and separately, the latter involving Dr. Imelda Hayes and a handful of other people whose expertise blurred the line between physics and mysticism, after he had eaten an early breakfast and then made the excuse that he had left his ID back in the Locust, Alan returned to the craft in the hangar where they had left it.

He might not have considered the possibility had it not been for Hayes's probing questions about what had happened in the skies over Argentina. Apparently, though the comm link had gone down, mission control had still received read-outs from those systems that had not been compromised in the encounter with the cigar-craft.

That meant they had seen the weapons systems activated and selected. They had waited anxiously to see what would happen next, only to have everything return to normal, ship and pilots coming home all in one piece.

So they had gone through the interviews and Alan had told his story, leaving nothing out but his own uncertainty as to why he was suddenly able to control what Kenyon had called his gift. And when it was all over, he feigned losing his ID and asked to check out the Locust's cockpit before going to bed.

Except that he didn't get there. Not right away. He got lost in a maze of identical hallways, corridors that—inexplicably—were all marked with a double-headed axe motif, and the more turned-around he got, the more wrong turns he took, the closer he felt the pursuit of some large, menacing animal that ran on two legs.

"Can I help you, Mr. Young?"

Alan turned, breathing hard, and found himself outside the hangar, which was under guard.

"What?" he said.

"You okay, sir?"

"Yes," he said, glancing around him, listening. "Yes. I have permission to return to my ship," he said.

It was true, and after they had checked in with his superiors, and he had logged in with his retinal scan and fingerprints, he was readmitted to the hangar. Perhaps it was the strange paranoia of having felt lost in the hallways only moments before, but he found it impossible to not feel like he was doing something secretive and forbidden.

The escort waited for him at the base of the stairs, not having clearance to go aboard, so Alan returned to his seat in the bulging center of the triangle alone. He pulled the ID from his pocket where he had stowed it, balanced it on end on the control console and, very carefully, let go one finger at a time. The ID was a simple plastic card with his name and picture on it, a bar code and other data impregnated in a magnetic strip, the card attached to a shirt-pocket clip. It could not possibly balance on its edge. And yet, as he moved his final finger away, Alan knew that it would. Knew, in fact, that making it do so would be as easy as breathing.

He stared at it and then, with his hands clasped together in his lap, made the card spin up onto one corner and revolve slowly. He willed it into three complete revolutions, then sent it flying from the console to his chest, where he clipped it in place on his pocket.

Whatever I can do, he thought, *whatever odd gift I have received, I can do it more and better on board this ship.*

He wondered.

Because the ship gave you the gift in the first place?

Perhaps.

For a long moment he simply sat there, considering this and the odd disorientation he had felt in the hallways of the base earlier, and then got up, returned to the steps and down to the hangar.

"Got it," he said, touching the badge and nodding at the duty guard. The guard gave a brief smile of acknowledgment, touched, perhaps, with the merest whisper of disdain for what the over-indulged flyboys got away with at his expense, and together they walked away.

But with each step they took, Alan could feel the power of his gift fading, and by the time they were back in the corridor and heading to the bus, he knew that he was about as close to being ordinary as was now possible for him.

It wasn't a reassuring feeling.

MORAT
Central Mountains, Crete

THE HELICOPTER CAME BACK THREE TIMES, FIRST IN TWO short passes, then in a prolonged low circle that kept Morat pinned motionless as deep into a crevice in the cliff as he could manage. He felt like a bug on the wall waiting to be swatted away. He kept his head down and his hands close to his body. His now ragged and dusty suit afforded him the only camouflage he could muster and his only hope was in stillness.

And wind.

Clouds had heaped up over the mountains and a stiff breeze was blowing in toward the cliff, so the helicopter was keeping a wary distance. Minutes earlier he thought he had heard the barking of dogs, but they had not appeared in the meadow and were, he hoped, exploring other avenues.

The chopper seemed to hang there for an eternity, and he had no way of knowing whether they had lenses—or rifle scopes—trained on him. He could only listen for the sound of it moving off, and once again he had the curious impression that it was not a helicopter but an insect swarm gathering about him, feeling for him with a million quivering antennae, as if trying to determine whether he was friend or foe . . .

It was an unsettling thought. He remembered that odd moment back in Kazakhstan when he had looked at himself in the mirror through what felt like insect eyes. But that hadn't been real. It had only been a dream . . .

He held on to that idea like he was the holding the rungs of a tall ladder.

He waited a full minute after the helicopter had moved around the other side of the mountain before risking a look back and down to the field of wildflowers and grass, but there was no sign of pursuit. His forced stasis had made his muscles cramp even as he had recovered some of his wind, and it was an effort to begin climbing again. But ten meters up the sheer wall of rock became a slope again, steep and treacherous with shifting scree under his unsuitably fine shoes, but something he could walk up, albeit hunched over so that he was frequently pawing the ground with his hands. He scrambled on for another fifty yards, then traced an angled path scored roughly into the mountainside by whatever wild animals lived up here. Then the stones became a series of steps, unevenly spaced and frequently little more than knobs and spikes of rock carved out by the elements, but scalable. In a matter of minutes he had doubled his altitude above the meadow, and hope, slim and fragile as eggshell, was forming in his mind.

And then the rain started. The clouds had piled on top of each other, deep purple mushrooms gathering over the mountain and swelling till the evening seemed to speed toward them. The darkness would be a boon to him, at least until the helicopter came back with searchlights, but rain was even more so. It made tracking him difficult and miserable work. He couldn't say for sure how much it would mute his trail for the inevitable dogs, but it would help.

It started as it meant to go on, hard, driving rain appearing from nothing and coming down like stair rods, fat, heavy drops pounding the ground and bouncing. Puddles formed on every flat surface, and Morat was soon wiping his eyes and stumbling on amongst little rivulets of streaming water gushing down from the mountain. But he'd take the wet discomfort and the sudden gray haze of the unseasonal storm over being caught. Any day.

Maybe the ancient gods were smiling on him after all.

That idea came back to him when, forty minutes later and still uncaptured and, to the best of his knowledge, unseen, he stumbled upon a cave in the rock. The mouth was a narrow fissure, a tall slit just wide enough to squeeze through, but inside were a pair of connected hollows, the deeper of the two being the size of a pickup truck, and a little taller. The one by the entrance looked scorched, as if someone had made a fire there, but the marks were old and he saw no sign that anyone had been there for weeks or more, though animal droppings suggested that wild goats might shelter here in weather such as this.

He shrugged hurriedly out of his jacket and let it fall, then checked for the knife he always wore on the inside of his left shin. It would be too much to ask that meat on the hoof would wander in to feed him, but if it did, he would be ready.

The storm swelled and raged for another hour, and Morat heard no sign of the helicopter. He was pretty confident that whatever traces he may have left on his ascent, the stormwater would have washed away. At least in the short term, his escape was complete. Now he needed to focus on survival and extraction.

While the rain was still flowing down the rock, he risked a short sortie outside to drink from the shallow pools, sometimes scooping the cold clear water up with his hands, other times lying down and lapping like an animal. The rain tasted good: clean and with an earthy tang so that he wished he had a bottle to save more before it evaporated.

But he wouldn't be staying up here long. He had not come to Crete to hide in the mountains. This was a temporary predicament, and in truth he hadn't yet abandoned the idea of completing his mission. If he could still find whatever Tan and the rest were looking for, could still eliminate the opposition, that would go a long way toward wiping out any demerits his previous conduct might have earned from Maynard.

He returned to the cave refreshed from drinking, but saw nothing on the mountainside that he might eat. What he had started to think of wryly as the Convenient Goat had not yet showed up, and he knew the search for a killer would continue through the night. His best bet was to stay in the cave and hope no one found him. He had another couple of hours till nightfall, but after that he might consider going down, albeit by a different route and to a different part of the island. They would be circulating his picture by now and word would have spread. Anyone who saw him—tourist or local, regardless—should be considered an enemy combatant. He didn't want to have to start shooting again, but the knife sheathed against his leg would kill more than goats. Morat was good with a blade and knew just how lethal that made him, particularly when faced with targets who had foolishly absorbed enough TV crime drama to think they might disarm him before he did lethal damage.

What he could really use right now was an isolated house. Somewhere with supplies and a telephone. Somewhere a scream wouldn't rouse a neighborhood if he couldn't get what he wanted silently. Morat sat against the rear wall of the cave, laid the knife on his right and the revolver on his left, and waited for darkness to fall, listening. The rain came and went again twice more, each time accompanied by the distant timpani of thunder and enough lightning to see by, if only for a fraction of a second. For some of it he stationed himself like a sniper in the narrow fissure of the cave mouth, scanning the world below for signs of human movement, but he saw nothing. The search had either been postponed or it had gone in the wrong direction entirely. It was probably the former, but either worked for him.

As the artificial gloom of the storm gave way to genuine twilight and the oncoming darkness of the night, he readied himself to go. He had not slept, but given his concussion, that was probably just as well. He'd had no nausea, and his head was, he thought, clear, something he tested by rehearsing in his head sequences he recalled from schoolboy hobbies, like the up gunning of World War II tank weapons:

Pz I. Twin Mg 34s.
Pz II. Mg 34 and 20mmm cannon.
Pz III, 37mm (KWK 38 L42) through Ausf E.
Pz III Ausf F-J, 37mm (KWK 39 L60)
Pz III Ausf N, short 75mm (KWK 37 L24) . . .

And so on, all the way up to the Jagdtiger and Maus. He was confident that he had the litany right, the names and numbers precise and familiar as prayer. Strange that it should all come back to him now, the little fascinations of his boyhood that had occupied him while the other kids were playing football or demanding why he talked that way, where he was really from . . .

His left arm was painful and would be of minimal use, but he thought it merely badly bruised rather than broken, though some muscle or ligament damage wasn't out of the question. He flexed it cautiously, then decided that the less he used it, the faster it was likely to heal. His shoulder where the Greek woman he had killed had hit him with the ax was bruised but not, thankfully, cut. His leg felt stiff after sitting, but he was surer of that and was confident he could go a good distance on it before needing to stop.

That was as well. He had no idea how far he was going to have to walk before sunrise. His escape into the mountains had moved him toward the central spine of the island and he had made the decision to come down not to the north, where he had come from, but to the south. He knew the terrain there less well and suspected it was more sparsely populated, but that suited his needs. An isolated house was all he required.

Morat watched the sun disappear below the horizon, then set out, working his way around the cliff face along the mountain's east side as the shadows deepened steadily. A half-moon broke through the clouds and gave the hunched and rugged landscape a pale gray cast, which was just enough to navigate by. It took almost an hour to reach something close to a path, and another to trace its slow way south, dropping fast through the trees toward a minor road that wound through the hills. He followed this for another half hour without seeing a single vehicle, then rounded a corner in time to hear the thin mosquito whine of a small-engined motorcycle or scooter. A moment later a light, dull and yellowish, rounded a bend coming up the road toward him. He dropped hastily into the ditch by the road and thought fast, calculating quickly the advantage of taking the bike against the inconvenience of having to conceal a body so that it would go unnoticed for at least twenty-four hours.

It was, he decided, too good a chance to miss.

The motorbike—probably just a moped, judging by the sound—was doing no more than twenty-five miles an hour.

Morat looked quickly for a log or pole but there was nothing at hand in the dark. Again he ran through the calculations of pros and cons, swift and deliberate in spite of the adrenaline he felt spiking through him, like the soccer player who brings the ball to the edge of the penalty area and has to decide: pass, dribble, or shoot . . .

He crouched, his weight on his good leg, like a leopard timing its pounce, his right hand sliding the utility knife from its sheath. The gun would be loud and he needed his bullets. He breathed . . .

waiting, waiting . . .

and sprang up out of the ditch and into the road right in front of the bike, which was laboring on the incline. He flashed into the meager light of the headlamp, and the rider sent the machine swerving wildly to miss him. In the same instant Morat lunged with the knife, but the bike's hard turn took its rider clear to the other side of the road. Morat's stab in the dark cut nothing but air.

But the swerve was more than the rider could compensate for. There was no barrier on the road and no real shoulder, and the drop over the side, though not sheer, was steep enough that, in a second, bike and rider just vanished. Morat rushed clumsily across the road, suddenly alert to the dread of another vehicle coming around the bend and spotting him in its headlights like a rabbit, and peered down. It was dark, but he could smell oil and burned rubber where the tires had slid, and he heard groaning some ten feet below. Taking little rapid steps down the shifting and stony dirt, he made for where the rider was wrenching himself free of the twisted moped, and fell on him. The rider's movements had been dazed, confused, still unsure that he was being attacked. He was not wearing a helmet, a detail that somehow struck Morat as suitably reckless and oddly, even touchingly, trusting. A man. He turned into Morat's assault, a face of slightly mystified pain that was touched with something awkward that might have been politeness, an attempt to put a brave face on what he still thought might be some kind of bizarre accident . . .

The look lasted till Morat's knife found his heart. Twice.

Only then, as the dead man turned his face up to the sky and the moonlight hit him pale and full, did Morat realize how young he was. Sixteen or seventeen, maybe, the skin perfectly smooth, the wisp of beard fooling no one.

And without warning Morat was looking at a brilliant light filling the windows of an empty house, staggering back at what he thought was an explosion, though there was no sound beyond the insect hum in his head . . .

What the hell?

He blinked, and there was only the dead Greek boy in the night, the air full of the scent of blood and oil . . .

He didn't know where those other images had come from, but he felt he'd had a similar experience before.

Where? When?

In the church. Yes. When he had been lying on his back looking up through the broken tower from which he had fallen. He had sensed something similar then, though the feeling had been the reverse of what he had just felt, as if someone had been seeing through his eyes. Yes. That had been it. A foreign presence in his mind. Someone had been in his head. Someone or something.

It had been strange. The same kind of strange that he had sensed after the dreams, when he had felt his mind was being invaded, images of darkness, of insect presences, appearing in his brain but coming from outside himself. And now, as he processed it all standing here in the empty Cretan night with the dead boy at his feet, he felt it sharp and fresh, stronger than before and somehow bound to a place.

He felt the pull of the old shattered church, like it was somewhere he needed to be, somewhere he knew from long ago, and he felt sure there was more to it than Tan and his excavation. There was something there, something to which Morat himself was connected. Something not entirely of this earth.

He had been determined to get as far away as possible from that church and the police who were crawling all over it but now, suddenly, inexplicably, he felt the opposite.

He had to get back. He had to return, not simply to complete his mission, but because whatever was there in that half-excavated field was about him. It made no sense, in the same way that his producing the image of the Eiffel Tower during his interrogation with Rasmussen had made no sense, but it felt real, pressing, urgent, like heat against his skin. It could not be ignored. It would not.

Enough of this.

He got hold of himself and dragged the body clear of the mangled bike, cursing under his breath. The front wheel was badly buckled, so the primary reason he had committed to the attack—transport—was off the table. And now he would have to hide the bike. He considered the dead boy, realizing that the advantage of his victim being so young was that, almost certainly, he would have . . .

A cell phone.

He found it in the pocket of the boy's jeans. An Android, unbroken, but screen locked. He'd deal with that in a moment. First he had to deal with the body and the bike. He had neither the time nor the tools to do the thing properly, but he wheeled the wobbling moped to where a thorny bush was growing and rammed it as deep inside as he could. The body he dragged into some long grass. Neither would stay hidden for long, not if anyone came actively looking, but they would buy him some time.

Whether it would be enough, he couldn't say. As he pulled the boy's still-warm corpse into place, he wondered vaguely about the image he had seen of the house all lit up from inside like it was burning with some white, unearthly fire. It made no sense to him, but he allowed himself to wonder at it, so he wouldn't think about the boy he had killed.

Then he turned to the phone. He powered it down, then back on again, this time holding the down volume button as he did so. He used the volume button to pull up the device's recovery mode. When the green robot icon appeared, brilliant in the darkness, he pressed and held the power button, then tapped the volume up button. He used the volume buttons to activate the factory reset option, accepted the wipe of all user data, shut the phone off and on again. When it came on this time, he had access to all the phone's standard functions. He went straight to the keyboard and dialed Rasmussen's direct number.

His handler answered immediately.

"Yes?"

"Agent A23946B14, Morat reporting."

"What the hell happened? Why didn't you wait?"

"There were unexpected complications, and some collateral damage."

"So we're seeing. I'm assuming you expect extraction?"

"That would be appreciated," said Morat, his eyes on the road.

"I'm not sure you're worth the effort," said Rasmussen coldly. Morat sensed his anger, the shouting he had been doing moments before this call went through.

"You need me," said Morat.

Rasmussen actually laughed at that.

"Mr. Morat," he said, "you are perhaps under the impression that Maynard's collapse has left our organization destitute and powerless. I assure you that that is not even remotely close to the truth."

"I'm glad to hear it."

"In certain important respects, our arm has, in fact, grown longer as a result of recent events, though the opposition is yet to see just how far."

"I can still complete the mission," said Morat.

"I thought you wanted extraction?"

"Just from this . . . predicament," said Morat carefully. "Get me to safety before the search team tracks me down and I'll still find what you want. No one knows the area as well as I do. No one else knows what they are looking for."

"We can tell them what they are looking for," said Rasmussen. There was something guarded in his voice for all its defiance and certainty. He wasn't sure.

"You don't want to though, do you?" said Morat, coolly. "And besides, it's not like this is something you can simply *explain*." He let that last word hang for a second in the silence, then added, "Your arm may be long, and I have no doubt that you still have the resources you need to bring in any number of mercenaries from Turkey or North Africa, but you know as well as I do that this is not simply a matter of military action, or even intelligence. I am, as you well know, the only person who can lead them to the artifact. You need me."

If Rasmussen had demanded what he meant by that, Morat couldn't have answered, though he felt the truth of what he had said just as he felt the strange pull of the broken church. He was bound to whatever Tan was looking for and his handler knew it. Rasmussen's hesitation was momentary, and his voice tried to sound as hard and certain as before, as if he had not changed his mind, but it was still composed and knowing.

"You make the mistake of all your kind," said Rasmussen.

"Oh yeah?" said Morat, finding a little defiance. "What's that?"

"You put too much faith in yourself as an individual. The individual is merely a tool, a claw on the foot of something much larger and more complex, an organization which generates the thoughts and plans that the individual carries out. The organization is the mind, and the mind is multiple, an infinite series of connections which bind and transform all those individuals into something richer and infinitely more superior. The mind is collective, the mind is . . ."

"*The swarm*," said Morat. The word came unbidden to his lips, and it upset him, though he knew he was right. He felt it as he had felt the insect hum in the blades of the helicopter, the awful dreams of things watching him, things inside him looking out.

This time Rasmussen's hesitation was followed by something that was almost pleasant, almost—even—impressed.

"Very good, Mr. Morat," he said. "Though I prefer the term *hive*."

"Yes," said Morat, understanding settling into him, deep and wordless, like muscle memory. "But I'm right too, aren't I? The object you had hoped to recover. You don't know where it is, and I'm guessing that there has been no mention of it in Greek police reports of the crime scene."

Rasmussen didn't begrudge him that much.

"You are correct," he said. "And you believe you know where it is?"

"I do."

"Have you seen it?"

"Not with my eyes," said Morat.

It was the right answer.

"Very well," said Rasmussen. "Then we have an understanding. How long is this phone safe?"

"A few hours, perhaps less. I'll have to turn off the GPS tracker."

"Expect a text in thirty minutes. Be prepared to send coordinates."

He hung up without another word, but Morat grinned. There was light at the end of the tunnel after all.

Unbidden, the image of the strange house glowing brilliantly from within came to mind again, and though he pushed the thought away, it unsettled his composure momentarily, so that it wobbled like a motorcycle with a twisted wheel.

NICHOLAS
Near Fotinos, Crete

NICHOLAS COULD NOT SLEEP. TOO MANY HAUNTING images in his head, too many flashes of memory. And in truth, he was scared. He knew there was a police car parked outside his rooms with one man inside, and another was drinking coffee in his kitchen, but the security precautions made him feel not more safe but less, serving only to remind him that it wasn't over, that the killer was still out there and that, for reasons no one would explain to him, they thought he might come back.

In the end he got up and asked the police if they would take him back to the site and the abandoned church. He would rather be there, he told them, than in his rooms, though he could not explain why. The two cops consulted in low voices, eying him sideways as if he had requested something both strange and suspect, then talked into their radios for a while. Eventually they agreed, driving him back up the road from the village, though the night transformed the world outside the car so completely that Nicholas felt like he had never seen any of it before.

There were cars and news vans parked all the way along the road to the site, and a series of metal barriers had been erected and strung with yellow crime-scene tape like bunting at an old-fashioned fair. Nicholas thought the lightning had started again, before realizing that some of the reporters were firing camera flashes at their car as they approached. He kept his head down and tried to avoid their eyes. It worked okay till they got out, and then the flashes came as thick and hard as the shouted questions, so that Nicholas shrank away, as if he was being shot at.

Anastas was waiting for him by the white tent over the tholos, but he was surrounded by other officers clad in black tactical gear, many of them armed with the kinds of purpose-ful-looking rifles and submachine guns Nicholas had only seen in the movies. Anastas didn't look happy, and though he didn't seem to be blaming Nicholas, he was clearly in no mood to babysit civilians.

"I'm very busy, Dr. Tan," he said. "You can go inside, if you wish, but stay out of the way and do whatever you are told. If there is a way you can make yourself useful, please take it."

"You haven't caught him," said Nicholas. It wasn't a question.

Anastas's face tightened, then relaxed.

"Not yet," he said. "But that part of the investigation now needs my full attention, so if you wouldn't mind . . ."

He gestured vaguely toward the church itself, which had been turned into the base of operations.

Go away, in other words, thought Nicholas. He nodded and stepped inside.

The police officers had set up folding tables on either side of the chapel's central aisle and they worked there under over-bright work lights plugged into a noisy generator by the front door. It was cooler inside than out, but the place felt off somehow, the brilliant lights and computers feeling bizarrely out of place in the ancient place of worship.

Blasphemous, Nicholas thought vaguely, though he had never been religious himself.

Rain had streaked down one wall and pooled on the old stone floor, but enough of the roof was intact that the computers were safe from the weather. Nicholas was shown to a table at the back, right in the little apse where the altar sat on a raised wooden dais in front of the remains of the latticed screen. Nicholas tested the floor gingerly with his foot but, unlike the timbers of the weathered belfry, it seemed sound enough. At his request, he was given access to a laptop.

"When can we start digging again?" he asked the nearest policeman when he finished talking on his phone.

"No speak English," said the cop.

Nicholas didn't believe him, but nodded and smiled apologetically, wondering what he had expected, and what he was going to do now. The man they called Morat, the stranger who had killed Desma, had not been found, and the evening's storms would probably make things harder now. Perhaps he could look through mug shots like they did on TV, help them to identify the man, he wondered vaguely. But no one offered to help him with that, and for half an hour he sat there, scrolling through online news accounts of the attack, pasting the Greek text into Google Translate to see if the reporters knew anything he didn't.

Half an hour later he looked up, conscious that someone had stepped between his table and the glare of the lights. It was Professor Elina Nerantzi. She had changed into clean clothes—jeans and a subdued gray cotton top—but looked like she too had not slept. Actually she looked like she had aged ten years. She had a laptop in her hands, cradled like it was a gift.

"Hi," she said. "I didn't know what to do . . ."

She shrugged, lacking the energy to finish the thought.

Nicholas nodded.

"Me neither."

"Can I . . . ?" she nodded at the chair beside him.

"Sure," he said. "Yes."

She came around the table, laid the laptop down, and opened it.

"There is Wi-Fi?" she asked.

"Yes. You don't need a password."

"I thought I could search through the archaeological records made after the war," she said. "See if there is something about this site which has not been seen. Not seen exactly. I mean . . . I don't know the word."

"Noticed?" Nicholas supplied. "Seen to be significant?"

"Yes," she said, smiling faintly, and immediately catching herself. "Reports which have not been noticed properly. Everything is in Greek, but I can translate, if you excuse my bad English."

"It's better than my Greek," said Nicholas. He mimicked her earlier smile, and felt how strange it was, making small talk like this a hundred yards from where the girl was killed. "Has there been any news about Desma's family? The two men?"

Elina shook her head a little too fast. She didn't want to talk about it.

"There were seventeen known illegal Nazi excavations in Greece during the occupation," she said, her eyes fixed on the laptop screen, "including some on Crete. Even Knossos. But there may have been others we do not know about,

392

particularly if they were committed by treasure hunters rather than by scientists working for the German state. Many artifacts were captured and sent to Germany. Some of them were then *looted* . . . that is the word, yes?"

"Looted, stolen, yes."

"Looted again by the Russians when they reached Berlin at the end of the war. Some of these items were documented in Nazi reports and have been traced. Others, no. Many local people on Crete, also British, Australian, and other prisoners of war captured during the invasion, were forced to work on building projects, fortifications and such."

"Slave labor," said Nicholas. He didn't say that he knew some of this already. She seemed glad to have something to talk about.

"Slave labor. Exactly. Thousands of local people were killed by firing squad immediately after the invasion in 1941 and all the time until the end of the occupation in 1944. In one, er, *incident*, five hundred people, civilians, from the village of Viannos, including women and children, were brought together and executed; punishment for an attack on a German military base by the partisan resistance fighters." She hesitated, as if grasping for the first time the reality of what she had probably said many times before, and for a moment seemed to stare at the computer unseeing. "Anyway. Many were forced to work. But we have no record of any dig here. Ever. Not by the Nazis, not before the war or after. So we do not know who found the tholos or when it was excavated. But," she said, "now we have the badge information for the German officer whose body was found there. We have requested information from the German authorities to help track which company he belonged to and where he was stationed. The police said they would handle it, but I told the detective we could be useful. They just sent . . . this."

She clicked on an e-mail and opened it. It was written in Greek, but the attachment contained facsimiles of printed documents filled out by typewriter with hand-inked details in elegant cursive, each one stamped with a German eagle.

"SS Sturmscharführer Klaus Schneider," she read aloud. "Missing in action, 12th October, 1944. This is the man whose body you found. His service record, promotions . . . But look here. Related files include letters to Hans Ulrich von Seneberg."

"Who's that?"

"One of the archaeologists who worked most directly with the Nazis here in Greece."

"Looking for what?"

"Trophies and treasure," she said, with a shrug. "But also anything they might claim as evidence for their Aryan origins."

"In Greece?"

"Absolutely. The Nazis gave great value to the ancient world and wanted to have it, to *claim* it as their own. They wanted to prove that all great things came from their own people, so they tried to show that the glories of ancient Greece were . . ."

"German?" said Nicholas, making a face.

"Kind of, yes. They wanted to prove that modern German culture was closest to the ancients. They thought such things would show their natural superiority. This meant that they could claim to be the rightful owners of such things. Also, they searched for . . ."

The next word she said Nicholas didn't grasp.

"What?" he said.

She said it again. It sounded like *Oh*-coolt. He frowned, then figured it out.

"Occult!" he said.

"Right. Yes. Sorry. My English."

"It's fine. Not exactly an ordinary conversation word. Go on."

"So, yes, the Nazis searched for *occult* objects," she said, pronouncing the word carefully, imitating the way he had said it so that he couldn't help but smile. "Mysterious things from old legends. Things of power, religious and cultic items or things suggesting secret knowledge."

Nicholas stiffened in his seat. He knew as much, of course. All archaeologists did. But a possibility had just occurred to him. He was, after all, still processing why Timika had approached him in the first place.

"Atlantis," he said.

"Yes!" she said, clearly amazed. "Crazy. But, especially late in the war, they were looking for super weapons, things which would make them stronger than the allies, and one of the places the Nazis looked was in mythology and ancient history. They wanted power. Even mysterious power. Especially, perhaps. Like in the Indiana Jones movies," she added with a half smile. "Some of that is true. They really were looking for these magic things. Holy things."

Nicholas said nothing for a moment as she continued to scan the documents, and a silence descended on them. In the rest of the church, the policemen and women talked on phones and compared notes about modern things, real things, while Nicholas and Elina sat at the altar end with their ancient history and legends, their backs to the fragmentary remains of the stone screen, as if in a different world entirely.

Atlantis. Could that somehow be part of this, and was that why Timika had approached him?

"Okay," he said at last, "so now what?"

"So this Klaus Schneider, the man who was shot, was stationed very near here," she said. "I am trying to find any reports which mention him by name, but my German is . . ." She waggled her hand. *So-so.* "I cannot see anything relevant but there is much here. Going through it all will take weeks. Let me try searching for key words which might link his name."

"Minoan," suggested Nicholas.

She typed, then shook her head.

"Ancient," he tried.

Still nothing. He tried "Atlantis," with the same result. He suggested "tholos" or "tomb," then "statue," "gold," "excavation," and "archaeology." None of it produced more than clutter, though the last two at least suggested they were on the right track. Schneider had been, according to one report, a student of archaeology before the war. He had made some connections to von Seneberg before his deployment, though his standing in the SS suggested he was no unwilling conscript into the Nazi's military attempt to subdue the world. It seemed likely that he was continuing his studies while deployed in Crete, probably spade in hand and with pressganged local labor, but the documents associated with his detachment showed no interest in his digging, though it seemed that he enjoyed better conditions than others of his rank. Maybe he had the ear of people higher up after all.

"Try 'tablet,'" said Nicholas. "Inscription."

Elina gave him a curious look, but he said nothing and tried to look casual.

"I do not know the words in German," she said. "Let me check."

She tapped at the keyboard till she found what she was looking for and began a new search. Her face lit up immediately.

"Yes!" she said. "Schneider submits a requisition for transportation of an object to Berlin, October 11, 1944. He describes the contents to be transmitted as '*a carved tablet of significant historical importance.'* He specifically asks for a packing crate four feet long. The tablet must have been large. The requisition is approved . . . but I see no record of the shipment being confirmed. The unit departed Crete two weeks later."

She sat back, the eagerness in her face turning to bafflement and disappointment by the light from the laptop screen.

"What date was that again?" asked Nicholas.

"The requisition is dated October 11, 1944."

"The day before he died."

"You think he was killed by the local workers before the tablet could be moved?"

"Is it possible?" asked Nicholas.

"Perhaps. And the Germans were already withdrawing so the case went unsolved. Perhaps he had not disclosed where he was digging to his superiors. If he and the guard were the only Nazis present . . ."

"Then their story went untold," said Nicholas. "But someone buried the bodies."

"Quickly," Elina agreed. "The grave was not deep. But then why was there no report of the event after the war? Even if two of the local people who worked on the site were killed, someone buried the bodies. So they survived."

"Maybe they kept whatever was found for themselves," he said. "The survivor might have been a German or a local. He buried both, and took the tablet."

Elina considered this, then shook her head.

"If he was German he would still have to get the tablet off the island, and he could not do that alone. Not if it needed a four-foot crate."

"And if he was local?"

"He would have declared the find to the authorities," she said, as if nothing could be more obvious. "We Greeks are proud of our heritage."

"Perhaps," said Nicholas cautiously. "But this was a time of hardship. Poverty. Maybe greed got the better of him and he decided to keep it to himself."

She scowled at the idea. Then her face lit up again.

"Or," she said, "he did not survive the war! Maybe the only people who knew about the site died in the final weeks of the occupation. Many did. He buries the dead Nazis and the local workers after whatever happened outside," she said, nodding vaguely in the direction of the church door and the dig site beyond, "but in the fighting of the last few days he is killed before he can tell anyone what happened here. It is very possible, I think."

"Then where is the tablet?" asked Nicholas. "If he'd simply buried it with the bodies for recovery later, we would have found it."

Elina's face fell again.

"It could be anywhere," she said.

HENRY "HANK" BABISH
Western Pacific, the Bismarck Archipelago. July 16, 1962

H ANK BABISH HAD PROVIDED AS MUCH INFORMATION as he could to guide their course toward the fallen satellite—or whatever it was—and as he went over the transmitted data at leisure, offered minor corrections as things seemed to come into focus, he had to confess that Scottaline's pressuring him had worked. His gut feeling had been right almost immediately, even though the scientist in him would have preferred a day or two to examine the data more thoroughly. Now they were moving slowly through the waters of the Bismarck Archipelago with their limited sensor apparatus on full alert, closely shadowed now by the *Monahan*, their destroyer escort, which, at some five hundred feet long and a tenth of that across the beam, dwarfed the research vessel to an extent that made Babish feel paradoxically less safe. If they collided, the destroyer would run them over, its great blade of a prow cutting through them like a sword through an over-ripe melon. At least they were now almost static, swaying gently in the sea between Bougainville and New Britain, as they combed their way through.

There had been reports of some debris having fallen on the islands themselves, and there was talk of putting together a landing party, though that would take still more diplomatic acrobatics. Babish found himself increasingly driven to see what had come down, and though the dominant view was that it was either a US or Soviet satellite, he felt a prickle of excitement that pointed elsewhere, though he would not allow himself to even frame the terms in his mind. He was a scientist, and that meant he would follow the evidence, allow himself to be led by what they found, and would not put the whimsical, speculative cart before the material horse.

And then there were the Chinese, or rather, the Chinese with their Soviet advisers and observers. The first destroyer had been distantly visible the previous evening, just as the research vessel and its escort were beginning to slow down to commence their search. By morning, they both were alarmingly close, to the southeast, and well within what Doolan called "shooting range." The sub came in from closer to shore where it had, apparently, been waiting, and now hung somewhere to the west, watching them like a crocodile in the reeds. It was rumored that the Navy had requested air support, but it would be another day at least before anything could get there.

The mood aboard the research vessel had grown thick and silent as the various techs focused on the job at hand so as not to think about what might happen next. The captain roamed the deck, overseeing, but once the

submersible had been launched in a great flurry of crank-
ing cables and warning sirens, there didn't seem much
for him to do, and he brooded among the crew, chewing
his lip and muttering to himself. It was hot and humid,
the breeze down to nothing, the metal of the boat's deck
rail seeming to blister under its flat gray paint. Only the
elderly CIA man, Scottaline, seemed unruffled by devel-
opments, sitting sphinxlike in his cabin or watching the
water from the stern with no show of emotion, still wearing a suit and shades as if he were part of a DC security
detail.

They had been actively searching the water for three
hours, and Babish's patience was starting to wear thin as
the fading light, when a member of the scuba team that
had been making a series of dives from the dinghies broke
the surface with one hand in the air. Something like glass
or metal flashed in it, an L-shaped panel a little under two
feet across. Relief broke over the boat like a wave, and suddenly there was a bustle of activity as the crew dropped
ladders and swung hoists to get the men and their findings
aboard. Babish rushed to join them, but then Scottaline
was looming over them.

"All materials to be collected in the floating crates,"
he said. "No scrutiny by unauthorized personnel. Babish,
you're with me." Hank looked up, surprised. "The lab," said
Scottaline. "Now."

The research vessel's lab was located below decks
almost directly under the bridge. It was permanently
staffed by a pair of techs running low-level experiments
and equipment checks to ensure that the facility was at
peak readiness, but Scotttaline cleared them out as soon as
he stepped in. One of them, a young guy in horn-rimmed
glasses, looked up, startled, but read the CIA man's face

and did as he was told. Only when the door was closed and Babish was alone with him did Scottaline lay down the fragment of wreckage he had recovered from the diver and carried in a canvas bag. The two men sat on either side of the table, looking at it, an irregular sheet of metal no more than a foot and a half long. As Babish had thought, it was shaped like a ragged letter L but it curved in on itself fractionally along the stem.

It was still speckled with beads of seawater so that for a moment Babish thought that its strange phosphorescence was something to do with that, but when he patted it dry with a cloth, the curious ripple of color in the metal only seemed to increase. It pulsed with blue-green radiance, as if it was glass backed with foil, tilting and pivoting in the light, though it was actually lying perfectly still on the work top.

"What can you tell me?" asked Scottaline.

"I'll need to perform a series of chemical and electrical tests to determine the precise composition of . . ."

"Start," said Scottaline. "I'll bring more fragments as we recover them."

"I'll also need the Geiger counter from . . ."

"Get it," said Scottaline. "But I don't want anyone else seeing the results of your tests, is that clear? This is a matter of the highest national security."

"Yes, sir," said Babish. The intensity of the man's stare was getting under his skin and he was glad when the CIA man got up and made for the door. "Sir?"

"What is it, Babish?"

"What do you expect to find?"

"A way to turn the terrier into a wolfhound," said Scottaline, almost to himself.

"Sir?" said Babish.

Scottaline smiled that odd pursed-lips smile of his, and his eyes, which had been temporarily vague, as if looking at something only he could see, regained their focus.

"One day," he said, "when all this is done, Babish, remind me to tell you about my Uncle Jimmy's farm." When Babish just stared, bewildered, Scottaline added,

"I expect to find the future." He hesitated and added cryptically, "And the past."

Babish continued to stare, but before he could say anything, there was a dull thud that reverberated through the ship and sent it rocking.

"What the hell?" Babish muttered, putting his hand over the uncanny fragment of metal as lab instruments rattled and a glass beaker walked off the counter and shattered on the painted steel floor.

"We're under fire," said Scottaline. He twisted the door handle, lowered his head, and was halfway up the steps before he thought to look back. "If we're boarded," he said, "hide it as best you can, on your person if possible."

Babish watched him go in a sort of daze, and as he disappeared from view, there was another low boom. He felt it in his gut and his bones more than he heard it with his ears. It came throbbing through the hull of the ship.

Warning shots into water, he thought. *The Chinese.*

Moments later, as Babish stood trapped in his own indecision, there was another shot, quite different in tone and feel, a bang from close by, as the *Monahan* returned fire.

Another warning, he hoped, a token defiance shot across their bow or overhead. If the destroyer had actually fired on the Chinese vessels, things were about to get very bad indeed.

Briefly. They couldn't hope to stay afloat for long, particularly with that submarine lurking.

Suddenly the strange piece of luminescent metal seemed a good deal lower on his priority list than it had a moment before. Hank Babish locked up the lab with an unsteady hand and climbed the steps to the deck.

He had expected running and shouting, but it was eerily calm topside. The crew had stopped what they were doing and stood in frozen silence, watching the two Chinese ships as the sun set, painting the vessels a gaudy amber. Work lights had been lit on all four ships, and they seemed to glow in the swelling dark. Babish looked wildly around, but there was no sign of Scottaline or the captain. No one moved and, in a flash, Babish remembered his childhood fascination with model ships, especially the kinds in bottles, frozen in time . . .

Nothing happened.

No shots, no movement. It was as if the very air had been sucked out of the gathering night, taking all sound with it.

Babish made for the bridge, where he found the captain and Scottaline huddled, heads together, as the wireless operator relayed messages from the *Monahan*.

"Sir, we're being ordered to withdraw," said the radio op. "The Chinese vessels say they will permit our retreat, but if we stay or attempt to continue our mission, they will sink us. Response requested." He looked up expectantly, his face tense.

"Request course approval for withdrawal," murmured the captain.

"Belay that order," said Scottaline. The captain gave him a furious look but Scottaline held up a hand before he could speak. "Give me a second," he added. "If we can stall them till we get some air support . . . They don't want a shoot-out any more than we do."

"And if their air support arrives first?" asked the captain.

"Sir," said the radio operator. "It's already en route. The *Monahan* has detected two Chinese-owned Type 27s on intercept course. Approximate arrival time, thirteen minutes."

The Type 27 was the US reporting name for the Soviet-built Ilyushin Il-28, a twin jet engine bomber that sported 23mm cannons and anything up to 6,000 pounds of bombs.

"We have no choice," said the captain. "If we stand and fight, we're going to the bottom, and it won't stop the Chinese from recovering whatever the hell we came here to get."

Scottaline didn't speak, and though his face gave nothing away, Babish was sure he was thinking fast and hard, looking for an option, for some sliver of victory they might realistically shoot for. Babish waited for the pursed lips, the spark of fire in Scottaline's eyes, but nothing came, and when he stood up, his face was ashen. Silently, he nodded.

The radio operator took a breath, then spoke into the microphone.

"Roger that, Monahan," he said. "Agreed. Stand by to withdraw. Repeat stand by to . . . Wait."

Everyone stared at the radio man, his face creased into frowns, shaking his head as he considered his instruments.

"No," he said. "I see it too. No, I don't know what it is. It just appeared." He faltered, his eyes wide, then snatched the headset off and turned to Scottaline. "We have an unidentified bogey overhead," he said.

"One of the Chinese bombers?" said the captain.

"No sir," said the radio op, looking suddenly young and out of his depth. "I mean directly overhead and not in motion. Hovering."

"How did they get a helicopter all the way out . . . ?"

"Not a helicopter, sir," said the radio operator, abandoning the attempt to clarify. "This is . . . something else."

The captain hesitated, but Scottaline and Babish were already racing for the door and out.

It was dark outside now, or should have been, but the deck was bathed in blue-green luminescence that pulsed like a living thing. The light came from above, a great shimmering craft, roughly blimp-shaped, but metallic and segmented and long as a football field.

"Why did no one tell me . . . ?" Scottaline began, but an officer, speaking in little more than a whisper that was, nevertheless, plenty loud enough to be heard in the unnatural stillness, spoke up.

"Just appeared, sir. Lit up right where it is now."

"Alert the Monahan," said Scottaline. "Ready surface-to-air missiles!"

"Negative, sir," someone shouted back. "All munitions are off-line. Even the five-inch. Power to all systems has been interrupted. We are defenseless."

"And the Chinese?"

"Couldn't say, sir. I think they may be the least of our worries."

Scottaline turned to the speaker as if to reprimand them, but then gazed up, his face pale and ghostly in the throbbing glow. Babish stared, and in his heart he knew that this was what he had come to see, what he had known was out there, somewhere.

A beam of brighter, harder light almost as long as the destroyers raked suddenly down, scanning, probing, so that all physical things became sharp and white, and shadows vanished so completely that for a second that lasted an age it seemed they would never return. Then all was black again, and the glowing craft winked out for a moment, before a thousand laser shafts of green light flicked out, probing the sea and the faraway land, and Babish knew that each stab of energy found a fragment of the wreckage they had been seeking.

There was a hiss from the sea, and Babish saw, scattered all around, pockets of light in the watery depths that blossomed white, then green, each sending a roiling column of bubbles to the surface. Whatever had crashed here was being systematically vaporized with a thousand pinpoint stabs of energy as fine and surgically precise as the tip of a scalpel.

There was a distinct electric hum in the air, a flicker of light that gave the impression of confused movement, like film fed too fast through a projector. Then there was nothing.

The darkness that followed, shocking after the brilliance from above, softened slowly and then the night was as it should be, and there was nothing in the sky but the rising moon and a distant speckling of stars. Time seemed to struggle to reclaim the world, and then men were moving, some slumping to the deck with the strain of what they had seen, others, Babish among them, standing at the rail watching as the Chinese ships slowly began to move again, speeding away into the night.

ALAN
Area 51/Dreamland

"**G**OOD MORNING, MR. YOUNG," SAID DR. IMELDA Hayes, looking up from her computer as he entered the test facility. "I trust you slept well."

She looked somehow polished, her pale skin healthy and scrubbed, un-made-up. She was in a good mood.

"Fine, thank you," said Alan. He missed being addressed as Major. It wasn't a power thing. The rank itself didn't matter. But it had confirmed the way his private sense of self combined with a purpose everyone recognized. He was a pilot and, in the Marine manner, more. At Leatherneck he had been Maintenance Officer, and before his redeployment there with the Harrier squadron he had been a test pilot. *Mister* didn't convey any of that. The part-time janitor might be Mister. He knew he had formally resigned his military commission when he officially joined the CIA but on days like today, days when he felt that there was something he should be doing in the sky, rather than sitting in these damn test labs, he missed it.

And if he was being honest with himself, he didn't like this building anymore. He had gotten lost on his way to the test center again this morning, the same baffling sense of being trapped in the heart of a maze, the same sudden appearance of the ax-head insignia, the same primal fear of whatever it was that was grunting and stomping along the corridor behind him. He could rationalize it away, but in his heart of hearts he knew something was wrong. He just didn't know if it was him or the place.

"Will this take long?" he asked.

"That's up to you," said Hayes. "You could be out of here in a matter of minutes."

"Great," said Alan. "I mean, no offense, and I can't go into details, of course, but I probably should be flying."

"Yes, I heard about your Argentine adventure," she said casually.

Alan was surprised that she knew the details of his flying, and she read as much in his face.

"You need to get used to the idea that the various aspects of your training are interconnected, Mr. Young," she said. "This isn't some side project for which you happen to be a test subject. You do understand that, don't you?"

He didn't, not really. In his head he was a pilot. Everything else—particularly this, whatever *this* was—was secondary.

"Sure," he said. She gave him a shrewd look and he felt momentarily transparent. "So. What do you need?"

She turned her computer monitor to face him. The screen was blank except for a red dot the size of a penny that seemed to tremble in the center.

"I've turned the controls up to maximum sensitivity," she said. "The smallest nudge of the mouse will send the ball bouncing all over the screen. I just need you to set it in motion with your mind."

Alan sighed.

"Miss Hayes . . ." he began.

"Doctor Hayes."

"Doctor Hayes," he corrected, "we've been through this. You know I can't do this stuff in test conditions."

"You couldn't," she said, smiling professionally. "But your abilities have advanced since then. You have more control than you did. I'd like to see you use it."

"I don't think . . ."

"Just try, please, Mr. Young."

Alan bit his lower lip, then gave a cursory nod.

"Would you like me to dim the lights?" asked Hayes.

"It doesn't make a difference," said Alan.

"I will sit behind you so I can see the screen and be less of a distraction."

She gave him another little smile, more knowing and playful this time, and he nodded again. She got up from the desk with her folder, pen, and notebook, rolled her office chair to his side, and settled a couple of feet behind his left shoulder. She smelled faintly of citrus and soap.

"In your own time," she said.

"What exactly do you want me to do?"

"Just move the red ball."

"Up, or . . . ?"

"Just move it."

So he tried. The red disk seemed to be vibrating at great speed, as if the computer was picking up tiny tremors in the building or the movement of the air, but it stayed dead center. Alan tried nudging it to the right, then to the left. He tried simply focusing on the word *up* or *down*, sometimes with his eyes closed. As his frustration mounted and his sense of the watching Dr. Hayes peering from behind him became more acute and embarrassing, he tried to send the damned thing hurtling around the screen . . .

Nothing happened.

"Maybe I will try it with the lights off," he said.

"As you wish."

She flicked the light off and the room dissolved in shadow, other than the bright blue-white of the computer screen and the red dot in its center, trembling with anticipation, taunting him. He stared at it unblinking till his eyes watered. He gave it commands in his mind, mouthing the words. He directed all his anger at this waste of his time into that little red sphere . . .

None of it made a difference. After ten minutes he turned abruptly and Hayes snapped the lights back on.

"I can't," he said. "I'm sorry. I just can't. And there are other things I need to be doing."

"You will get to those things when you have completed the test," she said.

"I can't complete the test!" he said, letting his irritation show through. "That has to be obvious to you. I don't know why, but I can't do it."

"You can and you will if you want to fly again."

He stared at her for a second, processing what she had just said.

"Wait . . ." he said. "What?"

"You have a gift, Mr. Young, but you must learn to control it. Until you can, I will not authorize your return to the cockpit."

"You can't do that," he said.

She flipped open the folder and showed him an official-looking form letter with her own letterhead clearly printed at the top.

"I am your doctor," she said. "You fly with my say-so, or I'm afraid you don't fly at all. Why don't you go and get yourself a drink of water and then we will resume."

He gaped, then shook his head.

"I don't need a drink," he said.

"Yes, Mr. Young," she said pointedly, not smiling any more. "You do. Down the hall and to the right."

Alan left the room in a kind of daze, as Hayes returned to her desk and picked up the phone. The vending machine was farther than he had expected and when he got his water from it he sat deliberately, defiantly, on a chair beside it and cracked the top of the bottle. He sat, looking at nothing, sipping at the water and listening to the hum of the vending machine, which matched the white noise constantly burbling from the speakers mounted high on the walls.

What the hell was he doing? That craft he had seen over Argentina, the craft that had seen him, tested him, was still out there somewhere. He felt sure it could be wherever it wanted to be. It might be hanging directly over Dreamland right now, flickering in and out of real space, like it had one foot in two different dimensions. He had seen it with his own eyes, but instead of being up there, trying to gather data on the mystery vessel, he was playing mind games—*literally!*—down here with Hayes.

Her gambit or threat wouldn't help. However badly he wanted to fly, however much he wanted to stop doing these damned tests, it wouldn't give him the ability to move the red ball. He knew that as surely as he knew the ground would support him when he walked on it. It was a fact of nature, and only some deep and thoroughly unexpected disruption of reality would alter that. It simply wasn't in his power.

On the Locust, when he had shielded the weapons systems from Hastings, he had done it not just deliberately, but casually, knowing he could do it. The power had been his for the taking, as solid and predictable as concrete. Why he couldn't access the same confidence here, the same surety, he didn't know, but it was a fact of the universe that every atom of his being understood, and he was now wasting precious time trying to get Hayes to recognize the same thing. It was maddening.

He waited another ten minutes before returning to the test facility, accessing the room by retinal scan. At least he didn't get lost on the way this time. Hayes was sitting in the corner again, waiting for him, but she said nothing about how long he had been. In fact, he thought, she avoided his eyes as he took his seat and began glaring balefully at the computer monitor with the red dot, so that he was suddenly on his guard.

But.

Something about the room seemed subtly different. He glanced around but it looked as it had before: the same baffling on the walls, the simple desk, the computer. The furnishings were minimal. So why did it feel so different?

He sat down in the chair, feeling the presence of Hayes behind him. She had slipped off her lab coat and was wearing a cream-colored blouse and navy skirt that went just over her knees. The coat had not been draped over the back of her chair but folded over something on the floor behind her.

A large cardboard box.

Alan wasn't sure why this felt significant, but he realized that however much he stared at the computer, his mind was reaching behind him for something that had not been there before.

He risked a glance over his shoulder and saw, peeking out from under her carefully positioned jacket, a tiny, cracked opening in the top flaps of the box and through it a patch of yellow paint.

It was the crate from the Locust, he was almost sure. The container for the alien manikins.

Yes.

He felt it. Moving the red dot was almost an afterthought, an easy, casual thing requiring no effort at all. He sent it tracing the screen in a series of spirals, slowly at first, then fast till it was dizzying to look at. He heard Hayes's intake of breath as it began to zigzag between corners. Then, with a nuanced twitch of his mental control, the red dot became a line that flashed across the screen before forming words in elegant cursive.

What's in the box, Doc?

He turned to find Hayes white-faced, staring from the message on the computer to him, and before she could collect herself, he reached down and snatched the lab coat away.

Beneath it, nestled in the corner of the room, half hidden by the cardboard box it nestled in, was the familiar yellow crate.

It made a kind of sense to him. It fitted, or rather, it fitted as the beginning of an explanation. But there was more, and to see that he needed to open the crate. It was locked, but it was as if he could see the tumblers of the digital lock in his head. Mentally tripping them so that the clasp sprang open was as easy as thought.

"Mr. Young, you are not authorized to look in there!" said Hayes, recovering from the shock of the moment. But her heart wasn't in it.

"Then you should call security," said Alan, lifting the lid. He had known to expect the two diminutive alien manikins which, for all their careful execution looked like half-jokey souvenirs from some Roswell gift shop, and sure enough, they were there. He lifted them out, knowing their irrelevance, and found that they had been lying on a quilted fabric. He peeled back the first fold like he was carefully unwrapping a Christmas present whose paper he wanted to save, and hesitated.

He had not known what to expect. But the tablet of carved stone still came as a surprise. He had never seen the thing Timika had found in the underground vault, the tablet that she had been directed to by Jerzy Stern's diary, but he knew that this was it the moment he laid eyes on it. He felt it, its antiquity, its strangeness, and he knew that this was the reason he had had such pinpoint control of his psychic abilities on the Locust. Whatever talent he had, this curious slab of an ancient past spoke to it, magnified it, made it usable.

"How does it work?" he asked.

"I really have no idea . . ." Hayes began, but the prevarication was obviously false, and Alan felt his impatience turn to anger.

"Don't lie to me, Doctor," he said, biting off the words, and staring her down. "I've had enough lies and evasions to last me a lifetime. And I'm tired of being your lab rat. Answer the question. How. Does. It. Work?"

"I don't know," she said, and this time her guard was down so that she looked both weary and a little scared of him. "We don't know. We weren't sure that it did."

"But it was on the Locust when I went to Argentina?"

"Yes. We didn't know if it would make a difference but thought we might as well try. Judging by what happened during the mission, we thought it worked. Today's tests were to make sure and see if we could calibrate how much difference it made, or see if it gave off any kinds of readings. An energy signature, perhaps, or . . ."

"And did it?"

She shook her head.

"Not that we were able to detect."

"We?" said Alan. "It's just you."

The door opened and Kenyon entered, two uniformed men with submachine guns with him.

"Just you?" he said. "Come now, Alan. You're never alone in Dreamland. Come with me, please."

As Hayes watched, caught between apprehension and relief, Kenyon showed Alan out and down the long white hallway. It wasn't entirely clear if he was under arrest and was being escorted to some kind of brig, but the guards kept close, weapons at the ready.

"Where are we going?" Alan asked.

"Something has come up," said Kenyon. "You are needed elsewhere."

And that was all the explanation he was going to get. They walked the labyrinthine corridors till they came to what looked like an external door that put them in a kind of parking garage Alan had never seen before. An SUV with blacked-out windows and a solid panel between the front and the back was waiting for them. Kenyon got into the back and gave Alan an expectant look. When Alan hesitated, put off by the dark interior, Kenyon gave him a withering look.

"This isn't some Manhattan street corner where getting into a strange vehicle means stepping into unknown danger."

"You mean I'm in danger already?" asked Alan.

"I mean that if we wanted you dead, Alan, you'd be dead. Come on. We haven't got all day."

It was tough to argue with that. Alan climbed in, and as he pulled the door shut, he felt the car roll forward.

He had no idea where they went, but he thought they drove fast and some of it felt like they were riding on dirt baked hard by the Nevada sun. At last he heard the echo of their tires on smooth concrete and knew they were inside again.

Following Kenyon's lead, he got out and found himself in another hangar, though this one was loaded with heavy machinery where men in blue coveralls were working. In the center, sitting outlandishly like something off a movie set, was a battered and gouged flying disk, its silver bright as chrome where it wasn't buckled and smeared with dirt. Alan knew it well. They had dubbed it the sport model. It was the craft Alan had flown at least partly with his mind the fateful night Hatcher had been killed.

"It's ready to fly?" he asked, turning in disbelief to Kenyon. It didn't look ready.

"Not even close," said Kenyon, frowning at the ship.

"Okay," said Alan. "So . . . tell me when it's ready."

"It has to be ready now."

"Clearly that's not going to happen," said Alan, scowling at the crumpled paneling of the otherwise sleek silver craft. Then the urgency in Kenyon's tone struck him. "Wait. Why does it have to be ready?"

"The craft you saw over Argentina?" said Kenyon, stepping closer and speaking in a lower voice. "It followed you."

"What? Where is it?"

"Up there somewhere," said Kenyon, his eyes flicking to the hangar roof. We can't get a fix."

Alan stared. This was bad. But it was also way beyond his range of expertise.

"So what do you want from me?" he said.

"We need that disk airworthy. You're going to fix it."

"What? I'm not an engineer! I can barely change the oil in my car. I sure as hell can't fix whatever that is."

"Not by yourself maybe," said a familiar voice. "But maybe with a little help."

Alan turned. Standing at the back of the SUV was Barry Regis.

"A little help?" Alan asked his friend.

"From the team," said Barry, nodding at the pit crew milling around the crippled disk, "from me, and . . ." He looked pointedly at the yellow crate, which was being lifted down from the back of the car. "From them."

JENNIFER
Hampshire. England

JENNIFER STUMBLED THROUGH THE HALLWAY OF THE empty little house, unsure what to think, her mind full of strange images, the old woman watching her from the chair through compound eyes, the impossible light that had filled the cottage before her disappearance, the framed pictures of elves and fairies with their butterfly and beetle companions.

Except that the elves and their bugs weren't separate at all, were they? They were one. They had been painted separately because that's how people made sense of them, but the shining ones had always been somehow insects for all their magical glamor.

She didn't know where the idea came from or why it had struck her now and with such strange certainty. The word *glamor* seemed particularly right. In ordinary talk it meant merely allure, the sophisticated appeal that some people radiated when they were suitably dressed. But the word went deeper. In the fairy stories of her childhood it meant something like a spell, a magical veil that disguised the elves and goblins so that their true hardness and cruelty were lost in ethereal beauty. Fairies, or the Fey as they were sometimes called, were cruel and selfish creatures, and it was only their glamor that stopped people from recognizing them for what they were. They were prone to random malice, delighted in spreading chaos and disorder amongst humans, and their acts caused pain, suffering, even death.

Acts such as abducting children . . .

Jennifer stopped just as she reached the cottage door, considering that thought realistically for the first time.

No, she did not believe in fairies, so no, she did not believe Margery's tale that she had, as a baby, been taken by them. But she knew of something else she had not believed in until very recently that might take a child, something that might enslave her father, something bound to strange lights in the sky such as had been reported from time immemorial . . .

Even as she thought it she found that her sense of the cottage door was changing. It was no longer wooden and painted with flaking blue with a little window in the top. Now it was gray and metal and set into a cinder-block wall.

She was in a cell!

She put her hands against it and it felt cold and solid. But the hands were not hers. They were strong, female hands. But their skin was brown, dark as polished walnut and, since she was hungry, her mind was straying to a pastry shop on East Fifty-Third that served the most divine eclairs . . .

And then it was gone, and she was herself again, outside the cottage and alone in the Hampshire night, though she felt the lingering presence of someone else's anxieties.

Jennifer fumbled in her pocket for her cell phone and dialed Timika's number.

It took a moment for the call to go through, and when it was answered, the voice was male and unfamiliar.

"Hello?"

"I need to speak to Timika. Timika Mars."

"She is currently unavailable. Who is calling, please."

"This is Jennifer Quinn, and you need to unlock her right away!"

There was a staticky silence, then the voice said, "Hold please."

Jennifer paced up and down the cottage's dark and narrow hallway, caught between an urgent sense that she needed to talk to Timika right away and complete bafflement as to what they had to talk about.

"Hello?"

It was Timika. She sounded cautious.

"It's Jennifer."

"They said," Timika answered. "I can't believe they are letting me talk to you. What's going on?"

"You are being held against your will."

"Yes, though it's not clear what branch of the great US of A is going to claim me. Things are a bit weird right now. What did you say to them?"

"Nothing. Why?"

"I just don't understand why they are letting us talk. Why are you calling?"

"I'm not sure," Jennifer answered. For a second she didn't know what to say, then the words tumbled out. "Are they keeping you in a cell with a gray metal door?" she asked.

"Yeah," said Timika. "You got, like, FaceTime or something?"

"No," said Jennifer, strangely relieved. "I can just see it. In my head. Or I could a moment ago. You were thinking about buying chocolate eclairs from a place you know in New

York. I was . . . sort of . . . you. Oh, and I'm e-mailing you something."

She tapped at her phone's screen and waited.

"I have it," said Timika, still wary. "I'm downloading it now. It's . . . holy shit! That's the thing I saw!"

"It's called Raggety," said Jennifer. "It was a character in a weird book I had as a kid. It always freaked me out."

"And now it's freaking me out," said Timika. "Thanks."

"I'm seeing into your head and you are seeing into mine: memories, buried details."

"Huh," said Timika. "Okay, well that sort of explains something, without, you know, actually explaining it at all, and kind of scaring the shit out of me in the process."

"We're connected," said Jennifer. "Other people too, I think. Maybe . . . Timika, I think I am seeing inside Morat's mind. Yours too now."

"Remind me to keep my thoughts clean," said Timika.

"You don't believe me?" asked Jennifer, amazed at how lightly Timika was taking it.

"No, actually, it makes a kind of sense. I just don't like it. Look, they are probably listening in to this call so don't be surprised if we get cut off, but whatever Alan and Barry can do with their minds, I don't think it just came from the craft. I think it was there before that night, waiting to be, like, turned on."

"What? How do you know?"

"I don't. Not for sure. But I think they were experimented on as kids. Their DNA tweaked. I think they were being groomed for . . . whatever came later."

"So why am I in your head?"

"I think the same thing happened to me. Recently. When I was taken. Right before you found me in Nevada. Whoever took me did something. Took my blood. Injected something back into me. Changed me." Her tone, which had been almost flippant, was now loaded with something like horror. Jennifer stood in silence, listening. A moment later, Timika's voice came back. "Is it possible that something similar happened to you?"

And there it was, the truth that had been orbiting her slowly for days, waiting to be caught in her gravitational well and pulled in.

"Yes," she replied simply. "Long ago. I was taken too."

There was another pregnant pause, then Timika said, "Right. Sorry. I guess we have more in common than we thought."

"So why am I only feeling it now?"

"Don't know. Something to do with . . . what we went through in Nevada, I guess."

"I keep thinking about bees," said Jennifer, almost dreamily. One hand had moved to the flesh on the back of her neck as if she was looking for the place where the surgery had happened all those years ago. She was talking to suppress the sense of violation, of outrage, talking to stop herself shrinking away from the past, like she was cringing at the feel of a bug on her skin. "Buzzing around me. Keep dreaming of them. Golden bees. I kept seeing them. This image from Crete in particular."

"From Crete?" asked Timika, her tone suddenly urgent.

"An ancient Minoan necklace thing. Two gold bees."

"You sure they were bees?"

"I thought so. I suppose they could have been wasps."

"Like, yellow jackets?"

"I suppose. Does it make a difference?"

"*Does it make a difference?*" said Timika, now her old self, confident and wry. It was comforting to hear her like this. "Let's see. Bees pollinate crops and flowers. They make honey.

They live in symbiosis with mankind and—literally—sweeten our existence, so that everyone starts freaking out the moment we suspect the bee population is in decline."

"I suppose so," said Jennifer.

"Girl, we haven't even got started yet. Think about it; when a bee stings you, it loses a part of itself, like it's cutting off a limb or something. It stings you, it's gonna die. Not so for a wasp which, apart from making nothing but more wasps, is the insect equivalent of the guy who cuts you for looking at his girlfriend. Wasps are not our friends and they do not come in peace. You ever heard people worrying about a decline in the *wasp* population?"

"Can't say I have."

"And with good reason. Now, think about it for a second. These things in your head, in your dreams. Are they bees or wasps?"

Jennifer thought. Her answer was entirely based on impressions she could neither defend nor explain, but when she spoke it was with absolute certainty.

"Wasps," she said.

"Yeah," said Timika. "That's what I figured."

"What does it mean?" asked Jennifer.

"Means we're in trouble," said Timika. "And I'm really not sure what I can do about it here. I think if you can . . ."

There was a confusion of noise in the background, voices, and maybe the shift of furniture in a confined space. When someone spoke again, it was the man's voice.

"Miss Mars is busy. Don't bother calling back."

Jennifer stared at the phone as it went abruptly silent, feeling the welling up of all the feelings she had kept in check so far. Timika had a way of making everything feel manageable, obstacles to be overcome and sneered at as you did so, but without her voice on the line Jennifer felt suddenly overwhelmed with horror and confusion. All the baffled outrage that had been swirling around in her head rose like a tide and she knew that she could not ride it out.

She sat down on Margery Cullen's thinly carpeted stairs and put her head in her hands.

And slept.

Or so it seemed.

She came to with a jolt, unsure where she was. She stood up, looking around her, and the house looked the same as before, but it felt later. Much later. She pulled out her phone to check the time but it was dead, the battery completely drained.

That's not possible, she thought. The phone had been over half-charged before she had come to the cottage.

"Mrs. Cullen!" she called out. "Hello?"

There was no reply and Jennifer was, she had to admit, relieved.

The dank creepiness of the old house settled into her once more and she remembered how keen she had been to get out before. She had to hunt around in her head before it came back, the strange sense of being outside herself, or inside someone else. She called Timika. And then . . . ?

She wasn't sure. Her eyes fell on the little hallway pictures of the elves with their bug escorts and, shuddering, she moved quickly to the cottage door and pulled it open. She stepped out into the night.

But was it the same night?

The thought alarmed her, in part because she didn't know why she even wondered about something that seemed so preposterous. It was dark outside, as it had been before, but she felt disoriented and, now that she thought about it, hungry.

Just how long had she been sitting on the old cook's stairs?

Assuming, of course, that the house still belonged to the old cook and not to the things depicted on her hallway walls.

Another mad thought.

For a moment Jennifer squeezed her eyes closed, forcing herself to be composed and rational, trying to decide what to do next. She felt lost as only a child does, completely out of her depth and looking for a sign from someone older, wiser, who would tell her that everything would be okay in a way so sure that she would believe it unquestioningly.

But her father, who had been there at the beginning of all this, was gone, and the only other person who gave her a sense of strength was a woman she had only known for a few weeks and who was currently incarcerated by the US government. The phone call to the States came back to her in snatches, like something from long ago, and Jennifer seized it with both hands and held on to it. She marveled at Timika's unflappability, envied it. She wanted to call her back, but the phone was dead, and who knew how much time had passed since they had spoken? In truth, she was amazed they had let Timika talk as long as they had. Indeed, the more she thought about it as she walked, dazed by all she had heard, back along the street to the stile and the path through the fields, the stranger it all seemed. She had to assume that, far from wanting to keep Timika silent, whoever had taken her prisoner wanted to hear what the two women had to say.

She wondered if she felt different now that she knew what had happened to her childhood self, and decided she didn't. How could she? If she had indeed been somehow altered when she was a baby, taken by whoever flew the mystery craft, she had lived with that change almost her entire life. She may only be feeling it now, but it had been in her, sleeping all this time. Again, she felt the shudder of nausea, a wave of revulsion that turned to anger as she thought of the violation.

Taking an infant and messing with the basic building blocks of her existence . . .

And adding what? Some grotesque insect trait, some leaning toward a hive mind that would link her to other, similarly violated people?

She shuddered again, as if she had found a cockroach in her hair.

Her father's business cronies had known what had happened, and had threatened worse. That was the chain they had wrapped around him, the tether that had pulled him from whatever course his life would have otherwise taken. She thought of Herman Saltzburg and the rest, savagely wishing he was still alive just so she could kill him all over again.

She gritted her teeth, closed her eyes once more, and breathed in the night.

The same night? What day is it?

She needed to find a way to use what she had discovered, to turn it into action, and she needed to shut out those other presences in her head. Because Timika was right. They weren't bees, benign and homely; they were wasps, and they meant her harm.

No, she thought, with that same inexplicable certainty, *they mean us all harm.*

She paused to consider this, trying to unpack her own thoughts as if they had come to her from someone else, and laid them out where she could see them clearly.

Yes, she decided. It wasn't just she who was under attack. *The world itself and all its people.* We are at war. Have been for years.

And the enemy . . . ? The enemy is . . .

She heard the humming in her head as she had heard it in the museum, and first it sounded like helicopter blades but then it sounded like . . .

Voices?

Not English-speaking voices, or any human language. These were an altogether different brand of foreign. They chirped and scratched and buzzed, rising and falling in pitch and volume, throbbing wave-like pulses of sound that whispered, simply, one word:

Swarm.

She paused to consider the implications of the word, and in that instant, distant but distinct, she heard the thin insect whine coming from the thatch of trees to her right, and looked up in time to see an uncanny, green luminescence drifting over the black treetops like toxic smoke. Shifting within it was something large and solid and spherical, something that sparkled like coal inside the glowing emerald mantle, something, she felt sure, that was looking for, *hunting* for, her.

MORAT
Central Mountains, Crete

THE TEXT CAME EXACTLY ON SCHEDULE, AND MORAT responded with his coordinates. His instincts had been right, though he was pleasantly surprised by the specifics because they suggested in no uncertain terms that Rasmussen hadn't been blowing smoke about Maynard's continued reach. A Mil Mi-17 helo was on its way from a private airfield near Tobruk in Libya, with a squad of eight heavily armed mercenaries and a Maynard field agent. It was an older but capable aircraft that could look after itself if necessary and would be able to deposit the troops and return to base without refueling.

Just.

Like a lot of things on this mission, precision was going to be of the essence. The helo would come in low, doing its best to stay off local radar, banking on the assumption that the sound of its approach would be put down to the Greek police's ongoing search for the fugitive shooter. A designated landing zone had been identified on the north side of the mountain barely a mile from the church and dig site. Morat would meet the squad there and they would secure the excavation on foot, eliminate Tan and anyone with him, and load the cargo into the helo. They would then fly northeast to an abandoned airstrip near Fethiye on the Turkish mainland, from which they would head east by private jet. In a few hours, he'd be back in Kazakhstan. Morat would have been nervous, but Rasmussen had included one more detail that put all his fears to rest.

Strelka support.

The arrow code name meant that when the helo came into Greek airspace it would have at least one predatory protector watching over it, a waspish protector that would evade conventional detection systems but could become very much involved if necessary, a protector whose sting was shaped like a great black arrowhead . . .

Suddenly things were looking up.

Morat checked the time and began his cautious trek back to the cave. He figured he could rest there for a couple of hours before returning to the meadow where the helo would touch down. With an assault team at his disposal he may not have to do much more than lead the way, but he would like to be mentally prepared.

He had, perhaps, overplayed just how confident he was about locating the missing artifact in his previous conversation with Rasmussen, but he was not worried. As time passed his sense of the church's importance swelled in his mind, and though he did not know precisely what the artifact was, he knew he would feel its rightness the moment he laid eyes upon it. He also had a pretty good idea where it was, though he could not have explained where that impression had come from.

The phone buzzed again. Rasmussen. A second call was unexpected and Morat frowned at it before answering.

"Yes?"

"You suggested you planned to return to the scene of the crime, is that correct?"

"To part of it, yes. The church."

"I thought as much. You should be advised that the local constabulary has set up their base of operations in that very building. You should expect multiple officers, some of them armed."

"That's not an issue," said Morat.

"Agreed, but I thought you should be aware that, according to radio chatter, Tan and the Greek archaeologist are currently located in that very building."

Morat tensed up. If Tan found what they were looking for before the team arrived, that could complicate things.

"Problem?" said Rasmussen.

"On the contrary," Morat lied easily. "Just means we won't have to go looking for him. Two birds, one stone."

"Understand that if you fail to exit with the artifact, your aerial escort has orders to vaporize the entire location."

"Understood," said Morat.

"Your fellow operative will give you a communication device on his arrival. I expect constant updates regardless of your success or failure."

"Absolutely, sir."

"And Mr. Morat?"

"Yes, sir?"

"Make sure it's success."

NICHOLAS
Near Fotinos, Crete

NICHOLAS DIDN'T SMOKE. NEVER HAD. BUT AT TIMES like this, he wished he did. It would be an excuse to step outside into the cooling night air and be alone with his thoughts. His eyes moved from the accumulated papers on the makeshift desk to the laptop screen and back, as the cops continued their bustle in the body of the church, but he wasn't learning anything new. In fact, most of the police had gone home for the night when Anastas left, and apart from the eager young lady cop with the slightly hawkish face who was still sorting through files and occasionally making phone calls, the only other officer Nicholas could still see was a disconsolate-looking young man loitering in the doorway. At first Nicholas thought he was guarding the place, but as the cop's gaze kept straying to the busy—and pretty—lady cop, he wondered if something more personal was going on. The female officer didn't seem especially aware of him, though that might be a performance, Nicholas supposed, a professional or teasing strategy to keep him interested.

Or, Nicholas reminded himself, *it might be no more than it looks like and would explain why the guy looks so miserable.*

He was over-reading again. Hard not to given the way he'd spent the last few days, pawing the ground and sniffing for clues like a bloodhound, trying to string together the links of a chain long broken.

If it really is a chain, and not just a bunch of isolated fragments . . .

That too.

Elina looked ready to fall asleep. If she hadn't been so afraid of being alone, she would have gone home hours ago. It wasn't like they'd made any progress since. A cot had been set up for the duty officers to take turns dozing: an army surplus thing, all telescoping steel rods and a stretched canvas panel for a mattress. Elina eyed it for a moment, caught Nicholas watching her and, shrugging apologetically, made the decision. She spoke, in Greek, to the policewoman, who nodded her assent while making it clear that it was both fine and slightly annoying that she had to give permission. Elina stood up and walked over to the cot, sat on the edge gingerly, then lay down and pulled her legs up, avoiding Nicholas's gaze as if embarrassed, as if needing to sleep after all that had happened and before they had solved their various riddles somehow showed weakness.

Lack of moral fiber, thought Nicholas, smiling vaguely to himself, not entirely sure where the phrase came from.

Elina rolled over to face the plastered stone wall. At the same time, the lady cop stretched at her desk, stood up, and smoothed her starched shirt over her chest, then spoke to the man at the church door in Greek. He replied hurriedly, fumbling in his pockets for the inevitable pack of cigarettes as she came to join him.

Nicholas was jealous. As they stepped out of the glare of the work lights they almost vanished except for the quick flare of a lighter. Nicholas listened vaguely to their distant mutterings, and thought he heard the woman laugh briefly, though he couldn't understand what they were saying. Then he realized he was hearing something else: a distant, whining sound that seemed to swell and echo in the church, like the drone of an insect or . . .

A bicycle wheel.

That was it. It sounded slightly labored, like something was rubbing against the rim, or it had been connected to a dynamo that powered the back light, like the one he had as a kid . . .

He turned slowly. With Elina sleeping, or close to it, and the two cops outside smoking, he had the little church to himself. It was still unnaturally bright under the floodlights, and outside he heard the steady chirp of crickets in the long grass of the site, but the place felt unreal. The sound of the bicycle was coming from behind the screen.

He got up cautiously, and went around the latticed stonework and the roughly carved stone block that was the little church's altar, the wooden floor groaning under his footsteps. He was inside the tiny curve of the apse where the priest would have conducted services a century or so earlier. And there was his mother, working as before, eying the slight wobble of the overturned bicycle's wheel with one eye shut, her face only inches from the spinning tire. She had a pry bar in one hand and was pressing its edge gently against the rim, feeling for irregularities.

"Ma?" said Nicholas. "What are you doing here?"

His mother looked up and smiled, that wide, open smile of hers that was almost a laugh. Man, he missed that smile. She was small and frail, birdlike, her face wrinkled till she looked far older than she really was, but that smile! Five hundred watts or more.

She answered, but at first Nicholas couldn't hear anything except the noise of the bike wheel. When he focused the sound sort of faded in, though it was out of sync with what he was seeing. It was like when you stream a video but the audio track is a little behind the picture, like a plane breaking the sound barrier, which you see go overhead in silence only to have the roar of the engines come following after it a second or two later. Her voice unwound not so much from her mouth as from the church itself, so that it sounded like she was speaking into an invisible microphone and her words were being piped in over the PA.

"I'm sorry," he said. "I didn't get that. What did you say?"

"Not level," she said. "Look! See? Wheel wobbles."

"It looks okay to me," he said, peering at the bicycle, which was red with flame decals, half scratched off, on the struts. One of the neighbor kids' bikes. She was probably fixing it for free. "You need another gauge? Wrench?"

"No," she replied. "Gauges fine. Floor not level."

"The floor?"

"Not level," she said. "See?"

"Not sure I can help you with that, ma," he said.

"Yes," she said, smiling at him with trust so deep that his breath caught and he found himself tumbling through joy and into grief. "You can."

He stared. He blinked.

And she was gone.

Nicholas was alone behind the altar's partial screen. He rubbed his eyes, finding them wet and painful, and turned quickly to see if Elina had seen, or if the two cops had come back in, but the church was silent. The Greek professor was curled up on the cot, her face to the wall as before, and the nave was otherwise empty.

Nicholas didn't know if he was relieved or disappointed. His mother had been here. Again. It hadn't been a dream. He had been standing, walking . . . And if it was a hallucination it was a curiously specific one.

He frowned at the wooden floor, feeling again the strangeness of the vision and wondering what it all meant.

"Floor not level."

His scowl deepened.

Floor.

The altar was a block of solid stone with a single cross cut into it, but the ground around it was series of interconnected wooden platforms forming a stepped dais. They weren't as old as the body of the church, and had probably been carpeted at one point, but the wood was whole, not worm-eaten and rotted like the floor of the belfry. It had been well protected by the dome above, which still looked completely intact.

He stared for a moment, then moved decisively, striding back into the nave all the way to the vestibule, where the excavation tools were stacked. Dimly aware of the two cops chatting outside in Greek, he chose a sturdy mattock whose earth-polished bit was bright as silver, and returned to the altar. He selected a seam in the wooden floor panels, worked the bit into the gap, and pried it like a lever, till one panel rose enough that, with the mattock handle braced under his arm, his could get his fingers into the crack. He straightened his back and pulled upward with both hands till the panel moved. He tried again and, when it snagged and creaked, forced it higher, gritting his teeth till he heard a corner splinter and the panel came free.

Underneath the floor were stone flags on which the panels had been laid, and in the center, half covered by the next panel, was one with an iron ring—brown with rust, but still solid—set into the stone.

Floor not level, he thought, the idea circling his head with feverish heat. She had pointed him to this. He knew it.

Nicholas worked the mattock into the gap between wood and stone and heaved the second panel up as if it was a great door in the floor. It banged against the rear wall, but no one called out to ask him what he was doing. If they came to see, he wouldn't even have to speak: just step back and point . . . because the stone beneath the wooden floor was now revealed, as was the slab of rock with the ring in it, a slab that was very clearly some kind of a trapdoor. For a second Nicholas just stared, drinking it in, feeling the taste of the word in his mouth like triumph:

Crypt.

JASON GREENWOOD
Wednesday, November 15, 1967. Hull, England

PETER AND MICHAEL GREENWOOD, THE FISHERMEN who saw lights in the sky over the Humber, were long dead. Their children and grandchildren were dead too, as was much of the fishing industry that had fed them. But while some of Peter's descendants had moved away, seeking factory work over the county line in Lancashire as the great Victorian steam age came to clanking, filthy life, traces of the family persisted on the Yorkshire side, and one, a boy of twelve called Jason, looked uncannily like him. There were, of course, no portraits of Regency-era trawler captains that might have survived till later years, and photography was still several decades away when Peter Greenwood died, but if his image had survived into this strange and different time, the resemblance between the fisherman and the boy

437

would have been unmistakable. It was the eyes, blue and clear and wary.

Jason grew up on the Longhill estate, a grim and dreary expanse of identical council houses, with few trees and less grass. It was a mere two miles north of the spot where his ancestor had watched openmouthed as the lights danced in the night sky over the river some 166 years earlier. A tiny distance, but it was not so unusual for families to live a stone's throw from where their forebears had lived, and it would be another two decades before that pattern changed significantly. Until very recently the only way from Longhill to Holderness High Road, the closest thing to a major street in the area, was by crossing a plank over a ditch. The residents had bought their food and supplies from mobile shops that had driven around the area at erratic intervals as post-World War II privation dragged on, seemingly forever. Those days were, mercifully, over, but Longhill was still a bleak, gray place to grow up.

Jason's ancestor had never again seen the lights he watched that night in the first year of the nineteenth century, but a century later Hull was once again witness to strange nocturnal visitors. In 1909, a Mister Walker, himself distantly related by marriage to the long-dead Peter Greenwood, reported seeing a strange cigar-shaped object in the night sky as he walked along Coltman Street, a sighting verified by others who contacted the local police. Four years later, a similar object was glimpsed again, and one was the subject of a mass sighting confirmed by numerous civilians and police officers as it hung for an hour and a half directly over Paragon Station, in Hull's town center. The object, again cigar-shaped, and marked with red and white lights, was reported elsewhere over the ensuing months and became part of the so-called "scare-ship" craze, later explained away with talk of German zeppelins performing training and reconnaissance exercises. Such airships would become a new source of terror bringing death from the air in World War I, though whether Ferdinand von Zeppelin's feared vessels had reached the necessary level of technological sophistication to have executed such missions in the immediately prewar years remains debated.

Jason Greenwood knew none of this and would have thought it all ancient history. He was playing football in the park with a ragtag band of friends, relegated to goalkeeper because his shooting was rubbish and his passing not much better. He wasn't much better in goal, if the truth were known, but they had Jimmy Clarkson, easily the best player on the uneven, weedy square they were pleased to call a pitch. The opposition hadn't mounted a serious attack for twenty minutes, and with the light fading fast, they wouldn't get many more opportunities. It got dark fast and early at this time of year. So Jason stood loyally in between the two piles of mounded pullovers they used as goalposts, desultorily humming "When I'm Sixty-Four." He might not be much of a footballer, but thanks to his older brother Terry, he knew all the new music and that made him, in his way, cool. The new Beatles album was odd, odder even than *Revolver*, and there were bits of it he didn't really like, such as "Within You And Without You" which kept starting up again just when you thought it was finally over, but the record had caught his imagination all the same. When Terry, on the third listen in their shared back bedroom, pronounced it great, perhaps the best Beatles album yet, Jason decided to agree.

So he was just standing there, trying to remember the lyrics and muttering along to the tune in his head, watching his mates running and shouting and falling over, when the object appeared over the bare and scraggy trees of Sutton Park. It was long and thin and silver, like a series of oil drums connected on end, but massive, fifty, sixty yards long or more. It was hard to tell. It had lights at both ends, and some along a line in the middle that might have been windows.

And it was coming down.

Jason hadn't seen it approach exactly. One moment it wasn't there, and the next it was, but it looked solid and real and impossible all at the same time, so that he stood pointing and shouting till his friends stopped, letting the ball run off the field, ignored. They stood there, gazing upward, and as they did, a new light came from it, like a great rod had lit up below the belly of the great craft, and it painted the ground below it with light. The damp and ragged grass flashed green and the kids threw long shadows, their arms up in front of their faces to shield their eyes, as the light played over them.

For a moment nothing seemed to happen. Jason and his friends were locked in silent wonder and then, as suddenly as it had come, the white brilliance that bathed them vanished, though the ship itself—if that was what it was—continued to hang in the sky above. Its lights went out, but the shape was still visible, black in the gray dusk, so that what happened next was quite clear.

"It's coming down," said Norman Salworth.

"Buggar me," muttered Jimmy Clarkson. "It is an' all."

The lightless vessel descended directly through the treetops, an almost lazy downward drift, though it seemed to angle in the process, as if turning to fit an opening between the branches and trunks of the park's chestnut and sycamore trees.

"Let's go see," said Norman.

"Are you mental or what?" said Angie Cavendish, the only girl allowed to play with them because she was as good as Jimmy with the ball.

"You got a better idea, Cavendish?" demanded Norman.

"Better than being eaten by aliens and what not?" said Angie, squaring up to him.

"Aliens don't eat ya. Everyone knows that. They like . . . probe ya and stuff."

He didn't sound very sure.

"Well maybe I don't want to be probed," said Angie.

It was almost funny and Jason, who had always thought Angie was the best of them in more ways than football, took a breath that was almost a gasp.

"So what?" Norman fired back. "We just stand 'ere?"

"Nope," said Angie fiercely. "We get a copper."

Jason knew his eyes were almost as wide at the prospect of talking to a policeman as they had been looking at the ship.

"What like, *'scuse me officer, but a UFO just came down in Sutton Park woods?*" sneered Norman. "Right. They'll think you're talking bollocks. And besides," he added, warming to his theme, "where are you gonna find one?"

"There was one by't swings, o'er yonder," said Jason, speaking up for the first time, mostly to support Angie. Norman gave him a withering look, but he shrugged. "Big kids 'ad wrapped 'em round 't top bar and 'e were fixing 'em, like."

The story passed muster, and Jimmy nodded sagely.

"That were Pete Walker's dad," he said. "I saw 'im."

"'e will be gone now," said Norman, as if he was scoring a fine point of logic.

"Nah," said Jason, braver now that Angie was watching him with what he chose to see as respect. "He does a second beat as't street lights come on. 'e will be o'er there."

He nodded toward the road and, as if on cue, a tall man in black with big shoes, silver buttons on his jacket, and a tall copper's helmet strode around the corner with an easy, swinging gait.

Angie Cavendish flashed Norman a look of triumph and then took off running toward the policeman, shouting as she went. She ran, as ever, like a gazelle, like she was about to streak past the rest of the racers at the school field day, which she always did, and Jason watched, his heart in his mouth. The copper turned to face her, stooping fractionally as adults did when they talked to kids and wanted to seem taller than they were, then turned toward the rest of them. Moments later, he was following her back toward them briskly, almost jogging.

"Now," he said, "what's all this about?"

They all answered at once, but when Officer Walker quelled them with his hands, Angie took over, and the rest stood in respectful silence, nodding.

"It came down o'er there," she said. "Behind them trees."

"Crashed?" asked the policeman, quickly holding up his hands for silence at the chorus of no's. "Alright. Wait here." He stepped away, and made a big performance of activating a portable radio, still a new device in 1960s Yorkshire. He talked overly clearly into a mouthpiece, putting on a slightly posher accent than usual, and they heard the crackly response but could not make out the words, particularly since he turned abruptly away, as if embarrassed or secretive. When he finished, he looked troubled and more alert than he had.

"What?" said Angie, the truth coming to her even as she spoke. "Oh, someone else saw it, didn't they?"

"There has been another report," conceded the officer. He looked less sure of himself now, as if he had merely been indulging them to this point and now didn't know what to do.

"Well?" said Angie, fearless as much in the face of law enforcement as she was in the face of one of Jimmy's crunching tackles.

The policeman's face set and he nodded. "Show me," he said. "But I lead, all right? You stay behind me and do what I tell ya."

There was some muttered agreement and furtive looks. In the policeman's presence, *helping him with his inquiries*, as it were, they were all braver and more sure of themselves. Even Norman had forgotten his objections and shot Angie a secret grin which, Jason was slightly annoyed to see, she returned, their differences apparently forgotten.

They crossed the playing field and the tarmacked path, climbing the slick ridge to the trees in a black huddle. Jason's heart was beating fast and hard, more with excitement than excursion, and when Angie—without warning—stuck out her hand to him, he grabbed it. It was soft and warm and very slightly moist, but what it meant, he had no idea, so that for a moment he almost forgot what they were doing and turned to stare at her in the gloom.

"Thanks," she said, clambering over a mossy log.

He nodded, realizing too late that she had just wanted a little help over the wet ground, and clung on to her hand a fraction too long, so that she gave him a quick look, peering questioningly into his face. Her eyes were big and dark, her skin pale in the failing twilight so that she seemed to shine . . .

"Over there!" said Norman, who had somehow gotten to the lead position in both literal and metaphorical terms.

He was pointing to a light among the trees. It wasn't like the dazzling radiance they had seen before. It was small and yellow and unsteady, and it was not, now that Jason had surmounted the ridge and could see the whole stringy copse of trees, alone. There were four others, evenly spaced.

Fires, he thought.

Of the great cigar-shaped craft which had drifted down here, there was absolutely no sign.

For a second, they all just stood and looked down into the thin patch of trees he had once thought a forest, and Jason saw by the light of the fires just how small it was, how poorly the natural world was represented in what must surely have once been a wild and fertile place. In a moment he felt older, a sensation that brought a wave of disappointment so that when the policeman turned to scowl at them, he was not surprised.

"Is this your idea of a joke?" Officer Walker snarled. "I ought to take you all in for wasting police time and," he added, gesturing vaguely at the fires among the trees, "arson."

"We didn't do nothing," Angie grumbled. "We saw what we saw and told you, that's all."

"It's true, Mister," said Jimmy. "We didn't set those fires."

"That's *officer* to you, Jimmy Clarkson," said the copper warningly. "And don't think I don't know who you are and where you live. I'll wager your parents wouldn't want to hear about this."

In other circumstances, the veiled threat would have sent terror through Jason, but as it was, and for reasons he couldn't explain, it didn't seem to matter.

"What she said were true," he said, surly, meeting the policeman's eyes and holding them. "*And* you said other people had reported it, an' all."

"Well where is your UFO now?" said the policeman.

Jason shrugged.

"Space?" he suggested.

Jimmy looked horrified but Jason was almost sure he saw Angie grin, though she hid it quickly.

"I'll be speaking to your mam, Jason Greenwood," said the policeman. "Now, I 'ave to get back to mi beat. See that those fires get put out, and don't be wasting any more police time."

They watched him go, turning back to look toward the makeshift football pitch.

"Told ya," said Norman sulkily. "Said it, didn't I? Knew 'e wouldn't believe us."

"Yeah," said Jason. "But it were still true."

It was too dark to see if Angie was looking at him, but he felt an approving silence as if he had crystalized something they had all been fumbling toward for years.

"Gotta get mi ball," said Jimmy. "See ya at school."

Unevenly they spilled down the ridge, but Jason considered the line of sputtering, dying fires, feeling the November night beginning to mist.

Just 'cause they don't agree, don't mean it isn't true, he thought again. *Doesn't make you a liar.*

"Walk me 'ome?"

He turned, startled out of his reverie. Angie Cavendish had waited behind. It was too dark for her to see his blush, his sudden jubilation.

"Aye," he said, very grown up. "All right."

ALAN
Area 51/Dreamland, Nevada

"**T**HIS MAKES NO SENSE," SAID ALAN. "I REALIZE WE'RE IN a tight spot if that cigar ship is close by, but I'm a pilot, not a mechanic. Let me take a Locust up and I'll bring back what intel we can."

"Hastings can fly the Locust," said Kenyon. "We need you in the disk."

"The disk isn't airworthy!" said Alan. "Look at it! You've been working on it for weeks and it still looks like it got T-boned on I-95. I can't fly that!"

The so-called sport model was a classic Flying Saucer design with a windowed central dome, but otherwise featureless chrome curves. One side was badly crimped and battered so that almost a quarter of the ship's surface area was distorted and collapsed, while its underside was scored and streaked from Alan's forced landing. It looked much as it did the night he had been dragged from its smoking remains, except that it was now surrounded by gantries and hooked to various computer devices and workstations. It trailed cables and hoses and looked, to Alan's eyes, like a patient on life support.

"We're gonna fix it first," said Barry.

Alan gave him a disbelieving look.

"You remember when you rebuilt your parents' lawn-mower?" he said.

"Started first time," said Barry, grinning.

"And promptly caught fire. Then blew up. Didn't so much cut the grass as turn it into a black and smoking crater. No offense, Barry, but you're no more of an engineer than I am."

"No one is asking for you to do the actual repairs," said Kenyon. "We just want you to provide some guidance. And while this jokey reminiscence is fun and all, we're kind of on the clock. So let's stop debating whether you are going to follow orders or not, and get on with it, okay?"

Alan looked from him to Barry and back.

"You're serious?' he said.

"Never more so," said Kenyon. "I believe you know Mr. Riordan?"

He indicated a freckled, red-haired man who had been head of the ground crew at Papoose Lake. Alan remembered him as capable and level-headed. He greeted him with a handshake, still trying to adjust to what was apparently being asked of him.

"So you want me to try to remember how I flew this thing?" he said. "I'll be honest, it was all a bit of a blur and a lot of it was kind of intuitive. Not sure how helpful I'll be when it comes to explaining it."

"Not as such, Major," said Riordan, who had always called him by his old military title. "We're trying to visualize the structure in peak flying condition, but the technology is . . . not all familiar to us."

Alan felt Barry give him a significant look.

"We need to know how things should be, and in some cases we have to reshape the exterior metal without further damaging the internal components, remaking broken circuitry and the like . . ."

"Okay," said Alan, still confused. "But, I'm sorry, I still don't know how to help."

"Same way you flew the ship," said Kenyon. "With your mind."

The baldness of the statement took Alan off guard, and he immediately looked sheepishly at Riordan and the three other engineers in earshot, one of whom he recognized as his former instructor, who Alan had nicknamed Professor Beaker. No one seemed remotely surprised or skeptical.

"All right," said Barry, taking charge. "Let's get to this, shall we?"

Alan wanted to say simply "How?" but he followed his friend's lead, if only to show willingness. It was only then that he saw—wearing her lab coat, glasses, and an air of rigid professionalism quite at odds with their last encounter—Dr. Imelda Hayes entering the hangar. Alan half expected some guard to step up, tell her she didn't have clearance to be here but, as he was quickly learning, her participation in the program had always been far more central to the whole than he had suspected.

"Can we focus on the lower left quadrant," said Riordan, taking a position on the elevated platform that jutted out over the fractured disk. "This is where the most profound damage seems to be."

Alan didn't like that *seems*. Riordan and his men were good at their jobs, but they had clearly made little real progress on the repairs since the crash.

"Move that into the craft itself, please," said Hayes. The *that* in question was the yellow crate, which had been placed on a wheeled dolly. Her eyes met Alan's briefly, but while she gave nothing away, he began to realize what they wanted of him.

"I don't know if I can do this," he said, half to himself.

"Follow my lead," said Barry. "I need to touch it," he said to the room as a whole. "Everyone okay with that?"

When no one responded, he climbed over the rail of the gantry and stepped gingerly onto the crumpled disk, squatting carefully, his face close to the metal and his eyes closed.

"Alan," he said, extending a hand. He spoke softly but the room was utterly silent and everyone heard.

Alan faltered and then, very slightly embarrassed, followed him, lowering himself onto the bulge of the cockpit and taking his friend's hand.

One moment he was feeling slightly ridiculous, acutely aware of everyone in the room watching him, and the next there was only the craft and his own mind blurring into Barry's. The intensity of it, the intimacy, was so startling that he almost let go, but Barry's grip was strong, and a moment later, Alan was barely aware where he was.

He was in the ship. He *was* the ship.

His former impression that the craft was an anaesthetized patient came back to him, though he knew that the consciousness he was sensing was really his own and Barry's. Even so, he felt the disk like it was his own body, blood coursing, synapses firing, gas exchanging, bowels digesting, muscles responding, all the unnoticed functions of a resting body suddenly clear and conscious in his head, but somehow mediated by the ship, as if their minds had given it life and they felt what it felt. The craft was suddenly vibrant, interfacing through them, speaking its pain, its crippled dysfunction.

For a moment it was almost too much to bear, and Alan gasped and sweated, close to sobbing with the electric agony of the thing, and then it receded and became, somehow, schematic, like he was inside a 3-D blueprint. This was Barry's doing, he knew, but as he scanned the details, he could see quite clearly the gap between what was and what should be. With his mind he reached out to one network of nerve-like connections that had been cut cleanly and, as he visualized them whole again, they reshaped themselves and made themselves complete. He felt it, a curious, organic shift. It was, he thought, as if you could feel your own hair growing or sense the way your skin re-formed over a wound. He felt atoms and molecules rearranging themselves at his behest as the disk reknit itself from within.

It was a godlike feeling, but he felt only awe and humility.

Dimly, in the world outside himself, he thought he heard voices and the sound of labor and machinery responding to what he and Barry were doing, but it all seemed very far away. And once, when he looked up, he saw, sitting on the bulged canopy like a model on the hood of a sports car at some over-the-top auto show, a girl in a pink bra and matching garter belt with black fishnets.

Candy Cane.

She tapped her wrist and wagged a schoolmarm-y finger playfully.

"Get a move on, boys . . ."

THEY WORKED LIKE THIS FOR HOURS, AND WHEN THEY STOPPED Alan found himself so utterly exhausted that he could barely stand. As he was helped into a Humvee bound for his quarters, he tried to look back at the disk, but it was too crowded with engineers and half draped in tarpaulin, so that he could not tell how much difference they had actually made.

"Sleep," said a bleary-eyed Kenyon. "We're going to need you in the pilot's seat unreasonably soon."

"Where's Barry?" asked Alan looking woozily around.

"He'll be catching his z's en route to Quantico. Something has come up involving mutual friends of yours, including a shooting in Greece."

Alan started to get up, but Kenyon pushed him back down.

"Your friends are all fine and there's nothing you can do about it, but you may be heading over there as soon as we can spare you."

"To Greece?" asked Alan. He was barely coherent now. "What about the . . . the other ship?"

"That's our first priority, but yes, I think Greece is in your near future. Crete, specifically. We've received some new information derived from another source."

Alan gave him a questioning look.

"You wouldn't believe me if I told you," said Kenyon.

Alan made a dubious face. At this point anything seemed possible. Kenyon conceded the point and shrugged.

"Crop circles," he said. "I know how it sounds, but some fields in Iowa seem to be sending us coordinates. We wouldn't have trusted the intel but it squares with the shooting that happened over there."

Something in his manner snagged on what remained of Alan's conscious mind and pulled him back from the brink of slumber.

"And you think it has something to do with me," he said. "Why?"

Kenyon sighed. He clearly hadn't wanted to get into all the specifics just yet.

"The shooter," he said. "Fingerprints on the weapon recovered by the Greek police match a former employee of ours. The man you know as Jean-Christophe Morat."

Rage coursed through Alan and again he tried to get out of the car's backseat.

"It's in hand, Alan," said Kenyon. "Get some rest. We'll need you alert and ready sooner than you'd like."

Alan slumped back in the seat, thoughts and ideas blurring together as he gave in to the crushing, leaden exhaustion that smothered him like a blanket. His last lucid thought, fumbling its way to the front of his mind, was that if the shooting was in Crete, what the hell was Barry going to do in Quantico? He tried to ask the question but the words would not form on his lips. By the time the Humvee was pulling out of the hangar and into the desert night, Alan was sound asleep and dreaming of a maze of corridors marked with a double-headed ax, trying to stay one step ahead of the lumbering beast in the hallways behind him.

JENNIFER
Hampshire, England

JENNIFER RAN, EVERY THOUGHT DRIVEN FROM HER HEAD beyond the certainty that she did not want to be caught by the strange light in the sky. She had turned off the flashlight and was pounding along the uneven dirt track that ran along the pasture toward the wood and, eventually, home. Each step was heavy, clumsy, and she had to fight to maintain her footing in the dark. Her father had called it the joy of the country, the uncanny blackness, so hard to find in England, when you were far enough from towns that the night was untouched by the thin bleed of the light from street lamps.

Could use it about now . . .

The light in sky, a kind of emerald cloud with something harder and brighter inside it, seemed to slide sideways over the treetops, and from time to time, a shaft of whiter light cut through the air to the ground.

Searchlights?

Maybe. But then it seemed too much to hope that whatever was up there in the poisonous green haze needed light to see her.

Not that she was going to make it easy for them. Hiding might be futile, but she would do it anyway.

It was impossible to say how high the object—if it truly was an object—was, because she had no sense of how big it was. It didn't seem to grow larger or smaller as it moved. She saw no signs of jets or rockets, heard no sound of rotors or engines or noise of any kind. It just moved, drifting like some uncanny balloon in a fog that smeared the night sky with iridescence like some improbable deep-sea fish or a cloud of light-emitting plankton. It seemed to glide through the air, pause to consider, and then move off again. The searchlights stabbed down seemingly at random, columns of brilliance that filled the night with splashes of color. Grass and trees went from charcoal gray swatches to perfectly detailed flashes of yellow, green, and brown in light as bright as noon. A rook rose cawing from the treetops, disturbed, flashing black into the shafts of implausible light as it flapped heavily away.

Jennifer reached the stile into the pasture and clambered over, dimly aware of cows lowing their alarm from all over the field. She had been afraid of them as a girl, dull and gentle though they were, and she felt an extra prick of anxiety, as their uneven chorus rippled through the night. There was a five-barred gate on the other side, but the path across was little more than bent grass stalks, and she was suddenly struck with a terror of being trapped there because she couldn't see the gap in the hedgerow. She looked hard, set her sights on what she thought might be the gate, and stumbled across the tussocky ground, her head down.

The cattle, already disturbed by the peculiar lights in the sky, seemed to be further roused by her presence, and their lowing increased till it was a thick and steady choir, bristling with tension. She could sense those big, glassy brown eyes sucking in the light all around her, and once when the searchlight seemed to glance into a corner of the field only a hundred yards away, she glimpsed them in the gloom, black and white and motionless, casting long, ungainly shadows in the grass.

She swallowed, looked up for a moment to track where the thing in the sky was going and, in that moment, put her right foot down awkwardly, turned on it, and crumpled to the ground with a grunt of pain.

For a moment she grasped at her ankle, waiting for the initial pain to pass, her breath held and teeth clamped together, till she could tell how badly hurt she was. As she did so, one of the searchlights seemed to cut low across the field, as if the craft, or whatever it was, had dropped into a hover only a few feet above the ground, so that the yellow-green stalks leapt out of the darkness in a long, fading line. She kept still, afraid that movement would give her away, but saw by the angled beam that the gate was farther to the right than she had thought. She would need to adjust her course.

She rotated very slowly, listening as the light went out and the darkness was suddenly deeper and more complete than ever before. The field fell absolutely still. There was no sign of the craft overhead, and the night seemed—it was hard to believe—quite normal. Cautiously, she put a little weight on her twisted ankle, winced very slightly, but pressed some more, till she was sure it would bear her weight.

Keep still, she told herself. *Wait. Then sprint: a hard dash across the field, over the gate and along into Steadings' expansive gardens.*

Perhaps it was absurd to try to outrun whatever seemed to be tracking her, but she had no other option. In her head she thought of Margery, the ancient cook her father had trusted, with her odd elf-fixation, and the way she had vanished from her cottage in a blaze of light.

Into that? she wondered, looking cautiously up as she remained squatting in the grass, scanning the heavens for signs of the mantled object that had been haunting the woods. It seemed at least possible.

But the ship, if that was what it was, was still nowhere to be seen, and the field was wrapped in the thick and absolute darkness she had been craving only moments before. For a brief and glorious moment, Jennifer began to consider the possibility that she had escaped it.

And then the light came on.

It was a hard, white light, like a stage light but impossibly bright and tight. It hit her from directly above, pinpointing her position in a brilliant shaft, a rod of energy precise and crisp as surgical steel. It pooled around her, and by its light she saw, silent and close enough to touch, the eyes of the cows.

They had crowded in on her, surrounding her, having moved utterly noiselessly, creating a tight circle around her, evenly, unnaturally spaced. They were all facing her, as if they had been arranged like toys. They had stopped lowing, and their silence was almost as unearthly as the light from above, so that Jennifer felt frozen by their eerie and unblinking stares.

For a long moment, nothing happened.

The cows did not chew the cud or shift their bulk from foot to foot. They did not moo or toss their heads. They were not, in other words, like cows at all. They merely stared at her, like models of cows, though she could hear them breathing, and it felt like they were thinking—thinking not as individual beasts, but as a group that shared a single consciousness.

Slowly, very slowly, Jennifer got to her feet, standing tall, but with her arms by her side so that she would not touch the wet, black muzzles of the great beasts surrounding her. Then, just as slowly, she turned her face up into the light, willing herself to take her eyes off the strange, silent cows and stare straight into whatever was hunting her.

TIMIKA
Quantico, Virginia

IMIKA HAD BEEN LEFT ALONE IN A CELL. SINCE HER clothes and effects had been confiscated, she was wearing the papery blue jumpsuit they had given her and felt, as was surely the intent, like a criminal. Her cell had a stainless steel toilet bowl and sink, and a concrete bed shelf with a plastic mattress. The walls and floor were preformed concrete. No windows. There was a single central light she couldn't control.

She didn't know if it was day or night, and wasn't entirely sure where she was. She had been taken there in the back of a van, her hands unceremoniously cuffed and shackled to a rail behind her, then bundled out, past various checkpoints and guard posts, through silent corridors to the little box where she had been ever since. There had been, she thought, a major Marine brig on the Quantico base, but she had a vague idea that that was gone now, and she imagined that the Feds had facilities of their own anyway, but whether she was being held in a minor jail that couldn't keep her for more than thirty-six or seventy-two hours, or was in a much larger facility equipped to keep her indefinitely, she had no idea.

Timika did not scare easily, but as time ticked away she began to feel increasingly forgotten, as if she were some terrorist who had been caught doing dreadful things but did not have information worth extracting. She began to worry that she might be left there to rot, not so much because of terrible things they thought she had done, but because she was a minor embarrassment best kept out of the way. When she had blustered about her rights, about demanding to see a lawyer, about what constituted lawful incarceration for a US citizen, some stone-faced duty officer had given a formula response about the suspension of normal legal proceedings in the face of a threat to homeland security.

In other words, she was being held in a legal loophole, the kind that tightened as you squirmed.

It might as well have been a noose.

She had been allowed to speak to Jennifer, presumably because her captors wanted to listen to what they had to say, but she had not said where she was being held. She didn't know why: a kind of vanity, perhaps, a desire to show herself cool and together to her rich English friend. That seemed pretty stupid now. It might be days, weeks even, before anyone stateside raised any kind of alarm, and considerably longer before she was tracked down through normal channels. And then what? She was in the nation's blind spot, suspended between rear and sideview mirrors like a cyclist coasting beside an eighteen-wheeler. Worse, it wasn't just that no one could see her. They didn't want to. As long as the days progressed as they usually did, the average American didn't want to know what was done on his or her behalf in the name of national security.

No wonder she was scared.

And what *had* she done?

Timika turned this over in her head in the hope that focusing on the specifics of her alleged crime would keep her from outright panic. She had asked questions, pried into things she wasn't supposed to know about, but her only real crime had been misrepresenting herself. How long could they hold her for that?

But that isn't why you are in prison, is it? she cautioned herself.

This wasn't about what she had done. It was about what she knew and who she might tell. It was about what had happened to Barry and Alan as children, tests performed upon them without their knowledge, something she had already mentioned almost casually to Jennifer over a nonsecure phone . . .

You are such an idiot.

But so what? If this was the great secret they were trying to hide, she had already given it away. She had no hard evidence she could take to the papers, and could be threatened with treason if she tried. So what did they hope to get from keeping her locked up? And who the hell were *they* anyway? She been brought in by the FBI but Quantico was like a huge cabinet with dozens of separate drawers, each one devoted to a different subagency or operations group, some clearly military, some intelligence, and who knew what secret drawers the cabinet contained . . . ?

Timika sat on the mattress, her back to the wall, staring at the cell door, body still, mind racing. Because there was also the small matter of her own genetic makeup, the possibility that when she was drugged and bound in that snowbound—Russian?—facility a few weeks ago, things had been done to her that had altered her basic humanity.

"What are you?" Doctor Vespasian had asked. He'd seen something in her lab work that made her different, and he was pretty damn sure it hadn't been *him* messing about with her genetic code . . . As a result, she and Jennifer were seeing into each other's heads, but mostly they were getting subliminal horrors, cartoon twig figures and swarming wasps.

What a nightmare.

Later—an hour? Two?—she was still in the same position when the door opened, prefaced by a lot of insistent warnings and announcements, like she was a homicidal maniac who might have fashioned any number of shivs or shanks from the seemingly harmless detritus she had found or smuggled in.

Criminal! Terrorist!

She kept very still as the cell suddenly filled up: two uniformed guards with batons, tasers, and handguns, a young man in a lab coat who might have been a junior science officer or a secretary with an ego, and—most alarmingly—Doctor Vespasian.

"Hey fellas," said Timika. "Pull up a concrete couch. Can I get you something? Beer? Copy of the Bill of Rights?"

Funny, she thought, watching herself, the way she pushed her fear and uncertainty way down when other people came in, even when they were the ones she was afraid of.

Her reference to the couch seemed to make them aware that there was nowhere to sit and for a moment they seemed to hover awkwardly, unsure what to do, till Vespasian gave one of the guards a look and muttered "Fetch a chair." The guard hesitated, checking Timika as if she might use this moment of advantage to take the other three on, but eventually decided to risk it. As he ducked out the others dithered, watching her, until the guard returned with three stacked plastic chairs.

"Just one," said Vespasian. "The rest of you will be waiting outside."

The junior scientist looked slightly affronted and the two guards exchanged wary looks, but no one objected. A moment later, Timika found herself alone with the elderly doctor, who sat down with a folder, thumbing through it, then looked up and gave her a pleasant smile. The cell door had been left cracked, in case the guards needed to get in in a hurry.

"Miss Mars," said Vespasian, still smiling and showing brownish, uneven teeth arrayed like chisels. "It seems we rather got off on the wrong foot."

"These things happen when you throw people in jail without trial," she returned tartly.

He waved the suggestion away languidly.

"Come now, Miss Mars," he said. "Let us not waste time with idle posturing."

Iduw postuwing.

Timika said nothing.

"Who do you work for?" asked the doctor.

"Myself. I own a website. Investigative journalism."

"Ah yes," said Vespasian, consulting his notes and smiling still wider. "*Debunktion.* Most amusing. And a useful cover. A minor journalist, poking around, asking questions. Your real employers must be very pleased."

"I am my only employer," she replied, nettled by that *minor journalist.*

"And these others: Audrey Stanhope and Marvin Schrank. Do they also work only for you?"

Timika shifted fractionally.

"You leave them out of this," she said. "They work for the website. Nothing more."

"Whereas you have extracurricular interests," said Vespasian. He drew a slightly pixilated image of Timika at the hospital, clearly pulled from security camera footage. She looked furtive.

"I like those shoes," she remarked, feigning casualness. "I had better get them back."

"Tell us what we need to know and you can have them back on within the hour as you walk out the door."

"Why don't I believe you?"

"Too much time debunking, perhaps."

"Perhaps. But you're making a mistake if you think I'm carrying secret information I could just give up if I felt like it. I don't. You know as much as I do. More, I suspect. Like what you were doing to Barry and Alan when they were kids."

"Let's focus on you, Miss Mars," said Vespasian.

He had seemed irascible before, a loose cannon, but he seemed to have gotten himself under control and kept smiling in a vague, serene kind of way as if he liked nothing better than chatting to her. She liked him better when he was a little off the rails and likely to give things away, and decided she'd try to push him back there.

"Your blood, as I'm sure you know," he remarked, "came back with certain anomalies."

"I didn't know, actually," she replied. "Not till you told me."

"Indeed?"

"Indeed."

"And could you hazard an explanation for said anomalies?"

"I don't even know what they are. How should I know how I got them?"

"Very well," he remarked, as if this was a game they were playing. "Your genetic code has been, shall we say, tweaked. Modified. Rendered nonstandard. According to a traditional and absolute definition we might debate whether you are, strictly speaking, human."

Timika forced herself not to move, but the effort took all she had. When she said nothing, Vespasian prompted her.

"Can you offer an explanation for this?" he said, laying out the charts of chromosome pairings with the oddities circled in red pen.

"You mean, can I explain how this happened to me when you didn't do it?" she tried.

His gaze froze for a second, and then, with a half look over his shoulder to be sure there was no one at the door, he smiled again, a small and knowing smile.

"This," he said, "as you well know, is not my work."

"But it's similar," said Timika. "Right? Like what you did to Barry?"

"I've been trying to determine what this particular tweak might do for you," said Vespasian, ignoring her question. "Do you have . . . abilities, instincts which other people might consider unusual?"

"Oh, I'm all kinds of remarkable," said Timika.

"No doubt, but you know what I mean."

"Like Barry, you mean?"

Vespasian's brows contracted and he leaned forward in a way that looked not so much eager as hungry.

"Mr. Regis has unconventional abilities?" he said. "You've seen this?"

Timika adjusted.

"Oh," she said. "I get it. You did the work, back in the day, but you haven't exactly been kept in the loop since." She saw the truth of her remark in his face. "So you want to hear what I know that you don't. Oh, doc. How long have you got?"

"All the time in the world," he said, rallying, digging in.

Timika shook her head.

"I don't think so," she said. "I think you have until other people well up the chain of command figure out what you are doing, and then they're gonna come down on you like a ton of the proverbial bricks, and when they do, it's not gonna be me who's worried about falling afoul of national security. It's you. I might even ask who you think you're working for, because, minor journalist though I am, I got a sneaking suspicion that I might just outrank you."

For a second Vespasian's face clouded and the anger she had glimpsed in their previous meeting flashed in his eyes, but he bit back whatever he had been about to say and, instead, pulled a digital voice recorder from his pocket and hit a button. Timika's own voice, tinny and indistinct, came back to her.

"I think the same thing happened to me. Recently. When I was taken. Right before you found me in Nevada. Whoever took me did something. Took my blood. Injected something back into me. Changed me."

"Your little chat to your English friend," said Vespasian, checking the file, "Miss Jennifer Quinn. Quite a lot there to unpack, wouldn't you say? In what way exactly were you *taken* and by whom?"

"I was abducted. I don't know who by."

"Nationality?"

In spite of herself, Timika actually laughed.

"You think that matters?" she said.

"Do I think the United States should pay attention to guarding its sovereign soil from foreign incursion?" Vespasian replied, mockingly. "Yes. Don't you?"

"I think you have no idea what you are up against," she said.

"But you do?"

"No," she admitted. "Not really. But I'm pretty sure they don't define themselves by lines on a map."

"Meaning?"

"Not all our enemies think of themselves as nation states."

"Ah," said Vespasian, recovering his wry amusement. "This is some leftist screed against global capitalism and corporate power. I should have expected as much. Isn't it strange how selective you people are with your conspiracy theory busting. Is the government also dousing its populace with chem trails and operating child sex operations out of the basement of a DC pizza parlor?"

"Don't be absurd."

"But you expect me to believe in your tales of multinational conspiracies."

"False logic," Timika shot back. "Doubting one piece of received wisdom that everyone else accepts as true doesn't mean you doubt everything you're told, so don't lump me in with the crazies. I have come to believe in some things most people would think are nuts. Doesn't mean I think Earth is flat or that climate change is a hoax perpetrated by the Chinese."

"So you're a selective skeptic?"

"Best kind."

"Then tell me about the manner of your abduction."

"I am not at liberty to say," she said.

It was true. She had signed a nondisclosure agreement about the events in Nevada, and the only reason she hadn't hidden behind it before was that she had assumed he already knew all about it. The fact that he didn't, while it bought her a line of reasonable defense, worried her.

Just how official was this incarceration? Who knew she was here and who exactly was this man, with his secret medical procedures? After all, just because she was in a government facility didn't necessarily mean the man sitting opposite her was a government operative. Her own argument about multinational enemies proved that, just as her view that some conspiracy theories were crazy and some were not meant that the good doctor here might be pursuing an agenda different from and ignorant of whatever Alan and Barry had been involved in at Area 51.

"I'm not sure you realize just how much trouble you are in," Vespasian said, patching over the cracks in his composure. "I don't know what higher power you think you have access to, but right now this is my investigation and you will remain here as long as I . . ."

There was a hasty tap on the door and it was pushed open by one of the guards.

"Sir?" he said to Vespasian, inviting him to speak outside.

"I'm in the middle of something here!" Vespasian shot back.

"It's urgent, sir. Perhaps if you would step into the hall?" said the guard, giving Timika a significant look.

"Just tell me, man!" Vespasian shouted, all his careful professionalism crumbling.

"We've been told to ready the prisoner for immediate transfer," said the guard, unblinking but knowing he was entering dangerous waters.

"Nonsense!" said Vespasian scornfully. "This is my prisoner and I'll turn her over when I am satisfied that . . ."

"Sir, with respect, the orders were clear and emphatic, sir. There is a delegation en route . . ."

"I've a mind to put you on report for countermanding my wishes in this matter," Vespasian retorted.

The guard opened his mouth to respond, but before he could say anything, Timika heard a commotion in the hallway outside: footsteps, regular but insistent. The guard stepped back out of the doorway deferentially. Pivetti appeared in the doorway looking harassed. There were two other men with him, both in dark suits. One of them was flashing a CIA shield in Vespasian's face while his own was granite hard and dark as thunderclouds.

"Hey there, Doc," said Barry Regis, his eyes flashing, as he absently thumbed the wrapper off a green Jolly Rancher. "I'm told your prisoner misrepresented herself while interrogating my mother. Now, Timika is a remarkable woman, but unless she held a séance, that would have proved tough."

"What?" said Timika, unable to stay quiet.

"June 19, 2012," said Barry, his flinty eyes not leaving Vespasian's face as he popped the candy in his mouth. "That was the day the Alzheimer's took her. So, what do you say, Doc? Got some answers for your favorite patient?"

MORAT
Unidentified landing zone, Crete

THE HELO CAME IN GROUND-HUGGINGLY LOW. SO LOW, IN fact, that Morat watched its final approach from his vantage on the cliff and frequently lost it below the ridges and trees of the rugged terrain. It had to come up to find the meadow, rising like a dragonfly over a pond. Up close it was loud, the rotors thrumming in the night like a giant insect swarm, but the locals would think it part of the search team, and by the time the Greek police realized it wasn't one of theirs, he and the squad sent by Maynard would, he hoped, be well on their way. If they'd been flying nap-of-the-earth like that all the way from North Africa, there was a good chance they'd avoided ship- or ground-based radar and AWACS surveillance. Even if they'd been spotted, they'd be hard to track, particularly on the south side of the island, where they wouldn't have to deal with whatever hardware was on the alert around the Souda Bay NATO base up on Crete's northeast corner.

He began his hasty descent to the grassy plateau, then jogged toward its center, hands raised and waving as the Mil Mi-17's lights came on. It was an ungainly bird, chunky in the body, spindly in the tail, and without much concession to either aerodynamics or the brute power of more modern helicopters. But it had been getting the job done, in one variant or another, for forty years, and Morat had a soft spot for the type. Given its port of departure, this one may well have been left over from the Libyan civil war in which both pro- and anti-Gaddafi forces had used them.

Even handed, Morat thought, liking the idea. *Unencumbered by ideology.*

The helo set down, its distinctive clamshell doors peeled back, and its troops spilled out, weapons at the ready, like bugs disgorging from a split carcass. In combat, it would be up again in seconds and speeding away, but the powers that be had decided it was best to sit where it was till they were done rather than risk attracting attention by circling the mountains. That was probably as well, Morat decided. It was going to take them a half hour to reach the church from here. Whether they would return to this spot or call for the chopper to collect them from there remained to be seen.

A lot was going to happen in the next sixty minutes.

Morat had felt the pull of the church swelling within him like lust or hunger. He needed to be there, and not just because he fully expected to find Tan there. The other target—the real target—was there too. He could feel it. It was calling to him.

That wasn't all. He sensed other people coming. He got strange images flashing through his head as if he had thought them up himself but couldn't follow or imagine the train of thought that had produced them: an old woman riding a giant stag beetle, the inside of a small jet littered with candy wrappers, the empty eyes of a cow . . .

None of it made any sense. But beneath it all, through it, humming like insect song, was the knowledge, the certainty, that what he wanted—not just Maynard, *he himself*—was back at the church.

Under it.

He didn't know why he felt that or how it was even possible, but he was sure of it, and if getting to his prize meant blowing the ruined church and everyone in it off the map entirely, so be it. He wasn't sure what kind of firepower the helo packed, but he'd check before they began their little hike.

And he was something of a force to be reckoned with all by himself. He intended to prove that much. He was a cultured man, Jean-Christopher Morat, but at heart, in the dark when no one was looking, he knew he could just as easily have been a monster.

He'd be letting the monster out tonight.

Crete was a good place for it, a place once associated with the myth of the maze-like labyrinth and the deadly, bull-headed Minotaur that hunted in its shadows . . .

Yes, he thought, grinning to himself at the aptness of the image. *He could be a monster.*

The squad got clear of the chopper and dropped to one knee, professionally watchful and expectant, as the leader—a man Morat recognized as Milo Sigorsky—hurried over to meet him, a duffle bag over his shoulder.

"Mr. Morat," he said, offering his hand. They had to shout over the noise of the helicopter, though the engines were already shutting down.

"Sigorsky," said Morat. "You have a phone for me."

Sigorsky handed it to him.

"And a weapon," said Morat.

"You're going in with the team?"

"Absolutely."

Sigorsky looked momentarily put out, as if this was unexpected and unwelcome, but he knew better than to argue.

"I assume you have something to spare," said Morat, unblinking. "I'd like to keep this quiet if possible," he added, thinking of the PSS he'd left in the church, "but I'll take getting it done over getting it half done silently."

"Got you covered," said Sigorsky, unzipping the duffle bag and revealing—along with a comm headset—a Heckler and Koch MP5SD submachine gun with built-in suppressor, black and purposeful.

"Perfect," said Morat, taking the weapon and a couple of magazines. "This will do nicely."

"And the target?"

"A carved stone tablet. Very old. You'll find it in a wooden crate in the crypt below the church."

"You know exactly where it is?" said Sigorsky, bewildered.

"I believe I do," said Morat, checking his weapon and walking away.

49

NICHOLAS
Near Fotinos, Crete

NICHOLAS STARED AT THE IRON RING IN THE FLOOR, AND A dozen possible courses of action raced through his head. He should tell the cops chatting outside the church. He should wake Elina. He should call Timika or Anastas, whose card was in the pocket of his jeans. He should run.

He didn't know why he thought that last one, but he felt it strongly, a sense that something he had thought—or had pretended to think—was over, had just restarted, and that if he got out of here now he could leave it all behind. He could almost see his escape window closing, and when it shut completely it would bring darkness and suffocation . . .

But he was just as sure that he would not follow that instinct or, he suspected, any of the others. He was an archaeologist. He had put up with the training and the study, much of it tedious, he had endured the disdain of his peers and the

473

ignorance of the general public, he had made do with lazy, corner-cutting students in his classes, and faculty who didn't think his work trendy enough. Most important, he had taken a chance on this dig, one that might torpedo his struggling career, and had watched people die as a result.

He was going to open that damned crypt and he was going to do it alone.

Besides, a wild inner voice added, *your dead mother nudged you toward it.*

That sent a slightly mad ripple of mirth through him, but he managed to suppress it before it came out as an actual giggle, and he stilled himself, the full insanity of his predicament settling on him like wisdom. For a long moment he shone his flashlight on the flagstoned floor and just stood there, reconsidering the options to wake Elina, to call the cops, to run . . .

Nicholas worked the bit of the mattock under the ring. It was rusted in place, but came free the moment he put a little weight on the handle. The stone slab to which the ring was fastened was only a couple of feet square, but it looked thick and solid. He wondered vaguely if he would need a power winch, or a couple of other strong backs with crowbars, but in the end he lay the mattock down and got hold of the ring in both hands. He dropped into a half squat, the flashlight held between his teeth, braced himself and pulled, gently at first, testingly.

No point giving yourself a hernia.

The slab moved immediately, shifting so that the dusty groove around its edge broke and became a distinct crack. It moved almost silently, but Nicholas still glanced back into the church, around the remains of the altar screen, to make sure no one was watching. Elina had not stirred in her sleep and the cops were still outside. He returned to the stone slab, kicking the mattock closer so he could shove it under the flagstone if he couldn't get it all the way out.

He pulled again, stepping back as he did so, and the flagstone tipped up on its lower edge like a hatch. For a second the stone blocked out whatever was beneath it, and Nicholas had to walk the slab clear and lay it down before he could see what it had been covering.

He had half expected simply a recess in the foundation, a reliquary where some fragment of bone or other holy object might have been placed when the church was first consecrated. It might have been a vault for the church's chalices or even the tomb of its priests, merely a stone box below the chapel floor.

But it wasn't. Until Nicholas could get the flashlight on it, it was merely a black square, a hole, and when he stood directly above it and shone the light down, he saw steps that began some four feet down. He considered this uneasily. Indiana Jones was all well and good, but the prospect of climbing down into that cramped and claustrophobic space, which might be packed with bones or who knew what, was suddenly less appealing than it had been a moment before.

Again he glanced back into the chapel, then put the rubber-clad flashlight between his teeth once more and sat on the edge of the hole, his feet dangling. Cautiously, he transferred his weight onto his elbows and lowered himself in. Nicholas wasn't a big guy, but it was tight all the same, and he had to turn carefully to face the altar before he could walk down the steps, dropping slowly to his knees in the dark, and feeling with his hands for the low roof so that he wouldn't crack his head open. He was able to take two steps down before ducking under the stone roof of the passage, and only then could he see the way ahead.

There was no grand tunnel or vault. The crypt was small and simple as the church above it. There were ten uneven steps down, and even at the bottom Nicholas could only stand with his shoulders hunched and head bent low. The roof seemed to be solid and natural rock, the crypt itself a kind of cave in the earth. It may even have been why the site had been chosen for the chapel in the first place, and the archaeologist in Nicholas wondered if, given its proximity to the Bronze Age tholos, the place had once served some other ritual function; religion evolved, after all, adapted to culture, temples to Artemis and Athena repurposed as chapels to the Virgin Mary . . .

He swung the light around. The crypt was half the length of the church above it, and the rock ceiling sloped so that the corners were low, making him feel like he was standing inside a subterranean dome. On his left the natural rock was mostly solid and naturally formed, though the rear had been hollowed out into squarer angles by human hands. The right side had been more obviously worked, cleared and refilled with what seemed to be tomb-like stone boxes marked with carefully etched crosses. Mostly they looked comparatively modern, like the church aboveground, late nineteenth century, perhaps a little earlier but not much. Nicholas wasn't sure how much the Ottoman occupation had restricted the construction of Christian churches and monasteries, but a site like this—unless it had remained hidden throughout that period—might also have served as a mosque at one point.

He squeezed past the low stone tombs toward the back. Here the floor was uneven and, again, was natural rock occasionally leveled with mortared stone. A couple of the graves back here looked rather older than those at the altar end, their masonry rough, their angles soft. One was marked with a coarsely etched and slightly asymmetrical cross, but his eyes slid off it to where, propped against the wall at the very back, was a wooden crate marked with a swastika.

It was lightly built from the kind of timber Nicholas associated with forklift pallets and was about that size, though it was only about eighteen inches thick. He got down on his haunches and tested the wood, wishing he had brought the mattock down with him. The cave-*cum*-crypt was quite dry, but the wood had aged poorly nonetheless, and when he found an uneven board and pulled at it, the seam split. Underneath was packing straw, pale and dry. He got his fingers below the next panel and ripped it free from its wire nails, then the next, till the top cover was gone. He brushed the straw away, shone his flashlight on what lay below it, and marveled.

Inside the crate was a single slab of stone, yellower than the grave markers in the crypt and surely older. Etched carefully into the tablet was a symbol quite unlike the cross on the tombs.

The relief carving showed a central, vertical shaft flanked by two rounded lobes so that the whole looked like a stylized butterfly, its wings spread flat. It was the ancient *labrys*, the archetypal symbol of Minoan Crete found throughout Knossos and in ancient sites all over the island, rendered in bronze and gold, painted onto ceramics, and carved—as here—into stone. Its name was built into the myth of the labyrinth, the complex of tunnels beneath the palace of King Minos prowled by the bull-headed Minotaur. It was a maze so dense and disorienting that Theseus had only found his way out after killing the monster by following the spool of thread he had unraveled as he went. Four thousand years ago the *labrys* was a symbol of power and strength, but it was also simply a tool and a weapon for both military and ceremonial purposes.

Nicholas considered the symbol: a broad and sweeping double-headed ax, balanced, perfect.

CAPTAIN LIU
July 7, 2010. Hangzhou, China, at 8:40 p.m.

CAPTAIN LIU REVIEWED THE INSTRUMENTS OF THE Air China Boeing 737-700 series, and corrected for their final approach to Xiaoshan Airport as Wang, his copilot, radioed the tower, switching from the Wu they had just been speaking moments before to Mandarin. As Wang gave the flight number and the time they had left Xining, Liu found himself looking forward to getting home for a couple of badly needed days off. Since getting married, he had come to loathe the long trips away, and now that Yuru was pregnant, every hour away felt like two, his absence loaded with the possibility of disaster. How it would be once the child was born he hardly dared think. It wasn't like he could stop flying. They desperately needed the income.

It was odd to think of it like that. He had always wanted to be a pilot and still loved to fly, the miracle of it, up there with the world laid out beneath him.

He just loved his wife more.

It really was that simple. Wang thought him sentimental, even a bit stupid, but Wang, whether he admitted it or not, was miserable at home, as his gleefully secret affairs when they were out of town attested.

"Landing checklist," Wang prompted.

"One second," said Liu, lining up with the runway, the lights of which were just visible ahead. "Okay. Landing gear?"

"Down," said Wang. "Three green lights."

"Flaps and slats?"

"Thirty-five, Thirty-five, Set"

"Spoilers?"

"Armed," said Wang.

"Autobrakes?"

"Three."

"Landing checklist is complete," said Liu. "Guess we're going home."

"Hold it," said Wang. "What's that?"

"I don't see . . ."

But then he did. Directly over the airport, hanging in the air without any clear means of support, was a long metallic object with lights along the sides. It was not moving and seemed suspended, though by what, it was impossible to say.

"What the hell?" muttered Liu.

Wang got onto the radio immediately, speaking fast, not so much amazed or baffled as annoyed as he gave the call sign, launching directly into a non-protocol rant.

"This is CA 1910," he snapped. "We have an unidentified craft directly over our runway. Was someone there going to warn us about that? We're coming in now. You either get that thing out of the airspace ASAP or we're going to have to abort and come around again."

There was a heavy pause as Liu considered how long they had before aborting, then air traffic control came back.

"Negative, CA 1910. We have no aircraft on that runway. Please check your instruments, over."

"I'm checking with my eyes," Wang shot back. "You might want to do the same. And I didn't say on the runway, I said above it. Over."

"Roger that, 1910, performing visual check now. Hold your course."

In the silence that followed, Wang fumed.

"Performing check," he scoffed. "They mean someone's looking out the damned window. What the hell *is* that?"

Liu said nothing. It was no conventional aircraft, that was for sure, no rational aircraft. Something that shape just couldn't stay up. It was hard to gauge its size and altitude because it was, well, just too odd to fit any normal schematics. It also wasn't showing on their instruments or, apparently, on the air traffic control system. He didn't like the implications of any of this.

"CA 1910 this is Xiaoshan control, abort landing. Repeat, abort landing. Over."

Wang didn't need to be told twice, and together they reversed their descent, pulling up so that for a moment they looked to be on a collision course with the unidentified object. As they did so, Liu saw the lights of the cigar-shaped cylinder oscillate, and a beam of light opened up along its length, splashing the runway below with startling radiance. The 737 climbed steeply, and Liu gave it more speed to prevent stalling, but both pilots were watching the object—craft?—falling away beneath the passenger jet's nose. For a second they held their breaths and exchanged worried looks, sure that something strange and possibly cataclysmic was about to happen as they lost sight of the thing hanging over the runway.

For a moment there was nothing, and then there was the buzzing of the internal phone as the flight attendants called in to see what the hell they were playing at.

"People on the left side are pointing out the window," said the flight attendant over the cockpit intercom.

"I'll bet," said Wang. "Hold on. We'll see what air traffic control tells us."

They banked east and began tracing a lazy circle in the hope of a second attempt, but the news from the tower, when it came a minute later, wasn't good.

"Yeah, sorry 1910, we're going to have to redirect you to Ningbo or Wuxi. Hold on while we plot you a course. We'll lay on ground transportation for passengers who need to get back here, but we're shut down effective immediately. Nothing in or out. Over."

"But what is that thing?" said Liu.

"Undetermined at this time," said the air traffic controller. "We're waiting for updates from higher up."

"Higher up where?" asked Wang, unease giving a sharper edge to his customary belligerence.

"Just wait for instructions, 1910. Tell the passengers there was a spill on the runway and we're closed for cleanup. Safety precautions. Over."

"That's bullshit!" said Wang. "They saw it! They know there was something in the sky."

"Negative," said air traffic control. "Say nothing till we've heard from . . ."

"Higher up," said Wang. "Yeah, we know. We're the ones looking at it, in the same airspace. Who the hell is better positioned to tell us what it is?"

"Hold on, 1910. We have a message coming in now."

There was what felt like an interminable pause during which the 737 completed its slow circle and, with no landing clearance pending, began another. They were halfway around before the radio came back to life, the air traffic controller's voice, which had been a notch more excitable than usual, now carefully level and professional.

"1910, we have your course to Ningbo planned out. Over."

"Copy that," said Liu. "No option to land at Xiaoshan?"

"Negative, 1910. We're done for the night. We have some previously undisclosed military tests taking place in the area. Sorry for the inconvenience."

"And the military didn't think to tell you about them till they had already started?" snapped Wang, disbelieving.

"It's a readiness protocol thing," said the tower operator. "They have to be impromptu. We're sending you your revised flight plan now."

Liu and Wang exchanged looks.

"Goddamned military," muttered Wang. "No consideration for how their games affect the rest of us."

Liu opened his mouth, but caught himself. Wang looked scared, and Liu couldn't blame him. He didn't know how much of their off-air chatter was monitored, so they had to be careful what they said, but the copilot's fear was more than an anxiety about being seen to be unpatriotic. He didn't want to think about the incident any further. He was embracing the bogus military exercise story because it was easier, safer to do that than reflect on what they had just seen.

Liu nodded once, and Wang, for all his bluster, looked quickly away like a chastened child. In the same moment, something sped past them, trailing light so wide and bright that for a moment the rugged hills below leapt into hard and brilliant color as if painted by lightning. One moment it was there, and the next it was gone.

Liu stared straight ahead, thinking of his wife, the child she carried, their future rolling out before them like a brightly lit landing strip extending through rugged terrain as far as the eye could see.

"Course correction received, air traffic control," he said. "En route for Ningbo."

"You planning to file a formal report of what you saw up there, 1910?" said the tower. "Given the nature of these exercises we'd prefer to not discuss them but if you insist on documenting . . ."

"Negative," said Liu hastily, his eyes on Wang, whose silence was approving. "We can't be sure what we saw. Best leave it alone. Over."

"Roger that, 1910. Probably for the best."

Liu swallowed and looked at Wang again, but neither man spoke except to run through their checklist protocols, saying nothing else till they were safely on the ground. Once there, Wang began discussing which of their flight attendants was cutest. As if nothing had happened.

Neither Wang nor Liu ever said a word about what they had seen over the airport in Hangzhou, and a week later Wang was reassigned to Beijing. They would never see each other again.

ALAN
Area 51/Dreamland, Nevada

ALAN WAS WALKING THE MAZELIKE PASSAGES OF THE Papoose Lake facility, their walls marked with the strange ax-head symbol. Except that instead of a complex of intersection hallways and dead ends, the corridor was long, straight, and unbroken, extending as far as Alan could see. This seemed so normal and unsurprising to him that the idea that it had ever been confusing, labyrinthine, now seemed almost impossible to believe, so that Alan feared his memory had been playing tricks on him. He felt a sense of satisfaction, knowing that all he had to do was keep walking straight and he would reach his goal, though what it was he expected to find had somehow slipped his mind.

Something important. Vital even.

But the straightness of the hallway meant that there was now nowhere to hide. He hadn't heard the beast-man coming after him for a while, but he knew he was still out there, hunting him. Perhaps he would have one of those double-bladed axes.

Or horns.

Yes, he thought. *Horns, sharp and spreading like those of a great bull.*

But the black girl in the silver-green bodice and tutu was in front of him. Gretta. As before, she wore cream satin ballet shoes with the ribbons crisscrossing her legs and she rose gracefully onto the very tips of her toes at his approach, hands above her head, left leg in front of the right. Elegant, even angelic, she stood there, motionless, then put her heels together and executed a perfect plié, bending her knees, hands clasped formally and demurely across her stomach. When she came up again, a smooth, vertical movement with no bend in her waist, she opened her mouth.

She did not speak exactly. Instead, eyes fixed on Alan, she hummed a high and level tone that sounded clear and bell-like, as if she had drawn her finger around the rim of a wine glass. But inside the tone, somehow, were words.

"Left of the castle, vault the gate or you must enter the top hat."

She closed her mouth and the unearthly sound stopped abruptly, whereupon she extended her arms out to the sides and became not a girl but a great raven, wings wide as the night, so that Alan flinched away. When he looked again he was no longer in the corridor, but outside, and though there was darkness around him, the bird-girl—now strangely slender and taller than Alan—was hovering above him, and glowing white.

"Wake up, Alan."

It was Kenyon.

"What?" said Alan, rubbing his eyes. "What time is it? Is everything . . . ?"

"Sorry to rush you, Alan," said Kenyon, "but we need you suited up right now. Hastings is taking the only airworthy Locust. We need you in the disk. We have a situation."

Fourteen minutes later Alan and Kenyon were barreling into a familiar hangar, the tires of their blacked-out SUV squealing on the painted cement. Alan, who had mostly dressed in the backseat as they sped blindly through the desert, half rolled out, tossing the bottle that had contained the energy drink he had just sucked down onto the seat. Kenyon had briefed him as they drove and Alan had asked only one thing:

"It has to be the disk?"

Kenyon, reading his apprehension, just nodded.

They had no way of knowing that the hasty, unconventional repairs made under Alan and Barry's trance-like instruction were safe, but that wasn't really the issue. Flying the disk was unlike flying any craft Alan had ever piloted, and that included the Locust. In fact, it was hardly like flying at all. In that cockpit he became part of the machine, and did so with such organic and immersive seamlessness that it became hard to think of it as a machine at all. It was a part of himself. The only time Alan had piloted the disk he had lost himself in it, felt fused with it at the level of consciousness. And frankly, for all the extraordinary ways that it had enhanced his flying, the maneuvers he had been able to execute, it had been terrifying, and though he had been hankering to get back up in the air for weeks before the Argentine mission, his focus had always been on the Locust, the triangle craft which, for all its remarkable capacity and handling, still felt like an aircraft.

The disk was something else entirely.

It sat there now, round and slender, its rim blade thin, and even in the drab and tinted florescent light, it seemed half alive. Light cavorted on its surface in ways that seemed like more than mere reflection. With its sleek, mechanical perfection its mesmerizing surface almost took away the preposterousness of the thing's stereotypically UFO look.

Almost.

The hangar was teeming with the familiar ground crew, including Riordan and, he noticed, hovering at the perimeter, her face tense and watchful, Dr. Imelda Hayes.

"Straight inside, please, Major," said Riordan. "That's it, guys. Finish up," he added to the pit crew.

"What about the crate, sir?" said one, a young black man in regulation coveralls. He was looking to the corner of the hangar where a number of familiar yellow boxes were stacked, each one loaded—presumably—with little alien manikins.

"There's no time," said Riordan.

"Do it," said Hayes, stepping forward. "That's an order, Mr. Riordan. But not those. This one."

She indicated another crate, identical to the others, but sitting on a dolly by the pedestrian entrance. Riordan's brow creased, but he bit back whatever he wanted to say.

"You heard the doctor," he barked at the staff. "On the double."

As Riordan checked his watch anxiously, Hayes's eyes met Alan's and he nodded with mute understanding, some of his unease shifting, calming. Now that he could see the crate he could almost feel its presence on the edge of his mind like a distant sound or an aroma from childhood. It was, somehow, comforting, and not only because he instinctively sensed that it would aid his mental interface with the disk.

"Let's get you in, sir," said Riordan.

The hangar wall was rolling up. Alan put his hand on the almost frictionless metal of the disk, then took hold of the short ladder and climbed in. Just before he dipped his head under the hatch he turned back and looked at Hayes and

Kenyon who, unnervingly, stood to attention and saluted. Alan returned the gesture automatically, and suddenly the ground crew were all doing the same, grim-faced and pale. Alan didn't know why, but it felt like they were standing at the side of a grave as the coffin was lowered.

52

JENNIFER
Hampshire, England

JENNIFER DID NOT MOVE. SHE TRIED NOT TO LOOK INTO the blank, hypnotic eyes of the herd pressed in around her, the cattle unnaturally silent and still in the bright, hard light from above. They stood in a ring facing her, casting shadows on the grass like bizarre black-and-white standing stones. Above her she could see nothing but light, though she felt a strange electric prickling in the night that made her hair float, as if everything on Earth had shed its weight, its matter, reduced to something close to energy with the merest wisp of a gravitational tether.

She was not sure how long she had been there like that, her vision full of the bovine faces considering her, heart pounding with fear. She had always been afraid of the cows, but they had just been cows, chewing, lowing, wandering aimlessly about the field, spooking easily. Now they were . . . Something else.

She had a powerful sense of the beehive again or—remembering what Timika had said—of swarming wasps: lots of legs, lots of eyes, but one controlling mind. But she did not feel the malice of the swarm, the danger of its myriad stings.

Which doesn't mean it isn't there.

The night was utterly noiseless. No owls hooted or foxes barked, and Jennifer wanted to speak just to make sure that the light above her hadn't somehow sucked all sound out of the world. But she didn't, because talking might make something happen, and she felt sure that this, strange and awful though it was, was preferable to what might happen next. But the stillness meant that the footsteps, when she heard them, were clear and distinct, even though they came from all the way back at the stile.

She turned her head slowly, still watching the cows in case they might—what? Surge forward. Trample her. Bite. She knew cows didn't bite, but these weren't cows. Not anymore.

The footsteps came closer, the grass stalks breaking under human feet, and then she caught it, the faintest sweetness of pipe smoke on the air. She turned all the way then, her feet shuffling awkwardly as she rotated, while the cows watched, impassive. But then they were adjusting, shifting. At first she wasn't sure what was happening, but then, with another dreamy shock, she realized that they were bunching together in order to create a clear path for the walker with the pipe.

She sucked her breath in and held it, tears springing to her eyes. Because she knew what that scent meant, knew it deep in her heart long before the cows parted and revealed, strolling toward her, smiling softly, Edward Quinn. Jennifer opened her mouth, bit back the sob, and spoke into the still night.

"Dad?"

53

TIMIKA
French airspace

TIMIKA STRETCHED OUT, DELIGHTED BY HOW ROOMY THE Gulfstream jet was compared to the crowded airliner she had used to make this trip last time. Fast too, and without all the usual airport security hassles. They'd be on the ground and out in another hour or so. She pulled the window screen down and gave Barry a look.

"If you're trying to impress a girl . . ." she said, smiling suddenly, "this is pretty good."

"Glad you approve," Barry replied.

"You doing okay? That stuff with Vespasian must have gotten under your skin. No pun intended."

Barry grinned mirthlessly.

"I'm okay," he said. "Angry. Anxious. But okay. There's still a lot to learn about what exactly they did to us, who authorized it, and what the results might be, but for now, yeah, I'm okay."

Timika hadn't understood much of what Vespasian—badgered and weary—had confessed about the artificial modification of codons and amino acids in the human genetic code. The doctor had tossed the terms out scornfully, knowing they wouldn't mean much to the layman, all that stuff about CRISPR—Clustered Regularly Interspaced Short Palindromic Repeats—and Cas9. That had been intended to obscure rather than explain. But Barry had worried at him like a dog with a chew toy until Vespasian had used less opaque but rather more troubling terms like *targeted genome editing.* The Chinese were doing it, he said, as if that made everything okay. It was a huge leap forward, a monumental progression in molecular biology with all manner of applications, a field in which he had been an unsung pioneer . . .

But what it all added up to, Timika was still unsure and so, Barry thought, was Vespasian. He had tweaked people's genetic code, rewritten the building blocks of their humanity, but what he had achieved in the process or why he had done it, he couldn't—or wouldn't—say, and when Barry pressed the matter, Vespasian had merely become hungry for information.

"What can you do?" he said. "What triggered the change?"

Barry said nothing, but the hunted look in his eyes was all the confirmation Vespasian needed, and while the doctor wouldn't give up anything further and left under guard, he did so with a look of almost serene triumph on his face. He didn't know what he had done. Not really. But seeds he had planted decades before had sprouted and that, he had decided, was validation enough.

Timika and Barry had boarded the plane in somber mood, but Barry was less upset than she had expected and seemed almost relieved that the truth was out where he could see it, even if that truth was unsettling and incomplete. There was a great deal more still to be revealed, but he seemed somehow lighter, as if the secret was something he had been dimly half aware of all his life. Now he could tackle it and its implications head on.

Or he would be able to when this other business was concluded. Assuming it was another business entirely, and not merely part of the same thing.

That was an odd thought, and Timika wasn't sure where it came from, but it felt right. Whatever Vespasian had done to him as a child, and whatever they were doing now on this CIA transport to Crete, they were connected. She felt it in her bones.

"I'm sorry about your mom," she said. "You know who the woman in your house is?"

"Some ex-military set up to hold the fort, in case someone came nosing around," said Barry with a rueful smile. "Sounds like she'd only been there a few hours when you got there."

Like they knew she was coming.

"Yeah, about that . . ." Timika began.

"It's fine," he said. "I get it. And in your—admittedly fairly pushy way—I think you had my best interest at heart."

Timika was about to protest, but the smile in his eyes had a note of warning and she knew better than to push her luck.

"Yeah," she said. "That's fair."

Barry's smile widened.

"You know what I learned today?" he said.

"What's that?"

"I learned all about candy," he said.

"Candy?"

"It has been in my head for weeks. Constantly. There was this stripper . . . Doesn't matter."

"I'll bet," said Timika.

"No, I mean it really doesn't matter. I wasn't interested in her as a stripper. I was interested in her because of her name. She had this lollipop . . ."

"I'm not sure I want to hear this story."

"No, but that's the point. I didn't care about her. Not in that way. And even though I was craving sugar-candy all the time, Jolly Ranchers, stuff like that, I didn't particularly like it."

"Strippers rot your teeth," said Timika wryly.

"So then I started wondering that if it wasn't sexual and wasn't about the taste, maybe it was something else."

"Like what?"

"Like the word itself," said Barry looking pleased with himself. "Candy. So I looked it up, learned about the etymology of the word, its derivation from Arabic and Sanskrit words for sugar. That didn't really get me anywhere, so I tried looking elsewhere. And guess what?"

He fished what looked like a guidebook from his backpack and opened it to a page whose corner had been turned down, then read aloud.

"In the year 820, after 900 years of Roman and Byzantine rule, the island was made an Emirate by Andalusian Muladis, and its Arabic name was replaced with Khandax or Khandakas, known to the Venetians who later conquered it by its Latin derivation, Candia, and—to the English and French—as Candy, by which name the island was known internationally until well past the Ottoman occupation of the late seventeenth century, before becoming more widely referred to by its modern name . . ." He flipped the book over to show the cover: "Crete."

Timika made a face.

"Is that important?" she asked, adding—at his thoughtful nod—"Why?"

"Because something in my brain that I don't understand has been trying to tell me to go there for a long time."

"And your Jolly Rancher craving?"

"Gone," he said simply.

Timika considered this.

"If you didn't know that Candy was the old name for Crete till today," she said, "how could your brain use that word as a clue?"

"Exactly," said Barry, his smile fading. "How indeed?"

MORAT
Near Fotinos, Crete

THE MERCS—OR, AS THEY PREFERRED TO BE CALLED, PRI-
vate military contractors—were an eclectic group which,
Morat observed to himself, was a polite way of saying
motley. They operated by code number, P-1 through P-8, with
Sigorsky as C-1 (command) and Morat as R. At least it wasn't
colors. Introductions were terse and formal, and none of the
mercs removed their helmets, face masks, or night vision goggles, but Morat caught just enough dialect to identify a Brit,
at least three Americans, a couple of sub-Saharan Africans
and a pair who he guessed were either native to the Libyan
base where the team had been formed or were from very close
by, Algeria maybe, or Egypt. He'd bet money the Yanks had
been—or still were—Blackwater. Sigorsky was Russian. There
was a lot of work for private contractors these days; more than
enough to go around, and if you had the skills and followed

orders, ethnicity or nationality was, appropriately enough, not an issue.

The world was no longer divided by lines of geography, ancient treaty, or family bloodline. Maynard had proved that.

Still, Morat had always disdained mercenaries, though as they hiked unspeaking along the ridge and down toward the church, Morat wondered vaguely if he really was just one of them: he did whatever he was told to regardless of his own background or beliefs in search of a paycheck. He didn't like the idea, but a couple of days ago he would have struggled to come up with a good reason as to why it wasn't true. Things were different now, of course. The hum in his head, which had pointed him toward the church in the first place, spoke of a different kind of investment. It wasn't an ideology exactly, but it was the kind of identity and sense of belonging that the mercs would never have.

The squad, minus members P-7 and P-8, who had been stationed to guard the extraction point with the helo, moved swiftly over the terrain with that familiar military brand of caution and efficiency, their movements sure and economical. Without their night vision goggles, and in his inadequate shoes, Morat felt less sure-footed, but he was content to follow their lead in the dark, and in any case, bringing up the rear had its own strategic responsibilities. It also meant that he was the first to hear the distant hum of rotors.

He had gotten so used to that occasional insect droning that it took him a second to raise the alarm, tapping his headset and saying simply:

"We got helos incoming."

The cops continuing their search? Or had the mercs' own chopper raised an alarm after all?

He listened hard and this time he picked up something else. It was sound, he supposed, but he was also sure that it came from beyond the range of his ears. He was sensing it with something other than hearing, though it registered in his brain as noise. Specifically, it was the noise of jet engines.

This was no routine police search.

Someone knew they were here, knew Greek airspace had been breached, and were sending the cavalry. They were a long way off, far too far away for him to be able to hear their approach, but he knew beyond doubt that they were coming. Fast.

But then Morat had been promised some air cover of his own, hadn't he?

He grinned bleakly, secretly into the darkness, and immediately felt almost bad for the pilots of whatever the Greek air force was sending in. The poor buggers wouldn't know what hit them. Literally.

NICHOLAS
Near Fotinos, Crete

NICHOLAS SAT BACK, STARING AT THE DOUBLE-HEADED AX motif in the bluish glow of his flashlight, then worked his fingers carefully under the stone slab and, very carefully, lifted it from its bed of straw and turned it over. Fortunately, it was neither as big nor as heavy as the crate suggested, and he was able to pivot it on one corner, flip it, and lower it down reverse side up, without difficulty or danger. The last thing he wanted was to risk breaking it during his first look at it.

He had set the flashlight down to turn the tablet over, so he didn't know what he had till he got the light on it. He gasped, his mind reeling.

Two features immediately leapt out. The first was that this face of the tablet was covered with fine carving. Not Ugaritic. Something else entirely. Nicholas couldn't read it, but he recognized the curious script. It looked like a form of hieroglyphics, too simple to be pictograms, not enough recurring patterns to be writing in the conventional sense. Some of the logograms looked like the simpler Chinese characters, while others looked runic.

"Linear A," he muttered.

The scripted language of Minoan Crete, dating from somewhere between 2500 and 1450 before Christ.

Unlike Linear B, which showed up on the Greek mainland shortly after and was the written script of the Mycenaean Bronze Age, Linear A—though it may have been one of the parent forms of the younger language which, in turn, gave rise to Classical Greek—had never been deciphered. It was a remarkable find, no doubt, but what it said neither Nicholas nor anyone else would ever know. And that was doubly unfortunate because Nicholas dearly wanted to wrest the tablet's secrets from its ancient stone.

Because the other thing that struck him right away was the border that ran around the inscription. It was inlaid metal, a ribbon of some bluish material that looked like heat-tempered steel and, as he gazed on it, seemed to pulse with a faint but distinct radiance, so that Nicholas shut off the flashlight for a moment, and sat there in the dark to be sure his eyes weren't playing tricks on him.

For a moment the blackness of the crypt seemed to swallow the stone up entirely, but then a bead of pearly iridescence winked on, coursing around the panel of text like a droplet of water. If not for the distinct blue tint, shimmering between teal, cobalt, and aquamarine, he would have thought it was mercury, quicksilver. It ran as if the tablet was being tipped and pivoted, making the seemingly liquid energy move and sparkle, but the stone was quite still, and the movement—or illusion of movement—seemed to come from the metal's own peculiar energy.

Strange, he thought, *that you should think of water*, because there was more rain coming, though he wasn't sure how he knew that. That wasn't all he knew. Someone else had been thinking about the double-headed ax motif on the other side of the tablet. He could see it as they saw it, a printed insignia on a white-walled corridor among other white-walled corridors that connected and intersected till they formed a kind of maze. Nicholas didn't know who this person was, but he felt his unease, his certainty that the labyrinth in which he was trapped held a monster that was hunting him . . .

Unnerved by the clarity of the insight, Nicholas turned the flashlight back on and stared at the ancient text, willing it to turn into something he could decipher, wondering vaguely if it was worth all he had been through, all the others had lost, this baffling and mysterious artifact of . . .

The sound of footsteps on the stone stairs that led down from the church snapped his head around. Someone was descending into the crypt, flashlight in hand.

56

ALAN
US Airspace

OMPARED TO THE LOCUST, WHOSE CONTROLS WERE SO heavily computerized, the disk felt more like an actual aircraft, albeit one that was an outgrowth of himself. It banked and climbed with him, bonded to his very thoughts, speeding through the air so that he could almost feel it rushing past his ears. Getting back into the Locust's seat had felt like a kind of homecoming, and in spite of the quantum leap forward in terms of hardware and operating systems, it had seemed to be a natural technological evolution. The disk was not like that. The disk made Alan feel that it was he who had evolved, and the step forward was also a step sideways into an altogether different kind of future, not the straight-line movement of a chess rook or bishop, but the odd, dogleg attack of a knight. He careened through the night sky as if on his own wings, steering, accelerating, and maneuvering with his mind.

He remembered the sharply building exhaustion he had felt last time, and had left the ground of Dreamland apprehensively, but while he felt the pull on his mental focus, the weariness had not yet begun to register. He wondered to what extent the yellow crate was a factor in this, or rather the stone tablet it contained, and though he did not understand how that could be possible, he felt sure it was a factor. Such things, however, had to be merely accepted, not scrutinized. Not now. There would be time for that another day.

If he lived through this one.

The "situation" Kenyon had woken him for took the form of a familiar cigar-shaped object that had winked into being directly over Papoose Lake at precisely oh-three-hundred hours at a height of forty-five thousand feet. One minute it wasn't there, the next it was. It triggered no warning, no trace on radar or any other instruments. Not till it wanted to be seen, or so Alan felt. Then all hell broke loose: lights, sirens, every warning system in the place all suddenly screaming their collective hearts out.

Hastings's Locust was already up, trying—and failing— to initiate some sort of communication. He was under orders not to fire unless ordered by ground control, not because they were trying to play nice or be diplomatic with whoever was up there, but because their prior encounter had left them with an uncomfortable doubt about their ability to engage the cigar in any kind of conflict. Its mysterious, sensor-evading appearance had reminded them of that.

So Hastings had been sent up to talk and monitor, scan for signs of hostility or of intel sweeps of any kind directed at the base below, but nothing had happened. The cigar-craft, shimmering on and off of sensor displays without warning, hung in the night, canted at an angle for reasons only it knew, sometimes clear as some zeppelin from a century ago, sometimes not obviously there at all.

Until Alan went up. After twelve minutes of continual tracking with nothing to show for it, the disk's ascent apparently changed the situation instantly. The cigar-craft moved steadily off to the northeast, fluttered, and was gone only to be picked up by a radar station in Wyoming two minutes later.

"Go after it," said Kenyon over the radio. "Monitor only. Do not engage and keep weapons systems off-line. Repeat: do not engage."

"Roger that," said Hastings. "Moving to within a thousand meters."

Alan followed suit, willing the disk to slide through the sky and coming to rest in a still hover some two hundred meters above the Locust, watching. The cigar pulsed with light, rippling along its length.

"This is Magnus," said Hastings, using the squadron call sign. "Target gone from all instruments. He's not here anymore."

Alan half closed his eyes and tilted his head. He was moving the disk before Hastings's voice cut through the radio again.

"Hold that thought," he said. "He's back on long-range sensors. But he's moved another three hundred miles and is now in Canadian airspace. Please advise. Over."

"Engage all counter-detection measures and pursue," said Kenyon. "Previous orders stand. Do not engage."

"Roger that," said Hastings. "But I don't think he likes Alan's ride. He's running."

No, thought Alan, the idea emerging clear and sharp as glass. *He's not.*

"He's leading," he said. "He wants us to follow."

There was a thoughtful silence, then Kenyon's voice came back.

"Roger that, Phoenix. Be careful up there."

"You think it's a trap?" asked Hastings.

"Just stay alert, Magnus," said Kenyon. "You too, Phoenix."

"He's moved again," said Hastings.

Alan didn't need telling. The cigar was drifting high and black over the cold, turbid waters of the Atlantic. He could feel it. He nudged the disk with his mind and it skipped through the air at implausible speeds and emerged from a bank of cloud two hundred yards off the cigar's port side. He could see it looming there, inscrutable and still and then, as if it was waiting to be sure he had seen it, it was moving again.

"Where the hell is it going?" muttered Hastings as the cigar shimmered out and reappeared over northeast England.

"Greece," Alan breathed, recalling the mythic labyrinth, the dream of being hunted by a monstrous, horned figure back in Dreamland. The Minotaur. "Of course, it is. It's going to Crete."

"That's right," said Gretta, the little ballerina standing at his shoulder. "That's right."

57

JENNIFER
Hampshire, England

THE COWS HAD PARTED, THEIR EYES BLANK AS EVER, FORM-
ing a surreal corridor along which Jennifer took her faltering steps toward the man with the pipe. It wasn't her
father. She knew that. It couldn't be. It looked like him—
exactly like him—but Edward Quinn was dead and nothing
could bring him back.

"Jenny."

He said the word and it was him, her father, as if he had
just been away on some business trip.

He looked younger than he had been when she saw him last.
A decade or more. As he had been when they had been closest.

She walked between the silent cattle, her eyes locked on
him, fighting the tears back.

"You're not my father," she said. It was supposed to be
defiant, but it sounded merely sad.

"No," he said. "But I was."

"I don't understand."

"Walk with me," he said.

He turned his back on her then, strolling back toward the stile, but though his legs moved, she had the impression that that was just a kind of mimicry, and that he was really floating just above the ground. The scent of pipe smoke had changed now, become something like ozone or electricity, and almost on cue there was a dull rattle of distant thunder, a ripple of light in the sky, and it began to rain. It was a strange storm, and Jennifer was almost sure that the raindrops were falling slower than usual so that they felt like a curtain she was stepping through.

The man who looked like her father had somehow already climbed the stile and stood waiting for her, his head turned over his shoulder toward her, the same wan smile on his face. It looked sad and thoughtful, like happiness in defeat, and it reminded her so fiercely of her father that it was very nearly more than she could bear. But she went after him anyway, glad to leave the cattle pasture behind, hurrying to catch up as he turned not toward the house but, inevitably perhaps, toward the woods and the old fairy ring that they enclosed.

As she reached the tree line the rain droplets had slowed so much that she could look up to see them coming and could move around them. It felt like a dream, but it was also absolutely real. She was outside, standing among the black trees just beyond her dead father's Hampshire home, and it was night, though she doubted there had ever been a night as strange as this.

Not, at least, since she was very small.

That had been a strange night too. She remembered it now, though that was impossible, and it had been a lot like this, the great light in the sky following her father down through the woods and into the fairy circle.

He had been carrying her. He had been whispering baby nonsense about elves, showing his infant daughter the woods he so loved, and they had been there, as they were now, pale and bright and beautiful but not, she thought, what they seemed, whispering to him their promises and demands.

Insect voices. The swarm that thought as one trying to make sense of the individual human and its solitary, fragile offspring. What power that gave them over him!

Jennifer faltered, overcome with the terror of that memory, the deep and long-forgotten revulsion of the eyes that had beheld her tiny childish form that night so long ago. She clapped her hands to her mouth as if the scent of the memory was enough to make her vomit.

The man who looked like Edward Quinn turned to her now, and his face was serious.

"These are not those who took you," he said. He sounded almost like himself, though the voice was richer, more musical and resonant than it had been in life. "This visitation, our coming to this place, is merely a habit of memory, a way to make impossible things manageable. I am not who I look like. I am no one. We are no one. But we are not what took you. Can you feel that?"

"Yes," Jennifer whispered.

It was true. She felt the presence around her and it was ethereal and strange but she felt none of the watchful insect malice that had come with her memory like the stink of things rancid and hidden out of sight. This was different, as the silent cows were different from the swarm. She stepped deliberately through the frozen raindrops in front of her, as if to wash her face, and on contact with her skin they stopped being whatever they had been, becoming water and running down her cheeks like tears.

As she stepped through, half clambering over a fallen tree limb, listening to the rustle of the leaves beneath her feet—the only sound in the world, it seemed—she realized that she was almost across the thinnest stripe of the copse, and that before her was the fairy ring. Inside the broad circle of tiny mushrooms it glowed a vivid and vibrant green, lit brilliantly from above, and now the man who looked like her father had stepped inside the round and was walking into its center. When he reached the middle, he turned to face her, extending his hands toward her in invitation.

"It is time, little Jenny," he said. "Join us in the ancient dance."

She stepped clear of the trees but hesitated at the edge of the mushroomed rim of the turf.

"But if I join the fairy dance, I will be whisked away forever," she said, the words coming from some childish corner of her memory.

The man who was not her father smiled sadly and shook his head.

"We are not fairies," he said. "You know that. And we are not what took you. Come. You can still see them."

Jennifer, her face wet, needing to know, to see, took a long breath of the warm, wet Hampshire night, and stepped into the circle, reaching for her father's pale hand.

But as she crossed the line, she found that the hands extended toward her were no longer his. They were not the hands of any human.

TIMIKA
Souda Bay, Crete

THE GULFSTREAM LANDED AT THE SOUDA BAY NAVAL BASE, where the US Naval Support Activity was housed. From there Timika and Barry were hurried toward a waiting Navy chopper like visiting dignitaries. But Timika felt rushed, and wished they could stay on the base for a little while, feeling the ground beneath her feet. Twice on the plane she had glimpsed the twig-demon Jennifer had called Raggety out of the window.

Psychic projection, she had thought dismissively, closing her eyes and willing it away, but the image bothered her all the same, and not just because it was creepy in and of itself. She had seen it as she first sped toward Crete, and again in the car right before Elina had called to say that Morat was en route to the dig. Minutes later, people died. So however much she could dismiss the raggety imp as the residue of Jennifer's literary childhood, the trauma had transferred to her now and it meant something. It threatened bad things coming. Promised them, even. Timika couldn't say how that could be or why she was sure of it, but she was. Something beyond themselves was speaking to them, pulling from their subconscious to send them . . . what?

A warning? A threat?

One of the two. Either way the implication was clear. She and Barry were running headlong into danger. Why the herald of that danger had a vaguely insect form she couldn't be sure, but she thought that relevant too.

"You can't get a squad of Greek troops to come with us?" she asked Barry as they approached the helicopter.

"They already have a police presence there," he shouted back over the noise of the rotors. "We can't justify a military deployment without telling them things top brass doesn't want to talk about."

"There are US servicemen stationed here. Why can't we use them?"

"Same reason," said Barry. "In case you hadn't noticed, the US isn't real popular in Europe these days, and that makes our job a hell of a lot harder. A sovereign nation isn't going to let you send armed fighters into their territory unless you have their absolute trust. Combine the nation's current political profile with our need for secrecy on all things military and intelligence related, and we risk an international incident just by showing up."

"They may get an international incident whether they want one or not," said Timika broodily.

"You don't think I can look after you?" yelled Barry, checking his sidearm as they hurried, heads bowed, and climbed aboard.

Timika rolled her eyes, but the barbed and ironic quip she would normally have at hand wouldn't come. She shot him a look full of doubt and apprehension, but said nothing and belted herself in, nodding to the pilot who had his thumb raised expectantly.

Ready?

No, she thought, even as she nodded. *I'm not. Something is coming. We're not ready.*

They rose slightly unsteadily and then sped through the darkness only a couple of hundred feet above the black tree-tops. She was almost glad of the darkness because it meant she wouldn't see that awful stick figure clinging to the sides of the chopper, grinning at her, promising death and disaster to come . . .

They were ferried to the north side of the village, where Timika had eaten the best feta cheese and black olives in her life not so very long ago. The chopper set down in the tiny, wedge-shaped waste ground behind the most modern building in the area, a brilliantly lit green-and-white pharmacy. The helicopter wobbled in its descent and settled slightly off kilter so that Timika had to steady herself as she clambered out, her head bent lower than was strictly necessary to avoid the rotor.

"You know where you're going from here?" Barry asked her, as the helicopter rose into the night once more.

"Yes," said Timika. "It's walkable from here."

As they set out on the road past the taverna and out of the village, Barry's phone rang. He took it out, frowned at the display, and answered it.

"Where are you?" he asked, turning quickly to Timika and mouthing "*Alan.*" He pressed the phone to the side of his head, listened for a moment, then said, "Seriously? Okay. What do you need?" There was another pause, and Barry's feet slowed. Timika followed suit, and soon they were standing quite still in front of an old stone house, which might once have been a barn. "*Gretta?*" said Barry into the phone. "No. Never. This a person you're trying to find or . . . A *child*? No. Sorry man . . . Like Candy Cane, you mean? No."

Gretta.

The name resonated like the recording of a bell played backward in Timika's head, beginning with the faintest of reverberations but swelling in volume and clarity. Memories came back to her, things she hadn't considered for years, and with them an emotional piquancy that brought tears to her eyes as she traveled back to the girl she had been, all her old yearnings and pained, lonely sadnesses suddenly as sharp and vivid as they had been two decades earlier.

"Who is he asking about?" she managed to say.

Barry shook his head, implying that she couldn't help, but saw the shine of her eyes and stopped.

"Hold on," he said into the phone. "I'm putting Timika on."

He handed her the phone, watching her warily, concerned for her, but also apprehensive, troubled.

"Hi," said Timika into the phone but still looking at Barry. "You wanted to know about Gretta. I'm not sure, but I might be able to help. What do you know?"

"Er . . . well," said Alan. His voice was clear but it had a metallic, echoing quality and she wondered where he was. "I've been seeing a girl. A ballerina. Maybe ten years old." He seemed to hesitate, then added, slightly embarrassed, "Black. She said her name was . . ."

"Gretta," said Timika. She blinked and the tears rolled down her face.

"She wears a green dress . . ."

"A tutu," Timika corrected. "Forest green with a silver bodice." The words came to her precisely though she had not thought of them for years. Hadn't let herself think of them. "Cream satin ballet slippers with ribbons."

"Who is she?" asked Alan.

Strange that it should be him, a man she barely knew, talking to her over the phone from God alone knew where . . .

"Me," she replied. "Kind of. That is, I made her up. When I was a kid. She was what I wanted to be. How I wanted people to see me." She took a short, gasping breath, then recovered herself. "Does that help?"

"Yes," said Alan, as Barry put a cautiously protective arm around her shoulders. "Yes, it does."

MORAT
Near Fotinos, Crete

NO SIGN OF THEM YET, THE ENEMY, BUT HE KNEW THEY were coming.

The terrain looked quite different in the dark, but Morat's recall of the route down to the dig site was close to perfect. He shifted to the front, from where he led the team with confident speed. They moved in silence, but Morat could feel their tension, their strained, eager listening.

He spotted the tower of the little church just as the helicopters thrummed in over the coast. It glowed faintly with the light that bled out of its little windows and the patchy roofing, the top of the tower itself and the doorway little pale spaces in the night. To the rest of the team it would show green in their night vision goggles, and he sensed it in a similar way that went beyond ordinary sight, as if he was one of those snakes with the heat sensors, a pit viper tracking its prey.

Three helicopters. He paused to watch them as the team took cover. The fighter support he had guessed at—or sensed—would be entering a patrol vector, on the assumption that the helos were enough. Still, the Greeks weren't taking any chances, but that was hardly surprising if they'd managed to plot the team's helo in from Libya. In other circumstances he'd be pissed, but he was confident of his advantage and knew that the important thing was to stay focused on the job in hand, not to be distracted by whatever happened in the sky overhead. His waspish protectors would handle the fighters easily enough.

It was a toss-up whether the Greek authorities would have connected the earlier shooting to the unauthorized helo incursion, and that meant they might still not be watching the church. From his position, squatted behind an ancient, half-collapsed wall, he could see two people standing in the light of the church door. Police. They seemed to be looking up at the sky, watching the helos coming in, but taking no action of their own. They might have been civilians, mildly curious about something that didn't concern them.

Still, better to be prepared.

"There's only one road in," he said over the comm, as the field spread out in front of them. "P one through three secure that entrance and make sure no one comes in. P four take the east perimeter of the field, behind the church. Ensure that no one leaves that way. P five set up a sniper watch where you can see the whole field from this vantage. P six and C one, you're with me. There's only one way into the body of the church, so we're going in the front door. Hold your fire till I give the word unless your presence is discovered. All people outside the team should be considered hostiles. All hostiles are expendable. Priority one is the artifact. If Tan can be taken alive, that's priority two. Clear?"

They sounded off in sequence, Sigorsky bringing up the rear. If he resented Morat's taking charge, he hid it well. They were all watching the Greek helos now, trying to decide if they'd been seen or if the choppers were making for the extraction point where their own helo was waiting for them.

"Stay focused," said Morat. "The air support is not our problem. Got that?"

It wasn't radio protocol, but he didn't care, and they heard the command in his tone.

They kept still as the helicopters buzzed overhead, their searchlights coming on and splashing the ground with sudden color as they swept up the ridge and on toward the meadow to the southeast. For a split second, Morat wished he was in the arrowhead triangle he knew was lying in wait, unseen, undetected, lethal as a snake in the dark. Then the night erupted in sound and light, the first helicopter falling from the sky and bursting like a great fiery egg on the mountainside, and Morat was giving the order to go.

NICHOLAS
Near Fotinos, Crete

THERE WAS NOWHERE TO HIDE IN THE CRYPT. NICHOLAS braced himself, watching the erratic beam of the flashlight bouncing wildly off the walls, but there just wasn't anywhere to go. He crouched where he was, his eyes wide as the light found and held him in place.

"When did you find this?" said a voice. Female. Greek. Drowsily amazed.

"Elina?" he asked.

"Oh," she said, self-consciously flicking the light toward her own face. "Yes."

"Just now. See this?" he said, edging away and turning his own flashlight onto the stone tablet. "Linear A. It's what they found in the tomb and hid. It's what the killer wanted."

"Why?" she asked, shuffling carefully through the cramped space, her head bent low.

Nicholas shook his head.

"I don't know. I mean, it's very old, beautiful in its way. Valuable. But . . ."

"We can't read it," Elina concluded for him. "So why . . . ?"

"Shh . . ." said Nicholas suddenly.

Not much sound penetrated the crypt from above, but the explosion had been unmistakable. He hadn't so much heard it as felt it rumbling through the earth. Something had happened. Something terrible.

"I heard helicopters," said Elina. "As I was coming down. You think one of them . . ."

"We should run," said Nicholas, not wanting to think through the implications of her question. He still didn't understand what was happening, but this was far bigger than he could have imagined and he wanted to be gone. The distant sounds of gunfire around the church seemed to emphasize the point.

Running suddenly seemed like a very bad idea. Perhaps they could seal themselves in again? Pull the wooden dais over the trapdoor. Stay down here in the dark till it was over. No one knew about the crypt. They might yet be safe . . .

But even as the possibility occurred to him, his eyes went back to the stone tablet and he bit his lip. It had called to him. It had shown him his dead mother and told him where it could be found.

That made no sense. The carved stone was no more than that: an ancient slab of rock, and to think otherwise was not the thought of a legitimate archaeologist, a scientist of the past. But he couldn't shake the idea.

It called to you. It found something in your head that you would listen to, and it led you to this place.

Which raised a dreadful possibility.

What if it had also called someone else?

ALAN
Greek Airspace

THERE WAS NO SIGN OF THE BALLERINA IN THE COCKPIT NOW, but Alan didn't worry about that or what her sudden appearance and disappearance meant. His conversation with Barry had banished such doubts. The little girl was an imaginary aspect of Timika, a snapshot of her own past and the person she had once wished she was. He didn't know why this made perfect sense to him, but it did. The ballerina was a kind of warning, a friendly one he instinctively knew that he could trust.

"Left of the castle," she had told him, "vault the gate or you must enter the top hat."

He had no idea what that meant, but perhaps later . . .

"Phoenix, this is Magnus," said Hastings over the radio. "We're getting reports of hostile aircraft of unknown specification engaging Greek aircraft over the island of Crete. I'm heading in to assist. Request backup."

"Right there with you, Magnus," said Alan. "You have a reading on the cig?"

"Negative, Phoenix. You?"

"No," said Alan. "One minute it was in front of me, then it was gone. I've got instruments primed for its signature should it return, but for now our priority seems to be those bogeys. What are you seeing?"

"I have a pair of arrowheads on viewer," said Hastings. "There were three helos reported but I only see two airborne. Make that one. The other is taking fire and going down."

"See if you can save the last one," said Alan. "I'm right behind you."

"One of the arrowheads is moving to intercept a pair of Greek F-16s, location . . ."

"I see them," said Alan. "I'll look after them."

In fact he didn't so much see them as feel their presence. They were on his display panels, but he could almost see them better with his eyes closed. The arrowhead was dropping on them like a stooping falcon, but it hadn't opened fire yet. He tightened his focus and the disk slid through the Greek night, cutting through the air as it dropped thirty thousand feet in under two seconds, and came up shooting.

He remembered at the last second the full destructive force the disk could muster, how his own anger had seemed to fuel the weapons he had used to shred the arrowheads that had killed Jackson a few weeks before, and he tried to make the strike surgical. In place of the stream of light peppering the enemy craft, a single point of energy, blue and hot, sped through the air and caught the diving arrowhead squarely behind the cockpit. It fizzed briefly and dropped, directionless and turning in the air, like so much scrap.

Alan banked and climbed again, unsure if the jets had even known they were under attack, and as he did so, he felt the terror of the arrowhead's pilot as the craft hit the black waters of the Aegean below and broke apart.

He tore his mind free of the struggling pilot, feeling the sweat break out on his forehead as he brought the disk around to help Hastings.

Their enemy—Maynard, or whoever was now holding the purse strings and giving orders to the likes of Morat—had not expected them, and Hastings's initial assault had caught the other arrowhead unawares.

"Magnus, this is Phoenix," said Alan. "Is it down?"

"Not down, but out," said Hastings. "Tagged him on the port side as he went to engage the final helo. He spun off west, losing speed and altitude. Pilot may have lost consciousness, or directional control might have been impacted. Looked pretty wobbly. Should I go after and finish him off?"

"Let's be sure there's nothing fresh incoming first," said Alan.

"Well, we took as big a bite out of their fleet last time as they did from ours. I doubt they have a whole lot more craft to deploy," said Hastings.

He sounded jubilant, which was understandable in the circumstances.

"Let me check in with our people on the ground," said Alan.

It didn't feel right. Not yet. Battles that felt "too easy" only happened in movies, and he knew that any fight you walked away from was a good one, but his instincts said he wasn't done. He brought the disk arcing back over the humped mass of the island that was Crete—Candy, as it had been, home of the labyrinth—and he saw the sudden mass of cloud that had formed around the central spine.

It had not been there only minutes before. He frowned, wondering vaguely about minotaurs and other stranger monsters. The thick and smoky storm clouds were heaped up and swollen, purple and black, heavy with rain and electrical discharge. The place positively hummed in his mind with vibrating and barely contained energy. The center of the cloud was tall and solid, its billows strangely hard-edged and vertical, so that it looked like a fortress rising over the darkened island.

A castle.

Alan banked the disk to run around the flank as the lightning began to ripple and surge, and he saw in the center a shape that, if the cloud bank was like a castle, would be its gatehouse, where a portcullis or drawbridge might stand.

He stared at it, flashing past at speed, thinking vaguely about the imaginary ballerina and her advice, but he didn't go in. He didn't try to—as she had said—*vault the gate* because he was needed out here, because Barry and Timika were down there somewhere and this was not over. So he flew north of the ominous cloud, committing to going past the castle-like cloud rather than entering over its dark, swirling gate, but as he did so he had a sudden feeling that he had made a mistake. His instinct had been right. It wasn't over. There was more for him to do up here . . .

He brought the disk to a sudden halt, but still he paused, distrustful of what mind and body were telling him for which he had no real evidence, no readings in his sensors, no orders from base or observations from anyone else. The cloud was supercharged with lightning which, for all he knew, might play hell with his craft. He could be blind in there, and who knew what might be lurking inside, ready to pounce. All logic and experience told him to stay out here where he could see what was going on, poised to act if needed. Only his gut told him to vault the gate and enter the cloud bank. His gut and Timika's imaginary childhood dancer . . .

But he had said he could trust her, and he knew that he had to. He brought the disk around and aimed it at the cloud castle, but his deliberation had cost him. As Hastings began to shout over the intercom, Alan saw them zipping out of the cloud, weapons blazing. Not arrowheads. Worse, much worse than that.

There were ten bright spheres but with a single mind between them, so that the word that insisted itself on Alan's consciousness as he set the disk shooting away in a hard, desperate retreat was *swarm*.

62

JENNIFER
Hampshire, England

THE WORLD SHE KNEW HAD VANISHED. SHE STOOD IN light, bright but gentle enough that she did not need to squint. The figure that had looked like her father was tall and pale as the stars, and his resemblance to anything human and ordinary was coincidental, a final cloak to make their interaction easier.

But if he was not human, neither was he the insect swarm, the things that had buzzed waspishly in her head for days, the things binding her to Morat, the things—she felt sure—that had taken her from this spot when she was a child. This creature was distinct from her, different, and though it was not human, it was also single and its mind was its own. It was wise and watchful, but while it did not have the casual cruelty, the malice of the swarm that had abducted her, Jennifer felt more curiosity than kindness from it. There was power here, but she would have to be careful of it. This thing might not be her enemy, but neither was it clearly her friend.

"What happens now?" she asked.

"That depends on you," said the being of light. "What do you want?"

The answer came instantly and without thought.

"To help my friends," she said.

The creature seemed to consider this approvingly.

"Once," it said, "we bestowed gifts upon your people. Long ago, as you reckon it. They were for you. Not for the others."

"The swarm," said Jennifer.

Again the pale creature seemed to think about this and inclined its almost human head in agreement.

"If what you call the swarm were to acquire these objects," it said, "the consequences would be dire."

"For you?" asked Jennifer.

She felt its smile, and it was as if she was a child who had been asked what two plus two were and she had answered with something not just wrong, but entirely inappropriate to the question: lemon, perhaps, or ambulance.

"Dire," said the creature, "for you. Your people. Your world. You should prevent this from happening."

"Can't you do it?"

"That is not my way. Our way."

"My friends are in Crete," said Jennifer. "That is a long way from here."

"No," said the pale creature. It extended a long hand with slender, sensitive fingers, and as it moved she saw that the light that bathed them came from the being itself, so that as it moved it lit the air around it with pearly radiance. "It is very close. Look."

The hand opened and beyond it, where the woods around the fairy ring should be, she saw a blasted field, barren except for a few stumps of olive trees and, a little farther away, a ruined church or chapel.

"Can I go there?" she asked.

"It would be very dangerous."

"I know."

"And yet you still want to go?"

"Yes," said Jennifer, feeling sure, insistent.

"Why?" asked the creature, its head tipped toward one side musingly.

"Because I sent them there," she replied, the truth of it lodging hot and bright as a star in her mind. "They are my friends and I sent them there. People have already died as a result. I need to go, to help."

"Your enemies are already there. They have weapons. Your friends will not survive."

"Then I must help!"

"And if you cannot?"

The question pulled at Jennifer's mind and she wondered if she had always heard it or almost heard it, felt it hanging in the air at the very limits of her consciousness. She had grown up rich, a person of wealth and privilege, even of status, but she was not sure she had done what she should have. Always on the edge of things, always a champion of causes, of issues, but always safe in her ability to walk away, to return to the wealth she professed to despise, even as she knew it had made everything in her life possible. She had resisted, in her way, but if her money—her father's money—went away, what would she be worth? Who would she be? What would she have achieved?

Worth had to be more than a bank balance.

Yes, she thought.

"If I cannot help," she said, "then I should stand with my friends as they fight."

The creature of light considered longer this time, and she thought she sensed its wonder and confusion. But just as she expected it to say no, to close the circle and release her back to the woods on the grounds of her father's house, it gestured with its hands, and the image of the barren field shifted, as if a veil had been lifted. It was real now, not an idea or an image, a projection or a vision of something far away. It was there.

Ten yards at most.

Jennifer took the first step. Then another.

She looked back, to where the creature of light was watching her, feeling its strange and unearthly curiosity, as if it was watching animals at play.

Three more steps and she was through, listening to the thrum of bullets coursing through the warm Cretan night.

TIMIKA
Near Fotinos, Crete

ARRY HAD KEPT TO THE STONE WALL AS THEY ROUNDED THE corner where the road widened and stopped at the edge of the field. That had saved their lives. The bullets skipped sparking off the uneven hunks of rock, spitting chippings and grit from the wall. The guns weren't as loud as she had expected, but they were fast, spewing near-white flashes of fire in an almost constant stream. The shots had been as sudden as the rain that had broken over them without warning and now fell hard and thick.

She dropped below the wall, her crouch bringing her hands to the dusty ground, as Barry paused, listened, and went back up firing his pistol. Two shots, then two more, and she heard one of the machine gunners go down with a grunt. She heard more gunfire from farther away, and Barry huddled down again and pulled out his phone. He hit a preset number and handed it to her.

"This is Timika Mars," she shouted over the rain as soon as someone answered. "I'm with Barry Regis on the edge of Nicholas Tan's excavation site. We're getting shot at."

"Number of assailants?" said the voice, businesslike.

"Hard to say. Several. With machine guns."

She didn't know what else to say, or who she was talking to.

"Withdraw to cover till we can get support to you," said the voice. He sounded military and American.

"Which will be how long?"

"Half an hour," said the voice. "Minimum."

"No way," she said. "I have friends in there."

She wasn't sure how she knew that, but she did. She felt Nicholas's presence in the church and knew that he did not have a half hour.

"The Greek police will get there faster," said the voice. "You should wait till . . ."

"Not gonna happen," she said.

She wasn't being brave. She just knew she couldn't leave Nicholas, even if there was precious little she could do to help. She hung up and gave Barry a look. He was thinking, calculating, but he met her eyes and nodded almost imperceptibly, then straightened up again and squeezed off three more rounds. A machine gun opened up again and he ducked behind the wall, frowning as the bullets zipped through the air above them.

"There's still two of them," he said, as lightning lit the sky overhead. "We're stuck."

"You have a spare piece?" she asked.

He looked doubtful, but his left hand went to his shin and patted it. The rainwater was starting to pool at their feet.

"Can you shoot?" he asked over the thunder.

"Seen a lot of movies," she answered.

He managed a tight smile, the rain running down his face.

"Yeah," he said, "that's not gonna do it."

"So what do we do?" she whispered. "We're pinned down."

"Stay here and I'll see if I can outflank them."

"I'm coming with you."

"Timika, I don't have time . . ."

"I *said*, I'm coming with you."

She gave him her flintiest stare and he turned away.

"Okay," he said. "But stay out of sight. These guys are serious."

She'd only had a glimpse of them, but she had seen the black gear, the night vision goggles, and didn't need telling. There were more distant shots from some other part of the field and she crunched in on herself, making herself small, wishing she was a little lighter, more athletic.

Gretta.

She hadn't thought of that in years. It would be just her luck to die musing on a version of herself that had never existed.

"Give me the gun," she said, tapping his ankle holster, squinting her eyes to keep the rain out.

"I told you . . ."

"Just give it to me," she said, not pleading, not angry. Businesslike. As if choosing a difficult solution that made logical sense.

He frowned, but his hand went to the pistol and drew it. He slapped it into her open hand, butt first. A snub-nosed revolver.

"Emergency use only," he said. "Don't cock it. Just point it and pull the trigger if you need to."

It was heavier than it looked, and warm from his body, and it felt dangerous so that for a second she almost wanted to give it back to him. But Barry was moving, vaulting the wall in a kind of roll, then charging toward the gunmen. They came up shooting, but were surprised and couldn't find him. As they redirected their fire in the direction he'd gone, forgetting or ignoring her completely, Timika edged out, sighted, and fired.

The gun kicked in her hand, but her target crumpled into cover, not dead, but startled and hurt.

Badly enough to stop him?

She wasn't sure, and, suddenly struck by the possibility of having to kill him where he lay, she was overcome with dread and terror. She squatted down behind the stone wall hugging her knees, the pistol all but forgotten.

More gunfire, close this time. The cannon crack of Barry's service weapon, then the oddly muffled rattle of the machine guns. Another shot from Barry, then a long, agonizing silence.

Timika squatted in the rain, trying not to sob, listening, waiting.

A sudden stream of shots. Not Barry's pistol. The suppressed machine gun. It fired, then stopped, and there was no answering report.

No, she thought. *Barry. No.*

And then, through the driving wind and rain, she heard the sound of footsteps coming toward her.

64

MORAT
Near Fotinos, Crete

IT WASN'T CLEAR WHAT WAS GOING ON. TWO OF THE THREE
Greek helos had gone down in flames but the third seemed
to have gone on toward the extraction point unmolested.
Morat had heard the distinct hum of what was euphemisti-
cally called "nonconventional" weapons fire, followed by the
keening of the air when something equally nonconventional
moves at speed. He couldn't see, but he felt sure their arrowheads were under attack by whatever remained of the US's
Locust fleet.

Alan Young was up there. Almost certainly.

It changed nothing, of course, not for their mission on the
ground, and probably not much in the air either. Maynard—
or whatever he was supposed to call them now—would have
to reveal their allies a little sooner than they had wanted to,
and that would really put the cat among the pigeons. He

looked up from the deep shade of the church wall, wondering if it had already started, but it was hard to see anything through the rain and the lightning-laced cloud.

An odd storm, he reflected, *which had erupted out of nothing. Something to do with the swarm, perhaps.*

He shuddered involuntarily, but put the response down to the rivulet of rainwater that had found an opening at his jacket collar and run down his back. There was fighting at the road head, but he thought his men could hold it for long enough. One of the cops who had been guarding the church door—if you could call what he was doing "guarding"—had stepped out, shouting, and P-4 had dropped him with a single shot. The policewoman who had been with him had screamed, fired blindly, then ducked back into the church, which made her smarter than her buddy. She would be calling for backup, but that didn't matter. This would be over long before the police reinforcements arrived.

He nodded to Sigorsky—AKA C-1—to make sure he was ready, wondering vaguely who the shooter on the road was, and for a second his mind strayed that way, bringing him up short, genuinely surprised.

Timika Mars.

The woman who had befriended Quinn's daughter was here. He couldn't imagine why. It was a bad choice on her part, and it would almost certainly cost her life. That was no skin off Morat's nose. Actually, it was a bonus: one more loose end tied off.

"What?" said Sigorsky.

"Nothing," said Morat. "An old acquaintance of mine is here."

"Problem?"

Morat grinned.

"Not in the slightest," he said. "On my mark."

He raised his hand, listened for another second, then lowered it. The two men made for the church door, moving quickly but bent over. Sigorsky stepped up with his machine pistol, but Morat put a hand on his shoulder and, when he had his attention, shook his head. Sigorsky watched as Morat's hand went to Sigorsky's own belt and unsnapped a grenade, one of the old Soviet F-1s, but more than adequate for the job.

Sigorsky nodded. There was no point getting into a gun battle with the lady cop.

Morat flattened himself against the wall by the door through which he had crawled not so very long ago, gripped the release lever tightly, pulled the pin, and flipped the grenade inside. He heard it bounce off the wall and skitter on the tiled floor. The rain was too loud to hear if she ran or spoke, and a moment later there was the dull boom of the explosion. He turned his head away from the blast as the shock pulsed out of the open doorway with a flat hard flash, followed by a plume of smoke. Then he brought the machine pistol around and led the way inside to mop up.

As he waited for the smoke to clear, Morat thought he heard something high in the night sky above him, something on the edge of hearing, beyond the rain and the thunder and the gunfire. It was simultaneously satisfying and terrifying, the thin and malevolent whine of the swarm.

NICHOLAS
Near Fatinos, Crete

ICHOLAS DIDN'T KNOW WHY HE WAS SO SURE THAT THE
shooting outside had something to do with the man
they called Morat, the one who had killed Desma, and
even less idea why he was sure the killer had come for the
tablet, but he knew one thing for certain: Morat wasn't going
to take the ancient carving with him, not if he could help it.
Maybe it was nothing more than pride and defiance, a determination that the assassin would not get what he wanted.
But it felt like more than that. He didn't know why the tablet
mattered, but his instinct said that it did, and nothing that
mattered should be allowed to fall into the hands of people
like that.

But the killer would come down into the crypt. That
seemed certain too, though he could not say how he knew.
And while Nicholas had survived one encounter with the

killer, he thought a second meeting, down here where there was no place to hide, no room to move, was pushing his luck.

"We need to go," he said to Elina. He hefted the tablet and found it lighter than he had feared, light enough to carry a little way. The Greek woman looked scared, but she had no better idea and followed him to the tight little steps up into the church. "Wait," he said. "If I take this with me, they might not come down here at all. Not if they see me. You should stay here."

She listened wide-eyed, then shook her head, though he suspected that had more to do with not wanting to be alone than it did about trying to help.

"Yes," he insisted. "Stay here."

While she was still deciding, the thud of the grenade ripped through the nave above them. Nicholas shrank back for a second, holding the position to see if the whole church was coming down, then started back up the steps, even though in his heart he felt the pained certainty that he had missed his chance. They were here now and there was nowhere for him to go. The very last thing he could do was keep Elina alive, even if he could not do as much for himself.

Yes, said his mother, whispering into his ear. *That's right, Nick. Look after her.*

He pushed up through the hole in the altar floor, the stone tablet clasped in front of his chest, smelling the smoke, the acrid tang of gunpowder. The police work lights had gone out in the church, but it wasn't completely dark. The altar screen gave him cover from the main entrance, and he emerged stooping to find the policewoman sprawled facedown on the wooden dais. She was bleeding from shrapnel wounds across her back and wasn't moving, though he thought she might still be alive.

Maybe she had seen the bomb or grenade and got almost far enough away; maybe she was partly protected by the altar screen.

He felt oddly calm, as if he was considering the thesis of an academic paper. Scooting around the altar stone, he risked a look through the stone lattice, suddenly aware of the drumming on the patchy church roof.

Rain. When had it begun to rain?

The soft glow in the body of the church came from a battery lantern and a computer terminal. There were two men veiled in smoke in the entrance, both black-clad, both armed.

Nicholas tore his gaze away and his eyes raked the prone body of the policewoman. She wore a small black automatic on her belt. He snatched at it, knowing he was being stupid, knowing it would probably get him killed, and tried to figure out where the safety catch was, his eyes back on the cautious men at the end of the nave, no more than ten yards away but indistinct in the gloom.

One of them was not wearing the night vision glasses, and though the church was dark and still billowing with smoke, Nicholas recognized him.

The assassin. The man they had called Morat.

It wasn't a decision. It was anger. He stabbed the pistol in the killer's direction and pulled the trigger. The gun jumped in his grip and he was unprepared for the noise, the flash, and the smoke, which made it harder to see what he was shooting at. And then they were returning fire with faster weapons that lit the nave and sent ricochets whining off the stone.

The screen shattered, pieces of its frame kicking out at his face, and he dropped, scurrying behind the altar stone as the guns blazed around him. He was still cradling the stone tablet in his left arm and he sat now, his back to the altar, hugging it to his chest like a child with a teddy bear, fighting back the sense of inevitable defeat. He prayed that Elina would stay where she was so that she wouldn't suffer the fate marked for him.

He had minutes at most. Seconds, probably.

"Throw the gun out here, Dr. Tan," said a cultured voice. Morat. It had to be. "You know what I'm here for. You know I'm going to take it. But you needn't die in the process, and I would prefer not to risk damaging it with another grenade. Toss the gun, leave the tablet, and you can walk out of here a free man."

Liar, thought Nicholas with bitter certainty, and for a moment it was almost like he was in the killer's head, waiting for his opportunity, machine pistol at the ready, and absolutely no mercy in his heart.

ALAN
Somewhere over Crete

THE BRASS SPHERES CAME SCREAMING OUT OF THE CLOUD castle, weapons flashing. Almost without thinking Alan sent the disk into a steep, spiraling climb, feeling the laser blasts shredding the air around him, as he tried to angle back into the muddying fog of the storm. Hastings's Locust was slower to respond, and his evasion more predictable. He was hit twice almost immediately and fell into a rolling dive, smoke pouring from his port side. The best Alan could hope was that Hastings would survive. He was out of the battle.

Alan was alone and outgunned. The spheres had the same instantaneous maneuverability as the disk, the same impossible speed. One-on-one it might have been a fight, but outnumbered like this, Alan had only one option.

Run.

But to where?

He swooped and slid, angling hard, his mind inventing ever more elaborate jinks and dodges as the sky around him exploded, but time was running out. He came to an abrupt halt, reversed, dived, but the spheres matched him move for move, each one mirroring the others as if they were the tentacles of a single beast.

Then Alan saw it, the curious bulge of cloud west of the main front. It rose like the crown of an old-fashioned top hat, and without wasting so much as a thought, he sped for it, climbing all the way until, directly above it, he dived like a cliff-borne gannet into the mouthlike barrel of the storm cloud.

Vault the gate or you must enter the top hat . . .

It might buy him no more than a few seconds, but it was, he was sure, what the ballerina had told him to do, and he would not hesitate this time.

Immediately, his sensors seemed to stall and flicker as he became part of the swirling mass of electrical energy. He didn't need to look around to know that the spheres were coming after him, but there were shadows here, corners in which he might skulk for a time, and with the rare jubilance of hope, he spat back a pulse of lethal energy that turned two of the spheres, blasting them off course and sending them dropping, lightless and spent.

It was a tiny and short-lived victory, but he celebrated it nonetheless, roaring his defiance as he sent the disk cutting this way and that while the swarm reconfigured behind him. He sensed their momentary concern as they gathered, used it to speed deeper into the heart of the cloud, but then they were coming with new, vengeful deliberation.

The strain on Alan's mind swelled, as he felt the presence of the one behind him, divided though it was between different ships. He could hear them buzzing in his head, could almost see their antennae, their long, sticklike limbs ending in hook claws reaching into his own ship and, for something less than a second, he gave in to fear and revulsion and the sense of imminent disaster.

It was enough.

The disk quivered, not a projection of his mind now but a physical flying object that had been struck. It spun, listing to his left, losing speed and altitude. Blinking through sweat, Alan fought to level the craft out, to recover control, but he was hit again, and again, and he knew it was over.

67

JENNIFER
Near Fotinos, Crete

ENNIFER STEPPED INTO THE FIELD AND THE RAIN WAS THE
same rain that had been falling on the English woods of
her home, though she could not feel it. Jennifer was and
was not there. She walked but the grass did not bend beneath
her feet and the raindrops, though they sparkled in the gleam
of her, went through her.

My body, she thought absently, *stands in the fairy ring. My
soul is here.*

It was dream logic, the kind that only makes sense from
within, and becomes strange when you wake.

She could hear the gunfire. She could even smell the wild
herbs, the ozone whisper of lightning, the gunpowder, and
when she held her hand out in front of her and willed it hard
enough, the rain seemed to well in her cupped palm for a
moment before running through.

She knew where she had to go. The church was dark and silent. It felt shrouded with death as well as age, and she wondered if it would not have been better that the tablet they had found here had been lost and forgotten. Long ago—long ago as the humans reckoned it, she thought vaguely, as if she was not really one of them—it had been a gift to humanity.

Language. Writing. An exponential evolutionary leap forward in culture and technology.

And though long forgotten, the tablets—for there were several of them—still had the power to stretch humankind, to tease and provoke the mind and make it more potent, more suited to the next great evolutionary leap. She saw this as the creature of light and energy had seen it, as if she too was standing, musingly, her head to one side as she watched some insignificant single-cell organism learn, expand, and evolve. Even when the process was complete that organism would be so far beneath her that it remained a mere curiosity, a dog that had learned to do a trick.

And yet.

She was still Jennifer Quinn. She had loved her father—an emotion the creature of light did not seem to fully grasp—and she cared for her friends, even those she had just met.

Not dogs, then. Not single-cell organisms.

She took another step toward the church, and there was a body on the ground. A policeman. Young, she noted sadly. Not someone she knew.

She wondered why that mattered, but she was at the church door now and she sensed terrible things about to happen, many of which were well outside her control. She hesitated, turning back toward the road where she knew her friend Timika was huddled in despair, and she sensed the presence of the creature of energy within her.

"You can go back," it said. "To the fairy ring. You are at risk in this place. There is no need for you to be here."

She considered this, then shook her spectral head so that the light from within her splashed the stone of the ancient chapel.

"Yes," she said. "There is."

And she stepped through the stone doorway and into the chapel.

TIMIKA
Near Fotinos, Crete

THE FOOTSTEPS STOPPED AND, RELUCTANTLY, Timika looked up, resigned to what would happen next.

Barry Regis stood over her.

"You coming?" he said.

She gaped, sensed his composure, and got unsteadily to her feet.

"I thought you . . ." she began. "I heard the gun. It wasn't yours, so I thought . . ."

"Yeah," said Barry, grinning bleakly as he swung the suppressed machine pistol around. "Took this baby off the other guy. MP5SD. Love these things."

"You . . ." but she couldn't find the words and, caught between the impulse to kiss him and the impulse to punch him hard, said nothing.

"There were three down at this end of the field, but I saw two go into the church and there's at least one more in the trees over there. We need to move carefully. I still don't think you should . . ."

"I'm coming."

"Keep to the shadows and whatever cover you can find," he said. "And when we get there . . ."

Timika glanced past him toward the church.

"What was that?" she said.

"What?" he replied, turning.

"I thought I saw . . . Look! There! That light."

Barry tried to follow her line of sight and froze.

"What the hell?" he said. "It looks like . . . a person!"

"Like *Jennifer*," said Timika, and now that she had said it, she knew it to be true. She could feel the woman's presence, though it was strange as the light that seemed to suffuse her. "Why is she here? Why does she look like that? What is happening here?"

"I don't . . ." and now it was Barry's turn to freeze, to look momentarily distracted, lost in thought.

"You okay?" Timika asked.

For a second Barry did not speak. He seemed curiously absent, as if he was not fully conscious, or was far away.

"Barry? You're freaking me out. And we need to move."

He blinked then, and stooped to look her full in the face.

"We should leave," he said.

"You mean go into the church? Yes."

"No," he said. "I mean run. Get out of this place as fast as we can."

"What? We just got here! Nicholas is in there. Maybe Jennifer too . . ."

"We can't save them," he said. "I'm sorry, Timika. We can't. And if we go in, we'll die."

"You can't know that."

He seized her by the wrist and leaned in close, his face gripped with an intensity of feeling she had never seen in him before, so that she was chilled into silence.

"Yes," he said. "I can. We're all going to die. I've seen it."

MORAT
Near Fotinos, Crete

MORAT COULD FEEL THE PRESENCE OF THE ANCIENT tablet on the other side of the altar screen with the archaeologist, though it wasn't a pleasant sensation. It resonated on the edge of his consciousness like a high-frequency whistling or the deep rumble of a generator, the kind of sound you pick up less with your ears than with your bones. It was a distant, smoldering radiance and he felt sure it was trying to mute itself from him, like an animal breathing shallowly lest the hunter hear it . . .

It did not want him to find it.

Even there, submachine gun trained on the hapless Nicholas Tan making his futile last stand, the thought struck him as intriguing. The stone could not think, could not feel. Of course it couldn't. But some ancient consciousness had imprinted itself into the rock and metal. Perhaps. It had a sense of purpose, of power, and wanted—if that was not too strong a word—to be used by the right people.

Not him. Not Sigorsky. Not Maynard and most definitely not whoever was feeding them, holding their leash. Not the swarm.

Interesting, he thought. *And, for the tablet, disappointing.*

Because Morat was going to take it, was going to hand it over to Maynard, was going to add it to their arsenal. What would happen after that, he couldn't begin to guess but it would, he thought, be glorious and terrible. The kind of thing you needed to be on the right side of.

Good thing his loyalty, which had wobbled for a moment back there, was clear again.

Sigorsky punctuated his thought by firing another quick burst with his MP5. One of Tan's wild shots had knocked out the lights, so the machine pistol fire lit the dark chapel like the flicker of an old movie projector. Morat heard the brass casings clatter and roll, heard the chips of stone and plaster shower down from the altar screen, and heard Tan's whimper of defeat as he shrank away, the forgotten pistol dropping uselessly from his hand.

Tan knew.

There were only seconds to go now.

And then the dim nave was aglow with a new light source, pearly and soft. It came in through the front of the chapel. It *walked* through the door. It wasn't a person holding a light. The person *was* the light. She was tall and slim, ethereal, and with a thrill of disbelief, Morat realized he knew her.

Within the unearthly glow was Jennifer Quinn.

He did not hesitate, turning his weapon on her, sighting down the barrel, and firing a dozen rounds on full auto. Every bullet hit its mark.

She did not go down. In fact she seemed barely aware of what had happened. The shots went through her because she was not really there.

Astral projection, he thought vaguely. *Something like that.*

But that just meant she couldn't do anything but be a kind of distraction, and he had come too far and gone through too much to be distracted.

"What the hell?" said Sigorsky in Russian, staring at the glowing figure.

"Ignore it," said Morat, listening to the hammering of the rain on the roof. "It's not real. Just a kind of hologram. A projection. Get Tan."

Sigorsky edged down the dim nave, his weapon raised and ready as if he was storming some insurgent bunker, and then Tan was stepping into the light, his arms folded over the stone tablet in front of his heart like it was a shield. His face was pale and his eyes turned down. He might have been crying.

Sigorsky hesitated and, when satisfied, took a step back so that Tan could come around the screen and into the empty heart of the chapel, stepping around the body of the prone policewoman.

"Over here, if you don't mind," said Morat. He saw the way Tan's eyes had gone to the spectral silent figure of Jennifer Quinn, which was illuminating the nave. "Ignore the light show," he added. "It's not relevant."

There was a series of popping sounds outside. Not thunder. Gunfire.

Morat half turned to the door, then nodded to his colleague.

"Sigorsky, there's someone still out there," he said. "Cover the doorway and check in with the team."

He returned his gaze to Tan, who was staring at the thing that looked like Jennifer Quinn, while Sigorsky went down the squad list over the comm. P-1 through P-3 were missing. That meant someone had come up from the road, Timika Mars, presumably, and whoever was with her.

Barry Regis.

Of course it was. He should have sensed the former Marine's presence earlier. Regis was a real fighter, but that was okay. If he and his lady friend were making for the church they had just walked into the sniper field of P-4 and P-5.

Morat, smiling grimly at Tan down the barrel of his machine pistol, wondering vaguely if he would feel the moment they died. In the same moment he sensed the presence of the others, his masters, buzzing through the universe, imminent now, poised; clawed feet and stings at the ready.

The swarm had arrived.

ALAN
Somewhere over Crete

THE DISK TREMBLED LIKE A STALLING BIPLANE AND ALAN
sensed another hit from the pelting spheres as they
swooped from the swollen, ominous cloud. They moved
like a school of fish, like a murmuration of starlings, swoop-
ing and adjusting as one, so that the individuals were revealed
as a cloud with a single purpose.

He could not outfly them or outthink them, and the
effort was killing him. He felt it in his wavering focus, his
sudden drowsiness. He had survived this long because of the
stone tablet in the crate, but whatever benefit he had derived
from it, he had exhausted its resources.

Sorry, he thought, to Barry, to the world in general. *I just
can't hold them off.*

And then the swirling cloud rippled with new color unseen
in any normal storm: green and gold, blood-red buckling and

cracking into teal as the heavens roiled and burst. Something was coming. He felt it even as his ship limped directionless toward it.

More laser fire. More damage.

His control of the disk died. It left him as if a fuel line had been cut and all the energy that made the thing work just drained away. Like the opening of an artery.

In the same moment the great cloud castle ruptured and there was something new and solid in front of him. Something metallic and rippling with light in the heart of the maelstrom.

It was the great cigar-shaped craft he had first seen over Argentina. The same ship that had led him here, though for what purpose it was impossible to say. Maybe there was some logic, however strange, however alien, that his ship must come apart in this spot and in this moment. Maybe it mattered to someone or something that Alan died here.

TIMIKA
Near Fotinos, Crete

S HE COULDN'T LEAVE. SHE WOULDN'T BLAME BARRY FOR making the right tactical choice and withdrawing, but Nicholas was here because of her and she wouldn't leave him, even if the attempt to save him was certainly suicidal.

Almost certainly.

Barry had seen the future before and then averted it. She had heard the story of the almost–road accident in Nevada. If it could happen there, it could happen here. And besides, Timika didn't believe in destiny. The future was hers.

So she nodded, then began running through the rain toward the church, dimly aware that the storm above had changed, become strange. She looked up into the sky and saw something huge and gleaming, its surface shifting in light and color like opal. It sat, it seemed, at the heart of the storm, and around it the rain seemed to be slowing. Not easing off, but actually slowing down as it fell. She hesitated, openmouthed, but came back to herself as the gunfire recommenced, distantly at first, from somewhere north of the church, then close by.

Barry had come with her after all, and was strafing a clump of trees.

"Down!" he shouted, dropping to one knee.

She threw herself headlong in the wet grass, feeling the improbably slow raindrops breaking on her skin.

He fired again, then pivoted in place to retarget on a point to the south where a black-clad figure had appeared behind the crumbled remains of what might have been a stone animal pen. The figure crumpled, hit.

"Okay," said Barry. "Go."

She scrambled to her feet, the revolver still in her hand, and launched into a bounding run toward the church, whose doorway glowed with the kind of soft whiteness she associated with gaslight.

Jennifer, she thought. *The light is coming from Jennifer.*

Which made no sense, but seemed true nonetheless. And if such things could be real, then surely Barry's vision of the future could be rewritten. She would get Nicholas out. She owed him that.

The thought was fresh in her head when the church door, only yards away now, suddenly darkened as another man stepped into it. Her feet stuttered, unsure what to do, and in that half second she saw the flash of his weapon, saw it before she heard it, before she heard Barry scream in agony, before she felt the bullets rip through her own chest.

72

NICHOLAS
Near Fotinos, Crete

ICHOLAS CRIED OUT. TIMIKA CRASHED THROUGH THE
church door, the force of her run bearing her forward,
but it was clear that she was dead before she hit the
ground. The man who Morat had called Sigorsky didn't even
look at her, but redirected his fire outside and pulled the trigger, the shell cases arcing out as he emptied his magazine.

Morat gave him an approving look, then peered past him
to the darkness outside the church.

"Barry Regis, as I live and breathe," he said, grinning.
"Too bad you don't. Not anymore."

And that was when Nicholas really understood that it was
over, that their rescue had failed and they would all die. If he
was lucky the killers would leave without finding Elina, but
even that was a long shot. As for Nicholas himself, there really
was nothing left to do and nothing else to save.

Indeed, he thought, *destroying might be better.*

He shot a glance at the uncanny, spectral woman who was now the church's only light source, raised the stone tablet above his head and threw it at the stone floor with all the force he could muster.

"No!" shouted Morat, sweeping his weapon around.

The assassin's anger was almost worth it, as was the shattering of the carved slab the killer would never get. But without the tablet to shield him, the bullets ripped Nicholas Tan apart.

73

JENNIFER
Near Fotinos, Crete

"**I** COULDN'T HELP," SAID JENNIFER. SHE WAS STILL NOT herself, not entirely there, and it was more than her body that was missing. She watched and she knew that the people she had come to save were dead or dying around her, but she saw it as she might see a failed chess move, as a minor frustration, not entirely unexpected, nor without interest. She saw it, in other words, as *they* saw it, without emotion or personal investment.

It didn't feel right.

She saw the blood the people needed to stay alive, splashed on the walls and floor of the curious building where people had once gathered to say words and sing songs, though she could not remember why.

I am becoming them, she thought.

And that didn't feel right either.

Though it was, perhaps, what they had always wanted.

Yes, she thought. *That was correct.*

They had planned this moment decades ago, though for them that probably felt like yesterday. Or tomorrow. Or now. They did not see time as she had once done.

As I do, she insisted, holding on to her humanity, though she wasn't sure why.

Decades ago . . . They said they hadn't been the ones to take her, but how could she know for sure? How could she tell the difference between the bright, wise being that had looked like her father and the insect swarm that called to her and tried to kill everything that got in its way? Maybe they weren't so very different, and even if they were, what use was that to her if she had to stand by and watch her friends die?

The thought stirred something swirling deep in her consciousness: passion, perhaps. Anger. Grief.

Yes.

She gasped the air into her actual lungs, though she knew they were in her body a thousand miles away, and she felt the juddering tear of her heart as she looked upon the bodies in the church.

My friends. My failure.

And she wondered again, what use were the beautiful beings of energy if they could not stop this, if they did not care to try. Perhaps they had indeed waited decades or longer for this, knowing it would happen, and doing it anyway, because these humans were nothing, their lives winking out in a few years, little more than mayflies. What value could such creatures have for beings that lived outside time?

Time.

She thought of the storm in the fairy circle where her body stood, the raindrops suspended.

"This can be changed," she said.

In an instant her father stood before her once more. Not her real father, of course, and he glowed with the pearly luminescence that looked like holiness, but the creature had his face, his voice, and that was something.

"You are creatures of time," he said. "You move forward through it, or so it seems to you, and you cannot go back except in memory."

"You can," she replied, surer of herself now. "You must. Thirty seconds. That is all."

"It would make no difference," said the thing that looked like her father. "It would merely delay the inevitable, and make you watch it all over again."

"No," she said. "Do it."

"You are not one of them anymore. This does not matter."

"It does to me. Thirty seconds. Do it."

ALAN
Somewhere over Crete

THE DISK DID NOT FALL, BUT IT WENT STILL AND SILENT, gliding to a halt. It seemed suspended in an energy field, held lightly in place by something outside itself, and it fluttered very slightly as the tremors of the storm raging outside shook it. Alan glanced wildly around. In combat the disk had become transparent so he felt little beyond his own body and senses, and was able to turn to where the spheres were hurtling after him. They were close. But they too were suspended motionless in the air. Some had been caught in the act of shooting, but their laser blasts had been severed before they reached him, a millisecond before impact.

There were raindrops all around him, but they were not falling, and hung in the air like a spangled curtain.

At first he thought that gravity had ceased to function, but then, scanning the great bruised mass of the cloud, he saw a streak of lightning, frozen like the laser blasts, and realized with horrified amazement the stranger, simpler truth.

Time had stopped.

TIMIKA
Near Fotinos, Crete

"**O**KAY," SAID BARRY. "GO."

Timika scrambled to her feet, the revolver still in her hand, and launched into a bounding run toward the church, whose doorway glowed with the kind of soft whiteness she associated with gaslight.

Jennifer, she thought. *The light came from Jennifer.*

Which made no sense, but seemed true nonetheless. And if such things could be real, then surely Barry's vision of the future could be rewritten. She would get Nicholas out. She owed him that.

The thought was fresh in her head when the church door, only yards away now, suddenly darkened as another man stepped into it. Her feet stuttered, unsure what to do, and in that half second she saw the flash of a weapon from inside.

The gunman in the doorway crumpled as if deflating, and fell.

76

NICHOLAS
Near Fotinos, Crete

NICHOLAS CLUTCHED THE STONE TABLET TO HIS CHEST, staring in stunned disbelief as Morat considered the machine gun in his hands as if he had not seen it before. It was smoking from the stream of bullets he had fired into the man he had called Sigorsky. Nicholas could feel his bewilderment as if he was halfway into the killer's head. Morat frowned at the gun, and then his eyes grew wide with the realization of what had happened.

The glowing phantom woman had moved close to him a moment earlier. Not just close. She had moved into him so that her own glowing figure was gone as she had become him. Nicholas felt that too, as he felt the minds of Timika and Barry, whom he had never met, and the pilot, Alan, who was up there somewhere . . .

They were bonded. The stone had not just given them unusual insights and abilities. It had connected them, because that was how it—or whatever had been using it, manipulating it—understood communication.

The swarm.

They did not talk to individuals. They did not recognize the single, the solitary consciousness. They sought connection and unity because that was what they were. That was how they were seeking to shape humanity.

But in the process they had given a gift to Nicholas, to Alan, Timika, Barry, and Jennifer. They had, inadvertently, bound them to each other, let them into their different minds, conscious and subconscious. Somehow, through the stone or the craft Alan flew, or something more basic and essential . . .

Blood, DNA manipulated at the most fundamental level . . .

Morat had been made part of that collective too. Not the swarm, though it had tried, but a human hive that had its own principles.

Somehow, Jennifer Quinn had used it to step into Morat's mind just for a second, and in that second he had cut down Sigorsky.

Morat was back now, eyes shut, wrestling with the invader in his head, trying to redirect his gun on Nicholas. The weapon trembled in his hands as his eyes opened and the light that had been the spectral Jennifer Quinn blazed out of him.

MORAT
Near Fotinos, Crete

JEAN-CHRISTOPHE MORAT, THE NAME THAT HE HAD USED for just long enough that it felt real, tightened his trigger finger, staring along the fat suppressed barrel of the machine pistol into Nicholas Tan's face.

He understood now, the way the swarm had made him vulnerable, the way the spectral figure of Jennifer Quinn had gotten into his mind, but that was finished now. He would shove her out. He would kill Tan. He would cover the church door and kill the Mars woman and the Marine. It just required a little presence of mind.

Quinn was in his head, but he was the killer, the monster prowling the labyrinth with his two-headed ax. They were trapped. At his mercy.

He just had to pull the trigger and she would be gone.

JENNIFER
Near Fotinos, Crete

I T HAD ALMOST WORKED, BUT MORAT WAS STRONG. JENNIFER fought him, but he pushed back with a force she could not match, and as he did so, the gun barrel swung back to Nicholas.

"You should go now," said the being that looked like her father. "You have achieved as much as you can. Further delay will be calamitous."

"To who?" she managed, still locked in conflict with Morat.

"To you," said the creature of light, and for a moment it really was her father, and his concern for her, his love, was real.

It was all she needed.

She smiled, tears in her eyes, looking past Nicholas to where the Greek professor Elina was crawling unsteadily from behind the altar, the fallen pistol shaky in her hands. Morat saw her, but Jennifer hung on, though she knew what would happen next.

Elina's gun fired once.

Jennifer felt the bullet go through Morat's body, except that it was now her body too.

The chapel faded.

She slumped to the grass of the fairy ring, bleeding, knowing that no one would find her body till morning.

"It's okay," she whispered through her pain, glad to be herself again, if only for a moment. "Better this way."

And then she was gone.

ALAN
Somewhere over Crete

THE GREAT ZEPPELIN-LIKE SHIP PULSED AND THE SHOCK wave hit the disk and everything else, blowing it out of the cloud and through miles of space as real time collapsed back in on itself. Normality took hold and the disk was falling seaward.

Dazed and drunk with exhaustion, Alan searched for the brass spheres that had been about to shred his craft, but they too were blown away, and whether they were intact elsewhere or vaporized, he could not say.

Their old enemy, he thought . . .

And then his mind was empty of all but the instinct to right the disk before it slammed into the Aegean.

With the last of his mental strength he reached out to the crumpled rim of the disk and smoothed it out, as if he was rolling clay or tamping cement. The metal responded to his caress, and the disk leveled out a little, though it was still crippled beyond his capacity to repair it. He tried to find a place to set down, but couldn't make sense of the data that streamed unevenly into his head. He was coming down, harder than he would like, and whether he would survive the crash, he couldn't say.

Survive . . .

The word prompted something, a tinge of pain like a gunshot.

Jennifer Quinn was dead. He did not know how he knew this or what had happened, but he felt the certainty of it like a stone in his hand, hard and sharp, something he might squeeze till the blood ran.

TIMIKA
Near Fotinos, Crete

IMIKA FELT IT TOO. THEY ALL DID. SHE SAT IN THE CORNER of the chapel, both hands over her mouth, her eyes staring, listening to the distant wail of approaching sirens and, moments later, the arrival of the first helicopter. Barry slumped beside her a short time later and they sat in silence, oblivious to the activity around them for a while, as the police and ambulances came, their lights strobing over the church's old stonework.

The policewoman was alive. Concussed and with shrapnel injuries, mostly superficial. She was stretchered out on a gurney with an IV already in place. Nicholas, Elina, and the rest were checked over for injury but were left where they were while the police, led by Detective Inspector Anastas, pieced together their story.

It had holes in it. No one mentioned Jennifer for obvious reasons, and Timika found the weight of that secret oppressing her with grief and guilt. It seemed disloyal not to say what the Englishwoman had done, even if no one would understand or believe it.

Alan was missing and presumed dead, said Barry. His craft had sent every available distress signal but the readings had been confused, the disk clearly undergoing significant damage. It vanished from radar over the sea.

"Did you feel it," asked Timika, "when he died?"

"No," said Barry.

"But you did when Jennifer died?"

"Yes."

"See, that's good," she said.

He nodded, but seemed wary of hope.

"There'll be an extensive search and rescue operation," he said. "But he could have come down anywhere, and there's no way of knowing what sort of shape the craft was in by then."

He said it blankly, matter of fact, but it took all his considerable will and strength to do so. Timika took his hand, rested her head on his shoulder, and closed her eyes. They stayed there, unmoving, till the Navy officers arrived. It was they who supervised the moving of the stone tablet, now repacked in its Nazi crate. Nicholas wasn't so sure they were allowed to do this, but the servicemen said they had authorization from the State Department who would, they had been assured, handle any wrangling over ownership with the Greek government later.

From that moment on they were insulated from the Greek police who, in turn, seemed more interested in taking care of their own. Two of the mercenaries who had worked with Morat had survived their wounds, but the United States had declared them terrorists and enemy combatants, something else the Greek authorities seemed happy to relinquish. What would happen to them was unclear, but Barry had a feeling that cells in Guantanamo figured in their immediate future.

When the interviews were done and the documents signed, Timika, Barry, and Nicholas were flown to the American embassy in Athens, then put up for two nights in a neighboring hotel while the powers that be decided which questions to ask and which to ignore. The DOD figured extensively in those conversations and, after a series of frank debriefings in which they told their stories—unexpurgated this time—to a dozen interrogators, several of them from the very Nevada base where Alan and Barry had been stationed, they were told they were done.

The three of them flew to England for Jennifer's funeral, a surprisingly small affair run by a man called Deacon who had worked for Jennifer's father and who was in his dignified way shaken by her death. It was a simple service and was followed by the revelations of her will, which had been altered privately the night before she died.

"The money lady to the end," said Timika, stunned to see her own name among the beneficiaries. But that wasn't right, not as an assessment of all Jennifer Quinn had been, and though they had not known her long, and Nicholas not really at all, she felt that they, perhaps alone among the many guests at the palatial Hampshire estate, were there as friends who had known her worth.

It was the kind of too-late realization that hurt like a fine blade.

For the second time in a matter of months, Timika found herself wondering what would happen next, where she should go, what she should do. She had decided to like England. It was like living inside a model, everything a little undersized and not completely real, but then everything felt like that after New York. Maybe she would stay there a while. Maybe longer. She needed to talk to Marvin and Audrey soon, but wanted to be clear on what she was going to say first. She felt the need for change of the deep, thorough, and permanent variety.

Barry wasn't. He checked in with his superiors daily, waiting for news about Alan, but none came. On the morning of their fifth day in Hampshire, he told her that the agency had decided to initiate proceedings to declare Alan legally dead.

"Already?" she replied. "Isn't it usually, like, years later?"

"Not if they were considered in 'imminent peril' at the point of disappearing," he said. "It was a 9/11 thing, so that the families of the missing didn't have to wait years to start filing for death benefits and such."

He said it flatly, avoiding her eyes.

"You want to keep looking for him," she said.

"You think I'm crazy?"

"No," she answered. "If I can help, I will."

He considered her, then smiled for the first time in a week.

"Thanks," he said.

"Got to stick together, right?" she said, as if it was nothing, as if it didn't really matter, as if it wasn't the only thing keeping her from screaming till her throat bled.

"Right," he said.

NICHOLAS
Hampshire, England

PROFESSOR NICHOLAS TAN WAS, HE REALIZED, UNLIKELY to get tenure on the strength of his Cretan expedition, however remarkable it had been. The discovery of a new Linear A tablet was, of course, an achievement, but unless he could somehow figure out how to read it on the flight home, it wasn't going to help him all that much. Besides, the carving itself had been impounded by the CIA, unphotographed, undocumented, and spirited away like the goddamned Ark of the Covenant at the end of *Raiders*.

"Academic journals," he had explained to Timika, "are annoyingly picky about sources and evidence. Meaning, you know, they expect you to have some."

"Won't just take your word for it then," said Timika, grinning.

"Alas, no," said Nicholas. "So the *what I did on my summer vacation* paper just went up in smoke."

"And you didn't find Atlantis," said Timika.

"That's right, I didn't," said Nicholas, matching her smile. "I had almost forgotten. All told, professionally speaking, not a ringing success."

"Made some friends," Timika offered.

His smile buckled at that, and there were tears in his eyes when he nodded emphatically and said simply, "Yeah."

AWAY FROM THE STONE SLAB, THEIR STRANGE PSYCHIC connection seemed to fade, as did the dreams, the moments of peculiar insight and anything else out of the ordinary. Nicholas was almost relieved, because he didn't think his heart could stand constant encounters with his dead mother, but he suspected such moments of strange mental capacity and connection weren't gone forever, that something had opened in themselves that, when needed, they would find ways to access it again. That made him feel better about the bad stuff, the things they had gone through, the people they had lost, and made him wonder if the dead ever really went away, or if some intangible presence lingered if only in the minds of those who survived them. The dreams—if that was what he should call them—about his mother repairing bicycles had been more than his own subconscious. There had been something else in them, something alive and thinking. Maybe it hadn't really been his mother, but then again, maybe it had.

After all the shooting and drama, followed as it was by all those weird meetings with the military and intel guys, Nicholas had expected to want nothing more than to go back to his Reno office and stick his head in a book, but when the time came, he found he wasn't ready to leave Europe. When, one night in what had become their local pub Barry started talking about going back to Greece to help hunt for his buddy's missing plane, he found himself offering to help.

"You serious?" asked Barry.

"For a little while at least," Nicholas replied. "My semester doesn't start till the end of August and I already have my classes planned."

Timika took a sip of her drink and gave him a shrewd look.

"He's hoping to find Atlantis in the process," she said.

"I think that if it was sticking up out of the Aegean," Nicholas said, "someone would have spotted it by now. But hey, who knows?"

"Maybe that's where Alan is," said Barry, trying to go along with the joke. "Maybe his craft took enough damage that it had to go back where it came from: the Atlantis UFO foundry." He grinned to show that he was kidding, but no one laughed. "Sorry," he said.

"Get yourself a beer, big fella," said Timika, patting him on the arm.

Barry nodded and sighed and went to the bar, his shoulders practically filling the place.

"You okay?" she asked Nicholas.

"Yeah. It's just the world that got stranger."

"I'll drink to that," said Timika, doing so.

"It's like . . . I don't know," said Nicholas. "Like all the things I thought I knew . . ."

"Yeah."

"I mean, it really is okay," he said, "or, at least, it will be. I think. But . . ."

"Yeah?"

"If I do go back," he said, "to Greece, I mean. I think I'll go see Elina."

"Yeah?" Timika repeated, smiling again over the rim of her glass. "Good for you."

"I don't know if . . ." he shrugged, letting the sentence hang unfinished in the air, then caught her sideways grin and laughed. "Life, eh?" he said. "What a weird ride."

And when Barry returned with beers for all of them, they drank to that too.

THE END

ABOUT THE AUTHORS

Tom DeLonge

is an award-winning American musician, producer, and director best known as the lead vocalist, guitarist, and songwriter for the platinum-selling rock bands Blink-182 and Angels & Airwaves. His home is San Diego, California, where he focuses on creating entertainment properties that cross music, books, and film with his company To The Stars... Check out his other multi-media projects at ToTheStars.Media.

▼   ▼   ▼

A.J. Hartley

is an international bestselling novelist whose work includes archaeological thrillers, the *Darwen Arkwright* children's series, the Will Hawthorne fantasy adventures, novels based on *Macbeth* and *Hamlet*, and two upcoming young adult series, *Steeplejack* and *Cathedrals of Glass*. He is also the Robinson Distinguished Professor of Shakespeare at UNC Charlotte. His website is www.ajhartley.net.